UNCAGED DESIRES
UNCAGED DUET

MADI DANIELLE

Copyright © 2025 by Madi Danielle

All rights reserved.

No part of this book may be reproduced in any form or by any electronic or mechanical means, including information storage and retrieval systems, without written permission from the author, except for the use of brief quotations in a book review.

This novel is entirely a work of fiction. The names, characters and incidents portrayed in it are the work of the author's imagination. Any resemblance to actual persons, living or dead, events or localities is entirely coincidental.

Designations used by companies to distinguish their products are often claimed as trademarks. All brand names and product names used in this book and on its cover are trade names, service marks, trademarks and registered trademarks of their respective owners. The publishers and the book are not associated with any product or vendor mentioned in this book. None of the companies referenced within the book have endorsed the book.

Cover Design: KBGDesigns

Editing: KMorton Editing Services

❀ Created with Vellum

To my therapist, I don't think you read my books, but if you happen to come across this one…skip it.

PLAYLIST

You Ruin Me - The Veronicas
DARKSIDE - Neoni
BLOSSOM IN THE DARK - Diana Goldberg
Pretty Distraction - SkyDxddy
Met Him Last Night (Feat. Ariana Grande) - Demi Lovato
Kerosene - Rachel Lorin
Downfall - Massie
MAKE THE ANGELS CRY - Chris Grey
Little Girl Gone - CHINCHILLA
Psychofreak (Feat. Willow) - Camila Cabello
The Smallest Man Who Ever Lived - Taylor Swift
Fire Up the Night - New Medicine
Whispers - Halsey

Often - The Weeknd
Unthinkable - Cloudy Jane
The Lonely - Christina Perri
Fallout - UNSECRET & Neoni
Die With A Smile - Lady Gaga & Bruno Mars
Who Am I Living For? - Katy Perry
Who's Afraid of Little Old Me? - Taylor Swift

TERMS AND ABBREVIATIONS

BJJ - Brazilian Jiu Jitsu.
Gi - jiu jitsu outfit.
Muay Thai - fighting style in MMA that originated in Thailand.
MMA - Mixed Martial Arts.
Cage - Enclosed space where fighters compete against each other.
Submit or "tap out" - When a fighter yields resulting in defeat.
Full mount - Grappling position where top fighter is on top of opponent with their legs wrapped around the opponent's torso.
Arm bar - Submission hold in MMA that hyperextends opponents elbow.
Triangle choke - Choke that encircles opponent's neck and one arm with legs.

CONTENT AND TRIGGER WARNINGS

This book has some dark themes and elements, so please take care of yourself. Content and triggers include:

- Anal Play
- Explicit Sex Scenes
- Light Bondage
- Dub-con
- CNC
- Non-con
- Somnophillia
- Stalking
- Primal Play
- Masturbation
- Breath Play
- Violence (on page)
- Domestic abuse
- Abuse of a child (referenced)
- Group Sex Scenes
- Snake Play

CONTENT AND TRIGGER WARNINGS

If any of these will cause you distress please don't continue. Do what is best for yourself and your own mental health.

NATIONAL DOMESTIC VIOLENCE HOTLINE

If you or someone you know needs help, please reach out to someone.

You can reach the National Domestic Violence Hotline at 1-800-799-7233(SAFE).

PROLOGUE

Whenever I drive through an old town with rundown buildings, the remnants of what once was is still evident, I think about what it may have been like in its prime. That club with the writing on the chalkboard outside and the cocktail sign in the window.

I wonder if people look at me the same way. What would I have been if all my pieces weren't shattered? My life altered and my feelings shut down. I guess we will never know. And just like the buildings, I need to rebuild myself. Stronger and better.

CHAPTER 1
MAXINE

"**F**uck you!"

I jackknife up in bed. Feeling like the words were spoken just now but I know that's not true. He's not here. He can't hurt me. But that doesn't stop the memories from finding me in my dreams. It doesn't matter that I managed to get away. I feel like I'm always going to be looking over my shoulder. I'll never feel fully safe.

Which is why instead of trying to fall back asleep, I get up to double check the lock on the hotel room door and window before climbing back into bed. Pulling the blanket up to my ears like a shield, I can't seem to close my eyes because every time I attempt to, I see him. I see his raised fist. I see the spit flying from his mouth as he screams at me.

I hear his voice radiating through the room. I feel the pain from where his blows strike me. Worst of all, he's not the only person in my nightmares. There's the times I've run to my mom telling her about it.

"I can't marry him, he hurts me."

"If you would just listen, then maybe he wouldn't."

I pull the blanket tighter as the tears run down my cheeks. None of them can hurt me anymore. They won't find me, and if they do, I'll make sure they regret it.

§

I BARELY SLEPT, and by the time the sun is peeking out, I know I need to get back on the road. I had a plan when I left, this included trading my Mercedes in at a sketchy dealership for a Corolla. No one in my past explicitly said they had a tracker on me or my car, but my ex fiancé, Carson, always seemed to know where I was.

Better safe than sorry.

My escape had been planned for months and I wasn't about to fuck it all up that easily.

I stopped last night about halfway from Texas to my destination—the pacific northwest. I'd spent months researching places at the local library when I could sneak away since I couldn't risk my internet history being discovered.

After tossing a few things back into my bag, I check the window to make sure the coast is clear for me to quickly make my way to my car.

Once inside, I lock the doors and look around. I feel like I'm going insane with paranoia, but if there's one thing I know, it's that I wouldn't put anything past my ex. Or my family. If there's even the slightest chance of them finding me, they will.

Which is why I start the ignition, breathing out a sigh of relief when it starts and I take off toward my new home.

⸘

AFTER DRIVING for another couple of hours, I need to get gas. I hate stopping because every stop makes me uneasy. I do everything as quickly as possible. Bouncing on my toes as I watch the number on the pump get closer to the forty dollars I gave the attendant inside.

I jump slightly at the sudden noise as the pump clicks, signaling that it's finished. After I put the nozzle back where it goes I look up, my eyes catching on a tall lean man, and my heart rate kicks up.

No. It can't be him, he wouldn't know I'm here.

When the man turns to the side I see his profile and I feel like I can breathe again. It's not him, but it makes me jump into my car and drive off without looking back.

⸘

WHEN PEOPLE THINK of beach towns they think of sunshine, warm sand, and water. Not the Oregon coast. The end of January brings a chill to the air, the gray clouds covering the sky and the sun setting early in the day making the nights seem so much longer.

And it's perfect for my new life.

My cash is limited, but it's all I was able to take since I'm not able to use any of my credit cards. It'll be enough to put a deposit down on the little rental I found and to cover a couple months rent, but I'm going to need a job. Something I've never had before.

Not sure who's going to hire the newbie in town with no experience or work history to speak of, but I'm no stranger to talking my way into what I want. I hope that this won't be any different.

By the time I arrive in Seaside, Oregon—my new home—it's late. Everything is shut down as the darkness wraps itself around me. I'll get the keys to my new home tomorrow, but tonight I'll rent a room at a local hotel and enjoy sleeping close to the ocean.

Normally, I would have the patio door open to fall asleep to the sounds of the waves breaking on the shore, while inhaling the breeze that comes off the water sending the salty sea air through my room. But as I get into the room, I make sure every entry point is closed and tightly locked.

I can't have the doors leading to the balcony open. I can't listen to the waves or feel the breeze as I drift off to sleep. It doesn't matter that I'm on the fifth floor, I can't risk someone finding me and dragging me back home.

I'm not going back. I can never go back.

FIRST THING THE NEXT MORNING, I meet up with my new landlord. She's an older woman who's standing outside my new rental as I pull up.

"Maxine?" she asks as I approach.

I bite back my reaction to that name and nod just once.

"So nice to meet you, Maxine. I'm Rhonda." She shakes my hand and pulls out a keyring with a set of two keys attached. "Rent is due on the first of the month and please be respectful of the home."

I nod in response.

"Come on, I'll show you around." She opens the front door for me and we both walk in.

As she gives me a tour of the modest home, she starts to ask some questions, "What brings you to Seaside?"

"Fresh start," I answer, simply.

"It's not the typical time of year that people come here, have you been here before?"

"Uh, no." I shake my head. I know she's trying to be nice, but my skin begins to feel itchy at all the questions but I don't want to be rude by not answering.

"Oh interesting, and where did you say you're from?"

I hesitate. "I didn't. I'm from down south," I answer vaguely.

"It's a bit warmer there, I hope you won't mind the cold."

I give a small smile. "I'm sure I'll get used to it."

After we circle back to the front of the house, she announces, "That's it."

"Thank you." I hand her the deposit money I owe to move in as she hands me the keys.

"Feel free to reach out with any questions."

"Actually, I do have one…do you know anyone hiring around here?"

I see her cringe slightly, probably worried about my ability to pay rent if I'm asking for a job.

"Uh, hm, it is the slow season right now, but you can check in with George at The Tavern up the road, he may need some help. Ever worked in a restaurant or bar before?"

Instead of answering directly I say, "I'm a quick learner."

She nods at my response, I can see her questions forming. I watch as she bites them back, choosing not to voice any of them, which I appreciate.

"Well, you have my number if you need me." She sighs.

"Rhonda," I call after her as she goes to her car. She turns around and I play with the keyring between my fingers. "Call me Max."'

"Nice to meet you, Max." She sends a wave in my direction before driving off.

Turning back toward the house, I take in the two story home. It's not very big, it only has two bedrooms but seemed like the perfect spot for me. I open the front door and take it all in. This will be the first place I've ever lived by myself.

The quiet is both calming and unnerving. As the silence pierces through me, I can feel it wanting to pull the memories, and the pain to the surface—which is what makes the flashbacks start.

This is why I need distractions. First a job, and possibly a new hobby to make me find myself again. I just wish I knew what that was. I used to dance, but that's not going to happen again. It only reminds me of my old life and I'm going to have to find something else to fit my new life.

Maxine is dead. But Max doesn't know who she is yet.

CHAPTER 2
MAX

"So, you've never worked in a bar before?" the manager of The Tavern asks me.

"Technically no, but I'm not picky and am a quick learner," I insist, though he doesn't look convinced. He said his name is George, and he's a large barrel-chested man who appears to be in his late fifties or early sixties. He looks like someone who doesn't trust anyone, and especially not newbies in this town.

I stand my ground. At five foot one I may not look very formidable, but I raise my chin and show him that I'm serious and that his intimidation tactics aren't going to work on me. I've faced worse monsters than him.

"Alright, what kinda skills you got?" he grunts.

"I can make drinks," I lie, and hope it's convincing enough as I continue, "I can wait tables, and do dishes. Whatever you need, I'm your girl." I put my hands on my hips.

The side of his lips pull up in a smirk like he's amused by me, but I don't move.

"Alright, little girl." I try not to show my agitation at him calling me that. I'm twenty-five, not a child. "We'll do a trial run tonight. You can be behind the bar, and we will see if you can keep up or handle yourself with our crowd. You get through it; I'll give you a job. You bitch, cry, or run out, don't bother coming back."

"Won't be a problem. I can handle it."

George nods with a smirk. "Good luck. You'll need it."

§

I'VE BEEN THROWN to the wolves on my trial run. After about thirty minutes with the bartender showing me the ropes, he left me to fend for myself. I know that I'm being tested, probably more than normal, but I'm no quitter.

"Hey Red, another round," some asshole yells from the other end of the bar. He's a part of a group of men that came in close to when we opened. They are all middle aged and the second I saw them, I could tell they were going to be a problem.

My first issue is being called "Red" throughout the night. Calling someone a name based on a characteristic they have is a pet peeve of mine. But I'm good at dishing it right back. Which is why as I'm bringing the group the generic beer they've ordered and setting them down in front of him I say, "That'll be another thirty dollars, baldy."

His smug face contorts with rage, and he rears back. "Who the fuck you think you're talking to?"

"I could ask you the same thing. You call me by my hair color, I'd do the same, except you don't seem to have much left."

"I'll be sure to tell George his new bartender is a real fucking bitch," he threatens. "Then you'll be out of a job."

"Oh no, that supposed to scare me? I'm just doing my job." I extend my hand expectantly. "Thirty dollars."

I see him wanting to say more, but he digs his wallet out of his pocket and slaps his card into my hand. I send him a fake smile that drops immediately when I turn around to charge him and see the other bartender I was working with, David, standing there with his arms folded staring at the bald man. I'm annoyed that no one thinks I can handle myself when I clearly had it all under control.

I'm sure this bald asshole isn't going to tip me for shit, but that's fine. There are plenty of others around and before I get pulled into another verbal sparring match with him, some woman, who looks at me like I'm less than a piece of gum she just stepped on, is demanding drinks from me.

"Two gin and diet tonics," she orders.

"Be right up." I nod, already grabbing the bottle of gin. Other than the customers, I'm not sure why George was acting like this is the hardest job ever. Most people here have been ordering pretty simple drinks, like beers or ones with just a couple ingredients. I may not be a professional yet, but it's hardly rocket science.

It's when I grab the diet tonic the woman snaps at me, "I wanted normal tonic, new girl."

I look down at the bottle in my hand, my eyebrows creasing. "No, you definitely said diet tonic."

"You think I need fucking diet, bitch?"

If everyone could stop calling me a bitch today that would be great.

"You're the one that said it, not me." I shrug, trading out for a regular tonic bottle.

"Why are you even here, anyway?" she snaps as I pour the drinks.

"I'm working, what are you doing here?" I slide them over.

"Back off, Karissa, she didn't do anything to you. Take your drinks and leave her alone," another woman says, planting herself on a barstool in front of me. She looks to be about my age, her blonde hair falls just above her shoulders and her eyes are so blue that even in the low light of the bar they stand out.

Karissa sends the new woman a look before rolling her eyes, slapping cash onto the bar and taking her drinks back to a table somewhere else.

"Ignore her, she just doesn't like that you're new in town, pretty, and already getting more attention than her. I'm Danner." The new woman stretches her hand out to me with a smile. I can't tell if she's being sincere, but it seems like it.

"Max," I respond, shaking her hand.

"I love that, so what brought you here?"

"Work." I shrug, already moving to grab more drinks for the irritated patrons.

"No, I meant what brought you to Seaside?" She chuckles.

"Oh, uh it's nice here, I guess. I'm sorry it's so busy, can I get you something to drink?" I try to not be rude, but I feel the sweat dripping across my brow and down my back from the intensity of my shift so far. I'm really hoping to keep this job and can't be chit chatting the entire time.

"Yeah, I'm sorry, I'll take a Dirty Shirley." She's still smiling, and I wonder how someone can be so happy, but don't have time to question it.

I quickly make her drink, wasting no time as I pour the vodka in and top it with Sprite and grenadine. I start to tell her how much she owes, but she's already handing me cash. Suddenly, my eyes catch on the small group of men that just walked in and I freeze. It's five large men that all look equal parts scary and too sexy for their own good.

The oldest looks to be in his late thirties or early forties with arms that could crush me. As they move, I catch a glimpse of tattoos peeking out from his leather jacket, spreading onto his hands and neck. His salt and pepper hair is short and a little fucked up from the motorcycle helmet he's carrying, I assume.

The man behind him is around the same height, but looks younger, possibly twenties and his dark hair is longer flopping onto his forehead. His gaze scans the vicinity immediately like he's surveying it all. He looks slightly leaner than the first man, but just as muscular.

Another man walks further into the dim bar lighting and is towering over the first two men by inches. His body, though covered in jeans and a hoodie, looks like it could lift a building. He has tan skin, hair cropped close to his scalp and when he glances over at me his eyes are so light blue, they're almost out of place with how intimidating he is.

The two other men with them are both tall and built, but one seems younger than the rest, maybe in his early twenties. Though, my entire focus is on the first three that are holding my entire undivided attention.

They look like the kind of guys I would want. Guys that can give me the things I've always thought about. The things my ex said were gross and wrong. They look like they can be brutal. Unforgiving. Dirty.

"Oh shit, keep your panties on over there, Max," Danner's voice pulls me back to reality and away from the Adonis' that just walked in here.

I scoff, pretending like I wasn't just blatantly staring. "Panties are firmly on and will stay that way."

"Yeah, okay. I know they're hot; the whole town knows they're hot. But stay far away." She shakes her head. "It's not worth it."

"You dated any of them?"

"Nope," she pops the "P" dramatically. "But I know people who have. Well, dated isn't the right word, but just trust me. Keep your distance."

"Don't worry, distance is exactly what I came here for," I insist.

I finish helping someone else and as I'm returning their card to them, the large scary man of the group is leaning against the bar, his mesmerizing eyes looking right at me. It's almost uneasy how intense his stare is, but I don't let it show.

I open my mouth to ask what he wants when he speaks first, "I don't know you."

"And you're not going to," I snap. "What can I get you?"

He doesn't say anything, his stare is blank and emotionless even as his eyes trail along my body. The only show of emotion is a slight tug on the side of his mouth. "What are you offering?"

Propping my hands on my hips I say, "Whatever shitty beer or lighter fluid alcohol you usually get. So you better order now, or I'm helping someone else."

His eyebrows raise, but the rest of his face remains just as indifferent as before. "I don't drink beer," is all he says.

"Great, I don't remember asking what you don't drink." I roll my eyes, grabbing a glass, and slapping it down onto the counter, taking the drink dispenser and pouring it full of water while keeping my eyes locked with his. "There you go."

Without paying him anymore attention, I get back to dealing with the other customers. I glance over at Danner and see her sipping her drink to hide a smirk as she watches the giant man walk back to his table where his buddies sit watching our whole interaction.

That man looked like trouble; they all do. And the last thing I'm looking for right now is any more of that. I intend to keep my head down and focus entirely on me, myself and I.

CHAPTER 3
CAINE

I left the glass of water on the bar, returning to the table where the guys are relaxing with nothing in my hands.

"Thought you were getting us drinks," Drew complains.

"George hired some new girl," I tell him as an explanation. The other bartenders know us here, but for some reason this new one intrigues me. The little feisty redhead. The fucking *stunning* redhead.

I've seen David, the other bartender, running back and forth, but it's clear they're testing her. And I'm not in the mood to deal with that shit.

"Fucking A, Caine, you could use your Goddamn words to order the drinks," one of the other guys from the gym, Alexander, grumbles.

"Heard you don't drink beer," the new voice says from behind me right before the woman slides a tray full of cups with clear liquid on it. Everyone may think it's liquor, but I'm sure it's not.

"This dickhead doesn't, but the rest of us do. But right now, I just want to know your name, sugar," Alexander flirts.

I turn to see her reaction and notice how short she is compared to me. At six foot four I tower over most people and I'm guessing she's about five feet.

"Then these can all be for the dickhead. Enjoy," she smarts before walking back to the bar. My eyes catch on her full hips and round ass in her jeans that hug her perfectly.

"What happened?" Cal, another fighter at Uncaged, the MMA gym where we all train, asks returning from God knows where.

"Caine pissed off the new bartender, so instead of booze she brought us water." Drew folds his arms across his chest. "Only water."

Adam, our coach, sits quietly with his arms folded, just watching this all play out and I know he's not about to get any more involved than he needs to. Sometimes I think he likes to watch all of the drama unfold with everyone else and then goes home to laugh about it.

"Fuck all of you. I'm going to get a drink, I don't give a shit about you guys," Drew announces, standing up and walking over to the bar.

I pick up one of the glasses of water, inspecting it for any possible spit, and even though it may not be there, I keep my sights set on the little bundle of fire working behind the bar as I down the entire thing in one gulp. I catch her small smirk, and I can't deny the way it makes my body react. She's a sexy thing, and she fucking knows it. Too bad she probably couldn't handle me and what I need when it comes to sex. But fuck, I'd like to see her try. I bet she'd scream so pretty for me.

"Okay, well water may be enough for you, but not me." Cal slaps his hands on his knees, rising up and going to the bar along with Drew. Alexander stands to join him, leaving just Adam and me.

Shrugging, I pull out my phone to scroll through my contacts to see who I could see to get in a quick fuck or a blowjob. Every single name I pass bores me, I feel like I want something new. I want someone who can actually keep up with what I need, and it pisses me off that not a single woman around here can do that for me.

Frustrated, I toss my phone down and chug another one of the possibly tainted waters. Adam looks at me with some stupid amused look on his face.

"What?" I snap.

He shakes his head. "Not my business." He drinks one of the cups of water and doesn't seem to care that it probably has the spit of a pissed off bartender in it.

The rest of the guys return, drinks in hand, and I want something stronger, but I have a fight in two days and can't get drunk right now.

"What do you think her deal is?" Alexander asks and we all know who he's referring to.

"Probably a short timer, she seems like she won't stick around." Drew shrugs.

"Yeah, especially if Caine tries to talk to her again," Cal says as he shoves an elbow into my side, and I shove him away.

"Fuck off," I grunt.

"Danner is looking good over there, a lot prettier than you fuckers." Alexander stands, his eyes roam over to the blonde sitting at the bar that keeps talking to the redhead.

"She ever given you a chance with that ugly ass face?" Cal jabs and Drew lets out a chuckle.

"She wants to, just watch." Alexander downs his drink, before standing tall and walking toward her.

"This should be fucking good." Cal sits back like he's about to watch a show.

I don't give a shit about my buddy getting laid. I kind of want to leave, but I turn back and notice the way Adam is watching the same woman that caught my eye. Obviously, she's new meat and going to get some attention from everyone, but the way he's looking at her adds to how pissed off I am. Drew notices as well.

"I'm leaving," I announce to no one in particular.

"See you tomorrow." Adam nods and I don't say anything in response.

I risk one last glance at the new bartender. The new mysterious woman that's appeared in our town with an attitude leaving her fearless enough to stand up to me, even though she doesn't know who it is she's toying with. I don't even know her name, yet I can't deny that I'm curious about her. Intrigued, even.

She looks up and catches me staring at her, which is good because I want her to see. Again, instead of looking scared and cowering, she raises her chin slightly in a challenge. One I can't help but meet with a raise of my eyebrow. I walk out the door before she can see the look of amusement on my face.

Little killer looks like she may want to play.

Before I do something that some would say is reckless, I get on my Ducati Panigale and drive the short distance back to my house. I live about a mile away from the beach, but closer to the MMA gym where I train. When I have fights, I have to travel, usually to Portland or Seattle, but I never wanted to live there. Adam has a great reputation as a coach, and I knew I wanted one of the best. Being able to train and live here was a win-win to me.

I grew up in the suburbs outside Chicago and I didn't want to spend my entire life rotting in some place I don't like. Especially after I really decided to pursue fighting. My parents made it obvious how unhappy they were with that decision.

Good thing it wasn't their life.

We used to vacation in various places, but I always remembered Seaside and decided that would be the place I would start my adult life. It was a bonus that Adam Hayes happened to live here and had an MMA gym with an open spot for me to train. After giving college one half-assed year, I knew it wasn't for me and never looked back.

I get home and toss my keys and helmet onto a table in the entryway before kicking off my boots and immediately going to my pull up bar to do a couple sets. I'm pent up, even after practice, and hate that no one is at the gym to spar with.

I could go hit the bag, but it's not the same. I like it when they fight back—it's always more fun to have someone challenging you. With that, my mind immediately goes back to the bartender from tonight. Just the thought of her attitude is already making my dick harden in my jeans.

Frustrated, I rip off my clothes as I go to the bathroom and jump into a freezing cold shower to shock my system. Fuck, a little distraction like her…I'd break her and love every single second of it, but I have different priorities and dealing with some newcomer is not on the top of that list.

※

I SOMEHOW FIND myself outside The Tavern around closing time. I don't know why I'm here, hidden in the shadows waiting to get another look at her. Just a glimpse, I swear. I don't know what it is that's pulling me to her, but whatever it is, I won't let myself touch.

I really did try to sleep, but I just needed to learn more about her. See her again. Fucking something. I don't know who I am or what the fuck is wrong with me because I don't do this—obsess over someone—but I know I needed to settle whatever bullshit has my mind going crazy over this girl because I can't be this distracted and sleep deprived before my fight.

I shift my hood further over my head, covering my face from the fresh drizzle coming down. My foot is kicked up against the wall as I lean back on the wooden building that looks like it could've been here since the town was founded.

"You sure you don't need help getting home?" a voice I recognize as David, the other bartender, asks.

"Pretty sure I can manage a couple streets by myself," the redhead snaps, clearly annoyed. I tense at her tone.

"You sure? I don't mind," he tries again.

"I do. See ya later." She blows him off and the side of my mouth kicks up at her reply.

"See ya, Max," he calls.

Max.

That's when I see her walk out of the door; she doesn't even look in my direction, just heads in the opposite direction. She keeps a steady gait, pulling up her own hood to protect against the falling raindrops.

Kicking off the wall, I keep some distance as I follow her, not sure what I'm doing, but I can't deny the feeling that following her awakens in me. The dormant beast that hasn't gotten to play in a long time. The one that wants to close in on her. Grab her. Tell her to run from me. Chase her. Listen to her pleas to stop, all while her pussy cries with how much she actually wants it.

I step on a stick, and it lets out a loud crack and I watch her spine stiffen, but she doesn't look back at me, just increases her pace that's easy for me to match with my long strides. Stuffing my hands in the large pocket of my hoodie, I keep my eyes locked on her as she tries to rush back to wherever she's staying.

Part of me wants to fuck with her a little more. Scare her. If I can't touch her, then it's at least something. Get her blood pumping. Make her breathing speed up. Her shoulders tense. Maybe she'll even run. *Fuck*, I want her to run.

Taking out my keys, I hit the metal against the iron lamppost and hear her little gasp and it makes a small smile appear. Her pace picks up again, her shoes slapping against the wet pavement. I make the noise again and see her try to look back without seeming obvious. I duck my head slightly, so my hood covers most of my face.

She starts to run and the impulse to chase after her is so strong, the need so fierce it's pounding in my veins, begging to be unleashed. It's when she runs into a small house that I realize how long I've been following her. We made it off main street, where the bar is, down the boardwalk and to a residential street where evidently, she lives.

Staying in the shadows, I catalog the location for the future. Just in case this game escalates between us.

I'll see you around, Max.

CHAPTER 4
DREW

Mouths locked together, tongues tangled, we crash against the wall by my front door. We can't wait. There's a level of desperation that ramps up every time we do this. Like a race to make everything else go away to make each other feel good. It's a competition, who can drop to their knees first. Who can draw the pleasure from the other first. It's rough and dirty and so fucking hot.

I pull on his belt, working to undo his pants as quickly as possible while he pushes off his leather jacket and it falls with a thump on the floor. We didn't plan on ending our night like this, but lately it just seems to be what happens. Both needing the escape we find in each other that no one else seems to understand.

As I go to my knees to pull at his pants, he stops me. "No, you're not going to reinjure your knee because you can't wait to have my dick in your mouth," Adam insists.

I can't hold back my eye-roll. "It feels fine, and it's never stopped your dick from going in my mouth before."

"Never on the hard ground. You want this? Then get your ass to the bedroom."

I think about fighting back, but don't feel like arguing when I have a raging erection that desperately needs attention. Stomping off to the bedroom, he follows easily. He's used to being the one to call the shots as my coach and that doesn't stop him from doing the same when we're alone.

No one can know about us, though. Our sexualities aren't a secret—we both enjoy cocks just as much as we enjoy pussy. But he's my coach and while the people we know wouldn't have a problem with us being two guys, they would have a problem because of our roles in each other's lives.

Even though I'm injured and have been unable to fight for the last several months because of it. I fucking hate it and the man currently standing in my bedroom—stripping off the rest of his clothes—is the one not allowing me to do more than just coach because of said injury.

"Still desperate for my cock? Then you'd better get your ass on that bed," he demands darkly. And while I may not usually like being told what to do, I can't deny the shiver that goes down my spine in anticipation, making me want to do exactly what he says.

Yanking off my own clothes quickly until I'm just in my briefs, he continues to watch me as I climb onto the bed, sitting on the edge, leaning back on my hands. He smirks, taking his time to walk over to me, his hard length free from the confines of his pants and my mouth waters, not wanting to be denied again.

He stands in front of me, and I don't wait for him to say

anything because I want the desperation back. It feels better to be distracted because if I'm not then I'll argue with him about my fighting status again.

I swallow his thick cock, immediately pulling a groan from his throat as I run my tongue along the underside the way he likes. His hands grip the longer hair on top of my head tightly, the pinch of pain making me groan around him. His hips thrust forward, pushing himself further down my throat and I take it, wanting him to lose all control.

My own cock is hard as steel underneath my briefs and I can't help but press my palm against it for some sort of pressure, trying to find some semblance of relief.

"Fuck, your mouth feels so fucking good," Adam grits out, pushing me further down onto his cock forcefully.

I breathe through the gag my body wants to let out, but instead I swallow around him, and he throws his head back with a guttural groan. Reaching up, I tug his balls with one hand, grabbing his ass in my other, pushing him further down so my nose is pressed against his groin.

He pulls me off him with the grip on my hair, and I let out a sound of disappointment as the drool drips down my chin. His eyes lock on my mouth and seeing it makes his gaze blaze with heat.

"Fuck my face, you know you want to," I taunt him. Needing the loss of his control. Needing relief myself. Just fucking needing something more than him standing there staring at me.

"So desperate to be used like a pathetic fucktoy, aren't you?" His voice is dark, and it only makes my dick throb even more.

I press my hand against my erection again, needing just the slightest friction because I'm unbearably turned on. Dropping my mouth open and sticking my tongue out, I show him that I *do* want that. I want to be used the way I know he wants to use me.

"Are you gonna fuck your hand while you choke on my cock?" he asks, sliding his own hand along his length, using my saliva to help guide his movement.

"No, I'm going to make you come, then you get to be *my* fucktoy," I taunt, enjoying the exchange of power between us because he may like to be in control most of the time, but I know he likes to be used just as much as I do.

Before he has the chance to respond, I swallow him down again, doubling my efforts, using my hand to squeeze around the base of his cock as I lick and suck the rest of him. When I feel his control slipping, I let go, wrapping my hands around to his ass, my fingers grazing his crack, but not breeching between them yet as he thrusts forward burying himself to the hilt in my throat. I'm warmed up now and ready to take him as he fucks my mouth without holding back.

I choke and gag around him, all while moaning and craving more. It's when I push my finger against the tight bud of his asshole, not even pushing in, just adding pressure, he comes with a groan, holding himself inside me as deep as he can go, his grip on my head tight so I'm not able to go anywhere while his hot cum fills my throat and I swallow it down.

Pulling off him, I wipe my mouth with the back of my hand, smiling when I say, "My turn."

Adam kneels in front of me, I spread my legs to accommodate his large body between them. Leaning back on my hands I watch him grip the waistband of my briefs and lift up slightly to help him pull them down my legs. My cock is painfully hard as it bobs freely between us. Precum pools at the tip as I wait for him to touch me, and I'm seconds away from shoving his face onto my length and forcing him to take it.

He wraps his fist around me, dragging his thumb across the tip and swiping the liquid there, then gripping me even tighter as he pumps. He toys with each piercing, the six ladder rungs decorating my cock, which only adds to the sensation.

Groaning, I throw my head back at the feeling, finally getting some relief but it's not enough. I always need more—an extra level of pain to reach the peak and he knows it. Reaching out, I grab a fistful of his hair, pulling his mouth onto my waiting cock and he doesn't fight my hold as I push him down.

His hands grip my thighs as I hold his head down on me, thrusting up into his throat. His fingers tighten on my legs, his short nails biting into my skin giving me that bite of pain I crave while I use his mouth for my pleasure. When his teeth graze against my cock I moan loudly, feeling the impending orgasm barreling toward me.

All semblance of control is gone as I use him, and he gives me what I need. The fucked up parts of my mind that need the pain, the giving and receiving of it, take over as I find my release, holding Adam's head still as I come down his throat. I feel him swallow around me and it prolongs my orgasm. Especially when he grips my legs even tighter, there may even be a little blood, and *God* I hope there is.

He pulls off me, looking up with a raised eyebrow. "Feel better?"

I scoff, shoving him lightly away to pull my briefs back on. "I felt fine before."

"That's why you practically begged me to come back here with you, right?" He grabs his own clothes, already pulling them on because we don't do sleepovers. Our arrangement is purely physical. We get off, we fuck off.

"I didn't beg, you were the one looking at me all night like you couldn't wait to get me alone," I tell him.

He lets out a noise that I know is a chuckle, but Adam doesn't really laugh. "Hardly, but I know you needed an outlet after today."

I grimace at the reminder, the high of my orgasm fading quickly as I think about the day. Another day he hasn't let me practice due to my injury. I've felt fine, my leg hardly bothers me anymore, and yet Adam acts like I'm at a huge risk for more. I can practice without making it worse. But all he lets me do now is assist in coaching, stretch, and do light workouts.

And now, I'm pissed off all over again.

"Yeah, well, that's what happens when you take away my main outlet, I have to find something else," I snark.

He blows out a breath after pulling on his shirt. "I didn't take it away. I want you to be cleared before I let you fight again."

"You say that," I grumble with an eye roll.

"Is that why you continue to do this? Get me to come and

hope I'll be convinced to let you back into the cage before you're ready?" he fumes.

"That's fucking bullshit. Don't act like I'm using you anymore than you're using me."

"Caine has a fight in Portland this weekend, I'll need you to cover jiu jitsu classes on Friday," he says, not acknowledging my comment.

"Yup." I pull my sheets back up, getting ready to climb into bed the second he steps out of my room.

He looks like he's about to say something else, but just shakes his head, walking away. I hear the front door close as I lay down. Despite the annoyance and anger thrumming through my body I am tired. Even as I try to go to sleep my body fights the sensation like it always does.

My body and brain know that I'm vulnerable when I'm asleep and that's when the memories of the past assault me, and I can't fight back. Sleeping is when I'm weakest. Weak, the very thing I work hard not to be anymore, but it doesn't matter because once the state of unconsciousness takes over there's nothing I can do but succumb to the trauma once again.

Yet, when sleep pulls me under, I don't fight it anymore. I can't fight anything in my life anymore apparently, so I let it in. But for some reason tonight, as my eyes close, I think of the woman at the bar. She drew me in immediately the second I saw her. We didn't speak, but there was something about her that felt like it mirrored something in me. I felt drawn to her in a way I've never felt before.

Of course, Caine already pissed her off, that seems to be how he is with everyone. Barely speaks and when he does it's generally not anything good. Instead of cowering to him, she stood strong, and I liked seeing it. I don't know her name, or anything about her, yet her hazel eyes are the last thing I see before the depths of sleep pull me under.

CHAPTER 5
MAX

George was surprisingly shocked at how well I handled myself that first night. And by shocked, I mean he grunted something about seeing me again, which makes me think he was happy with how I did.

Another shift came and went the next night, and it was less exciting than the first, probably because I recognized some of the assholes that came in and had their drinks ready before they could say too much to me. Despite my quick service, the side eyes they gave me told me that they still aren't my biggest fans. Which is fine.

Danner also came back, and she seems determined to be my friend. The only people who didn't show up again was that group of unnaturally attractive guys who were there my first night. My lip quirks at the memory of giving their table a tray of water. One of them came up to Danner later trying to hit on her which made me laugh. She didn't go home with him from what I could tell, but he definitely wanted her to.

One of my goals since leaving Texas has been to get a job, and then the second is to do something for myself. Learn who I am and what I like without the influence of others telling me what I *should* like.

One of my ideas has been wanting to learn how to protect myself. I hope Carson won't find me, that no one from my previous life will. But if they do, I don't know the extremes they would go to bring me back. It's no longer enough to hope.

That may sound dramatic, but I wouldn't put it past him, or my parents, to hire a PI or bounty hunter to try and drag me—literally—back home.

Home.

Not anymore.

Part of me wants to find a dance studio and get my body moving in that way again. I've always felt complete when I would dance. The music carried me in a way that made me feel whole. I just don't think I could dance again. I used to enjoy it, but just like everything in my life, that's now ruined.

I did some research, but there's not much this small town has to offer, until I stumbled upon a gym that piqued my interest. It's an MMA gym. And after I fell down a rabbit hole of researching MMA, I only got more interested in pushing my body to do what I saw in the videos.

That's how I end up at Uncaged late this morning, ready to sign up.

I walk into the front door, and don't see anyone at first, so I'm worried that they aren't open, despite what their hours say online.

"Hello?" I call out to the large space. There's a desk right when you walk in that has a single computer and a phone. There's an enclosed area in the middle of the large space that I'm guessing is the "cage" from what I learned online, that's where the fights take place, or I'm assuming where they practice.

Behind that, I see punching bags lining the wall. The floor is covered in mats and there's various other items along other walls including exercise balls, giant tires, medicine balls, bands, and other equipment I've never seen or would even know what to call them. For a second, I wonder if I've gotten in over my head here, but then another memory assaults me. The pain in my cheek from a slap that feels like it just happened and it brings me back to the reason I'm standing in this gym.

I need this.

I need to do this, for me.

I need to take my power back.

I need to feel safe.

A large man walks out from a side room that I assume is an office. He looks shocked to see me and pulls a headphone out of his ear.

"I'm sorry I didn't know anyone was here," he apologizes.

I recognize him, but I'm not sure why, that is until he removes the baseball cap on his head, runs his hand through his black hair before placing the cap back on. Backwards. I want to moan and roll my eyes at the same time at the sight.

That's when it hits me why I recognize him. He was one of the men that came into the bar with that huge asshole. He wasn't rude to me, so I guess I don't have an issue with him, yet. But it's early and that could always change.

I shake my head before answering, trying to physically shake any of the dirty thoughts I have in regards to how he looks with that backwards hat and tight shirt hugging his body showcasing the divots of muscle that cover his chest. The way I'd like to lick those divots, especially on my way to discover what may be hiding underneath his waistband and—*no*. What the fuck is wrong with me?

"Yeah, I thought you guys were open. I was hoping to sign up," I say, trying to sound more confident than I feel.

He looks me up and down with a small smirk that I may have missed if I wasn't overly focused on his mouth already, even though I shouldn't be. I place my hands on my hips, ready to prove myself right here if I need to. Because the way he's looking at me makes me think he's about to be another person that underestimates me.

"Let's get you signed up then," he says simply, and I raise an eyebrow, but he walks up to the computer and starts typing.

I place my arms on the desk, leaning slightly, waiting for him to ask me things or give me paperwork or something.

"Name?" he finally asks.

"Max."

He looks up with a raised eyebrow, his green eyes are the color of moss, a darker green than I've ever seen before. I'm wondering if it's a requirement in this town for the guys to have unique eyes, because the dickhead from the other nights shining light blue ones assault my thoughts more than they should for someone I briefly met and definitely shouldn't think about again.

"That your full name?" he questions.

I roll my lips between my teeth. "Max Barclay." I hope with every fiber of my being he doesn't recognize my family's name. On the East coast, everyone knows who we are, at least who my parents are. I don't need this somehow getting back to them. Instantly regretting not giving a fake name that hope's obliterated with his next question anyway, and I know I wouldn't have been able to get away with that.

"Can I see your ID?"

Pulling out my wallet, I slide it over to him.

That damn amused look crosses his handsome face again, and I'm hoping he lets me have a session right now so I can practice trying to punch it off his face.

"Maxine Claudia Barclay?" His voice dances with humor and I scowl, snatching my ID back.

"Are you going to put out a bulletin about me or something?" I snark.

"Nope, just needed to verify you're who you say you are," he replies, almost like he knows I wanted to lie about my identity.

"Yeah, well, it's just Max so that better be what you call me from now on."

I catch the tiny smirk he allows, before focusing on typing my information into the computer. After about a minute of silence, the only noise between us the clicking of the keyboard he speaks again. "So, which class are you wanting to sign up for?"

"Um, jiu jitsu?"

He looks at me with a raised eyebrow. "That a question?"

"No," I correct. "I want to sign up for jiu jitsu."

He nods, typing and clicking on the computer some more. My mouth twists and I blurt, "Since you know my name, I should at least know yours."

He says nothing. It reminds me of his friend from the other night. Is there some sort of rule here where they can't speak more than a few words at a time?

"First name at least, it's only fair," I try again when he pauses typing.

"Drew," he answers.

"Short for Andrew?" I ask.

Drew grunts in response, turning to grab some papers and pushing them toward me. "Sign."

I sign my new signature on the designated line and hand it back to him.

"Beginner class is today at three, do you think you'll make it?" he questions.

"Yes," I tell him confidently.

Drew looks at me skeptically and I don't like it. I've been questioned my entire life, looked down on and thought of as incapable of doing things that I know I can. So, the way he's looking at me right now, like I can't make it back here in a couple of hours for some reason triggers something inside me. It might be a slight overreaction, but I don't care.

"Don't look at me like that *Andrew*. You don't know me; I'll be back in time for class. Actually, I'll be *early*."

He scowls, "Don't call me that."

"Don't underestimate me," I counter.

"We'll see how you handle class." He dismisses me, and I narrow my eyes at him. Clearly, he's an asshole just like his buddy and I can't wait to prove him wrong.

Turning to leave, I storm out and get to my car, slamming the door harder than necessary. The sound jolting me back to a memory.

"*Seriously Maxine, I don't know why you even try?*" Carson says immediately once he steps through the door, seeing what I'm doing. Trying to work on my latest project, refurbishing some frames I found.

"What? They are looking good." I look at the finished ones I've polished, and he steps closer, nose scrunched as he looks at them.

"They look like fucking garbage which is where I'm sure you got them from."

"No, I didn't," I responded softly, looking down.

There's a crash that makes my head snap up to see he's about to launch another frame into the wall to match the first one.

"What are you doing? Stop!" I reach out trying to stop him, and when the back of his hand makes contact with my cheek the pain blooms—

I bring myself back to reality. He's not here. He can't hurt me. He won't find me. None of them will.

CHAPTER 6
DREW

That woman, the one from the bar, she's even feistier than I thought. Now she wants to learn Brazilian Jiu Jitsu, and the thought makes me smirk. She's just a little thing and I bet she could be sneaky on the mats. She could also be thrown around.

Wonder if she would like that.

Shaking the thought away, I continue to prep the gym for the first class of the day. I didn't mind, but since my injury I miss being in the cage and getting to practice what I'm teaching. Training is the closest Adam lets me come to fighting. Even though I'm fine and my knee hasn't really bothered me in a month, he's convinced I need more time off of it and I can't risk a full-blown fight.

He doesn't know that I've convinced Caine to spar with me a couple of times and there's been no issues. It's starting to piss me off, though, that he thinks I can't handle it. If I didn't love this gym, and if it wasn't the only one in this tiny town, I would try to go somewhere else.

The first class is small, and the hour goes by quickly and then it's time for the one I enrolled Max in. I wasn't sure if she had work or something already planned for the day, which is why I wasn't sure if she would show up. Yet, she's the first one to walk in the door. She's wearing a pair of tight shorts that cover her thighs, ending just above her knee. Her torso is covered by a loose T-shirt that looks at least two sizes too big, falling off her shoulder and giving me a peek at the sports bra underneath.

"You made it," I state, keeping my face blank as usual.

"Looks like it." She folds her arms across her chest and narrows her eyes.

I nod toward the mats. "Start stretching while we wait for everyone else to show up."

She looks over at them and bites her bottom lip with a nod.

"There a problem, Maxine?" I ask.

"Max," she snaps suddenly, her face hardening. "It's just Max."

"There a problem, *Max?*"

"No problem." She walks away, dropping down to the mat starting some basic stretches.

I watch her for longer than I should, the way her limber body folds and moves already. I clear my throat, trying to also clear the thoughts causing my dick to start to harden. Luckily, I'm wearing a gi which is thick enough to not make it obvious. I don't usually train in one, but since today is just BJJ I decided to wear it, which was obviously the right choice.

"Hi Drew," another feminine voice coos, and it takes my attention from Max with a groan.

"Karissa." I nod, simply, not giving her any more attention than that. You give her an inch and she wants a mile. It doesn't matter who it is, she's always trying to get on someone's dick here. Mine, Adam, Caine, Cal, Alexander, she just wants the attention.

"Can you show me those stretches again, I forgot." She twirls a strand of hair around her finger.

I nod toward Max. "You can ask our newcomer, she seems to know what she's doing."

Karissa scowls over at Max. "Who is she?"

I ignore her, focusing on the other couple of people that are here for class.

"Alright, let's get started," I announce.

The group of students here for class stand up and wait for the first instruction I give. As I explain what I want them to do, I try my best not to watch Max too intently, but there are times I can't help it. She takes in everything I say without showing a single emotion. No confusion, no questions, no nervousness. I would almost think that she's done BJJ before if it weren't for the slight furrow of her brow when I tell them all to go practice.

But she doesn't ask for help. She just keeps trying to figure it out on her own with her partner.

I have them practicing a pretty basic guard and I can see she's struggling to get a good grip. I kneel down close to her before offering, "You need some help, little one?"

She scowls at the nickname. "No. I got it."

I leave her to it and check in with the rest of the class, since she doesn't need the help I'm not going to hover.

"*Drew,*" Karissa croons. "I need some help."

I hide my eye roll by running a hand down my face at her shrill voice and do my best to help her without losing my shit. She doesn't need help, she's just not trying. And if her tits were pushed up anymore her nipples would be out of the tight little sports bra she's wearing. Beginners don't tend to wear gi's since a lot of them aren't sure if they are going to stick with it.

I know this is Karissa's M.O., and even if it were Adam teaching the class, she would pull the same shit with him. And don't even get me started if Caine is practicing when she's here. The difference is, I'm pretty sure Caine has actually fucked her.

It's the curse of a small town, especially one that is mostly a tourist town. In the off season, the options are limited, and everyone knows everyone's business.

Except mine. I keep mine to myself, and the people I share that business with know that's how it's going to stay.

"What do you need help with, Karissa, looks like you have it?" I respond, dryly.

"Is it like this, though?" she questions, keeping a limp grip on her partner who looks just as annoyed as I feel.

"Tighten your grip."

Pouting, she says, "I think I need you to show me."

"I don't need to show you how to have a tight grip." I push off my knees, rising to walk back to the front of the room to continue with the class.

After it's over, everyone is sweaty and breathing hard. I watch Max try to hide it, but she doesn't do a great job. Part of me wants to stop her and say something, though I'm not sure why. That plan is completely derailed anyway by Karissa stepping in front of me, blocking my access to Max before she's walking out the door.

"How do I get some extra private training?" Karissa asks.

"Talk to Coach Adam," I blow her off, walking toward the office just to get away from her, really to get away from everyone. Luckily, this is the last class of the day so once I'm sure the coast is clear I lock the front door and clean up before heading home.

By the time I get home and eat dinner I realize I zoned out for who knows how long. I check my phone and see some texts from the guys about the fights tonight. Caine won, because of fucking course he did, and Adam asked how classes went today.

Drew: Good. New girl signed up.

Adam: New girl?

Drew: Yeah, the one Caine pissed off at the bar.

Adam: You think she'll stick around?

Drew: Hard to tell.

Adam: Guess we will see.

Tossing my phone to the side I scrub a hand down my face, annoyed that I'm not at the fight with them. I could be, and classes could've been canceled this week. But then I would want to be in a fight, and then Adam and I would argue. It's the current cycle with us. It usually ends with one of us in the other's bed, but it doesn't solve shit.

I need a distraction, and for a second I think about going to the bar to see if Max is there. I don't know why that's the first thing I think of but there's something about her. I don't know what I would even want to say to her, if anything. I should've worked the bag while I was still at the gym. Sometimes I go back when I can't sleep, and I need to clear my mind.

Without thinking about it too much I grab my keys and head out, fully intending to go back to the gym. So, when I actually end up in front of The Tavern I don't have an explanation. I don't drink much, not after I saw what it did to my dad. And ending up like him is the last fucking thing I plan to do.

Yet, here I am, walking inside anyway.

I don't immediately look toward the bar, instead I end up at a table toward the back. That's when I finally look in the direction of the bar and it's hard to not miss the flash of red hair that's pulled up in a ponytail that swings as Max works. It seems like she's getting less shit than she did that first night, but I notice she hardly smiles.

Most people I've ever seen working a bar act so friendly and flirty to try and get a good tip, but not Max. She keeps a straight face with most everyone. There's an occasional scowl, or eye roll. She intrigues me, and it's a feeling I haven't had in a long ass time.

In fact, I don't remember the last time I was intrigued by anyone.

Attracted, sure. I'm a fucking red-blooded male.

But there's something with her that's calling to me on some subconscious level, and it's fucking weird. Before I let myself wonder about her anymore and end up doing something I might regret, I leave without getting anything and go to the gym like I initially intended.

While I'm there, I beat the fuck out of the bag until I'm exhausted enough that my mind takes a break from trying to drive me insane with memories and thoughts of what would happen if I spoke to Max.

By the time I get home, I don't even have the energy to shower before falling face first onto my bed and going to sleep. But my mind decides that it wasn't as tired as I thought, because I'm still plagued by nightmares of everything I try to forget.

I can never forget it, can never fully escape it. It doesn't matter if it's been thirteen years—I'll never be fully free from it.

CHAPTER 7
CAINE

I won my fights in Portland, because of course I did. These were amateurs and I need more. I already told Adam I want to take him on when we get back just to at least *feel* like I'm getting some sort of challenge from someone. Drew used to be a good sparring partner before he got hurt, but now Adam doesn't let him spar and makes him take it easy instead.

Not that he always does, but Adam can't know that because it'll piss him off since it's on him if anyone gets hurt in *his* gym.

The guy that kicked out Drew's knee should've gotten more punishment, but of course he claimed it as an accident and didn't get shit for it. *Accident my ass.*

When we get back home it's late and I'm tired, but I can't deny the feeling of wanting to go see the new girl, Max. I don't know why, but I haven't been able to stop thinking about her the entire time we were gone. I want to get close to her again, to see how she struggles. How she would scream.

Bet she'd like it. *Fucking love it.*

That's why after I get home, I can't help myself from pulling on a hoodie and taking a walk. I saw the little house she's living in when I followed her home the other night, and that's where I find myself again. Standing on the sidewalk, my hood up as the drizzle of rain slowly seeps into the fabric of my jacket and the chill of the late winter wind tries to make me feel something. But it won't work, I don't feel any of it.

I haven't felt anything in a long time.

Even the hits and kicks during a fight barely phase me. I hardly feel anything. The rush, the pain, I'm numb to it all.

Except when I think of the spitfire on the other side of these walls I'm staring at. The woman who didn't look at me with fear, but with a challenge.

There aren't any lights on inside, not even the single light outside the front door. It's all dark, the sidewalk barely even illuminated by the streetlights. Everything is ensconced in darkness around me. The only sign of life existing is the faint sound of the ocean waves crashing onto the shore. The limited light around only reflects the lack of any life inside my body. At least in the morning some of the light from the sun may break through the gray clouds. The same can't be said when it comes to me. There's no light breaking through with me, not anymore.

I don't know how long I stay there, staring at Max's house waiting to see something, a glimpse of a silhouette through a window, a flicker of light. Anything that could remind me of what I felt the other night as I followed her.

Nothing happens. And for the briefest moment I think about trying to open her door, maybe she's dumb and left it unlocked, unfamiliar with the dangers that lurk around here waiting for a pretty new toy to come into town they can play with.

Dangers like me.

Maybe not tonight. She's safe for one more night. I refrain, turning on my heel and walking back to my house.

The same may not be said for tomorrow. The beast that sits dormant inside me is starting to wake up, and she's the one to blame for it.

See you soon, killer.

⚜

"AGAIN!" Adam barks as I submit Cal for the third time this session.

I lift up, and Cal groans, slowly getting himself off the floor once again. "For fucks sake, we get it, Caine," he grumbles.

"But do you?" Adam asks bluntly.

"Yes. I do get that Caine can kick my ass, thanks for the reminder, *Coach*."

"That right there is why you're going to do it again. It's not about Caine kicking your ass, it's about you making him work for it. It's skill, not strength."

As we get in position to start again, I smirk, my eyes locking on Cal's. He's exhausted and I've barely broken a sweat.

"Yeah, it's about skill, not strength. I just happen to have more of both," I taunt right as Adam starts the round, and with my taunting I easily overtake Cal's tired body, submitting him once again, not letting up until he taps, and I release my choke.

"Take a break." Adam shakes his head as Cal drags himself off to the side to grab some water.

Adam walks up to me, his back turned to the rest of the room, as he addresses me, "I'm not telling you to take it easy on them, but you could cut down the shit talk at least."

I shrug. "Why? It's as much a mental sport as it is a physical one. Gotta make sure to work out both, right?"

He scoffs, "Right. Go hit the bag."

I spray a stream of water in my mouth from my water bottle and go over to the heavy bags hanging on one side of the gym, adjusting the wrap on my hands before throwing combinations into the tough leather.

My mind empties in these moments, just me, my fists, and the bag. I continue various combinations until I feel the slight pang in my muscles. And then I don't stop, in fact I double down my efforts, dying to feel the burn in my arms.

"Caine!" My name is barked across the gym. I lift up my sweat soaked head to see it's Adam calling me back over. "You think you can tone it down a bit to show the beginner class an example of a pro?"

"Tone what down?" I fold my arms across my chest.

"Don't kill your sparring partner."

I huff. "Sure."

He looks at me skeptically before nodding his head once, trusting my word. I haven't *actually* killed anyone yet. Come close? Maybe.

But I'm not the only one.

"Hey." Drew saddles up next to me.

"Sup?"

"Adam tell you that the new girl joined the beginner class?"

My head swings in his direction because no he didn't. Not that he would have any reason to, I'm not particularly close with him or anyone here. Not like Drew. They may think they're hiding what they're doing, but we all know and don't give a shit. It's their business, not ours.

"Nah, she any good?" I fake nonchalance.

"Couldn't tell you, it's only been one class. Seems motivated, though."

I grunt in response.

"Maybe you'll scare her off with Coach's example."

"We'll see about that."

I hope I do scare her. I hope she runs. That way I can catch her. But it may be fun for her to stick around here a bit, learn how to put up more of a fight. The thought is way too appealing, and I need a distraction again.

"Cal," I snap, pointing back to the cage. "Again."

"Oh, for fucks sake," he groans, but I don't let him argue, climbing back up, jumping and shaking out my arms waiting for him to join. He's sluggish and tired, but I'm more energized than ever.

This new girl may be both the best and worst thing to happen to me, as long as the thoughts of her keep me fired up and not distracted. I can't afford distractions.

But motivation, that I can always afford.

CHAPTER 8
MAX

Uneasiness spreads over my skin as I shoot up in bed. My interrupted sleep is going to catch up with me one of these days. The exhaustion is going to take over and I'm going to end up passed out on the bar top just to get a couple extra minutes of sleep.

I can't even blame the nightmares every time because they don't appear every night. *Just most.* Yet, when I wake up with my heart racing and glance around my dark room, I can't help the feeling that there are eyes on me. Someone can see me, even though it's impossible.

I'm paranoid. Maybe on the verge of a mental breakdown. I'd say I'm about due for one considering everything I've been through. Everything I escaped. Add in the less than enthusiastic welcome I've had in this town, and it would make sense.

Dropping back onto my bed, staring at the dark ceiling, I can't shake the feeling, and it makes me restless. I close my eyes, seeing if that will trick my mind into shutting off and letting me sleep, but it doesn't.

Resigned to not sleeping, I grab my phone and find a song to play, I continue to lay here, even as the melody flows through me, urging me to move. Begging me to let it out and let the instinct lead me through the familiar motions of dancing.

I keep myself plastered to the bed, just listening to the music as my body screams at me to let the notes carry me across the floor, but I can't. I just can't do it yet.

"Dance for me, wifey," Carson sneers, snapping with one hand while the other cradles his whiskey glass. I think it's his fourth since he got home from work an hour ago. Maybe fifth.

"Not your wife," I grumble, attempting to storm past him into the bedroom. He's worse when he drinks.

His hand shoots out to grab my wrist and I gasp at the immediate pain from the tightness of his grip. "Not yet, but you fucking will be. I want you to dance, so do it."

"Let go of me," I insist.

He only squeezes tighter.

"You're hurting me," I try to keep my voice steady. I shouldn't have instigated him. I know what happens. It's what always happens. My mom's voice rings in my ears telling me how if I just did what he asked he wouldn't hurt me.

"Then fucking dance. Maybe then I'll fuck you how you want, like the disgusting slut you are." His face twists in repulsion before he

swallows the rest of his drink, dropping my wrist and I immediately rub at the sore joint.

Tears fill my eyes. I made the mistake of telling Carson what I may like to try in the bedroom, and he's never let me forget how gross he finds it. Especially because my needs don't matter. They never have and never will with him.

"I'm waiting, wifey."

Instead of trying to fight this battle more tonight, I do what he says, and I dance. I dance, hating every single second of it. I dance as the tears fall down my cheeks and he just watches. Smiling the entire time, enjoying the sight of me breaking right in front of him. Losing another piece of myself every second I perform for him.

This hasn't been for me in a long time, and it never will be again unless I manage to leave.

The song ends, and I'm crying, tears coursing rivers down my cheeks. Wiping them away, I shut the music off and turn over, forcing myself to try and sleep as the silence consumes me. But the uneasy feeling of being watched doesn't leave.

Though, it doesn't feel the same as when Carson's eyes were on me. This feeling of being watched sends fear trickling into my blood, but there's something else there—adrenaline. *Excitement.* Something I haven't felt in a long time. I'm probably just being paranoid, but despite that, my body eventually gives into the exhaustion as sleep pulls me under once again.

※

EVEN THOUGH I have to work tonight, I'm not about to miss my second BJJ class ever. This is something I need to stick with. Something I need to do for myself.

I arrive at the gym, ready for another class and to face Drew and his doubt in me once again. But it's not Drew that I see standing at the front. It's one of the other guys from my first shift at the bar, the older man with tattoos covering his arms, hands, and up his neck. His salt and pepper hair is cut short. He doesn't smile or greet me when I walk in, just looks at me expectantly.

"I'm Max," I tell him, stepping up to the front desk.

His eyes roam over me, but not in a way that makes me uncomfortable. It's like Drew last week, and I immediately feel like he's sizing me up because he doesn't think I can handle this. Which pisses me off because I've been underestimated my entire life. Just a figure to be looked at and admired. An *accessory*. First for my parents, then for Carson. And now, I'm here, and these guys think they're better than me just because I'm not six foot whatever and covered in muscles. I watched enough videos to see women in MMA to know that's not even necessary.

I go to speak but he finally says something instead, "Start your stretches on the mat."

"Okayyyy," I draw out the end of the word. "Can I at least know your name before you start barking orders at me?"

His eyebrow raises and I realize how bitchy that sounded, but I'm done letting men boss me around. I'm done letting *anyone* boss me around.

"You can call me Coach," he responds gruffly.

"Interesting first name, *Coach*."

I go over to the mats and start stretching. As I drop down onto the floor, that same feeling of being watched comes over me and I try my best to shake it away, obviously I'm in public and people look at other people in public.

But this is different.

I glance around trying to find the source, and that's when I see him again. The man from the bar. The asshole with the mesmerizingly blue eyes.

He's leaning against a far wall and there's no denying where he's looking because it's right at me. I debate flipping him off but decide against agitating him right now and go back to focusing on my stretches.

"Okay, everyone," *Coach* announces. "Before we get started today, you're going to watch a couple of my professional fighters go a round to show you what it's like."

Coach points over to the man who's been watching me. "This is Caine, he's one of our pro fighters here. He's going to be sparring with Cal."

Both men go into the cage, and I watch their minimal preparation, assuming because they've already done any stretching or whatever they needed to before this. Or think they are too good for it. Either way, it doesn't matter much to me.

Coach signals them to start, and they are circling around the ring, slightly bent at the hips with their hands wrapped and up, ready for the first move. It doesn't surprise me that the first move is made by Caine and then everything happens quickly as he maneuvers his body around Cal's who's trying to fight back.

He manages to get out of Caine's hold, but it isn't long before they are on the ground. Caine's legs are wrapped around Cal's body and his arms are around his neck.

Cal taps the side of Caine's leg, and he lets go. That's it.

"Alright, pair up," Coach calls out to the rest of us, and I linger, continuing to watch the two men as they stand back up. Especially since Caine's eyes find me instantly. His blank face pulls into the smallest smirk.

I turn away instantly, ready to focus on class and learning how to handle myself like that. I want to feel strong and powerful. To feel safe for the first time in my life.

I end up paired up with another guy in the class, he seems young—early twenties at most— around five foot six and has a shy smile. I can tell he's not used to this, the martial arts or the talking with new people. Eventually, I learn his name is Skylar and do my best to make him feel comfortable practicing the moves with me since that's why we are here.

Yet, the entire time I can't shake the feeling of eyes on me, and I know who they belong to. I refuse to acknowledge him for the remainder of the class. I don't even spare a glance in his direction as I leave the gym.

CHAPTER 9
ADAM

Caine can't keep his eyes off Max, and it makes my hackles rise. Caine is intense. He's unpredictable at times and I've seen what happens when he snaps. He tends to keep it in the cage, but the look in his eyes as he stares at the new woman in town reminds me a lot of what he looks like before a fight.

I shouldn't care. And I don't, not really. I don't think he would do anything too crazy, but part of me isn't sure.

It makes me think of Drew, how he believes he's a monster because of his past and what he's done. Yet, he's more in control than Caine, a man who was given everything in life and chose something else just because he could.

He never struggled like us, he got it all handed to him. Until he started fighting. This has been the first time he's had to work toward anything. You aren't just gifted with the skills, it's something you have to train and fight for. That's how I know what he looks like when he's motivated for something he wants.

And I think he wants her.

Which means he won't stop until he has her.

She surprised me today. She's clearly motivated and tenacious. When she screws up, she tries again until she gets it right. It's rare to impress me, but she did. It's different.

Now, here we are at The Tavern once again, Alexander and Cal already at the bar trying to talk to Danner. Caine, Drew, and I sit at a table toward the back keeping an eye on our surroundings.

Though, I feel like that means we're all looking at the same thing.

Max.

The mysterious woman who's arrived in town and caught too much attention in such a short time. And she doesn't even know it.

I watch her make drinks quickly—much quicker than she did that first night—and not put up with any shit from the patrons.

"What do you guys think of her?" Drew asks. Neither Caine nor I respond. "She seems like she's serious about her training."

That makes Caine scoff, but he still doesn't say anything.

Instead of responding, I push away from the table and approach the bar. I'm not even sure why my feet are bringing me up to the dark wood, sticky from having drinks spilled on it all night, but then I'm there. Staring down into the eyes of this fiery redhead.

"Hi, *Coach*," Max greets with a sneer. "What can I get you?"

"Water," I state simply. She rolls her eyes and mumbles something about "boring gym guys" before slapping a glass full of water on the counter in front of me.

"It's Adam by the way," I say as she starts to turn away.

"What?"

"My name. At the gym it's Coach, but outside of it, it's Adam."

"Enjoy your water, *Coach*," she says pointedly before returning back to serving other drinks that require a bit more effort than my glass of water.

As I get back to the table, Caine is leaning back in the chair that looks too small for him, with his large arms folded across his chest and his gaze locked on the redhead behind the bar.

"You both officially piss her off with your water orders?" Drew asks once I sit down.

"Something like that," I responded.

"Alright, well, if either of you end up running her out of the gym, then that's on you." Drew shrugs.

"So, you're telling me you were so nice and welcoming to her last week while we were gone?" I look at him skeptically. Drew doesn't take too kindly to new people either. He's as distrusting as the rest of us. We all have our reasons, and his are because he doesn't open up to *anyone*. Not even me.

Which is why what we have could never be anything more than just sex. Just the time for us to both get off and have a good time, then go our own way. No strings, no emotions. Neither of us could handle more than that, especially not Drew.

Caine on the other hand, scares almost everyone who meets him. And for good reason. Not me—I've met scarier. I've fought scarier. Lived with scarier. I've seen the darkest parts of humanity firsthand and came out alive.

He may think he's the scariest thing to walk around, but he's not. Not even close. The real dangers, the things that should scare you, are the things you'd never expect. The nicest people can be the vilest behind closed doors. The real monsters hide in plain sight, and you never know until it's too late.

"Whatever, I'm heading out." Drew stands up, looking down at me as he does, with a silent question.

We try to keep our situation to ourselves, it's no one else's business. Especially not the other guys. I'm a coach and Drew started off as just one of my fighters when he rolled into town five years ago. He started to help coach a year ago, and even more so now after his injury. But I know what people would think about us sleeping together. They would think he's using me or some other stupid shit.

So, we decided it's best to keep it just between us.

I answer Drew's silent question with a small nod. He knows what that means and accepts it with his own nod.

"See you guys tomorrow."

With him gone, it's just Caine and I at the table, sitting in silence. He has yet to look away from Max.

"You going to go talk to her?" I finally ask.

"Probably not."

I nod once like his answer makes sense. I'm not going to try and figure him out, or question what the fuck he's doing.

"Okay, I'll leave you to your staring contest then." I stand up, slapping a twenty on the table for a tip, despite not buying anything.

I step outside, the bite of the coastal breeze hits me before I pull on my helmet and swing a leg over my Yamaha YZF-R3, turning the key, letting out the clutch, and revving the engine before driving off toward Drew's house.

❧

DREW's front door swings open, and he's already shirtless, tattoos cover his arms and onto his chest, and I know they cover his back as well. The skin on his toned stomach is the only area on his torso untouched with ink. Unlike me, with practically every inch of my own skin covered with it, some of the artwork has meaning, stories from my life. Others are just there because I didn't care what the artist put on me, I just wanted to feel the scrape of the needle on my skin.

He opens the door wider, and I step inside, kicking off my wet boots as he walks further into his house. I shed my jacket, meeting him in the living room before draping it over a chair, pressing my hands against the top of it and leaning forward.

"Did I miss anything?" he asks, dropping onto his couch, his sweatpant covered legs spread out casually.

"Nah, I left not long after you."

"Okay, well then let's do what you're here for," he says casually and something about his tone irritates me. Like this is just for me. Like this is just a chore or something for him to check off a list.

"What the fuck does that mean?" I question, standing up straight, and folding my arms across my chest.

"What it always means—you're here to fuck, let's fuck so I can go to bed."

I narrow my eyes on him. "What is your deal?"

"Nothing, *fuck*." He slaps his hands against his thighs, standing from the couch and I refuse to move from my spot behind the chair.

"Then why the fuck are you acting like you don't even want me here? Because I'll leave, I don't give a shit." I grab my jacket, ready to do just that.

"Of course you don't." He shakes his head.

"Are you jealous or something? Suddenly wanting a relationship? What the fuck is going on?"

"No, I'm not fucking jealous, I'm pissed off, Adam. Every

fucking day you act like everything is fine, but you won't let me do anything. Won't let me practice or participate in anything other than helping *you*," he spits out.

"This is about not letting you train? Because I won't let you fight?" I ask, my tone dripping with annoyance. "Fuck me for not wanting you to get your other knee blown out, right?" I shake my head.

He steps up to me, getting in my face, his anger palpable and mine is close to matching his at this moment.

"Don't know if you've noticed lately, *Coach*, but I'm a big boy and know what I can and can't handle," his lip curling as he practically growls the words in my face.

"And as your *Coach* I know what I'm willing and not willing to let my fighters go through."

"That's all I am? That's all any of us are then? *Your* fighters?"

"Yes, and just so it's clear that's all you'll be." I let the anger take over, and am about to storm out the door because I didn't come over here for a fight. I thought we've been on the same page, but it doesn't seem like it right now and I don't know where any of this came from.

Instead of saying anything else, he grabs me by the back of my neck and slams his mouth onto mine. I want to fight him, to get to the bottom of this sudden anger, or just leave and let him be pissed off alone. But when he bites down, his teeth sinking into my lower lip, I realize this is going to be a different kind of fight.

This fight is the kind we're going to have like this, with our bodies seeking pleasure instead of pain. Our mouths are sealed and tongues tangled as we fight for dominance. We lick and bite as our hands grab and scratch. I work my hand into the waistband of his pants, gripping him roughly in my fist, squeezing his shaft, feeling the bulges of his piercings. He lets out a moan as I roughly run my hand up and down, jacking him off.

He thrusts into my fist as I swallow down his moans. His pace increases and I can tell he wants more; he wants to come. And he's close.

I break our mouths apart, dropping my forehead to his, using my free hand to hold the back of his neck tightly. I grip his erection tight at the base and he continues to thrust against me, trying to gain the friction I'm not allowing him to find.

"Seems like you just wanted to get off. Wanted to *use me* to get yourself off." I grip his neck tighter.

"So what? That's what we do. *Fuck*," he groans. "Move your hand."

I let out a dry chuckle. "No, you want to get off? You can do it yourself." I remove my hand from his pants and back away. Grabbing my jacket, I don't look back at him as I quickly slip my boots on.

"That's how you're going to leave things, then?" Drew asks from behind me, I can hear how pissed he is, and I know how explosive he can be. I also know how well he can bottle it up.

"Yup, finish yourself." I leave his house, and he doesn't try to stop me. Not even when I'm on my bike, about to drive off, all I see is the light from his living room through the window darken and know that's all the response I'm going to get.

Fine by me. Despite my raging hard on, I head back home. Knowing whatever has been going on between us isn't really over, but there's no denying it's changed. Who knows if that change will be good or bad.

CHAPTER 10
CAINE

There's music.

It's playing inside her house as I find myself outside, just like I have every night for the last week. This is the first time I've heard music. It's bass heavy, but not loud. I stand on the sidewalk, my hood pulled up as I wait to see if tonight will be the night for something new. A glimpse of her, a glimpse of *something*.

That's when I see it—it's still dark, but there's a soft glow in the room which highlights her silhouette in the window. Then she moves.

Actually, she glides.

She's dancing, I don't see enough and it's over before the song even changes. She freezes in place, for a second, I think it's because she sees me, but there's no way. Then the music stops.

And she's gone from the window, leaving me staring at the dark house again.

There's a buzzing under my skin, it's different than before a fight. This is something I haven't felt in a long time. There's this pull to get closer to her. To take it a step further. This feeling leaves me wanting more than to just stare at her house every fucking night. I shouldn't go in; I should leave her alone for a little while longer. I continue to wait until it becomes unbearable. This feeling of needing to be closer to her. It overwhelms and consumes me.

It's that exact feeling that brings me forward, testing her front door, and it's locked. Going around the back, I check the back door and notice a slight jiggle, the lock gives way easily and then I'm inside. Surrounded by her scent, it's sweet and floral and immediately I'm hit with the need to find the source.

Quietly, I make my way through the small home until I reach her bedroom, the door is cracked, and I can see her there. She's lying in bed, back turned toward me. Her red hair contrasts the white bedsheets, almost looking like blood.

I need to get closer to her. I need to touch her, to feel her, just once. I push open her door, led by this drive to conquer her, it barely makes a sound, and she doesn't stir.

Part of me was hoping I'd find her sleeping. The other part wants to find her awake. Maybe she'll scream, maybe she'll fight. Just the thought already has me hardening for the fantasy. I step through the threshold. She doesn't move. Not even as I get closer. Her chest rises and falls evenly under the blankets with each breath.

Silently, I get closer until I'm standing at the edge of her bed. I want to reach out and touch her. I want her to know I'm here. But I also don't want to ruin this. Not now. I just look at her.

How perfect she is laying there, her creamy skin is untouched, but would look so beautiful with my marks.

When she runs from me, she's going to know exactly what's going to happen when I catch her. When she screams for me, we are both going to enjoy every second of it. So, I'll be patient, which is why I leave her room, and her house for the night. But I'll be back, and maybe when I am, I'll make sure she knows it.

※

As I'm wrapping my hands, my mind wanders back to last night. Always back to her. What if I put this wrap around her pretty throat. Used it to tie her against the corner of the ring keeping her there while I used her body how I wanted. How long would she fight before giving in? How many times would she come for me, my name on her lips even though I know she'll insist she doesn't want it.

"Caine," Coach barks, pulling me away from my thoughts of her screaming my name because it doesn't sound as good coming from him.

I look over at him and he nods me over to the front desk. Standing behind the computer with him I see that he has a schedule pulled up for some fights for me to attend.

"All of them." I barely even look at the list. I want all the fights, all the exposure, and all the money.

I hate that I'm still living in my family's shadow. Most of the money in my account is theirs, and the only reason they haven't cut me off is because they're hoping I'll come back and admit defeat. That'll never happen. I won't go back there just to do what they want. Fuck going to law school, fuck following in my dad's footsteps. I'm going to continue fighting and make it on my own.

I hear Adam sigh from behind me as I finish wrapping my hands and start practicing. Drew is across the gym, working his upper body, probably because Coach will get on his ass if he does too much with his legs.

Personally, if he wants to fuck himself up more that should be up to him. It's his body to ruin if he wants.

As I start my combinations on the bag, I feel my body loosen with each punch and kick as instinct takes over. I hardly notice when Drew walks over until he's holding the other side of the bag I'm currently attacking, and it doesn't swing like it should.

I continue to try and hit the bag, but when it doesn't budge, I stop, shaking out my arms. "What do you want?"

"I want to spar. Later, after Adam is gone."

I'll never turn down the opportunity to get some practice in. Especially with an actually decent fighter.

"'Kay," I agree. "Now go away."

Something I like about Drew is he's never one to question anything, or to stick around too long. I also like that he's willing to go behind Coach's back to fight.

Once I'm done here with him, I can go by Max's house and see her again. I already feel the need to see her washing over me, and it's getting stronger. Soon, I'm going to need to touch her. Whether she's ready for me or not.

THE PUNCH LANDS across my jaw, and I smirk at the slight sting from Drew's fist. I go for a takedown, but he's able to get out of my grip. I don't take it easy on him. I'm not mindful of his knee and he doesn't act like he wants me to be.

My own fist lands against his face, making him falter, but even as I try to grab him, he avoids my hold. We circle around the ring, ready for whoever is going to make the next move. When I try, I stumble just slightly and any fighter with less experience wouldn't have noticed, but Drew did. And that's how he's able to get a grip on me and put me in a hold.

I fight to get out of it and manage to do so before he gets me into a full takedown. We continue on like this until we're both sweaty and getting tired. But even when my body starts to feel tired, my mind doesn't quit. Which is how I'm able to get him into submission until he taps, and I let up.

"Fuck," he grabs a water bottle, gulping it down. "I miss this."

"Just tell Adam to fuck off and you're going to fight anyway." *It's what I would do.*

Drew just scoffs, wiping his face down with a towel. Instead of trying to help him figure out his shit or listening to him complain about it, I gather my stuff to head out.

There's someone I need to go see.

CHAPTER 11
MAX

Every night it's been the same routine.

I get home from work and try to go to bed. Sometimes I'm able to fall asleep, other times I toss and turn. But without fail I'll always wake up at some point in the night. When something feels off, like someone else is there, watching from the shadows.

The weirdest part of it all is that I'm not scared.

The logical part of me knows it's not Carson, or anyone from my family. I don't know how I know, other than if it was them, I'd have been dragged out of here already, and that's mostly why I feel like I'm probably just going insane. That's why I turn on music and let it flow through me, sometimes I'm able to move with it, other times not.

This is my new normal and I don't hate it.

There isn't the fear of what I'm going to walk into when I come home. Fear that Carson has been drinking and how he's going to take it out on me or what he'll make me do. There isn't any worry about my parents and what they're going to make me do, dress up for, or who they will make me talk to.

It's a peace that I've never experienced before. Despite the feeling like I'm being watched, the peace is soothing.

After stripping off the clothes I wore to work, the smell of smoke, beer, and liquor lingers on my skin. I get into the hot shower to wash it all away. The water beats down on me, soaking my hair as I work the shampoo then conditioner through my long auburn locks.

As I'm rinsing the conditioner out, I feel like I hear a door closing, and jump. Standing still, I wait to hear something else, but nothing happens. I'm sure the noise was from outside. Continuing my shower, I get that feeling again. The one I get when I wake up every night, but this time I'm fully awake as it hits.

I turn off the water and just stand in the shower, waiting to see if I hear anything else. The water drips from the shower head, but the rest of my house is silent. Even as I step out into the bathroom, wrapping a towel around myself.

Hesitantly, I step into my bedroom and glance around to see if anything is out of place, still waiting to hear something else. Everything looks as it should, and no sounds are made.

Not even as I change into an old, ripped, oversized T-shirt. I always wanted to be able to wear things like this around the house and just be comfortable. Too bad I never could, because I was told that's not how a woman is supposed to dress.

And Carson liked silk.

Everything I wore had to be something *he* liked. Which is why I left behind all those silk pajamas when I left, because he liked them so much that he can enjoy them by himself now. Wear them, jack off with them, I don't care, it's not my problem anymore.

I do wish I brought one pair to burn, though, that would've been nice.

My phone dings from where I left it on my kitchen counter, since no one is really trying to get a hold of me, it's pretty surprising that it's going off at all, though I'm sure it's going to be Danner. She's nice and is essentially forcing her friendship on me. I didn't come here looking for any sort of connection, but I guess a friend may be nice once I actually get used to living a normal life.

As I walk into my living room toward my kitchen, my feet freeze and I stop dead in my tracks, staring at the large man leaning against the wall across the room. He's massive and not entirely unfamiliar, but it really hits me when I get a glimpse at his light eyes, the blue so bright that it's almost silver has me recognizing him instantly.

The guy from the first night at the bar. The fighter at the gym. Caine.

"What the fuck are you doing here? *How* are you here?" I stutter, looking around to see if he broke a window or something to be here, but everything seems to be untouched.

"I'm here for you," his voice is deep and I'm a little surprised he said anything. But it doesn't really answer my questions. For a second, I'm worried that he's here because he knows Carson or my parents. Maybe they sent him, but there's no way they would know where I am. And I met him during my first shift, so it would be impossible.

"Why? How did you get in?" I look around again, shaking my head. "Actually, it doesn't matter, get out."

It's my defiance that gets him to smirk, just the slightest pull of his lips, but it's there. And it makes me uneasy seeing him be anything other than standoffish. There's something sinister in that movement. Something that makes me feel like I should want to run in the other direction. But another part of me has me staying still.

Which is why I don't move. My heart rate kicks up the longer he looks at me, but I still don't move. Not even when his eyes roam over my barely covered body, my legs completely exposed, my nipples hardening into peaks under the thin fabric without a bra to conceal them.

I shift slightly, making my legs rub together, and I'm ashamed of the slickness I feel pooling there. But it's the reminder that I never sleep in any underwear and that's the reason that I don't have any on. Now, here I am with a somewhat scary looking man, standing in my house uninvited, towering over me while I'm practically naked. For some reason my body's reaction has *not* been to scream and run away.

No, my body has decided to react in a way it really shouldn't. As he stalks forward, I stay rooted to the spot. I can't even get my voice to work as he gets closer. His footsteps are heavy and seem to get louder with every step he takes closer to me. My breathing picks up, and yet I don't move. I can't. I'm stuck.

Pulling every bit of mental strength I can manage, I fold my arms across my chest, standing as tall as I can while he steps even closer. "Why are you here, Caine?"

He's standing so close now that if I reached out I could touch him, but I don't move, waiting for his response.

"I thought you'd be sleeping," he responds.

My eyebrows knit together at yet another non-answer from him. "So breaking and entering doesn't matter if the person that lives there is sleeping?"

He makes a small huffing noise, almost like the world's smallest laugh. If it were anyone else, I may think that's what it is, but I don't feel like he's capable of such an action. He probably doesn't find anything funny. Or amusing. Or joyful unless it's beating people to a pulp and watching them bleed out.

Or breaking into unsuspecting women's homes and trying to scare them.

He glances around briefly. "Nothing looks broken to me."

I breathe out an annoyed sound. "Okay, well, you're still in my house uninvited and I want you to leave before I call the cops."

"You're not going to call the cops."

I scoff, "Yes I am."

"With what phone?"

I glance behind him at the counter where my phone still is, and I know there's no way I can get to it without him easily grabbing me. That doesn't mean I'm not about to try. I dart past him quickly, and manage to get to the counter, grabbing my phone before I'm completely pinned by the large body behind me.

His legs and hips push against mine, holding me in place as he reaches around, plucking my phone from my hand despite my efforts to fight him off. My phone clatters out of reach as he pushes it away and spins me around to face him. Caine pins my hips with his, the counter digging into my back.

"Get the fuck off me," I screech, trying to swing my arms and legs to make any sort of contact with him. Unfortunately, I'm not able to with the way he's pressed completely against me.

"You really need to work a bit harder in training if this is the best you can do," he taunts, dragging his nose to where my pulse beats violently under my ear and inhales.

I scream out in frustration, attempting to land a punch against his face. Instead, he grabs my wrist in one hand and before I'm even able to try and swing with my free hand, he has that one as well. He manipulates my body with expertise until he's holding both wrists in one hand against my chest.

I continue to try and get him off me, but the hold he has won't budge. When I shift my hips slightly, that's when I feel it, the unmistakable hardness rubbing against me, and I suck in a quick breath.

"Let me go," I grit out.

His free hand falls to my exposed thigh, right where the hem of the T-shirt grazes my skin. "I'll let go if you make me."

He moves his fingers higher, taking my shirt with them as he slides up the skin of my leg and it renews my fight. I try to break my hands free, but all it does is make him tighten his grip more, making me whimper from the pressure. But not because of the pain, though I'm sure I'm going to have bruises left over, but because I feel how my traitorous body is responding, as the wetness between my thighs increases. My pussy throbs when he presses his hips against me again.

He's so much bigger than me, so much stronger. He could truly do anything he wants to me at this moment and I'm hardly even trying to stop him.

"Let me go," I repeat weakly as his hand continues to move up my leg, he's close to discovering that there's nothing between his hand and my pussy. Which means soon, he'll discover how wet this interaction is making me.

His head dips down to my ear, lips grazing against my skin and chills cover my body. Though, I can hardly hear him over the blood pounding in my ears. "I said make me, killer."

I scowl at the nickname. I double my efforts to fight him off, and I'm actually able to move my foot enough to stomp on his instep, but he's wearing shoes and I'm not, so it doesn't even matter. Then I'm back to being completely pinned and his hand has made it up to where my thigh meets my hip and is sliding forward.

"Please, let me go," I try. This time I actually get a laugh from him. It's deep, throaty, and full of smoke. The feel of it trembles down my spine, sending another set of chills running throughout my body.

"Not happening." He turns me around again so my hips are

pushed into the counter while he covers my back. "Especially when you came out here without anything covering your pussy. Almost like you were wanting something like this to happen," he says darkly.

"I'm allowed to walk around my house however I want to, you aren't supposed to be here," I rasp.

His fingers are at the juncture between my thighs now, they graze against my core, and I feel the rumble of his chest with the low growl he lets out as he discovers what I wanted so badly to hide.

"And you shouldn't be soaking wet," he teases, applying some pressure to my clit making me bite back a moan.

"Don't fucking touch me," I spit, attempting to throw my head back to hopefully do some damage, but all I feel is his solid chest and he runs a finger through my slit and my breath hitches right before he pushes it inside me roughly.

I cry out at the intrusion, and try again to get away from him, but he continues to keep me pinned between his brick wall of a body and the cold stone of my kitchen counter. I'm completely at his mercy as he roughly pumps his finger inside my embarrassingly wet cunt.

"Sure as fuck seems like your pussy wants me to be touching you." He punctuates his words by shoving another finger in and I scream at the sudden stretch. And because I know that I shouldn't want him touching me, despite the fact that I'm suddenly desperate for more.

The palm of his hand presses against my clit and it makes my knees buckle as a shot of pleasure shoots through me. Caine presses me harder against the counter and there's no denying the *large* erection digging into my back. The mere thought of that coming anywhere near me has my fear kicking up a notch.

It's that thought that has me struggling, fighting even more than the fact that there's a man I don't know in my house. A man that's essentially holding me hostage with his fingers knuckle deep inside of me.

Clearly there's something wrong with me.

But I guess I've known that for a while.

I feel him grip my throat at the same time he curls his fingers, hitting a spot on my inner walls that has me clenching and moaning.

"You like this don't you, killer? You like the fact that I'm taking whatever the fuck I want from you and there's not a damn thing you can do about it?" His gruff voice adds to the sensations I'm feeling, and I hate how my body is responding.

I hate that he's right.

"No, get the fuck off me." I try to buck against him, using my body weight to try and push him off once again. Though, it still doesn't work and only makes him push his fingers in rougher and squeeze my throat tighter.

My head is tilted back slightly with the grip he has on me, and that's when I realize my arms are free once again. Reaching behind me, I grab the back of his neck, digging my nails into his skin and he groans.

"That's right, fucking hurt me."

I do just that while he continues to work me with his hand, and I begin to feel the orgasm cresting from the way he's rubbing and fucking me with his fingers. I don't want it to come though, I don't want to give him that. I don't want to give him anything more than he's already taken.

Moving my hands from his neck, I dig my nails into the skin of his arms, but it doesn't make him move, it only has him tightening his grip so hard he's cutting off my air. The worst part isn't the fact that he could easily kill me right now.

No, the worst part is that it's the lack of air and fear that has my orgasm that was approaching, full on barreling toward me. I try to hold it back. I want to hold it back, but when Caine squeezes my throat even harder, I'm completely cut off from taking a breath, his deep gravelly voice says, "Give it to me." I'm done.

His grip on my throat lets up, so I suck in air the same moment my release slams into me. I'm clenching around his fingers, gasping for breath while crying out. He pushes my chest down on the counter, covering my back with his hard chest as he works me through the pleasure and I'm still trying to catch my breath as the strongest orgasm of my life racks through me.

Once I come down, he removes his hand from under my shirt, wiping his soaking wet fingers on the skin of my legs making me shiver. His lips graze against my ear when he speaks, "Next time it's going to be my dick you come all over."

"Next time I'm calling the cops," I spit back.

He huffs a breath that I think is supposed to be a chuckle as he lifts off me and I whirl around ready to try and fight him again, but his long legs have him across the room, almost to my back door.

"No, you're not. But you should really get this lock fixed," he says, opening the door and I gape at him. "Or don't, makes it easy for me, but I like a challenge."

"Fuck you," I seethe.

"Don't worry. You will."

Then he's gone.

I rush forward to lock the door he just left out of, and stare at it for a few seconds while I try to work out what just happened. I'm still throbbing between my legs, I can still feel the phantom grip of his hand around my neck, and my hips sting from where the counter was digging into me. Everything is so confusing, but I remember what he said about my door.

I jiggle the handle slightly and the lock pops open easily. Throwing my head back with a loud groan I know the chance of me getting any sleep tonight has all but vanished knowing I'm not secure here. Though, I've already faced one monster tonight, what's another one if I was somehow found.

Despite my annoyance, the soreness in my core, and the tinge of fear I can never quite get rid of, I lock the door again, shove a chair underneath the door handle, and turn on some music.

At first, it's just to take me out of my mind, but as the melody continues I feel myself moving. Before I know it I'm dancing without having the noise of my thoughts affecting it. For the first time in a long time, I feel freer than I think I ever have.

CHAPTER 12
DREW

I'm sore from sparring with Caine two nights ago, but I'm doing my best to hide it as I assist Adam in teaching a Muay Thai class. I think he notices I'm favoring my left side slightly, but he doesn't say anything as we continue with class.

Out of the corner of my eye, I notice Caine comes in and heads straight to the equipment to start lifting. He's not quiet about it, the weights clunking as he loads up the bar and starts to work. Luckily class is almost over. The asshole thinks he can do whatever he wants whenever he wants, and no one stops him.

Sometimes Adam tells him not to do this shit when there's a class going on, but it doesn't make a difference. And since he's considered the best fighter here, it's not like Adam is going to kick him out of the gym. It doesn't matter anyway; I don't give a shit.

Adam and I haven't talked about the other night, and I don't know if we are going to. This weekend Caine has a fight somewhere, Seattle, I think. I don't know and I really don't care. At least this time I don't have to cover any classes by myself.

Everyone from Muay Thai is leaving and Adam goes right to his office without a second glance at either me or Caine.

Works for me.

I step up to the front desk as everyone is leaving just to check when I can come back without talking to a certain someone. I'm hardly paying attention when I feel the air shift as someone steps up to the desk.

"What can I help you with?" I ask without looking up.

"I want to sign up for another class." I recognize that voice, though it sounds less snarky than I've heard it before.

I look up to see Max standing there, hands folded leaning forward, eyes locked on me, despite the loud thunk of weights I know come from Caine. She doesn't even flinch or glance in that direction.

"What class are you wanting to join?" I ask simply.

"Something where I can hit people."

I choke on a small laugh at her serious tone. She just raises her eyebrow and makes it clear that she's serious about her request.

"None of this is about hitting and hurting people, you know that, right?" I have to ask, even if that's why most of us started the sport. But that's not the point of it.

"Sure." She shrugs.

"Okay, well, if you're wanting to hit things." I give her a pointed look. "Then we can put you in a kickboxing class if you'd like."

"Who teaches it?" she asks quickly, her eyes darting over to Caine briefly and I can't tell if she's hoping I'll say his name or hoping I don't.

"Coach Adam," I answer easily. Boxing is his specialty, not everyone knows he was a professional boxer when he was young because he doesn't talk about himself a lot. He dabbled in everything else throughout his career, but boxing was always his main focus. That is, until he retired and trained heavily in BJJ and Muay Thai as well.

"Good. Sign me up." She nods.

"Alright," I agree. This time I don't need to see any of her information, because I remember it. I remember too much about this girl when I shouldn't.

As I get her enrolled in the class, I notice her gaze flick over to Caine again. That's when I see that he's stopped his routine, reaches down and flicks the buckle of the lifting belt open before dropping it, his eyes never leaving hers.

"Something going on there?" I ask, and I'm not even sure why.

She scoffs, looking back at me. "No."

The side of my lip tugs up in a small smile at her dismissal because that's not usually the reaction he gets. I hear the door to the office open behind me and for some reason it prompts me to do something I would've never thought I would do.

"So, you're single then?" I ask.

"Um, yes and not interested in that changing," she answers slowly.

I force out a chuckle that I hope sounds lighthearted. "One date wouldn't change it."

She looks at me skeptically and I don't blame her, I haven't exactly been *nice* before now. And really, I'm not thinking too much about what I'm doing other than seeing how everyone will react. With the way Caine is looking over here I know I'm getting at least one reaction.

"I'm not going on a date with you," she states seriously.

I lean forward, getting closer to her and I see her eyes catch on my exposed arms as I subtly flex them. "We don't have to call it a date then, we can just hang out."

"I'll pass, thanks."

"You don't want any friends?" I try, feeling everyone's eyes on us.

She must too because she glances over at Caine again, and I notice her body language change, softening as she leans in closer to me. "I don't know what it is you're trying to do, but leave me out of it."

"Not trying to do anything other than be a nice person."

She laughs loudly, tossing her head back dramatically before looking back at me again. "I don't think any of you around here are *nice people*."

"Maybe I am, and you've just caught me on a bad day before."

She leans back, keeping her hands planted on the desk with her arms outstretched as she puts distance between us. "I doubt that. See ya around."

As she goes to leave, Karissa bumps into her shoulder in a way I know was intentional. Max narrows her eyes at her.

"Gotta watch out with those wide ass shoulders," Karissa sneers.

"Pretty sure you just don't know how to walk straight," Max retorts, and without saying anything else she walks out.

I watch her leave, especially the sway of her hips and the way her tight jeans hug her round ass. My intention was to get a rise out of everyone, including her, but I feel myself having a reaction to her. I can't deny that it's tempting to pursue her a bit harder.

Karissa makes a disgusted look at her before turning with her eyes set on me, and the flirty look takes over. *Nope.* I look away at the exact same time Adam says the first words he's said to me since he left my house the other night.

"How'd that go?"

"Great," I grunt.

"Sounds like it."

"Jealous?"

"Nope, but I think someone else may be." He nods toward Caine, and I see him staring daggers at me.

I just smile at him in response.

Pulling out my phone, I make it look like I'm busy, but really, I'm entering her number that I quickly memorized from her profile into my contacts.

When I look up, Adam is gone, and I just shake my head. He may be jealous, but there's no way he's going to show it. Though I see Caine is still staring at me, his murderous gaze unwavering and I don't know why, but it makes me want to fuck with him more. Maybe it's because he seems to get everything he wants. Or maybe it's because I never do and being able to train and fight has been one thing for myself until even that was taken away from me.

Now, maybe it's time I take something from him.

CHAPTER 13
MAX

Something must be in the water at the gym because I thought Caine was the only crazy one, but it seems to have spread to Drew as well. First, they were assholes to me, and now they're hitting on me like that's completely normal.

Okay, Caine is still an asshole. And actually, insane since he broke into my house and fingered me while holding me hostage in my kitchen. Not exactly the same as Drew asking me on a date, but still, I feel like he's just as crazy.

Yet, the crazy intrigues me in a way that it shouldn't. And that's something I don't have the time to unpack. Especially as I head into work after my pit stop at Uncaged. I hope Caine realizes why I was there—it's so the next time he tries to touch me without permission, I'll be better prepared to put up a fight.

Even though it seems like that's exactly what he wants from me.

"Hey Max," George calls as soon as I'm inside the front door of The Tavern.

"Hi," I nod. George has been a bit nicer to me since I've proved to him that I can handle myself working here. It's like I've passed some sort of test.

"You're going to be alone behind the bar tonight, think you can handle it?" he asks and I hide my grimace. I've always had someone else with me since I started and I'm a little worried but refuse to show any sort of weakness around here.

"Yeah, I can," I state firmly. He gives me a look that tells me he's trying to see through what I'm saying and detect any lie, but I stand my ground.

"Alright."

As the night continues and I work my shift, I somewhat regret saying I'd be okay alone. I also don't think I had any other option. I'm not able to keep track of what time it is when I see Danner come in. She smiles at me before looking around, probably noticing my lack of help and frowning.

For such a small town, I swear this place is busier than it should be, especially for some random Wednesday. Though, I haven't been yelled at or called a bitch, so I count that as a win.

"Hey girl," Danner greets when I finally make it over to her.

"Hey, are you wanting anything?"

"Just a Jack and Coke, I'll make it easy on you," she answers easily, and I quickly pour the drink for her as she hands over cash. "Keep the change, babe."

My lips quirk in a small smile. "Thanks."

I turn to the register and my eyes catch on the man walking in and I roll my eyes. I'm surprised to see him alone, but it doesn't dampen the annoyance at seeing *any* of them. My irritation ramps up when Drew slides into the one open stool at the end of the bar.

Focusing all my attention on everyone else needing drinks, I try to pretend he's not there. Until he makes it impossible by calling me over by name, and it makes me want to punch him in the throat.

I'm sure that's not a move I'll be taught in any sort of training, but I know it, anyway.

"Maxine," he calls when I don't respond the first time, and I'm changing my mind about the throat punch and thinking a junk punch would be more fitting for him.

Stepping toward him, I fold my arms across my chest. "Do *not* call me that."

"I called for Max, and you ignored me." He shrugs.

"I was hoping you'd go away. What do you want?"

"A date would be nice."

"I already turned you down once today, it might be embarrassing to have to do it again." I narrow my eyes at him. "Tell me what you want to drink or I'm moving on to the next customer."

"Bourbon. Neat."

I can't help the tiny laugh I let out. "Oh, so one of you does actually drink then, huh?"

I pour the drink, sliding it in front of him when he slaps his credit card down. "Leave it open. I plan to stay here awhile."

"Great," I respond dryly, refusing to acknowledge him more than I have to.

I can't lie though; I'm wondering where his buddies are and a part of me would love it if Caine could show up and put Drew's face through a wall for hitting on me. I saw how he looked at him when I came to the gym earlier, like he was contemplating murder. I know there's something about that man that is a bit questionable…unhinged…*dangerous.*

The same thing could be said about Drew. Both feel dangerous in different ways and instinctively, I know that I should stay far *far* away.

The last thing I need is more danger in my life. Clearly, I already have enough if Caine feels like he can break into my house whenever he wants. Which reminds me of the new lock I bought earlier that I need to install before I go to bed tonight.

The rest of my shift goes by in a blur of faces, drinks, cash, and cards. My feet are throbbing as the night gets later and it's almost time to close. Danner stuck around for a while before leaving around midnight to go to bed. The one person that has stuck around the entire night, and is still sitting at the bar with only his second drink of the night, is Drew.

"We're closing up, you're going to need to leave," I tell him as I hand over his receipt, not giving him the opportunity to order another drink. I'm not staying here any later than I need to because he wants to play games.

"Let me walk you home." It's not a question.

"Absolutely not." The last thing I need is for both him *and* Caine to know where I live. Still not sure how he knew anyway.

"It's for safety."

"I'm taking classes *for safety;* I can handle it."

"I'd feel better if I walked you home."

I roll my eyes at his persistence and refuse to argue with him right now because all I want to do is close the bar and go home. Without saying anything else to him, I turn on all the lights and stand by the front door, folding my arms across my chest while tapping my foot.

Drew gets the hint, finishing his drink with one last gulp before standing and walking toward the door. Instead of walking out of it, he steps up in front of me, looming over me and I don't move a muscle.

"I'll be waiting outside." He's leaning down slightly since he's so much taller than me and I can feel his bourbon coated breath on my skin, and I work to suppress the shiver.

"Don't," I tell him.

He stands up straight, his eyes roam over my body once before leaving and I don't waste any time closing and locking the door behind him. It reminds me of the other night with Caine. Only less violating. But what I still don't understand from that night, is why I'm not more afraid. *I should be, right?* Any normal person would be terrified. But I'm not.

When I'm done cleaning up everything around the bar, I'm sure enough time has passed that Drew won't still be waiting outside for me. Collecting my things, I step outside, locking the door behind me and I feel him before I see him. So I'm not surprised when I turn around and he's there, leaning against the wood siding of the building.

"Let's go," he encourages. I want to argue more and refuse to let him walk me home, but honestly, I'm tired and just want to go home. So instead of fighting, I don't say anything and just keep walking.

I try to maintain a fast pace so maybe he'll give up, but it doesn't work because his long legs keep up with my strides easily. The one thing I'm thankful for is the fact that he doesn't say anything. However, I'm very aware of the fact that a man I do not know is walking me home claiming safety, when he could very much be the reason I'm unsafe.

Or he knows about Caine and that's why he's doing this.

My mind is tired from all this thinking and worrying. We get to my house, and I rush toward my front door without a word. He follows slowly as I unlock the door quickly, turning back toward Drew who's standing at the bottom of the small set of stairs leading up to the front deck.

"Thanks," I murmur with a wave.

"Goodnight, Max."

Rushing inside, I lock the door and peek out the small

window to make sure he leaves. When he does, my shoulders drop as I relax. Looking toward the back door, I remember the messed-up lock and the fact that I need to fix it.

My body and mind are both exhausted though, and I decide to leave the project for tomorrow. Which may be a dumb idea, considering that I know the risk. I know that I could wake up to someone in my house again. But it won't be the devil from my past, and anything is better than him.

That's why I drag myself up to bed, accepting that I might be inviting evil into my house once again. And for some reason, I'm not even worried about it.

I don't hear anything as I get ready for bed and climb into my cool sheets. Even as I start to drift off, I know he's not here. Which may be the case for tonight, but the voice in the back of my head tells me he'll be back. Maybe not tonight, but he will be.

CHAPTER 14
CAINE

I wanted to go to her. I wanted to find her in bed, crawl in there with her, hold her down, and feed my cock into her sweet mouth. I wanted to hear her choke on it and see the pretty tears streaming down her face as she cried for me while my dick was buried in her throat.

Especially after watching Drew talk to her earlier, I need to stake my claim, needing both her and him to know that he can't fucking touch her.

But I couldn't.

I had to go to Seattle for a fight. I tried to tell Adam we could leave in the morning, but he wouldn't even consider it and told me we needed to leave tonight or I wouldn't be fighting. So, my obsession had to take a backseat for now.

When I get back, she better be ready because I'm not taking it easy on her like I did the other night. That was nothing compared to the things I plan to do to her. And even though Drew is stuck back in Seaside while we are gone, I know he won't touch her. She wouldn't let him. She needs the push and he won't do it.

That's only for me.

I'm covered in sweat and blood, not all of it mine, at the end of the fight that I won with a knockout.

"Good work," Adam grunts out. It's the best compliment I can expect from him, which is fine by me. I don't need to be praised or some shit. I don't do that in the bedroom, and I don't expect anyone to do it with me at all.

I nod in response, already playing in my head how I can do better next time. What to adjust, what to change completely, where I went wrong, and what mistakes to never make again. I know a lot of fighters think about their fights after the fact, but I doubt they are as hard on themselves as I am.

My entire life I was raised to be a perfectionist, and that is how I continue to see myself. Especially when it comes to my goals in this career.

"Out of your head, go get cleaned up," Adam insists, pulling me out of my thoughts but it'll only work for a few minutes until I'm sucked back in on how I can improve my strategy.

Though, this time as I'm washing my body off, I see some of the faint scratch marks that aren't from the fight. They're almost faded against my tan skin, but it brings me right back to that night in the kitchen with Max.

I have to keep my erection down because this is not the place. But when I get back to the hotel I plan on replaying every feeling, every single sound she made, and every bite of her nails digging in my skin while I fuck my fist.

I need to get back home so I can have that in person again. I need it more than I need my next breath. After the event is over and we're back at the hotel, I think about how I wish I had a way to watch her while I'm away. Maybe at some point I'll figure out a way to do that.

For now, my memories will have to be enough.

※

THE DRIVE back home feels a lot longer than it normally does. I keep my headphones in with music blasting as Adam drives and I watch the road ahead, impatiently waiting to be back in Seaside. The small glimpse of the ocean, despite the fog that's coating the coastline, has me bouncing my leg, needing to get out of this car.

As soon as he drops me off, I go inside to drop off my bag, but I'm not staying. I'm sure Max would love to know just how close she lives to me. Though the sun is just now setting and I'm not sure if she's home, I still make my way to her house to check for myself.

I need to see her, I won't be able to settle until I lay eyes on her. Until I touch her.

Her house seems quiet, I don't notice any lights on or hear any music. Seeing her at work isn't going to satiate me enough, but I don't care. I head there anyway. The second I step inside the dark bar I seek her out, and there she is behind the bar.

Her long red hair is pulled back in a ponytail that is

begging for my fist to yank on it. She's wearing some tight little tank top, her tits pushed up to give me the perfect view of her cleavage and it makes me want to lick every inch of skin I can see right now. When she turns around, standing up on her tiptoes, I see the shorts she's wearing and a peek at the fishnets underneath. I want to rip them off with my fucking teeth.

Sitting at an open spot at the bar, I rest my elbows in front of me waiting for her to notice me. I don't say anything, just watch her. The other bartender working with Max moves around her and places a hand on her waist as he does.

My eyes home in on the movement and I want to break that fucking hand. If he thinks he can touch what's mine, he's going to learn how wrong he is. I don't even know his name, but when he appears in front of me asking what I want it takes everything in me not to yank him across the bar top and beat him into the ground.

"What I want is for you to keep your fucking hands off Max," I say lowly.

He rears back, surprised and a little scared. "Sorry, Caine, I didn't know she was your girl."

I'd be surprised that he knows my name, but everyone in this town knows my name. And soon they're all going to know that she's mine too.

"Now you do. Get fucking lost."

He does just that, running away from me, but I watch him go up to Max, clearly avoiding touching her in any way as he says something I can't hear, but nods his head in my direction. She looks over, noticing me for the first time and narrows her eyes, turning back toward the dipshit and shaking her head.

They talk for a few more seconds, she's clearly arguing, and I almost want to laugh. Or go over to her, throw her over my shoulder, and show her just how *mine* she is. Doesn't matter if she wants to deny it, she's wrong.

Finally, she steps up in front of me, the bar separating us and it's too much distance for me.

"What do you want and why did you tell David that I'm 'your girl'? I'm not *your* anything."

"I'll take a water." I ignore her other question because there's no use arguing about this right now. She'll remember later just how mine she is.

With an eye roll, I watch as she fills a glass full of water and her eyes light up for a brief moment before she turns around. Spinning back toward me, she slams the glass down, the water sloshing a bit, and I see the telltale signs of the spit she just added. The look on her face almost seems like a dare. I meet her challenge, grabbing the glass and drinking the entire thing at once, keeping my eyes on her the entire time. I set the glass back down in front of me while her mouth is agape.

"Delicious," I murmur.

She doesn't say anything else before turning away. I spend the entire time watching her and watching *David* to make sure his hands stay off her.

When Max leans across the wooden top to take an order, I see how she pushes her tits out even more. I look to see who the fuck is getting to see it, so I can add gouging their eyes out to my list of things to do.

That's when I see who they belong to and my blood boils. What the fuck is Drew doing here, talking to her. And *why* is she letting him look at her like that? When she slides back to get him his drink she looks over at me, and I shake my head slowly.

She just smiles and I fist my hands on the bar. It's tempting, the urge to cause a giant scene, one that ends with me fucking her on this damned bar just to prove to her and everyone else in here that she's off limits. Including Drew.

Especially him, particularly when I see the smile she gives him, and then he says something that makes her throw her head back laughing. Again. And I'm out of my seat, going over to them.

"What's so funny?" I ask her, not looking at him yet because if I do, he's getting punched in the face.

Her eyes shift to Drew, the humor still evident there and I feel my knuckles crack with how hard I'm fisting them at my side.

"None of your business," she shrugs, getting back to her job. I continue to watch her before addressing Drew.

"The fuck do you think you're doing?"

"Getting a drink, maybe you should try it some time," he says, taking a sip of the brown liquor in his glass. Speaking into his glass, "Maybe it would make you less of an asshole."

"Doesn't work for you," I retort, seriously seconds away from laying into him right here. "She's mine, lay off."

He scoffs, "Does she know that?"

"Yes." I look over at her to see she's not paying any attention to us.

"You're delusional. I'll leave her alone when she tells me to." He starts to bring the glass up to his lips, but stops, looking down at the marks on my exposed forearms. "Actually, no I won't, she likes a fight, huh?"

I don't acknowledge the existence of the faint scratches to him. "What does Adam think about you going after her?"

"Doesn't give a shit." His tone is emotionless and I'm not sure if I believe him, but I don't care about their situation or relationship or whatever the fuck they have going on. I just want him to back off.

"Well I do, so fuck off."

He smirks. "Might be good for you to learn to share."

"I don't share."

He smiles into his drink and it sends me over the edge. I go around the bar, stepping up to Max, caging her from behind as she rings out a customer. I catch the way she gasps and tries to turn around, but I don't let her. I'm instantly hard with how much this reminds me of the other night. Plus, the fact that everyone can see us only adds to it.

Leaning down to her ear, I let my lips graze her skin just

barely because if I get even the slightest taste of her, I'm going to end up throwing her down and fucking her on this disgusting floor without a single thought. "I'll see you later, killer. Don't let any of these assholes touch you."

I feel the vibration of her laugh on my chest and I can't help but lean into her even more. "Good luck getting in this time, I fixed the lock."

"Perfect. I was hoping you did. I like a challenge."

George comes out from the back just as I'm rounding the front of the bar again. "Caine, I better not see you behind my fucking bar ever again."

"I don't give a shit," I respond before clapping a hand on Drew's shoulder harder than necessary and leaning in so only he can hear. "If you fucking touch her, I'll make sure to take out both of your knees."

"Fuck you," he spits and I slap my hand on his back twice, roughly before leaving.

I'm not going far, though, I'll just be waiting for her to come home. If she decides not to listen to me, and there's anyone else with her, they're going to experience more than just a warning from me.

CHAPTER 15
MAX

"Fucking prick," I mutter as soon as Caine's body leaves mine. I don't look up to watch what he's doing; I take my sweet time running the credit card and getting the receipt. By the time I'm done, he's gone, and I let out the breath I didn't realize I was holding.

"You okay?" David asks hesitantly.

I shake it off just like I'm used to doing. "Yeah, fine."

Throwing myself back into work I eventually get back to Drew, "Need another one?"

He looks at the glass on the counter and shakes his head. His green eyes lock on mine. I can't exactly read him, but he looks serious. Deadly so. "If Caine ever bugs you too much, let me know and I'll take care of it."

I roll my eyes, waving him off. "I can handle it, that's why I'm taking more classes. I'm an independent woman and don't need any of you muscle heads standing up for me."

I mean that more than he could ever know. I've never had the chance to be independent, and now that I am there's no going back. It doesn't matter if I have to deal with some psycho that thinks he has some right over me and my body. At the end of the day, I'm the one that gets a say in what happens to me now. I don't belong to anyone anymore.

I was my parents'. Then I was Carson's. I'm not about to be Caine's, or Drew's, or anyone else's. I'll never allow myself to belong to anyone else. The only person I belong to now is me.

⚡

AFTER CLOSING up and forcing Drew out of the bar yet again, I'm glad to see there aren't any random MMA fighters waiting outside for me and let out a sigh of relief. The air is cold and there's an extra chill from the light mist of rain that's coming down. I pull on the hoodie I bring with me but never wear inside since the air in the building can be stifling.

It doesn't do much to help my practically exposed legs since I'm just wearing fishnets and shorts with my black Doc Martens on my feet. Luckily, the walk isn't far, and I've endured worse. I keep a quick pace as I make my way down the dark streets that are barely lit by the streetlights. Everything is closed and there's an eeriness around here with the brightly painted buildings that contrast the darkness around them.

I make it to the sidewalk that runs parallel to the beach and notice that the lights here are dimmer than the ones on the main road as I make my way back home. Once on my street, I pick up my pace as the uneasy feeling of being watched runs down my spine.

As soon as I reach my house, I quickly unlock the door, rush in, and lock it behind me. My chest heaves slightly with deep breaths and the feeling I was having of being watched still doesn't dissipate, even now.

My house is quiet, and dark, but I'm not alone. I know it, for some reason, even knowing that, I don't turn on the lights that could potentially reveal whoever is here. Because it's the same feeling I had the other night. The hint of fear, but the intrigue and embarrassing arousal dripping between my thighs.

Stepping further inside, I try to find the figure I know is hiding in the dark, but I don't see or hear him. I start to think that I may just be going insane, my paranoia finally taking over. Probably from the mix of exhaustion, cold air, and history of trauma.

With a sigh, I go into my bedroom and flip on the light, except nothing happens. I flick the light switch a couple more times with the same result—nothing. The panic comes rushing back, and my heart starts beating so fast I feel like I can hear it. I turn to go find the breaker box, but instead of walking out of the doorway I run into a large hard chest.

The scream I let out is immediately muffled by the rough hand closing over my mouth, and my chance of escape is stopped by the other arm wrapping around my waist, holding me tightly against the muscled body. I refuse to have a repeat performance of the other night and start fighting.

Somehow, I manage to catch him off guard by shoving my knee into his groin and after making contact, his grip loosens enough that I'm able to break free, pushing past him and rushing out of my bedroom. I don't know where I'm trying to go. I don't even know where I could go, but the only thing my mind is telling me is to *run*.

So that's what I do. Stumbling slightly in the dark as I try to find the front door, the dim glow shining through the small window at the top is my guiding light. When I think I'm about to get to it, still unsure of what my plan is other than running down the street like a madman, a body crashes into my back, crushing me against the front door and I let out another scream.

Bucking back against him, I try to get him off me, but he's like a wall with his entire body pressing me against the door. From the side of my face stuck against the wood, all the way down to my legs that are immobile from the weight pressed against me.

As Caine leans down to speak, I try to throw my head back to connect with his face, but he holds me still with a fist wound tightly around my ponytail. "Every time you run, I'm going to catch you. And when I do, I'm going to do whatever I want with you."

"Get off me," I mumble, my teeth grazing the inside of my cheek as I talk from how tightly he has me shoved against the door.

He chuckles, deep and menacing in response. His feet kick my legs apart and I whimper at how helpless I feel against him. I want to be strong. I want to fight back, and I want to be able to feel like I can handle myself no matter who I'm going up against. But he always makes me feel helpless against him and that I really am at his mercy.

The voice at the back of my mind reminds me just how badly I want this. How I told Carson I would like to try this in the bedroom—have my control taken away in a way that I *want*. He did not understand, and it was never how I wanted. He took advantage of me when I was vulnerable and it was never for my pleasure, it was only for his.

Unlike now.

No, I refuse it. I refuse to give Caine anymore of myself, especially openly when he thinks he already has me. He can't know how badly I really want this.

"Let. Me. Go," I grit out.

He only kicks my legs even wider apart, pressing himself harder against my back, his hand that's not in my hair is moving between my legs, pressing against the crotch of my shorts and creating friction against my clit. I try to hide my small moan, but with the way he thrusts against my back, I know he hears it.

"If I let you go, are you going to run again, killer?" he asks, pressing against me, the seam of my shorts biting into my clit.

I whimper softly, my hips thrusting involuntarily at his touch, seeking out more, even though my mind is screaming at me to fight, to get away from him. The rest of me is reacting in a way that is begging for him to keep touching me, to touch me more.

Take from me.

"No," I croak out softly.

He huffs out a disbelieving breath and his hold loosens slightly. The hand that was holding my ponytail is gone, running down the strands, while he backs up just barely. It's enough space for me to push past him and run again, trying to get to my room, and lock the door.

I hear the deep groan mixed with some noise of humor that comes from him, but I take off without a second thought. Yeah, I'm a liar, but I don't care right now, I just want to get away from him.

It doesn't take long before he snakes an arm around my waist, hauling me up and I screech, thrashing my body in hopes of hitting or kicking him anywhere. I'm sure I'm making contact, but he acts like it doesn't faze him at all.

"Come on, you lost your chance to make this easy." He grunts, shifting me over his shoulder, holding my legs down with an iron grip across my knees.

It doesn't stop me from continuing to pound my fists into his back as I attempt to swing my body off him. Doesn't matter if I land on my head at this point, as long as I get away from him. I'm caught between needing this—*needing him*—and wanting to get away. That's why I continue to fight it because I refuse to lay down and make this easy for him.

Even if my core is a wet and needy mess inside my shorts.

"Put me down!" I scream. I'm not sure where he's taking me, and it's not until I notice the doorframe we walk through that I realize we're in my bedroom.

"Not happening. You're going to see what happens when you give me complete control of your body just like I know you want to."

I hear the clink of what I think is his belt and I freeze, anticipating what he's planning to do next. Before I can think about it too much I'm thrown onto the bed. My back bounces at the contact and before I have the chance to get away, he descends on me, pulling my arms in front of me, keeping my wrists held together while he brings his belt around the back of my neck, and my panic surges.

I continue to try and fight him, even as he uses the leather to bind my wrists and neck together. I don't make it easy, but he acts like my attempts to fight aren't even the slightest inconvenience for him as he continues to do what he set out to do.

When he rises off me, I try to escape again, but I'm stopped by the fact that now when I try to move my arms, my neck goes with them.

"Wha—" I try to move again, and am completely stuck with my bound wrists.

"Look at that. Now that's a pretty fucking sight." I can only see his silhouette against the darkness, but it feels like his bright eyes, that are such a contrast with the darkness of his soul, are staring right through me. I have all my clothes on, but I've never felt so exposed.

I take that back, when he turns on the lamp on my nightstand, actually bringing more light into the room, I feel even more exposed. My chest is heaving both from nerves and anticipation as he slowly stalks around my bed while I lie trapped.

"What the fuck is wrong with you?" I spit at him, thrashing around to try and get free, even if there's no chance of it helping. Especially when I feel the slickness between my thighs. The way my own body is betraying me makes me want to fight against this even more.

"So many things, but you being here makes it worse."

I glare at him as he looms at the end of my bed, arms crossed and a crazed look in his beautiful eyes.

"Oh, I'm so sorry for offending you just by being here and literally doing fucking *nothing*."

Caine reaches down, adjusting himself in his pants and I watch the movement, hardly noticing when my legs rub together slightly.

"You've done enough." He looks at where I'm trying to move subtly, and I can tell he sees it. Which makes me want to kick him in the balls again. "Now, shut the fuck up or I'm going to stuff your panties into your mouth."

"Fuck off."

He smirks, reaching for my ankles and I start kicking at him again. He's able to wrangle my legs easily, holding my ankles with one giant hand, despite my efforts to keep fighting him off. He's undeterred as he manages to unbutton my shorts, pulling them down, along with my fishnets so I'm left only in a thong that's embarrassingly soaked.

After he pulls off the clothes, I slam my legs closed to try and hide the evidence of my body's betrayal. I'm hoping that maybe he'll stop here and that I'll get to keep this secret to myself.

Of course, I'm not that lucky because he pushes open my thighs easily, and I gasp, using all my strength to try and slam them closed. His calloused hands are rough on my inner thighs as he holds them open. He looks from wet fabric up to where my shirt has ridden up my stomach, to my heaving chest and eyes that I hope show the hatred for him that I'm feeling.

"So wet for me, like the slut I knew you were. I should make you choke on these." He snaps the fabric on my hip, and I gasp.

"Do it," I challenge. "Then you can do whatever it is you're planning to do to my dead body, and I don't have to endure the few seconds you can last with your tiny dick."

That earns me a laugh. An actual, full-bodied laugh from him, and it's worse than the blank stares I've gotten. "Oh killer, you'll learn there's nothing tiny about me soon. I'm so glad you've been thinking about my dick, though."

I smile disparagingly. "Only about chopping it off."

"Such a fucking liar."

He grabs the side of my thong and starts to pull them down, despite me attempting to fight him off, keeping my legs glued shut as he manages to wrangle the soaked fabric off me. Bringing it up to his face he takes a deep inhale, and I grimace and squeeze my thighs tighter together.

My mind and body are clearly at war right now and I'm worried about how I'm going to make it out of this. I try to pull my arms free again, but it only pulls at my neck, and I groan in frustration.

Caine tucks my underwear into his pocket, and I open my mouth in surprise, but snap it shut quickly when I remember what he said about making me choke on them. Despite what came out of my mouth, I would rather make it out of this alive. I may not be unscathed, but honestly, I wasn't completely unharmed at the beginning of the night either.

He pushes my legs open again and there's no hiding what he sees, his eyes look up at me showing how pleased he is with his discovery.

"I'm going to fuck this pretty little pussy tonight, and you may tell me no, but we both know how badly you want it."

Before I have the chance to say anything, his mouth is on me, and I cry out. It's rough and dirty and I can't do a fucking thing to stop him. My arms are restrained, he's holding my legs open and I'm nothing more than a body to him as he devours me.

I don't want to acknowledge how good this feels. I don't want to come again like the night in the kitchen. I don't want to give him the pleasure of knowing what he's doing is working. But when his tongue flicks my clit rapidly before sucking it into his mouth, any attempt I have at holding off is gone because the orgasm is barreling toward me. It's unstoppable and when it takes over, the cry I let out is both in pleasure and frustration. I don't want to give in to him, and for him to know that this is everything I've wanted.

On the other hand, is it really giving into him when I'm the one benefitting in the end?

Caine rises up, his mouth and chin soaked with *me*, and I want to kick him in the face.

"You come so easily for me; you know that?"

"I fucking hate you." I say the words I want to believe, but really what I hate right now is how badly I really crave him. How badly I crave *this*.

"Yeah." He looks down at my core that's still wet with my desire. "Sure seems like it."

"Agh," I groan, throwing my head back onto the bed in irritation, wanting more than anything to fight him off, but accepting my fate fully at this moment. He's going to do what he wants and I'm unable to stop him.

But this is what I've wanted, the control being taken away in a way I've craved. And it is. I've wanted a man to use my body for pleasure, to give me the pleasure I crave while treating me like I don't have a choice. I don't know how this man I barely know, who's only ever been an ass to me, is able to give me something I've always wanted, but he is.

"Eyes on me, killer. I want you to see what it is you were worried would be too small."

I look over at him, glaring as he unbuttons his jeans and starts to push them down. I can't deny that the thought of running away flashes through my mind. Curiosity also courses through me. And it's the curiosity that's sure to get me in trouble.

"Tell me something," he says, shedding his jeans, but leaving his boxers on before pulling off his hoodie. Once that's on the floor he continues. "You think Drew can give you what you need?"

He pulls off his shirt, revealing the sculpted muscles that cover his chest. It's free of tattoos, clearly a contrast to the other guys I've seen at the gym who all appear covered, but

Caine has nothing. Just stacked muscles covered by smooth, tan skin.

"Probably better than you can." I tilt my chin up in defiance.

He grunts. "You think so? You have a terrible read on people then. You know he practically killed his dad."

"What?" I rear back, but then he's pushing down his boxers and I'm speechless in more ways than one. First of all, I don't know why he would say something like that, but truly every thought leaves my mind as he reveals every inch of bare skin to me.

Especially the bare thick cock that's hard and pointed right at me. The fear is back, consuming me as I take all of him in. He's huge—like, concerningly huge. I shouldn't want this. I shouldn't want him. Because there's no way that's fitting. Maybe I'm going to die tonight after all.

"What do you think? Too *small* for you?" he asks, wrapping his fist around himself and pumping once, squeezing the tip.

My mouth goes dry as I open it to reply, but I don't even know what I want to say. I don't know what I could say right now. The only thing that comes out is, "I'm not fucking you."

"You're right. I'm going to fuck you."

I'm pretty sure the next words I speak just may end up being my last, "Not a fucking chance."

CHAPTER 16
CAINE

Fuck, what is it about this girl that has me so out of control? I've never felt so crazed around someone, so completely unhinged. The need to make her mine, to claim her in every way possible, is consuming every fiber of my being.

Especially right now, with the taste of her still on my tongue as she's practically naked on her bed, squirming with a look in her eyes that tells me she wants to kill me. Even though she just came for me like a dream. I squeeze the head of my cock even tighter as I look at her.

I'm not going to be able to take off her shirt and suck on those tight nipples with the way I've bound her hands, but that's okay. I have to save something for next time—and there will be a next time.

"You know, I thought about waiting until you were in bed tonight," I tell her, giving myself another stroke.

She pulls at her restraints again, growling in frustration at the way it pulls at her neck. "You're a psychopath."

"Yeah, I might be. But I know I would've found you bare under one of your T-shirts again, wouldn't I?"

She squirms on the bed, but fails to get anywhere without the use of her arms.

"I know I would have because you want to be found like that, don't you?" Another stroke. "I would've pulled down the blankets, and seen this pink pussy already wet for me because you're a needy slut, even in your dreams, aren't you?"

"Shut up," she spits, her voice is breathy, giving away how she really feels right now.

Another stroke.

"Yeah, you are. You would've woken up when you felt my cock pushing inside you, and you'd have tried to fight me off, but I would have held you down. Maybe tied you up again. It would've only made you more of a desperate little mess for me."

She sucks in her bottom lip, and I know it's to hide any noise she's making, but I continue.

"You'd take it so well. I know you would. Maybe I'd try to go slow, and let you adjust."

"Stop," she whimpers.

Another stroke.

"But I wouldn't be able to go slow, not with your tight pussy squeezing me. I'd lose control, just like I always do with you. Maybe you'd scream and try to fight me. *Fuck*, I love it when you fight me. It wouldn't work, though, and you'd just deal with me fucking you until you're soaking my cock with your release."

"No." She shakes her head, pulling at her wrists.

"And then, I would fill you up with my cum. I'd even make sure to push any of it back in that tries to drip out because every part of you will accept all of me."

"You're crazy."

I shrug. "Yeah, but I think you might be a bit crazy too."

As I start to lean down over her, she tries to kick me away and I make a mental note to tie her legs to something next time, even if I like the way she fights me. Though, I didn't like getting kicked in the nuts earlier. I manage to grab her ankles as she continues to flail her body around and I use my grip on them to flip her onto her stomach, trapping her arms underneath her. It further limits her neck movement, so she's forced to scream into the comforter as she continues to try and kick at me, but it's harder from this angle, especially with her arms bound.

Yanking her down to the edge of the bed, I force her legs apart before situating myself between them. Grabbing her ass in both my hands and kneading it roughly, pulling her cheeks apart to see her tight hole and dripping pussy on display for me.

"So needy for me, killer, you're soaking the bed."

She mumbles something into the bed that I can't understand.

"What's that? You gotta speak up and tell me what you want."

Turning her head to the side, she's breathing heavily. "Don't you dare touch me."

"A little too late for that, don't you think?" I slap my hand down on her ass and she cries out, grinding down against the bed. I rub the spot I just hit, feeling the heat of her skin under my palm. I graze my fingers through her soaked slit and spread the wetness up to her ass cheek before slapping it again.

She lets out a little growl that reminds me of a feisty kitten. "Stop fucking hitting me."

"Stop liking it then," I retort at the same time she grinds herself against the bed again. My patience is running thin, and my cock stands at attention for her, leaking from the tip and it takes every bit of restraint I have not to ram into her right now.

Taking my dick into my hand, I rub my head along her dripping slit, coating myself in her arousal. Pressing against her entrance without pushing in, I feel her tighten as her muscles tense.

"Caine." Her voice is threatening, and it only makes me press against her harder, the very tip of my dick pushing inside her soaking cunt.

"Yeah, killer?"

"Stop." She says weakly.

"No."

Without giving her a chance to say anything else, I slam forward and fully seat myself inside her tight channel with a single thrust. She cries out at the intrusion, and I groan at how tightly she's squeezing me.

"Fuck, you keep telling me to stop, but you don't realize how much your cunt floods for me every time you say that pointless word."

She moans, turning her face back into the mattress trying to muffle the noise, but I heard it and I know she likes this. Doesn't matter how much she wants to deny me, we both know this gets her off.

I grab her ponytail, pulling her head to the side again. She's panting as I rock into her, enjoying the feeling of being completely enveloped by her wet heat. I keep my thrusts shallow, not wanting to pull out.

Max arches up into me slightly and I groan, pulling harder on her ponytail as I push into her roughly making her yelp.

"Still want me to stop?" I ask with another thrust that makes her gasp.

"Mmm," she hums. It turns into a moan with another sharp thrust of my hips.

Reaching between her body and the bed, I find where we are connected and feeling us together has me close to losing it already, but I need to feel her come around me at least once. Moving my hand to her clit, I rub hard, tight circles as I fuck her roughly against my hand.

"You're going to come for me, killer. Your sweet pussy is going to strangle my dick because you love this."

"No," she moans and it sure as shit felt more like a *yes* to me.

With my grip tight on her hair, I shove her head back down, increasing my pace as I fuck her into the mattress.

"You take me so fucking well. You're fucking dripping onto my hand, and you want me to think you hate this." I breathe out a humorless laugh.

My hand works her clit, and I feel her tighten around me as she gets close, but she's holding back. I can't understand her muffled words, and I don't care to, I just want her to give in.

"Come on, killer, give it to me." I pinch her clit, and she detonates with a scream, her pussy wrapping so tightly around me I almost lose control.

Working her through her release, I do everything I can to hold back my own until she becomes limp under me, and I lose all restraint, fucking her roughly until my own climax takes over and I'm coming, filling her with a groan.

When I pull out, I immediately lean back to watch as my cum drips out of her drenched pussy, but I shove it back in roughly just as I said I would. She gasps, trying to move away from me. Her tired muscles and bound wrists make it impossible, and I push every drop back inside her.

I back up enough to flip her onto her back, and her tired eyes are still glaring up at me.

"I should leave you like this for the night and see if you're able to get yourself free." The side of my mouth pulls up in a small smirk, and my dick twitches at the sight of her. Ponytail in disarray, errant pieces sticking to her face from sweat and drool. Knowing she's got my cum inside of her has the beast inside me raging again. Damn, I might just have to fuck her again tonight.

"You wouldn't," she challenges.

"Actually, I would."

I start to pull my clothes back on, because I really would fuck her again right now. Even though leaving is the last thing I want to do, I know that I should. It's a good thing I hid a small camera in here before she came home so I can watch this back and keep an eye on her when I'm not here and need my fix.

"Caine," she growls as I pull up my pants. I see her shift around slightly and there's a look that crosses her face which is one of concern and confusion. "You fucked me bare."

"And I always will. Your pussy is mine and I'll fill it anytime I want."

"I could get pregnant, you asshole."

"Good, then everyone will know you're mine while you walk around with my baby in your stomach."

"Good thing I have an IUD then."

"For now."

"Oh my fucking God," she groans. "Take this belt off me."

I shrug. "No."

And with that, I leave her for the night, unsure of how long I'll be able to stay away. I'm already craving her again, and who knows how long the beast within will remain satiated. Watching her on camera will have to last for now before I need to feel her once again.

CHAPTER 17
MAX

Motherfucking asshole. Son of a bitch. Piece of shit, leaving me here tied up with his cum dripping out of me… I could kill him. I'm *going* to kill him. Who the fuck does he think he is breaking into my house, tying me up, and doing whatever he wants with me.

Agh.

But why did I like it?

It only makes me hate myself even more. After finally managing to get his belt off, my thoughts have been a jumbled mess, which just matches how I feel on the outside too. I'm sore, wet, and aching. I force myself into my bathroom, and turn the shower to scalding, shedding the rest of my clothes before getting in and scrubbing myself of the desire I had for Caine's hands on me. And his mouth, and his dick.

I want to forget this night ever happened and every feeling that has come with it. Especially the ones that tell me this was the hottest experience I've ever had, because those thoughts are traitorous and *wrong*. Right?

Yet, when I think about how he took control of me, and how I wanted him to, heat washes through me again. The way he played my body perfectly, commanded it, really. Just remembering it has my hand sliding lower, almost like it's out of my control. I throw my head back when the tip of my finger grazes my clit, still sensitive from Caine's touch.

The bite of pain from being overstimulated has me pressing even harder as I circle the throbbing bud. I can still hear the way his voice sounded as he spoke to me. The weight of him on top of me. The feel of him inside me. I moan, pressing a finger inside my wet heat and groan out my frustration that it's not enough. Not compared to him.

I can hear his voice talking me through what I'm doing now, *"I knew you liked it, killer. Show me how much."*

That's what sends me over the edge once again, and I'm immediately irritated with myself at how it was so easy to get aroused, and even more annoyed how easily I came. The need to deny what he does to my body has me quickly finishing my shower, making sure to scrub extra hard like I can erase the evidence of my own betrayal.

By the time I'm done, my skin is raw and red. I'm sure I've taken a layer off, but I don't care. The feeling of him touching me, and the memory of touching myself after, is now replaced with the burn from the water and washcloth I used. The frustration with myself still remains.

Part of me wonders if I'm going to find him standing in my room when I return, but I'm only met with silence. I pull on one of my oversized T-shirts and underwear because I'm not trying to make it easy if he does decide to come back. The exhaustion hits me all at once as I climb into bed, which now will always be tainted with the thoughts of him.

I should be worried about Caine coming back while I'm sleeping like he talked about. Just like I should be worried that he was so easily able to take advantage of me, to render me helpless and take what he wanted. I should be a lot of things, but somehow, all I am is tired, and unlike most other nights, sleep pulls me in easily. The weirdest part of it all is that I'm not even plagued by the nightmares that usually haunt me.

❦

WHEN I WALK into Uncaged for my first boxing lesson, I'm doing so well with my head held high and my eyes trained forward. I don't seek out Caine to see if he's here. I hardly look at any of the guys that are around. I just take a place on the mat and start stretching while I wait for class to begin.

The room fills with other people, but I don't look at any of them or pay any attention. The only thing that I look at is Coach Adam, when his voice announces the start to class. This is different than BJJ in many ways, but especially because we don't have to pair up constantly. The best part about this class is when we get to start actually punching the bag and I get to imagine it's Caine's face as I drive my fist into the leather.

"Focus on your form, not the power behind the punch," Coach instructs. I want to scoff and ignore him because right now, the strength behind the punches is what's going to keep me going. Especially when it comes to the possibility of breaking a nose.

When I don't say anything, he comes up behind me. Strong hands land on my hips suddenly, and the flex of his grip has me shifting slightly at the way he's directing me. Then, he's touching my shoulders, pushing them down from where they were bunched up by my ears. My breathing is heavy, but I still don't acknowledge him yet.

"Now try." His breath caresses my ear and to my surprise it's not completely unwelcome. At the two-word command, I take in a deep breath before attempting the combination we were taught once again. It feels better than what I was doing; there isn't as much of a strain on my muscles, and I feel myself not twisting my back as much.

"Better," Adam says quietly as his hands slowly slide off me before he moves on to the next person.

My vow not to look at any of the guys diminishes as I follow him with my eyes noticing that he doesn't do the same with anyone else. Doesn't touch them, doesn't say anything into their ears with his lips so close they almost touch. No, that was just for me. I refuse to think too much into it, but I also don't know why I wouldn't mind it happening again.

Shaking the thoughts away, I get back to practicing. Clearly, the mixed signals around here and my conflicting feelings about Caine are confusing my mind and body. This isn't my fault, it's theirs. Letting the fury lead me, I go back to practicing, only this time when I drive my fist into the bag, it's Carson's face I see.

As class wraps up, I'm gulping down water from my water bottle when Drew steps up in front of me. I narrow my eyes while my mouth stays on the bottle, continuing to drink because my throat is burning, and this water feels like it's sweet nectar from the Gods.

"Hey, how was class?" he asks, far too lighthearted for my liking.

Instead of answering verbally I give him a thumbs up. He huffs out a small laugh and I finish the bottle of water, twisting the cap on preparing to toss it. Picking up the towel, I wipe the sweat from my forehead while he continues to watch me.

"Okay, bye." I turn to walk away, but he grabs my wrist, and I whirl around. I'm not sure what it is with everyone touching me without my permission lately, but it's starting to get old.

"What are you doing later?" he asks.

"Working."

"You ever have a night off?"

"Nope."

"Well, maybe I'll just meet up with you after work then, that's what Caine does, isn't it?"

I yank my wrist from his hold, stepping up to this large man, having to crane my neck to look up at him as he towers over me. "You don't know what you're talking about."

"No? So, there's nothing going on there?" He smirks down at me like he knows something. I'm about to use what Adam just taught me today about throwing a good punch on the man in front of me.

"I don't know what you've heard in your weird little gossip

sessions that you guys are clearly having, but just know that your friend is fucking insane. And you probably are, too."

His smirk turns into a full-blown smile, it's almost sinister and reminds me of the comment Caine made that I didn't exactly have time to dwell on.

"You know he practically killed his dad."

With the way he's looking at me, I can almost see how that may actually be possible. Although, just like with Caine, instead of running away, I raise my chin to look him right in his green eyes that are burning with something resembling a threat.

"It's cute that you think we sit around and talk about you."

"Then why would you think something is going on between us?"

"It's also cute you think he's the only one that's watching you."

I don't get a chance to say anything because he's turning around and walking in the other direction. I want to call after him. To yell at him to stay the fuck away from me, but I feel like the more I say that to anyone here, the worse it gets. So instead, I gather my stuff to leave. Just as I turn to head out, I catch Coach Adam looking at me and I have a feeling that he just watched that entire interaction.

I'm almost tempted to ask him if he's following me, too, but pissing off my coach is probably a terrible idea. Instead, I duck my head and walk out the door right in time to run into a wall of muscle. When I look up, I can't help the groan that comes from my throat.

"That's not the greeting I'd expect from you, killer," Caine taunts.

"Oh my God, will you all just leave me the fuck alone," I say, exasperated.

I push past him, and he actually lets me this time. Taking advantage of the clean getaway, I head home. I have this feeling everything is only going to get so much worse. It's like I've woken up some sort of monster. Or a couple of them. And it's only a matter of time before they come after me.

CHAPTER 18
ADAM

Watching Drew with Max, and then Caine with Max, has me wondering what I'm missing. I know Caine is a loose cannon, especially when it comes to women, but Drew usually keeps any interest he has in anyone subtle. And he's *never* interested in anyone from the gym. Except me, but we have a mutual understanding as to what this is. Or was.

Plus things didn't start between us because of any hidden feelings or pining. It has been purely sexual from the start. Tension, frustration, and a mutual trust we built that we use to find release with each other.

Yet, I can't help but think that part of what he's doing is to make me jealous and is using Max to do it. Or to piss off Caine.

Or maybe he really is interested in her.

Not that I would blame him. She's beautiful and her attitude only adds to her appeal. She hasn't backed down once since she's been here. Not even when I touched her, which I almost never do with students, but I wanted to see how she felt in my hands. My skin, tattooed, covered in scars and calluses against her pale, smooth skin felt like it should be wrong. Like I was tainting her, yet it only drew me in even more. I was too close to her, and I knew it. But I didn't care.

All I know is that trying to figure any of this out right now is making my head hurt and I have a job to do.

"Caine, into the cage," I call out, distracting myself by getting to work.

He's still distracted, standing there, watching the direction Max went, even though she's out of eyesight. With how tightly he's coiled, it's almost as if he's going to run after her.

"Aldridge," I shout out his last name, and he turns with a scowl. He hates when I use his last name. I know it's because it reminds him of the family he wants to distance himself from. Which is why we rarely use it.

"Cage," I demand. I almost call him out for the way he was watching Max but decide against it for now.

Cal doesn't seem to care though. Especially as he approaches Caine who's wrapping his hands and says, "Caine is too busy eye fucking the new girl to give a shit about practice."

"Come in here and I'll show you why *actually fucking her* is making me a better fighter than ever," Caine responds, already in position, bouncing on the balls of his feet.

I groan inwardly, wanting to put a stop to this, but knowing that sometimes I need to let the guys run their mouths and allow it to play out like it should. I may have learned that fighting isn't actually an answer and shouldn't be used all the time. These guys are still young and need to learn their own lessons.

Cal joins Caine, his form much less practiced as he steps up to him, but I hang back. Drew comes up next to me, arms folded across his chest. We don't look at each other, both keeping our gazes forward.

"You just letting this happen?" he asks as Cal throws a sloppy first hit.

"For a minute."

We stand next to each other in silence watching Caine easily submit Cal in less than a minute. It's not awkward between Drew and I, though I can tell he wants to say something. But he doesn't and neither do I.

"Again!" Cal calls.

"No, that's enough. Let's get started." I climb into the cage in case I have to actually separate them. Caine isn't even out of breath as he steps back against the edge, leaning casually as he adjusts his hand wraps.

Cal already has sweat dotting his brow, showing just how much energy he's already exerted.

"Don't worry, man, I'll kick your ass any time you want," Caine taunts.

"Bag," I tell him, because he is clearly in the mood to be a shit stirrer. Which isn't entirely new, it's just something I don't feel like putting up with today.

On his way out of the cage he acts like he's about to start something with Cal again, making him flinch before he leaves.

"Playtime's over," I call, then we get started.

§

I'M FINISHING up with the last few cleaning tasks before stepping up to the desk. Drew stands there texting on his phone while he ignores me. For some reason, I glance at the screen and my eye catches on the name at the top—*Max*. I don't see any of their messages, but I say something anyway.

"You moving in on Caine's girl? Seems unlike you."

He scoffs. "He doesn't have a girl. And I'll ask again, you jealous?"

Shaking my head. "Not at all."

And I'm really not, we've talked about what it may be like to watch each other with a girl. What it would be like to bring a girl in between us. These are just a few things that we would discuss in the heat of the moment that I still think about.

The thought of it being Max between us sends a shot of arousal straight to my neglected dick. She doesn't even reach our shoulders; we would practically crush her and yet the thought of it only turns me on even more.

"I'm heading out, then." He pockets his phone, glancing at me and I just nod.

After he leaves, instead of doing the same, I end up in my office. Even weirder, I find myself pulling up Max's information.

I don't know what it is that I'm doing—or why—and it feels wrong, but I can't help it. I want to see what it is about her that's causing those two to show so much interest in her.

And possibly even myself.

Maxine Barclay. She's only twenty-five, which should make me feel gross about the thoughts I had while touching her today considering I'm forty-two. But Drew is only four years older than her and if anything, the age gap only adds to her appeal.

I find myself entering her name into Google and am shocked when I see multiple news articles pop up. It's the top one that catches my eye with its title. Once I click on it, my screen is filled with a picture of Max, her long deep red hair curled wearing a black dress that's tight against her body and is shining against the lights that are on her. She's standing next to a man who looks about a half a foot taller than her and looks like an entitled prick.

Clean cut, in a suit, hair greased back on his head and there's something about his beady little eyes that makes me want to punch him in the face. Or maybe it's the pull on his lips, the small smirk, like he knows something that everyone else doesn't.

My eyes catch on Max's hand that's resting on his chest and zero in on the large diamond shining on her ring finger. I haven't seen her wear a ring and if there was a guy with her, we would've known about it. Especially with the way his hand is wrapped around her wrist. That's when I see the way she's looking at the camera—it isn't a smile of joy, it's pained.

Maxine Barclay to marry Carson Bradford.
Both families are thrilled to announce the union between the two,
set to marry in January.

I furrow my brow, double checking the calendar, noting that it's February. Scrolling, I find no marriage article and she's here alone. It only makes me more curious about the woman that's new to town.

The more research I do, the more obvious it is that her family is well off. It only feeds into my curiosity and the questions I have about her and how she ended up here.

Eventually, I give up and head home. It's too late and I've spent too much time looking into Max. I feel like a creep and my eyes feel heavy from how intensely I've been staring at the screen.

Once, I'm home, I greet Athena, my piebald ball python in her cage. I find her sunbathing under the heat lamp. She's the first and only pet I've ever had. Once I moved out on my own, the first thing I did was search for the perfect color. That's when I found her. I've always had a fascination with snakes, even growing up, bouncing from foster home to foster home. Some of the foster parents I had would get freaked out with how much I would talk about them, but I didn't care. None of them let me have one, and maybe if they had, I wouldn't have gone out and caused all the trouble I did.

Who am I kidding, I still would've gone out and caused trouble. Street fighting turned into underground fighting. Anything risky and dangerous had my name written all over it. It was like that for a while. It's crazy to think about how much different my life looks now than it did back then.

Taking Athena out of her enclosure, my twenty-three year old snake slides around my shoulders easily as she always does. Her mostly white scales meet her patterned ones in spots on her body. She slithers around on me before moving down my body onto the floor to have some freedom. I leave her to explore the living room as I shower and change.

I'm reclining on my couch wearing just a pair of sweatpants when Athena slides up the couch and around to the back of it.

"Hey girl," I greet, knowing she won't respond. That doesn't stop me from talking to her, especially at times like this. When we are alone, like we almost always are. Ever since I got her, she's been my best friend. The one constant in my life that I can always count on.

I've questioned my loneliness many times. Wondered if I should have tried dating more seriously and settled down with someone. My life has been filled with purely physical relationships because they're easy, and I've never had the desire to deal with any of the drama that comes with a relationship. I've also never blurred any lines with anyone at the gym, except Drew, and I can already feel the drama potentially starting as a result of that.

Especially since Max is now involved. I sigh, looking at Athena who's starting to curl into a ball on the highest part of the couch.

"There's a new girl that's been coming to the gym and I think Drew is interested in her," I tell her, feeling like I need to get my thoughts out, even to a snake.

"Caine is too. She's beautiful, but I feel like shit is going to hit the fan at some point and I'm going to have a front row seat to all of it."

With another sigh, I get up and take Athena from the spot

she's settled on. She doesn't uncurl from the ball she's in when I set her back into her enclosure and turn her night lights on before going to bed.

My mind is a mess, and I know I'm just going to toss and turn, so it's not surprising when that's exactly what happens. What is surprising is the fact that I pull up the article about Max again and end up staring at the picture of her with another man for way too long. I don't even notice when I fall asleep, phone still in my hand with her picture still pulled up.

CHAPTER 19
MAX

That motherfucker.

The days following my first boxing class have been absolute chaos. I feel like the only time my mind is able to stop is when I'm so exhausted that I fall into bed, sleep pulling me under. Even then, it's hardly peaceful, as the nightmares continue to plague me and I wake up screaming in frustration. They leave me wishing that I could go back home and destroy all the memories by getting rid of all the people that have caused them.

Today is my first day off and I'm cleaning my house for the first time since moving in. It's when I'm dusting the top of my dresser that my eye catches on a tiny red light. Upon closer examination, trying not to be obvious about it, I see that it's a camera.

I know it wasn't my landlord who put it there. Which means there's only one other person who would have. The same man who thinks he has a right to my body. The man I've been anticipating being in my home every night when I get home from work. But I haven't seen him since the night he tied me up and fucked me within an inch of my life all while I fought him. The man I've craved since that very night.

I've only caught glimpses of him at the gym. Even when I'm at work, I'll sometimes feel his eyes on me, but when I look around, I don't see him. Honestly, it's making me a little insane, which I'm sure is his goal right now.

But now I know that he's been watching me.

Back to my "this motherfucker" comment.

As soon as I make the discovery, my phone goes off and I groan. I know exactly who it's going to be, because he's been texting me at least three times a day for the past few days. I only responded once asking how he got my number, a question he conveniently ignored.

Just like I've done to all his other texts.

> Drew: I hear you have a night off. I volunteer to entertain you.

I lock my phone, fully preparing to leave yet another text unanswered, but then I look up and remember the camera and an idea pops into my head. A stupid idea, no doubt. Something I will most definitely regret.

But I've been playing a part to please other people my entire life. Maybe it's time to put my acting to good use and do something for myself for once. Not that it would be a hardship. I've seen the man and to say he's hot is an understatement. I've been used and abused more times than one person ever should. My new life is about me taking control for myself. And that's exactly what I intend to do.

※

Drew's at my door when I answer wearing some cotton shorts and a tank top without a bra. I have a mission tonight and it's empowering for me. Plus it's also going to piss Caine off. So, really, it's a win-win.

"Hi," I greet, leaning my shoulder against the doorframe.

His eyes trail over my body, obviously, and I let him.

"Hey," he finally responds once his eyes meet mine.

"You said there would be entertainment," I tease lightly.

"Are you going to let me inside so I can properly entertain you?" His tone is playful, and I can't deny that it makes me feel comfortable with him.

We may have gotten off on the wrong foot but right now, he seems like the type of guy I wouldn't mind having a little fun with. Too bad I'm not wanting to get into anything serious right now. This is purely about revenge. I might be using him, but something tells me he won't mind it.

Stepping aside, I gesture for him to come in. Before shutting the door, I look out onto the dark street, wondering if Caine is out there already watching. *Did he see Drew arrive? Did he see him come inside?* I bite back a smirk, hoping he can see me. I hope he's watching as I shut the door, knowing the only way he'll get to watch is through that fucking camera he planted in my room.

Drew takes his jacket off, draping it on one of the chairs in my small living room and it leaves his toned, tattooed covered arms exposed. The white T-shirt he's wearing is clinging to his broad chest, stretching so tightly against his muscles that I can see the ink that extends onto his chest, and it makes me want to discover it all.

My nipples tighten and I can tell that he notices when his gaze flicks down and runs his tongue along his bottom lip.

"What did you have in mind?" I ask, folding my arms under my tits, making it known that I want him to see how my body is reacting right now.

He steps toward me, and I don't back away. He's almost as tall as Caine but not quite as bulky. It makes me think of the differences between the two. When it comes to Caine, I don't know what I want, and I have no plan. He sets me on edge in a way my body craves, the fear and arousal mixing like a dangerous drug. But right now, with Drew, I know what I want. I have a plan. I feel more in control with him, somehow, it arouses me just as much.

Shaking the thoughts of the other man away, I look up at Drew, his dark green eyes remind me of the deep green on the leaves of a pine tree. Strands of his black hair fall across his forehead as he looks down at me. I can't deny that this man is gorgeous, and I almost feel bad using him like this. *Almost.*

"You tell me. Want to watch a movie?"

I continue to keep my eyes locked on his as I shake my head slowly. I reach out to run my fingers along the hem of his T-shirt, barely grazing underneath, just a ghost of a touch.

"Are you hungry?" he tries.

Again, I shake my head, pulling my bottom lip in between

my teeth and moving my hand higher so my fingertips graze the skin of his abdomen. The heat radiating from him makes me want to move my hand higher. To feel how his sculpted muscles will feel under my palm.

"Are you wanting to practice some of what you've learned?"

I let out a low laugh, shaking my head again, letting my hand move higher. I trace the indents that carve a "V" on his lower stomach. Moving higher, I trace all the valleys of the muscles I find as I slowly push his shirt up his body.

"How about you tell me what you're wanting then," he suggests. I don't know why the way he asks what *I* want makes my body react in an extremely positive way. I tighten my thighs together slightly to ease the ache that's starting to form.

Actually, I know exactly why those words make me react this way. Because I think it's the first time a man has actually asked what it is that I want.

On the other hand, I can't deny the devilish voice in the back of my mind that's trying to scream out and demand that he takes that choice away from me. That he can do whatever it is he wants to do to me and to make sure I can't do anything to stop it.

I don't speak right away, instead, letting my hands continue their exploration of his body. When I push his shirt up enough to start revealing the ink on his chest, he reaches behind his neck and pulls the fabric off himself.

I have to stifle the needy moan that wants to escape at the visual of him in front of me. His body looks like it's been chiseled to perfection. Every indent of muscle shows the work he has put in. The black ink showing part of his story, things I don't have the brain capacity to try and figure out right now.

"Let's go to my room," I manage to say evenly. His eyes darken with a small nod.

"Lead the way."

I do just that, stepping around him and walking toward my bedroom, feeling his eyes on me and the way my hips sway with each step. I make sure to keep the lights on because I want to know that when Caine watches this, whether it's live or he's replaying it later, that he sees *everything*.

Drew follows, stepping up behind me when we reach the foot of my bed and I turn around, instantly reaching for his waistband, and unbuckling his belt and jeans.

He stops me, covering my hands with his own and I look up at him, annoyed.

"I said *tell me* what you want, little one. With your words." His voice is deeper, more demanding and *fuck* if it doesn't make the throbbing between my legs more intense. I try to subtly relieve it with the pressure of my thighs pushed together, but it's not enough.

"I want—" I pause, because it feels weird to have to say it out loud. I'm not a virgin…obviously. I've also sucked a dick before, but I've never had to *say* it. The words seem foreign even as they pass through my lips. "I want your dick in my mouth."

Drew lets go of my hands. "Then, go ahead and take it out."

The way he says it almost feels like a threat. It's that hint of danger, plus the anticipation that fuels me even more. As soon as I get his belt and jeans unbuttoned, I pull them down and drop to my knees in front of him.

I look up, his boxers tented with his arousal in front of my face. I want to see it, but I wait a beat, teasing him. Rubbing my hand over him through the fabric of his boxers, he groans at the feeling. I feel something weird on the underside of his shaft and furrow my brow.

"What is that?" I ask, the fear kicking up a notch.

His voice deepens and his lip quirks up, making my heart race and my underwear flood. "Why don't you look and find out."

I swallow roughly, gripping the waistband of his boxers and pulling them down his legs, wondering if this is a mistake. Maybe this entire plan is about to backfire on me. I let another strange man into my house and I'm giving him a piece of my body.

Except the difference is, I *let* him in and I'm *letting* him have this piece of my body. It still doesn't change the fact that he's essentially a stranger. Even as I pull off his last item of clothing, I can't help but think about the fact that I barely know this man. That makes this moment even hotter than it probably should.

That, and the fact that I'm probably a bit fucked up in the head.

When he's completely exposed, his cock bobs in front of me and that's when I see what I felt. Wrapping my hand around him, I feel metal pressing into my palm, and I take a moment to count the bars forming the ladder.

"One," I count, rubbing my thumb along the bar.

"Two." I repeat the motion with the next one.

"Three." I do the same for each of the six piercings as I feel each one individually.

"Four." He groans with my movement.

"Five."

After I reach the sixth one, I look up, moving my hand along his entire length, enjoying how the bars rub against my palm.

Drew is smirking down at me. "That's exactly how many seconds it'll take for me to get you off."

"We'll see about that," I retort.

Pumping his erection, I continue to see how they feel, and he lets out a groan. I bite back my smile, proud of the fact that I affected him so much. I love when a guy makes noise. Carson never did and it was like fucking a mime.

I want it dirty. Loud. Messy. *Dangerous.*

The piercings, plus the look in his eyes right now makes me think Drew may just give me exactly what it is I'm wanting. Especially when I stick my tongue out, running it along his slit, lapping up the bead of precum that's there. I hum at the salty taste of him, squeezing him tighter in my fist.

I look up as I run my tongue around his head. It's when I fist the base of his dick and lick the sensitive underside of his head that he snaps. His hand fists my hair at the back of my head, pulling at the roots and I can't stop the moan I let out.

"Is this what you're wanting?" He pulls harder and I squeeze around him even tighter.

I nod against him, which only makes the sharp pain of where he's gripping me even more extreme. The pain only makes me wetter and my mouth waters as I try to fight against his hold to taste more of him.

"Damn, little Maxine is a dirty, desperate whore, aren't you?"

I scowl at the name. Not being called a whore. *That* only makes me more desperate for him.

I pull my mouth off him to snap, "Don't call me that."

"Don't like to be told what a whore you are while you're on your knees, drooling for my cock?"

"Don't call me Maxine," I grit out, feeling the air shift around us, the lighthearted energy we had before has left and this is the real Drew. I wrap my fist around him squeezing tight enough that he lets out a pained hiss.

This is the Drew I should be afraid of. The Drew that I want to do whatever he wants with me.

"Okay, little one. Take what it is you're wanting then, before I force my cock down your pretty throat until you choke on it."

His words should make me want to run, but all it does is make me want him even more. So, I wrap my lips around him and suck him in as far as I can while he continues to push me down with his grip on my hair.

He grunts loudly, his hips thrusting forward, pushing himself even deeper. I breathe through my nose trying to fight my gag reflex. I swallow around him, and he lets out a loud groan that would make me smile if I could. He lets me pull back slightly, and I look up at him with tears pooling in my eyes and drool coming from my mouth.

"Shit," he grinds out quietly, his other hand finding its way into my hair, he holds the back of my head with both hands and pushes my mouth back onto his dick.

Running my tongue along the underside, I feel the piercings and revel in the way they feel against me. I can't help but wonder how they may feel inside me. He's big too. Thick, and I wonder if it would hurt as he stretched me, and those piercings rubbed my inner walls.

I moan around him at the thoughts running through my mind. I push myself further, wanting to take him deeper into my throat. I'm so lost in the moment that I forgot the whole reason I was doing this to begin with. I glance over to where the camera is and look directly at it, knowing Caine is watching the whole thing.

I want him to know that I know. I want him to see this. I want him to see that I'm doing this because *I* want to.

It's why I put on a show.

Pulling back, I look up at Drew. Every muscle in his body that I can see is tense. I know he wants more. And I want him to give it to me.

"Fuck my mouth," I tell him softly, almost innocently as the words still feel foreign coming from my mouth.

His lips lift in a sinister smile. "With pleasure."

I hardly have time to debate if this was a bad idea when he shoves me back down onto his length, my nose kissing his groin. I choke and gag around him, trying to ease the panic that threatens to take over, but he doesn't let up.

His hips move at a punishing pace, doing what I asked, but with a violence I didn't expect. His groans grow louder and the sloppy sounds coming from him fucking my mouth mix with my own moans. I'm soaking wet and dying to be touched, to get some sort of relief from the arousal I feel.

Keeping one hand on his thigh, my nails dig into his skin as he uses my mouth and the other hand dips into my shorts as I swipe my fingers against my clit. I moan around him at the sensation.

"Are you touching yourself? Oh, *fuck*." He moans when I nod my head slightly. "I'm close, your mouth feels so fucking good. Are you wet for me?"

I hum around him with another nod, swiping through my wetness again before lifting my hand up toward him. My fingers are enveloped in his warm mouth as he sucks and licks the digits. His hips stutter and I know he's right there. My tongue runs along his piercings again and this seems to be what sends him over the edge. His loud groans fill my room, and he holds my head down on him as my throat and mouth are filled with his cum.

I struggle to swallow, and he doesn't let up as he floods my mouth with his orgasm. I dig my nails into his skin trying to pull away, but he doesn't let me, and I feel the spots starting to cloud my vision as my air continues to be cut off. I want to gasp, but I can't because I'll choke even more. My fear kicks up even more causing my own arousal to flood between my legs and I realize something must be seriously wrong with me.

Drew pulls on my hair hard enough that I release his dick with a pop, finally taking air into my lungs while my drool, tears, and his cum cover my face. He hooks a finger under my chin, forcing me to look up at him. His thumb swipes at the liquid on the side of my mouth before pushing it back inside. I swirl my tongue around his rough thumb, tasting even more of him.

I can't help it when my eyes drift over to the side as I make a show of licking and sucking Drew's finger before he pulls it from my lips.

"That was fucking gorgeous," Drew praises, running his thumb along my cheek to gather the tears that have fallen.

"Hmm," I hum not really sure what else to say. And I don't get a chance before a banging sound comes from the living room making me jump.

"What the fuck was that?" Drew asks, clearly more annoyed than scared.

"I don't know," I answer dumbly. He yanks on his boxers and pants quickly before going to the source of the noise.

I move a bit slower, even though I'm still fully clothed. I know I should be worried about what's happening, but for some reason I'm not. Maybe it's because Drew is here and he's a big guy so anyone would have to deal with him first, and that would take quite a bit of work.

I also don't think there's any real danger beyond a very pissed off professional MMA fighter. No big deal.

I turn toward the camera, walking closer to it so when I say my message to him, Drew won't hear from the other room.

"Hope you enjoyed the show." I wink before taking the camera, and tossing it into a drawer of the dresser it was resting on.

I'll come back with a hammer to destroy it later.

CHAPTER 20
DREW

Nothing like a life changing blow job leading to an unbelievable orgasm. Then add in an adrenaline high right after? What a night.

I've never done drugs, but if I had, I feel like this would feel better than any of them. I have seen too much shit in my past with friends choosing drugs over everything else and I always knew I wouldn't follow that path.

I have my fair share of vices, but none of them will ever include that shit.

Looking around Max's living room I try to find the source of the noise that interrupted us. I was about to drop down, to join her on the floor and eat her pussy until she screamed so loud her neighbors called the cops.

Then, there would be no way I could prevent myself from shoving my dick inside her and fucking her until she passed out. Even then, I wouldn't stop. I'd fuck her limp body all night, make her come for me over and over, even unconscious, until her body couldn't handle it anymore.

To say I'm pissed we were interrupted, would be an understatement. I'd love to handle whatever—or whoever—caused the noise and then go back to what we started. Maybe there'd even be blood on my hands, and she would let me run them all along her body. My blood soaked touch would bring her pleasure over and over again.

Fuck, and now I'm hard again while trying to possibly find some creep.

There's nothing out of the ordinary and Max joins me about a minute later. She has her arms wrapped around her stomach as she looks around.

"What was it?" she asks.

I shake my head. "I don't know, I don't see anything."

"Hm," she hums, continuing to look around. I notice that for a moment, her eyes catch on a window and linger for a second longer before she looks back at me with a shy smile. "Must've been the wind or something."

I look over to the same window, and I swear I see a dark figure out there. But the light is dim and maybe I'm just wanting someone to blame for the reason that I'm not balls deep inside her right now.

"Well thanks for checking, I think we should call it a night." She draws my attention from the possible figure, and I give her a questioning look.

I step toward her, watching as she looks me over. I know she likes what she sees, so I feel like I can convince her that I need to stay.

"I don't think you want that."

She presses a small hand to my chest, stopping me from coming closer. I want to grab her wrist and twist it around to her back so I can shove her down over the arm of her couch and prove to her just how much she *doesn't* want me to leave.

"I think that we should save something for next time." Her voice is seductive, and she runs her hand down my chest, lingering over my abs. My skin flames everywhere she touches, and when her fingers slide off, I want to grab them and put them back.

"Well, I think you should at least get to come." I step forward again, invading her space.

She raises her chin up to meet my eyes. The slight hesitation she's had since walking out of her bedroom is gone when she confidently says, "Next time."

I want to push but decide not to. Not tonight. My gaze flicks to her lips; I realize I haven't tasted them, and all I can see is how they looked wrapped around my cock.

Leaning toward her, I'm stopped again with her fingers lightly pressing against my mouth. Despite the gentle touch, I want to grab her and be anything but with the way she keeps stopping me.

"Next time," she says again.

I straighten with a smirk, wanting to do so much more, and also feeling like maybe I shouldn't leave her alone. But this is her choice, and if this is what she really wants then, I'll give it to her. For now.

She follows me to her front door as I grab my shirt and jacket, pulling them both on.

"Last chance to change your mind for tonight," I tell her.

"I think I got what I needed for now." She runs her tongue across her bottom lip, and I bite back a groan. "See you around." She opens the door for me and everything inside of me is struggling to fight against the dismissal. It seems like the more she denies me, the more I want to do something about it.

But I manage to hold back, just barely.

"Goodnight, Max."

"Goodnight."

The door closes behind me before I've even reached my motorcycle, and when I'm pulling on the helmet, I feel eyes on me.

Looking around I try to see where they are coming from. That's when I see the figure, and I know it's really there this time. The large build gives away exactly who it is, even though the dark and his hood cover most of him.

"Guess you're going to have to learn how to share because I don't plan on giving her up," I say to the darkness. "Especially not that mouth."

He doesn't say anything. Doesn't move. Not even when I'm on my Honda VFR800F, revving it before taking off. Maybe I should be worried about what he's planning to do to Max once I leave. I know that me being there wouldn't stop Caine from doing what he wants to do. And she wanted me to leave, so whatever he's going to do isn't my problem.

CHAPTER 21
CAINE

I deserve a fucking award for my self control tonight.

If she wants to play, then let's fucking play. I watched as Drew came to her house, and I waited to see what would happen. When I couldn't see anything more through the window, I pulled up the camera in her room. It took everything in me not to go barging in there the second she dropped to her knees in front of him.

She touched him.

She had him in her mouth.

He got to know what it felt like before me, and that's something he will pay for.

So will she.

I watched the entire interaction like a fucking train wreck, my eyes unblinking as he held her head and thrusted into her open mouth. How she drooled and cried for *him*. I couldn't take it so I pounded my fist on a window so they wouldn't do anything more.

Because if they had, I might have actually murdered him. As much as I wish I could get away with it, I don't think I could. I'm good, but even I know I'm not that good. Even my dad, one of the most well-known defense attorneys, wouldn't be able to get me out of the charges that would come from a murder as brutal as the one I would commit.

I watched to make sure he left, and I heard what he said, but refused to react. I'll deal with him, but she's first. She's alone. Probably wet and needy since she didn't get to come. Too bad she's going to be left that way. Because tonight, she's going to be punished.

But only after she falls asleep.

༄

I CONTINUE to watch her through the window, waiting. I'm not normally a patient man, and this entire night is testing every bit of control, patience, and restraint I have. Honestly, I'm pretty proud of myself.

I continue to watch while standing in the darkness outside, when all the lights in Max's house turn off, indicating that she's going to bed. I continue to wait to make sure she goes to sleep. It's a real test of my self-control.

After about an hour, the last little bit of restraint I've had is gone and I enter her house as easily as I would my own. She may have fixed the lock on her back door, but no lock is foolproof. They all have a weak spot. Just like my little killer.

Once I'm inside, I close the door quietly because I don't want her to know I'm here before I'm ready. I go to her room, immediately fixating on her sleeping form. She has one leg kicked out of her blanket that's resting between her thighs. Her soft breathing fills the air and it's the only sound in the room.

My heart is threatening to beat out of my chest along with the beast that's begging to take her again. To not give her the chance to wake up and fight me off, even though I like it when she does. I want her to know who's touching her and I want her to love it, just like last time. Even if she denies it, we both know the truth.

I step up closer to her, as if there's this invisible pull that draws me in every time I'm near her. Once I'm close enough to touch, I feel my fingertips practically vibrating with the need to feel her soft skin under them.

Reaching out to graze her exposed ankle, I run my fingers up her calf lightly, feeling relief at the smallest touch. I get to her knee, and she stirs slightly. I look up to her face to see if she's going to open those hazel eyes and catch me, but she doesn't. Instead, I look at her mouth and my anger is back.

I remember watching her with Drew. Watching how she dropped down willingly for him, how she let him do what he wanted with her mouth and how she liked it. How she touched herself and then let *him* taste what's mine.

Fuck that.

I pull the blanket from her body hard enough that I'm sure it'll wake her, but it doesn't. She adjusts slightly, lying on her back while turning her head to face me, but her eyes remain closed, and her breathing stays even.

She's so fucking pretty like this, so helpless. I could do whatever I wanted to her right now. I could wake her up with my dick inside her which would definitely piss her off. I could force her mouth open and make her take me down her delicate little throat and erase the feeling of another man there.

Instead, I undo my pants, reach in, and take my dick into my hand, pumping myself roughly while I stare at her sleeping form. Her nipples are peaked under her tight tank top, and they rise and fall with each breath she takes.

Squeezing the tip of my dick, I let out a low groan before reaching out to slide up her shirt and palming her bare breast in my hand. She squirms slightly and I continue to pump my length while touching her. She moans quietly, her hips move like she's searching for me, but I continue to fuck my hand until I feel the orgasm starting at the base of my spine.

Pulling her shirt up over her tits I don't hold back the loud moan as I unleash my release onto her chest, coating her in my cum, hoping she wakes up. I want her to catch me like this. I want to see her reaction to how I've marked her as mine.

She whimpers, her hips continuing to search, but she remains asleep even as I finish. I rub my hand through the cum coating her pretty tits, and massage it into her skin, making sure she's thoroughly covered.

Tucking myself back into my pants, I don't fix her shirt or the blanket. Lingering, because I want to take in the sight for a little bit longer, I'm almost tempted to take a picture. But I don't, because if anyone got ahold of my phone and saw this, I would kill them. This view is only for me.

Which reminds me, I go to her dresser to pull out the camera she hid. I expected her to destroy it, but she didn't. I make sure to relocate it to a spot that she'll struggle to find, and couldn't reach even if she did. The best part is it gives me an even better view of her entire room.

"Don't worry, killer, this isn't your entire punishment," I tell her unconscious body.

I leave her house the same way I came in, making sure to relock the door. When I get on my bike, I make sure to be as loud as possible with the engine as I drive off down the dark streets back to my house.

As soon as I'm in the door, I pull up the camera. She's in the same spot I left her and I smirk, leaving the camera open on my phone as I get into bed, because I want a firsthand view of her reaction in the morning.

And then, I'll deal with Drew.

CHAPTER 22
MAX

Something is off, I know it as soon as I start to wake up. My body is cold, which is weird because I wouldn't have kicked my blankets off, since I always burrow into them. I reach out blindly, trying to grab them to cover myself so I can fall back into a deep sleep, but it's not just the blanket that's missing. I start to wake up a bit more and realize my shirt is pushed up over my chest which is strange—I don't think I've ever done that in my sleep before.

Reaching up to tug the fabric back down, I feel something foreign on me. Hardened…sticky…*what the fuck?*

My eyes shoot open like I'm going to see the reason for this standing in my room, but I don't. It does confirm my suspicion though. Caine was here. His cum is on me. I know it was him.

I let out an annoyed scream, jumping out of bed, ripping off my clothes, and getting into the shower before it even has a chance to heat up. I scrub my body until it's practically raw. I continue to mumble threats to the man that clearly has a death wish.

After I finish cleaning myself up, I throw on a hoodie, leggings, and low-cut boots before storming out of my house. I head straight to Uncaged, because I'm fucking *done.*

I know it's because he saw me with Drew, and I don't give a shit. He doesn't have a right to me or my body. Drew was rough, and I loved every single second of it. Caine can know now that if I'm making a choice on who gets to have my body, it's not him.

When I bust in the front doors of the gym, the only man I see is Coach Adam standing behind the desk at the front. He just raises an eyebrow at me. My words get caught in my throat for a second, seeing how his bulky arms are exposed in a cut off shirt. The sides are completely open, showing off the tattoos that cover him from the snake on his neck, down his arms and hands, and seem to extend over his entire torso.

"Can I help you?" he finally asks, which makes me realize I've just been standing here staring at him.

"Where's the big asshole?" I snap.

Now he looks slightly amused. "Which one?"

Fair question.

"Caine," I practically growl, annoyed that I'm having to say his name out loud at all.

"Not here yet." He folds his arms across his chest. "Why are you looking for him?"

I hesitate, not sure how much to tell him. I should tell him everything, right? Maybe then he will kick him out of the gym. He'll probably tell me to go to the police and file a report.

Then I remember the reality of my situation and realize that he knows Caine a lot better than he knows me. He would probably take his side over mine, think that I'm lying and all of a sudden, I'm the town loon.

"He left something at my house," I say instead of explaining that he's taken advantage of me three times now. *Or that I've enjoyed it.*

He looks amused again, and I'm regretting coming here. "What did he leave? I thought you were seeing Drew."

My mouth opens, but nothing comes out because I don't know what to say. It's not like I can say the thing he left behind was his cum on my body while I was sleeping. Great, not only am I about to be the town loon, but instead I'm going to be the town slut, too.

"I'm not seeing anyone," I answer honestly and now he looks at me like I'm lying. "You know what, never mind. I'll figure it out myself."

I turn to leave, shaking my head, but he calls out my name. I hesitate before turning around, because I'm sure he's about to laugh in my face or something.

"I'm not sure what your situation is, and I don't really care. But I know these guys and if you want to have some extra training time without them here, just one on one, let me know."

Again, my mouth opens, and nothing comes out at his offer. I just nod before turning and leaving. That made it sound like he knows how Caine is, and he wants to…what? Help me defend myself? I guess I was right about him siding with Caine.

But the extra training couldn't hurt, and while Adam may be prickly as well, he doesn't seem like a complete psycho. Maybe I'll take him up on that offer. If anything, to just add to my list of things to piss off the man that keeps sneaking into my house.

"Maybe," I finally answer. The adrenaline is coming down as I walk out of the gym.

I decide to do something I haven't done enough of since moving here, I go to the beach.

It's early and cold, so there aren't many people here. I've seen the advertisements for this town in the summer, it looks so bright and happy. There are events and fun things to do, but right now, in the dead of winter, the layer of fog makes it impossible to see too far in the distance. The chill in the air is heightened by the ocean breeze as I walk closer to it.

Toeing off my shoes, my bare feet sink into the cold sand with every step I take. There are remnants of ashes in the sand, probably from bonfires last night, and I carefully avoid stepping on any charred wood pieces. When I finally find a clear spot, I toss my shoes onto the ground and sit next to them, hugging my knees to my chest.

I watch as the tide comes in, how the waves break before reaching shore. The clouds above me threaten to rain any minute, but I don't care. I want to feel it, to let the chill seep down into my bones. The quiet surrounding me is peaceful, but with peace comes memories. That's when they choose to haunt me the most.

"Why the fuck would you tell me that?" Carson snaps and it immediately makes me cower deeper into the leather chair he has in his office.

I'm not even sure why he has this chair, it's not like anyone comes in here.

"Well, because my mom said I should tell you everything I want, and that it would be easier on our marriage." I feel stupid even saying the words and my voice trails off. I knew I shouldn't have told him this. I knew he would judge me.

He scoffs. "She wouldn't say that if she knew her daughter was a fucking freak. Are you really that much of a slut that you'd want me to...what? Chase you around, hold you down, or tie you up to fuck you? That's fucking disgusting, Maxine."

I sink even lower. I knew it had been a long shot, but I thought maybe bringing up sex with Carson and sharing what I want might actually have been something he would've liked to talk about. He always complains that he wants me to fuck him more, and yet this has only made me feel worse about my fantasies.

"Never mind, it was a dumb idea." I shake my head, starting to stand up and wanting to go to bed. Alone.

"Yeah, it fucking was," his voice echoes from behind me as I try to leave as quickly as possible. "Don't ever talk about that shit again. And make sure you get your hair done before the engagement party this weekend; it looks like shit."

I don't respond to him—there's nothing for me to say and if I do, I'll just end up crying. Even if I scream at him, the tears will fall, and it'll only make things worse.

I know I need to leave. That I need to get out. I need a plan.

I hardly notice the silent tears streaming down my cheeks as I stare straight ahead at the waves lapping at the beach. I wipe them away, refusing to give that man or anyone from my past anymore of my pain or energy.

I got out. I made a plan, and I followed through and made it out.

Still, I wish I felt safe, but I don't. The danger I feel now...it's a different danger, it's almost a *wanted* danger. I crave it. And maybe that's why I remembered that conversation with Carson about some of my sexual fantasies.

It doesn't slip by me that some guy I barely knew was able to fulfill a fantasy I suppressed better than my "fiancé" ever could. My mind is a fucking mess, and I just want peace. I close my eyes, taking in a deep breath, inhaling in the cool salty air and letting it fill my lungs before letting it back out.

I'm finally in charge of my own body, my own life. Everything is mine for the first time ever, and that's what I hold on to. And I'll never go back.

※

Work isn't as busy tonight, which I'm thankful for. I feel like everything that's been happening has exhausted me physically, mentally, and emotionally. So, it's nice to not have a chaotic shift filled with assholes tonight.

Danner's here, as she usually is, and I can't help but think it's because she's really trying to be a friend, which I should probably accept. I just don't exactly know how. I've never had a friend before. I wasn't allowed. My parents, mostly my mom, would tell me that I couldn't have friends over and then would poison my mind with reasons why I shouldn't have them in my life.

My dad never cared enough to say anything about it.

Carson didn't want me to be close with anyone, because I could go to them and reveal how shitty he was to me. I've spent time learning about abusive partners and how isolation is one of their main tactics. Of course, at the time I had no idea that's what he was doing. I'm ashamed at how sheltered I was, and it didn't take much to expose the truth about the hell I was living in.

"So, how is it training at the gym?" Danner asks after I finish helping the other person at the bar.

I shrug. "It's fine."

She looks at me like she knows there's more. She doesn't know about any of my run-ins with the guys. One somewhat willingly, the other, not so much.

"Have you beat them up yet? Please tell me you've punched someone in the face."

That makes me laugh softly, shaking my head. "Attempted to, but not quite."

"Is there a reason I've seen Caine staring at you like you're his next meal?"

My heart rate kicks up at her mentioning him and that she's

even noticed him watching me. But I do what I do best, deny, deny, deny.

"Probably because he looks at everyone that way right before he kills them and stores them in his basement freezer."

"True." She chuckles. "Now, what's your excuse for Drew also being interested in you?"

I look at her with wide eyes, and she looks like she knows more than she's letting on.

I shake my head. "What are you talking about? I think you're seeing things."

"Mhmm." She sips her dirty Shirley. "All I know is that I've lived here my whole life. I've seen a lot of things, including when those two came into town. And I've never seen them watch someone the way that they watch you."

"Are you a private investigator or something?" I question, jokingly. "Wait, what do you do for work?"

The second important "d" after deny is divert and that's my plan B.

"Wouldn't you like to know?" She winks.

The bar door swings open roughly, and I half expect to see one of the guys from the gym walk in, but instead it's a middle aged man with a beer gut in a police uniform who looks around like someone's pissed in his cheerios. I've dealt with guys like this when they come in here, and it means I'm about to get annoyed.

"How can I help you?" I ask him, and he looks over, his eyes trailing up my body and I fold my arms across my chest instinctually, because the vibes I'm getting from him are concerning.

"Just looking for someone," he grunts.

"Who?" Danner snarks and he narrows his eyes at her.

"Someone not here."

"Well, if you let us know who it is then maybe we could let you know if they show up Officer…?"

He doesn't say anything in response before leering at me before leaving.

"Fucking prick," I murmur, not sure what that was about or who he thought he was.

"We call him Officer Doogie." Danner says, deadpan.

I choke out a laugh. "Why?"

"His name is Doug and he's an asshole, so…" She shrugs.

"Do you know what that was about?"

"Probably Adam. Doogie seems to think he's always up to something."

I scoff, thinking about how Adam's probably not the guy he should be after. "Well, is he?"

"Eh, who knows. Probably not, unless being incredibly good looking becomes illegal."

I cough out a laugh, shaking my head at her comment because I'm not about to agree with her. Though, I've never had a thing for older guys, especially ones that are so…rugged. But Adam is hot.

"Speaking of, did anything happen with you and that other guy from the group?" I redirect the conversation.

"Absolutely not. Never have and never will." She fiddles slightly with her drink, which makes me think there's more there that she's not telling me.

"Been there," I say under my breath. *And we see how that has worked out.* Looking for a distraction, I decided to take a chance. "Hey, we should hang out sometime, but not here."

She perks up. "We should. We could have a movie night or an old school slumber party where I can share all the deep dark secrets of this place that I can't share where others can overhear." Danner looks around like she's scoping the place out, and I chuckle.

"Sure, I mean, I've never been to a slumber party before. I wouldn't know what they're like, but sure."

She rears back. "What? What kind of childhood did you have that didn't include slumber parties?"

I huff out a breath, if only she knew. "A shitty one. Count me in, though."

"Just tell me when and where and I'll make sure you have the best first slumber party ever. It'll be even better than having one as a kid because now we can have booze."

I bark out a laugh, shaking my head and getting back to work. I can't deny that might end up being the perfect distraction.

CHAPTER 23
ADAM

The guys are training, and I watch. I'm always watching. I watch their form, the moves they make, and how they can improve. Whether it's the combinations, blocks, takedowns, or hits. My eyes remain locked on even the smallest detail so I can help them get better.

Caine is lifting while Drew assists me with class and it's not one of the classes Max is in, which is why Caine is actually focused on his own training for once. Drew is short with everyone, grunting out his approval or making small adjustments himself. I just watch.

Watching is how I've noticed everything going on recently with Max. I've seen how Caine stares at her, how tense he is when it comes to anyone coming near her and the look in his eye when she looks at him. I know how he is when he wants something and that he doesn't have any boundaries to tell him he's going too far.

That's why he trains as hard as he does. He wants to be the best and his top priority is to get to the UFC and win.

I offered Max the extra training because I saw how pissed off she was when she came in and I've seen how Caine has his sights set on her. He's gone too far, I'm sure he has. I don't think he's actually hurt her, but I wouldn't be surprised if he does at some point.

And I'm no stranger to wanting to push and go too far. What I want is primal and dirty, rough and raw. Drew can keep up with me and my needs like not many can. I can't help but wonder if Max could. If she can handle Caine, maybe she could handle me.

Would she want to?

Of course not, I'm too old for her, she wants things I could never give her. But I can give her training, and that's where any time spent together will stop.

"Alright, cool down," I announce to the class, which earns me a glare from Drew because he hates when I take charge after I tell him he can lead class.

I give him a look, wondering if he's going to say anything since we've barely talked since our little blowout. He doesn't. Instead, he walks to the front while everyone finishes up. I wait until everyone has left before I join him.

"Hey," I say simply, and he looks a little surprised, but is trying to hide it.

"Uh, hi?" I'm sure I caught him off guard with my casualness.

"How've things been going?"

He turns toward me, his arms crossed. "What're you doing?"

"Asking you how you've been?"

"Why?"

"I don't know actually," I brush off. It doesn't feel weird between us since our fight. Tense, maybe a little, but it isn't awkward.

"Hm," he huffs, turning to type on the computer.

Caine's fist hitting the bag echoes around us, especially with the silence since everyone has left. I don't know why I decide to say what I do, maybe it's to get a reaction from Drew. "Let me know if Max plans on taking me up on my offer for extra training."

I head to my office without waiting for him to respond. My comment may be immature, but I want him to know I offered that to her. Caine would probably kill me if he knew—at least he'd try.

Drew follows me into my office, shutting the door firmly behind him so it's just us.

"What do you mean you offered her extra training?" Drew asks, his face blank and not giving away any of his emotions. He's always been good at hiding how he feels.

"You're not blind, you've seen how Caine is fixated on her and I'm sure whatever you're doing isn't helping. I just offered some extra training time for her so she can defend herself if needed."

"She's fine," he insists.

"If you say so." I sit in my chair behind my small desk.

"Are you trying to make me jealous, now? Because that seems below you."

"No, and if I was, I don't think I would use some girl that you two are clearly already pursuing to do it."

"It just seems weird is all. You never offer extra training to anyone."

"And you don't know everything I do or don't do."

His eyes narrow on me like he doesn't believe me.

"What are we doing?" Drew asks, and it takes me back slightly.

"What do you mean?" I ask, genuinely confused.

"Are we done hooking up? Because if we are, then I'd rather that be settled and we can go back to normal." He shrugs.

I didn't really think about it one way or another. This was never a relationship; it wasn't ever going to be, it was just sex. Both of us comfortable with each other and with similar schedules who are able to fuck when we need. Him asking if that's done shocks me because I would've still fucked around regardless of what happened the other night. Shit, regardless of whatever fire he's playing with, but if he wants to stop then that's fine too.

"Did you want to be?"

The moment between us is tense, and I can't tell if it's the kind of tense that may lead to something sexual which is how it all started anyway, or a tense that's going to end in us trading blows. I'd rather not fight him; I know he still spars when he thinks I'm not around, but he shattered his knee when that guy kicked it out and that's not something you easily come back from.

He raises his chin. "What if I say no?"

"Then we won't be." I shrug easily.

"What if I say yes?"

"Then we will be," I say just as calmly.

"And what if I'd want Max to be involved sometimes?"

That earns him a reaction, my eyebrows raising.

"I'd say you may have a death wish with Caine."

He scoffs. "He doesn't scare me."

"Me either, but I'm not fucking around with someone else's girl."

"She's not his girl."

"Is she yours?"

"Maybe she will be."

I lean back, my arms folded across my chest, just staring at him. I can't quite tell if he's serious, and I also don't know how we got here, or why. Eventually I shake my head.

"If she's your girl, then I'm not getting involved. Have your fun," I dismiss.

"Yeah, but if you change your mind, the offer may not stand," he says, leaving the office.

I smirk because something tells me that offer will always stand. We talked about sharing a girl between us before. It would be fun, I know that it would, but I'm not about to get caught up in any of the drama potentially brewing here. Uncaged is my safe space, it always has been, and it needs to stay that way.

The gym has always been my peace, ever since I first stepped foot in one after my first coach yanked me from the streets. He had told me to knock my shit off with the underground fighting and that he would show me how to *really* fight. Of course, I didn't give a fuck at the time as a pissed off nineteen year old who had never known an ounce of stability. But after a particularly brutal fight, I came to him battered and bloody and told him I didn't want to die somewhere alone because I lost a bad fight.

He took me in and taught me everything I know now and trained me until I was one of the best. If it hadn't been for him, I wouldn't be where I am today. And it's something I can never repay, even if he was still around to cash in on any payment.

I sigh, pulling up the cameras in the gym and don't see Drew anywhere. Caine is in the cage with Alexander, and I sigh, knowing I'm going to need to go out there so they don't take it too far. Which is why I do one of the things I do best, I watch.

CHAPTER 24
MAX

After debating for a few days on if I should take Adam up on his offer for extra training, I have my first session tonight.

Even though Caine hasn't made himself obvious to me anywhere other than at the gym, I still feel him at night when I'm in bed. I feel my body prepare for him, the adrenaline and fear sends wetness between my thighs and I'm ashamed when my fingers make their way there. I'm even more ashamed when I actually rub myself to release while thinking of being held down by my throat. Or waking up to someone fucking me, finding them over me, their rough touch bringing me to the brink of orgasm before I'm even conscious enough to recognize it.

But he doesn't touch me or leave his mark on me again. It doesn't matter, because I know he's there. I feel him watching me while my eyes are closed and he thinks I'm sleeping, but I'm not. I'm waiting to feel his hands on me, or his mouth. My heart races at the possibility, yet it hasn't happened again.

Drew texts me every day and I actually reply. It seems like I keep doing things I probably shouldn't and yet I can't stop.

The presence of both of them looms around me at all times and it's suffocating, but in a good way. It's like I'm suffocating with anticipation at all times. And the way my body reacts, is concerning.

At the gym, I feel Caine's eyes on me while Drew lingers close by, and I'm waiting to see what will happen. Will Drew touch me? Will Caine do something about it, or will he touch me first?

Nothing happens.

I'm becoming a pro at hiding how crazy it's making me. The worst part is that the mind games they're clearly playing are starting to work. I've never felt this before, and it's odd. All the anticipation and smothering I've felt at the hands of Carson was always both literal and metaphorical.

Anticipation of him coming home and whether he had a good day or a bad day. A good day would mean I would be safe —at least until he started drinking. A bad day meant I would hide. But he had always found me.

Until now.

"Ready?" Coach Adam's gruff voice asks, pulling me from my mind and preventing another flashback from consuming me again.

"Mhmm," I mumble, dropping my bag by the front desk since no one else is here. With it being winter, the sun sets early and it's already dark outside. The overhead lights are the only thing illuminating the gym as they glow against the mats eerily.

"What do you want to focus on?" he asks, facing me, his arms folded and his legs shoulder length apart. My eyes are drawn to his throat and the snake tattoo there and with how it moves as he speaks.

"Whatever you think I need the most help with." I try to focus on why I'm here and not the way it feels to have him looking at me. He's so intense all the time, and I can't tell if it's because he's annoyed that I'm here or because he wants me underneath him.

Or maybe that's my own internal debate because I'm staring at him the same way.

He grunts in response. I want to say something snarky to his non reply. Before I have the chance he snaps at me instead, "Wrap your hands."

I do just that, somewhat relieved we're going to work on boxing today because I don't know if I could handle rolling on the floor working on any of the BJJ moves with him right now. And something tells me he might be feeling the same way.

Especially because he keeps his distance from me this time as he instructs my punches. Unlike the other day, when he moved me into the proper position and pressed his body into mine, he's keeping a normal distance today. It's a little annoying and a lot frustrating.

By the time we're done, I'm dripping with sweat while unwrapping my hands, sore from how many times I hit the bag today.

"Good work. Same time on Thursday?" he asks and I'm slightly taken aback. Part of me thought this may have been a one-time offer, another part is surprised he's asking about two days from now.

"Um, yeah, sure." Wondering if it was just a good guess that he knows I don't work that day.

He nods once and leaves me alone to gather my things so I can go. I almost call out to say goodbye before walking out but decide against it.

Once I'm outside, the feeling of being watched, of having eyes on me, is back. And just like every other time, I know who they belong to without even seeing them. And just like every other time, I silently dare him to do something.

Just to add to it, I pull out my phone, calling someone else while standing on the low-lit sidewalk.

"Hey little one," the deep timbre answers and I smirk into the darkness, even if he can't hear who I'm talking to.

"Hi, you busy?"

"Nothing I can't cancel."

"Good."

I go home, knowing I'm playing with fire right now. Yet, I'm not afraid to get burned. I've been through worse and survived.

DREW KNOCKS on my door not long after I get home. I was hoping to get into the shower, but he's here before I'm able to do that. When I open the door, he looks me up and down and has to comment on it.

"Why are you sweaty? Thinking about me a little too much and couldn't help yourself?" He smirks and I roll my eyes as he walks past me.

"I was doing some extra training with Coach tonight and you got here before I could take a shower."

"Adam?" he asks, sharply.

"Uh, yeah, unless there's another coach I'm supposed to be training with?"

"How'd that go?" His voice is even, almost like he's trying to mask any emotion, and it makes me curious.

"Why does it matter?" I fold my arms across my chest.

"Just curious if you think it helped."

I shrug. "Guess we'll find out. But I need to shower."

"I'll join you." The serious look on his face morphs into something more sensual and I hold my hand out to stop his advance.

"No, you can wait out here like a good boy," I tease. But it may have been the wrong thing to say because Drew grabs my wrist, and yanks me into his body, making me gasp as our chests collide.

"You should know one thing about me, and it's that I'm not a good boy and I never will be." He lets me go, turning me toward my room and swatting my ass. "Go get clean."

I glare back at him but walk toward my bathroom without another word. I know if I say anything, it'll probably end up being me asking him to join.

"Lock the door, though, because I'm bad at following rules."

His words send shivers down my spine, and I quickly go into my bathroom. After shutting the door and locking it quickly, I breathe out in relief, like he was chasing me. Even though I don't think he even took a step in my direction.

Hastily, I shower, where I usually like to take my time thoroughly washing my hair and enjoying the feel of warm water hitting my skin. I'm very aware that there's essentially a stranger in my house and I left him alone, trusting him not to snoop or do anything like install hidden cameras...*hah*. Too late on that one, I guess.

Once I'm finished, I peek out of my bathroom to make sure he's not waiting right there for me before dressing quickly in loose sweatpants and a tank top. Then I go into the living room and see that Drew is relaxed on my couch with his feet kicked up —shoes still on—while he scrolls through a streaming site on my TV.

"Make yourself comfortable, why don't you?" I snark, looking pointedly at his shoes that are currently kicked up on my ottoman.

"I did, thanks. You going to join me?"

"If you don't get your dirty shoes off my furniture, I'm going to kick your ass out," I threaten.

He chuckles, kicking his shoes off onto the floor and I cringe at him for still not putting them by the door because now, his gross, dirty boots are on my clean floor by the couch. I'm not super neurotic about things like this, but I can see the caked wet sand in the soles, and I know that's going to be a pain in the ass to clean.

"Come here," he instructs, patting the cushion next to him.

I saunter over, sitting about a foot away from him, putting my legs in between us, leaning back against the armrest with my knees bent in front of me.

He lets out a humorless laugh, his focus going back to the TV. "What do you want to watch?"

I'm a little shocked he isn't trying to push for anything right now. As much as I hate to admit it, the normalcy of the moment feels nice.

I've never had this.

Never just sat on the couch with someone just to watch something for the enjoyment of it. Carson would make me sit next to him when he would have some poker game on. I didn't know anyone watched poker games, but Carson does. And it bored me to tears.

"You ever watch hockey?" Drew asks, pulling me from my thoughts.

"Nope."

"The Denver Dragons are playing. It's the only sport I like other than MMA." He winks at me, and I hug my knees closer to my chest.

"I don't know anything about hockey or any of the teams."

"You'll like it. There's fighting." He smirks at me, putting the game on.

We watch silently for a few minutes, and it's hard to keep track of what's going on. The puck is so small on the screen and all I can see are the players skating back and forth with a lot of pushing and shoving.

At one point, Drew takes my legs and pulls them over his lap while running his callused hands along my skin. I have to suppress my body's reaction, but he doesn't act like he's affected at all. So, I won't, either.

I'm so distracted by his hands on me that I hardly hear him when he says, "Come here." When I hesitate, he moves me himself so I'm straddling his lap. That's when I learn he's not as unaffected as I thought, because his cock is so hard underneath me, that even restrained by his jeans I can feel him through the thin fabric of my pants.

Drew's hand moves up my spine to the back of my neck before he grips my hair in his fist, tugging slightly so I'm forced to look up at him. He leans forward, his lips skimming the skin of my neck as he speaks.

"I want to feel you rub yourself on my cock like this. You think you can do that for me, little one?"

"Like this?" I taunt, swiveling my hips slightly, feeling the bulge against my clit and it sends a wave of pleasure through me.

He lets out a low groan. "I know you can give me more than that. Use me to make yourself come. I didn't get to see it last time and I want to see how fucking pretty you look falling apart for me."

Grinding myself down on him again, only harder this time and I have to bite back a moan. "I'd probably look even better if I was coming on your tongue."

He chuckles, pulling my hair tighter, while using his other hand to help guide my hips. "Show me how you do it by yourself, then maybe I'll let you use my mouth."

"And you think you're not a good boy," I tease, swiveling my hips.

He yanks my hair so hard I yelp as my head is forced further back.

"Call me that again and I'll bend you over right here and force you to take my cock wherever I want and show you how *not* true that is. Now, be a *good fucking girl* and come for me so I can get to my meal. I'm starving."

I moan, rubbing against him even faster, the friction of our clothes between us heightening my arousal as I dry hump him. Drew keeps a tight grip on my hip, guiding me as I rub and move myself how I need to feel the sparks of pleasure.

There's a noise somewhere outside, but I choose to ignore it because I'm too focused on getting myself off on Drew's lap to care. He tightens his grip on both my hair and hip and it has me working myself even harder against him to find my release.

The noise comes again, only louder this time. I still don't care. I moan when he thrusts up against me, the added pressure to my already sensitive clit has me teetering near the edge. I tighten my thighs around him as my movements begin to lose their rhythm and my orgasm is cresting just as another loud crashing sound echoes around us. I'm already falling over the edge, crying out, as I continue to thrust my pussy against Drew's lap until it subsides.

"That was fucking cute," an annoyingly familiar deep voice says somewhere behind me, dripping with sarcasm. I'm breathing heavily and look up at Drew, who has a smirk on his face. He's not looking at me, no, he's locked onto the figure behind me.

"Glad you got to watch it. Are you planning to stick around to see what it's like when I have my tongue in her pussy too?" Drew asks, and my jaw drops at how calm he is about the other man who's just broken into my house.

"No," I snap, climbing off Drew's lap to face Caine. "You don't get to watch anything. Get the fuck out."

Caine scoffs, leaning back against the wall with his arms folded. "Nah, I think I want to see the show. You can fake an orgasm with him and then I can give you what we both know you really want."

I raise my eyebrows in surprise. "You want to watch us? You think you can handle seeing another man touch me?"

"Well, we both know it's not the first time I've had to watch you with him, is it?"

I steel my spine, craning my neck to look up at him. "So, you like watching?"

"I like seeing what I can do better. So, after he's done with you, I'll show him what it is that you *really* want," Caine says confidently.

"That may be difficult since I don't want *you* at all," I insist.

"You keep saying that, but we both know it's not true."

Drew steps up behind me and I feel trapped between the two of them, yet I find myself leaning back slightly against Drew. Maybe it's to prove a point, or maybe it's to poke the bear that is Caine a little more. Either way, Caine watches the move and his jaw tenses. It makes me smile, because he can pretend like he's okay with this and that he wants to watch, but we both know it's killing him.

He wants me to himself even if it means forcing it. But he's also proved that he's completely insane, and part of me wonders if this will lead to him murdering Drew and making me watch. The worry should make me stop this from going any further, but it doesn't.

Instead, I turn, keeping my back to Caine as I face Drew, our bodies grazing each other from how close we're standing.

"You heard him," I start. "He wants to watch. So, be a good boy and show me what you got."

Drew lets out a low growl, grabbing me roughly, and tossing

me over his shoulder and storming toward my bedroom. I push up on his back to see Caine following slowly. The deathly serious look in his eyes has me slightly worried, but I don't have much time to feel anything before I'm being tossed onto my bed.

Drew descends on me, his face less than an inch from mine and I think he may actually try to kiss me, which is something I've yet to do with either of them. But he doesn't. "What did I tell you about calling me that?"

"You going to hurt me?" I whisper, hoping Caine can't hear us because I'm sure he'll like that I'm asking, since it's obvious that that's what I'm *wanting*.

"I guess we'll see. It depends how much you can take." He moves off me, and I look around trying to find Caine, and just as Drew pulls off my sweatpants, I see Caine standing by the door to my bedroom. He didn't even bother to close it, which makes me feel weirdly exposed. Even more so than the fact that Drew is spreading my legs apart while the man who's been basically harassing me watches.

The second Drew's mouth is on me, I cry out. Especially as he sucks my clit into his mouth when I'm still sensitive from my first orgasm.

"What do you think, Caine? How many can I get out of her?" Drew taunts with a long lick up my weeping center that leaves my back bowing off the mattress.

"You get five minutes, and then I'm showing you how it's done," Caine threatens.

"You may have to drag me away from her, this cunt is dripping for me," Drew goads. "And *so fucking* sweet." I manage to look over at Caine, who has his eyes narrowed, every thick muscle seems tense.

Drew must notice that my attention has strayed because he grazes his teeth on my clit, and I try to back away from him. I'm trying to move myself further up the bed, but he wraps his arms around my thighs, pulling me tighter against his mouth so I'm unable to move, and I let out a small screech.

"Don't think you're getting away from me, little one. You're about to show him just how much your pussy prefers me and my mouth than his." Drew's eyes flash with mischief before he dives back in, licking and sucking my clit until I'm unable to move my focus to anything other than him.

My hands find his hair, gripping the dark locks and pulling, making sure to hold his lips against me as he continues to move his expert tongue in perfect precision.

"How does it feel, killer?" Caine's voice breaks through the pleasure induced haze I'm in. "Does it remind you of when I had my tongue inside you while you were tied up for me?"

Drew makes a noise that sends a vibration through me, and I moan, shaking my head like it can shake away what Caine is saying to me. But he doesn't stop, he just keeps talking while Drew continues fucking me with his tongue. And when I feel the pressure of him pressing a finger into me, I throw my arm over my mouth and sink my teeth into my flesh to suppress the scream that I'm desperate to let loose.

"Times almost up, you better work a little harder, Drew. She's not going to come for you, but you'll get to watch how well she takes my dick in that tight little pussy of hers. Or maybe I'll make her take me in her throat. How was it when she did that for you?"

Drew pulls back, continuing to thrust his finger in and out of me while he just watches the movement. He responds to Caine like I'm not even here. "Fucking amazing. I doubt you'll get to find out, sounds like she'd rather bite your dick off than suck it."

I chuckle, but it quickly turns into a moan when Drew curls his finger and leans down to suction his mouth onto my clit again. I drop my arm and let the sound of my moan fill the room. I do it so that Caine can hear that it's not his name coming from my mouth.

"Drew, fuck that feels so good, *please.*" I pull his hair tighter, while moving my hips to rub against his mouth while he pushes another finger inside me, and I start to see stars.

"That's it, come for me, little one. Show him what you really like and how I'm the one that gives it to you, not him." Drew's voice is lower, darker, like the first night when he was here with me. It feels like this is the side he keeps concealed, and I can't deny that when it comes out, my thighs clench and my core floods.

The threat of danger looming both between my legs and by the door of the room is intense and it shouldn't make me feel this way. But it does. Everything is heightened and when Drew growls, "Give it to me." I lose it.

My head falls back, and I can't suppress the moan that leaves my lips as the orgasm consumes me. I'm pulling at his hair, holding his face tightly against me while I rub myself against him as stars burst behind my closed eyelids and my thighs shake so hard while trying to slam shut. I think he's holding them open, and I think I hear Caine say something from his spot, but none of it registers. The only thing I'm aware of in this moment is how good I feel as the release works its way through my body, stronger than the one before.

As I come down from the high of my orgasm, Drew laps at my entrance and I try to push him away because the light graze of his tongue on my clit is too much and I feel like jumping out of my skin every time he touches it.

"Ah, too much," I cry when the tip of his tongue sends the slightest amount of pressure onto my sensitive nub.

Suddenly, there's a tight grip on my hair, pulling me to look to the side and Caine is there, looming over me. Drew hasn't left his spot between my thighs, but he's moved from kissing and licking my center to kissing and licking the insides of my thighs.

"Since he's had your mouth before me, I feel like he should have to watch me fuck your ass so he can see me claim another piece of you."

I glare up at him and squeak out a small noise when Drew nips the sensitive skin of my inner thigh and Caine tightens his grip on my hair at the sound. I see his jaw clench and I can tell that he wants to send Drew flying across the room because he's still touching me. But by some miracle he restrains himself.

"You don't have any claim over any part of me. You knew I wasn't a virgin when you fucked me. Yours isn't the only dick that's been inside me. It won't be the last either."

I yelp when he yanks even harder, pulling me up the bed, forcing Drew to lose his spot nestled between my legs and Caine forces my eyes up to him with his grip. My neck is almost painfully arched, and my eyes squeeze shut with pain.

"You don't talk about other dicks. You're lucky I'm not killing Drew right now for getting to taste you. But mine *is* the last that will be inside you. If you think I'll let anyone else fuck you, then you'll learn quickly that that won't happen."

"Drew," I squeak out, "fuck me."

Caine pulls even harder, his other hand collaring my neck.

"You want to see him die?" Caine threatens and I swallow roughly. I shake my head slightly, though the movement makes my scalp burn and my movement is limited from the grip he has on my throat.

I wonder if Drew can see how turned on I am from this. I wonder if he thinks I'm fucked in the head.

I am.

"You want to be fucked? Then it's going to be by me. He had his chance to touch you," Caine says, darkly.

"What if—" I stop myself. The thought that I almost spoke aloud is crazy, possibly from the lack of oxygen to my brain. Maybe it's from the two orgasms I just had that have left me stupid.

"Say it," he says, the words sounding like a threat on the air.

My eyes move from him to Drew, wondering if he's even still here since he's been so quiet. He's standing by the side of the bed, adjusting his cock that's clearly hard in his pants and I bite my bottom lip slightly.

"Say it," Caine commands again with another squeeze to my neck.

"What if you both fuck me?" My voice is quiet, and I can't believe I'm saying this. Have I thought about having more than one guy touch me before? Yeah, the thought of bringing two men so much pleasure that they both want me. This has been on the list of fantasies I've kept locked away because I knew I would be judged and shamed for them.

Right alongside the ones about being chased, thrown down in the dirt, and fucked while I act like I don't want it.

The way that Caine has a hold of me, the way he's looking at me and how he's talking to me? My pussy quivers with need. Add in Drew being here, and it's making me forget all the negative words that have been thrown at me when I've talked about my fantasies.

Even though one of these men thinks he has some sort of claim over me—that's not something that has ever been included in any of my fantasies. Probably because that's been my reality. Everyone's always felt like they had a claim over me. My parents, then Carson, and now Caine.

"Needy little whore, wanting two cocks?" Caine murmurs.

"Probably because yours doesn't give her enough. She knows I can give her what she needs," Drew chimes in and I bite back a smirk.

"Adam tell you that?" Caine asks over his shoulder.

I furrow my brow, confused by his comment. Catching Drew stiffen out of the corner of my eye. Caine catches the look.

"Oh, has he not told you about his little relationship with Coach?" Caine asks.

I don't respond.

"There's no relationship with him, don't speak on shit you don't know anything about," Drew threatens.

"So, is he okay with you fucking around with her too then?"

"He doesn't care what or who I do it with. And the same goes for him."

"I guess, you guys don't mind sharing." Caine looks back down to me, and I'm working hard not to question everything they are saying. "Too bad I do."

I roll my eyes, and Caine flips me onto my stomach so suddenly I gasp, almost dizzy from how quickly he moved me. He moves so his giant body is holding mine down, I can barely breathe from the way he's pressing me into the mattress, his lips graze my ear as he speaks.

"How about Drew holds you still while I stuff your greedy little cunt full of me. Then he can see what it's like when you're fucked the way you really like."

"How about you get the fuck off me," I bite out.

He lets out a low chuckle. "Drew, make yourself useful."

I think for a moment that he's not going to listen. Maybe he will even tell Caine to fuck off and do something to help me in this situation.

But then he's on the bed in front of me, kneeling by my head and grabbing my wrists, holding them in one hand, and when I try to look up at him to ask what the fuck he's doing, he moves my hair off my face to reveal a sinister smile. One that has chills run down my spine.

Caine is moving further down my body, spreading my legs despite my attempts to kick him away, which he easily avoids.

"Are you going to be a good girl for him, little one? I bet if you are, he'll let you come again." Drew smirks.

"I don't want him to. Get the fuck off me." I attempt to fight them both off, but I get nowhere. I'm completely helpless. Stuck and at their mercy.

And uncomfortably turned on. Achingly so.

"Fuck yeah, keep fighting and I will make sure to fill your ass, too. Bet you'd love that, like the filthy slut you are for me." Caine slaps his hand on my ass, and I yelp, burying my head in the mattress, ashamed that I'm in this position. I'm supposed to be getting stronger, learning how to defend myself, yet I continue to find myself in positions like this—where I'm helpless and being taken advantage of.

And the worst part is that each time, I end up liking it more than the last. Because I am strong, I know this in my core, but it's moments like these I may like to be a little helpless.

But that doesn't mean I'm going to make it easy for them.

CHAPTER 25
CAINE

Fuck, she's perfect. Even when Drew had his head between her thighs, even while I wanted to kill him and have her watch. She was fucking perfect.

The way she cries. The way she comes. The way she fights and struggles. How she takes my cock in her tight, soaking pussy. Which is exactly what I'm dying to do right now, but I also want to teach her a lesson about fucking with me, thinking she can do whatever she wants with whoever she wants. But no, she's mine, whether she wants to admit it or not.

Kneeling above her, I push my pants down my thighs that are currently pressed into hers to keep her spread in front of me. Her pussy is dripping, but I can't tell if it's all from her and how turned on she is or if it's also leftover spit from Drew. That thought pisses me off.

Drew. The same man that's holding her down for me right now.

"Flip her over," I command, shifting off her legs. Surprisingly, he doesn't argue with me, and uses her arms to flip her onto her back.

Max squeals, and the noise is both shrill and smoky, and it makes my cock even harder for her. She tries to flail around to kick me again, but I avoid her legs easily before wrangling them onto the bed, straddling her bare thighs, my dick standing straight as I work my fist over it slowly.

I push her shirt up so I can see her perky tits and puckered rosebud nipples. I reach down to pinch one between my fingers and she cries out, trying to fight us off with an annoyed growl.

"Get the fuck off me. Let me go!" She tries to buck me off, but all it does is make me want to shove my dick inside her. Somewhere. Anywhere. "Drew, please."

I smirk at the fact that she's trying to be sweet to him and that she thinks he's going to help her. She doesn't know him though, even if she thinks she does. Drew isn't the sweet guy she seems to think he is.

"Nah, little one, you wanted this, so you're going to get it how we want to give it." Max looks up at Drew, the shock and annoyance evident on her face. I want to laugh at how this may have ruined anything between them.

Good, there wasn't going to be anything serious there anyway.

"You wanted us both to fuck you, killer?" I ask, drawing her attention back to me. The look she gives me proves her annoyance, but the best part about it is the fire behind her eyes that I can see.

"I changed my mind," she grits out.

"No, you didn't. But don't worry, I won't fuck you tonight." She looks up at me, her eyes wide and surprised. I pinch her other nipple, which makes her yelp. "Disappointed?"

She shakes her head, but she's shifting around, and I know she's trying to find relief for her needy pussy. She's going to regret telling me to stop and get off of her, because I'm going to. Without giving her the relief she's clearly craving.

I continue moving my fist over my erection roughly, tightening over the head and working myself harder. She looks so good being held down underneath me, sweat on her brow, her skin flushing pink and her breathing labored. All while having that look in her eye that says she wishes she could kill me.

"Then let me go," she rasps.

I let out a low chuckle, fucking my fist harder over her, rolling her nipple in my fingers and tugging slightly.

"No, I'm going to remind you that you're mine. Doesn't matter if he has his dick in your mouth or if he touches you. That only happened because I allowed it. But you. Are. *Mine.*"

"I will never be yours." She narrows her eyes at me, and I lean down, sinking my teeth into the soft flesh of her breast. She tries to buck me off, but she can't with the way we're holding her down. I can't hold back my orgasm, and I let out a low groan, coming onto her exposed cunt.

I lean back, admiring how my cum looks on her skin. It's not the first time, but it is the first time that she's awake. I watch how it drips between her thighs; I can't help but take some onto my finger and push it into her. The way her thighs are forced together make her even tighter and she cries out at the intrusion.

"What the fuck is wrong with you?" she screeches.

I lean down, so what I say is only between us, despite Drew being close. "So much, killer, and you will never escape me. You're mine, I'm going to cover you with my cum, fill you with it, and do whatever I want to with you. The best part is you'll take it every time. You'll crave it."

She turns her head toward me, our lips almost touching, and I want to close the distance. I've never given a shit about kissing before, it's always seemed like a useless step into fucking and all I've wanted to do is get to the good parts, which is why I never have before.

If a woman had ever wanted to kiss me, I'd shove her to her knees and let her kiss my cock. I've never had a desire to kiss anyone on the lips. But right now, I do. She ruins it by opening those pouty lips to speak.

"Get. Off. Of. Me."

This time, I do, but not before taking more of my cum and pushing it inside her. Once I'm off her legs, Drew lets go of her arms and instead of fighting us immediately, she slumps down, and I wonder for a second if something is wrong.

But then she jumps up and I'm ready for a fight, wanting her to so I can have an excuse to hold her down again. Instead, she walks past us without looking up and goes into the bathroom, slamming the door shut.

The click of the lock sounds right before the shower starts

running. I don't want to look at Drew, but I can't help it. He just shrugs.

I want to stick around until she gets out, but I also know she doesn't want to see either of us right now. I'll just come back again once she's sleeping.

I nod my head toward the door, signaling to Drew that we need to leave. If he fights me, then Max is going to come out here and see me kicking his ass.

It's a good thing he doesn't, and we both leave. I make sure to relock the door, even if I'll be right back.

As we get to our bikes, I stop Drew after he puts his helmet on.

"Leave her the fuck alone," I threaten.

I hear him scoff behind his helmet. "You heard her, she wants both of us. If you think you're enough for her, you're a fucking idiot."

"And what? Are you going to bring Adam in on this? Fuck no." I shake my head.

"Learning to share your toys will be good for you, Caine. It may be about twenty years late, but better late than never." He straddles his bike, twisting the key and revving the engine before taking off.

I look up to Max's house, the light in her bedroom is still on and when I hear the music start to play, a slow smile spreads across my lips. Then, I kick up my foot, resting it on my bike, watching her window while I wait until she goes to sleep.

WE WORE HER OUT. I'm sure of it because it doesn't take long before her light switches off. Though, I don't miss the way her curtains move to the side as she peers out. I don't try to hide the fact that I'm still here. And she doesn't try to get me to leave. She's learning it won't take long for her to fully understand what it means when I set my eyes on something or someone I want. It means that it's mine.

Taking off my riding jacket, I toss it onto my bike before heading inside. I'm not going to need it and it's not like anyone is walking around here that will steal it.

It's not hard for me to get back inside Max's house. She really should be more concerned about how easy this is for me, but she never seems to be. She's always too busy telling me to get out, or to leave her alone. It's just shit I won't be doing so she's wasting her breath and we both know it.

Once I'm inside, I head to her bedroom. The door is cracked open, almost like she knew. Almost like she wanted me to come back. Interesting.

She's on her stomach, her auburn hair spread out on her white sheets. Her breathing is labored and it's clear she's completely passed out. I've seen this sight a few times now. While the urge to mark her skin again while she sleeps is strong, the urge to feel her against me is stronger.

Which is why I move the blanket from the other side of her bed and climb in. I'm not gentle about it—I don't really care if she wakes up and finds me here again. Actually, as always, I hope she does wake up and tries to fight me off. Then I can pin her down and fuck her since I didn't do it earlier.

Fuck, why didn't I? That's right. Because she let Drew touch her, let him make her come so I wasn't going to reward her. And I didn't. Just used her for my own pleasure and I don't feel an ounce of guilt about it.

Just like I don't feel any guilt about wrapping my arms around her middle, tugging her soft body back into mine and holding her there tightly. I'm a little surprised she doesn't wake up with how I'm pressed to her. Instead, she moans slightly, adjusting herself in my firm grip so her back is against me.

I let out a low groan as her ass rubs against my cock, already hardening for her. She doesn't wake up, not even when I rub myself against her because I can't fucking help myself. She's wearing little shorts, but I bet there's nothing underneath them, like the little teasing whore she is.

The urge to rip them off her body and shove my dick into her is almost unbearable. The restraint I show by not doing that should win me an award or some shit. I press my hand on her lower stomach, pressing her body even more securely against me, my dick nestling between her thighs. The tightness of them isn't as tight as her pussy, but right now it feels almost as good with how badly I want her.

She shifts slightly, creating friction between us and I grip her harder, digging my fingers into her stomach while my other arm wraps around her throat like a choke during a fight, but not as tight.

"If you're awake and keep rubbing yourself against me, killer, I'm going to fuck you into this mattress instead of letting you sleep like I was planning."

She doesn't respond and I don't know if she's truly asleep, or pretending, but she doesn't move again either. Somehow in the darkness of her bedroom, the only sound is her soft breathing, I do something I've never done in her bed, or any other bed before. I fall asleep.

CHAPTER 26
MAX

The other night, I felt it when Caine came back. I was half asleep, but unable to do anything about it. I anticipated him touching me, and taking advantage of me like he always has, using my body like I'm just there for him and not myself. The only thing I remember was his hard body pressed against mine. Him holding me almost too tightly, but I don't think he touched me, which is a first.

By the time I woke up in the morning, he was gone. The only thing that remained was the slight smell of him on my bed. The leather mixed with a hint of the ocean that seems to cling to everyone here.

It also could have just been a dream. I didn't have the energy to change my sheets after the activities of the evening, so maybe the lingering smell was from that. Maybe he only came back in my mind, because let's be honest—that doesn't sound like Caine.

My mind's been a confusing mess since that night. How everything had unfolded between the three of us. What I *wanted* to happen. What I'd asked for. That's never been me—Carson would have killed me for suggesting I wanted to be with more than one guy. For suggesting that he wasn't enough to satisfy me.

And yet, I find myself wanting it more than ever.

What would it feel like if they both held me down and fucked me at the same time? If they used me for whatever they wanted. If they took from me. If I was allowed to just be a body to use for their pleasure.

"Got it?" Coach Adam's voice breaks through the wild fantasy I was stuck in.

"Uh…" I can't form any words because I did not hear any of what he said. But I'm also not going to admit that to him. "Yup."

"Great, get into position."

Well, fuck. I can't exactly admit I don't know what the position is, highlighting the fact that I wasn't paying attention. I choose diversion and the words that come tumbling out of my mouth have me wanting to slap my hand over it.

"So, you and Drew are together?"

The look he gives me is lethal and I know I shouldn't have said that. I open my mouth to say something else, but his sharp voice beats me to it.

"Not that it's any concern to you, but no. So, you don't have to think he's cheating on me or something. Get in position."

Fuck.

"No, that's not why I was asking, I just—"

"Position. I didn't offer you extra training for a fucking gossip session, Max."

I gulp, my heart racing at his tone and how it feels like I was just reprimanded.

The weirdest part is the thrum I'm feeling between my legs from it. *What's wrong with me?*

I take a chance and drop down to my knees to guess the position for whatever he was talking about in my lust induced haze and the look he's giving me right now proves that I'm wrong. Very wrong.

"What are you doing?"

"What you asked." I bite back the sass, but I think he can still hear it.

"And that includes you getting on your knees? Wrong. Get up." He's so demanding and curt. His deep voice, the slight anger in it. I both want to stay on my knees and apologize and fight back and tell him to stop acting like I'm an idiot.

I don't say anything, I just let him command me like he has some right to. Because for once in my life, I want to listen. The air around him demands it, and that's probably why he's such a good coach. He's experienced, in control, and it boasts no argument.

And because my mind is in the gutter today, thanks to the two guys around here who refuse to leave me alone, I think about how that may translate to the bedroom. I wonder if he's the same way. I wonder if he would say the same words to me but mean them in an entirely different way.

"Get into position."

"Yes, sir."

"Do you even want to be here today?" he snaps.

"Yes, I'm sorry, I'm just tired." I scramble to my feet.

"I don't have to be here helping you."

"I know."

"Then if you're going to ignore me and do whatever the hell you want, you can leave."

"I'm not." I breathe out a tight breath to stop me from saying something I may regret just to get a rise out of him. "I'm not ignoring you. I'm just tired, but I want to be here."

"Good. We're going to work on your full mount. Due to your size, fully submitting an opponent bigger than you will take time, but we will get you there."

I nod in response, biting back the need to snap back at his comment regarding my *size*. I know I'm short. I get it every single day, but it's never stopped me before, and it's not going to stop me now.

He walks me through the steps, showing me in slow motion what I'm going to do and it's almost laughable how I'm supposed to wrangle this six foot one muscular professional to the ground and *keep him there*. But I don't dare show an ounce of hesitation.

Obviously, it's practice and he lets me do the moves as intended without doing anything to defend himself. After a couple slow practices, we work the moves at a more realistic pace, and I end up with him on the ground below me while I straddle his waist.

I know this isn't supposed to be sexual, but my mind is my own worst enemy, especially today. So, it's impossible not to feel the sexual undertones of the position we're in.

Plus, the fact that I can feel him through his shorts right now isn't helping. I don't think he's hard, but there's…*substantial* length hiding behind the fabric. I hop off him, ready to try again before I completely lose my mind and rub up against him like a cat in heat or something.

I've never been this…crazed. I don't know what's wrong with me, and I don't know if I like it.

We run through the move another handful of times before moving on to some kickboxing at my request. Hoping to eliminate some of the sexual tension in the air that I'm sure is because of my inability to control my raging hormones.

Except when I catch him watching me as I practice punching the bag, I see the flare of desire in his eyes. He blinks it away quickly, but it was there. It makes me think that maybe I'm not the only one feeling the tension that's swirling around us.

The piercing noise of my phone ringing brings me out of my daze once again and before I'm able to unwrap my hands and go to it, Adam picks it up off my bag, pointing the screen toward me where I see it says Drew.

My nerves kick up and I wonder how he's going to react, but he doesn't show any emotion. Not even when he answers it as I step toward him.

"Hello?" His deep timbre sends a chill down my spine.

He's quiet for a moment. I see the smallest smirk appear on his lips as he listens to whatever Drew is saying that I can't hear.

"Yeah, she's here. You two have plans?" Adam asks.

I tilt my head slightly, the question is mostly innocent, just a bit nosy, but there really isn't a hint of jealousy either. I want to yell at him for the massive invasion of privacy answering my phone, but for some reason I hold back. I'm not sure what it is about him that stops me from fighting back like I do with Caine and Drew, but there's something with him that keeps me stunned silent as I watch him have a conversation on my phone with his ex…fling? Current fling? I feel like I shouldn't try to figure it out.

"You can come get her if you want then." Adam shrugs and I narrow my eyes at him.

"I don't need anyone to come get me," I insist.

"You hear that?" Adam looks like he's biting back a look of amusement. "Your girl is independent and doesn't want you to come get her."

"I'm not his girl," I growl, and barely resist stomping my foot like a child, quickly growing sick of this game they are playing. "Give me my phone."

Adam passes my phone to me, and I hang up without saying anything to Drew.

"That was immature," I tell him, my only comment of rebellion of the night.

"I thought I was helping since you couldn't get to your phone," he answers simply, tone completely even.

"I wouldn't have answered, so it doesn't matter."

"That's rude."

"So is answering someone's phone for them," I retort.

"I'll remember that next time. We can be done so you can meet up with your boyfriend. Or is it boyfriends?"

I rear back like he slapped me. "Excuse me? What are you trying to say?"

"Nothing. Just trying to respect your time and plans."

I fold my arms across my chest, the previous feelings I've had about not fighting back are gone because I'm annoyed. I'm not sure why he's acting like this. He offered me extra training because he felt like I needed to be able to defend myself against the guys surrounding me like vultures at this fucking gym.

And now he's pushing me toward them? How can someone be so hot and cold for absolutely no reason?

"So, we're done for the day, then?" I ask instead of acknowledging him.

"If you want to be."

I nod, grabbing my stuff, including my phone and before I turn to leave, I can't help but have the last word. "Feel free to make your own plans with Drew, because he's certainly not seeing me."

§

WHEN I GET HOME, there's already a figure standing across the street from my house. He's leaning against his motorcycle, and I stop dead in my tracks, throwing my head back with a loud groan.

"What the fuck is wrong with the people in this town?!" I say to the sky.

When I look straight ahead again, I see the figure hasn't moved.

"Caine, I know it's you so instead of being a fucking creep in the dark just come here and do what it is you came to do," I taunt because I'm done with all of them tonight.

I'm done with all of them, period. I came here as an escape and so far, it's felt like anything but. I've been here for almost a month and have successfully gained a stalker, a man that I used to try and make the stalker angry who now won't leave me alone, and a coach that is slut shaming me.

Great job, Max.

Caine still doesn't move or say anything, and I decide this is the last straw for me tonight. I stomp toward him, not thinking of anything other than my anger between the gym and finding him here and I'm *done.*

I'm standing in front of him, and I can't hold back anymore. "What the fuck will it take to get you to leave me alone?"

To the surprise of absolutely no one, he doesn't say anything in response. I can see his bright light blue eyes in the moonlight, looking down at me. The black leather jacket over his black shirt and black jeans make him seem like an even darker presence than I already know he is.

"Seriously, Caine, I'm done with this game. I came here to start over. I came here for a fucking escape, and I'm done with you. Done with Drew. Done with the games. I just want to be left alone." I'm borderline yelling and waiting for a neighbor to come out and tell us to be quiet, but I don't care.

"What are you escaping from, killer?" he asks with an eyebrow raised and I let out a low growl, the temptation to slap him is almost unbearable.

"Right now, I'm trying to escape *you.*"

He lets out a low chuckle, it's dark and ominous and I know it holds no humor. "You'll never be able to escape me."

"You motherfucker, I swear to God if you don't—"

"There a problem here?" A man's voice cuts me off from letting loose on the annoying tower of a man in front of me.

I turn around and there's a patrol car that somehow pulled

up without me noticing. It's the same officer from the bar—Officer Doug, or Doogie I guess—I should tell him. I should tell him everything that the man in front of me has done. The breaking in, him taking advantage of my body, and I'm about to do just that, when Caine does something out of character and I'm a little scared with how quickly he shifts.

His arm wraps around my shoulders, pulling me into his chest and I try to push him away, but he's much stronger and I'm unable to do anything.

"Nothing to worry about here, Officer, just my girl putting me in my place."

"Not your girl," I mumble against him, but I know my words are muffled by the fabric of his shirt.

The officer looks at us for a minute and I wonder if he's going to take my side, but he just grunts before saying, "Keep it down."

Caine nods and I continue to try and push him away, but he doesn't let me go until the officer has driven away and turned the corner.

"You could've screamed," Caine says, letting me go.

"It's kind of hard to do that when you have my face shoved against your chest."

"Right. You can have your excuses, but I know you don't want me to leave you alone. You could've gotten rid of me."

"I've. Tried."

"Have you?"

"Yes!"

"Not very hard."

I grab my head in my hands; I'm losing it. Maybe I've already lost it. Maybe I'm living in a nightmare. Or maybe I died and this is the hell I've been forced to live in for the rest of eternity.

"I'm done. Okay? Leave me alone. Let me live my life. Go find another girl to torture," I say with finality.

He doesn't say anything, just gives me that smug look that I want to slap away. Even as I start to walk backwards toward my house, he doesn't say anything.

When I'm almost to the door he finally speaks, "I'll leave you alone…until you come begging for me again."

"Never in a million fucking years."

He lets out that low humorless chuckle once again before swinging his leg over his bike, pulling his helmet on, and slamming the bike into gear before taking off down the street.

I don't believe he's going to leave me alone. Not for a second.

CHAPTER 27
CAINE

Of course I'm not going to leave her alone. That ruins the fun. She's mine, she just needs a little more time to come around to it. Luckily for her, I have a fight out of town this weekend, so it looks like I'm leaving her alone. But really, it's because I don't have the ability to climb into her bed for the next two nights.

If I didn't have my fights to distract me, I'd probably go insane.

Fortunately for me, she still hasn't figured out where I've moved the camera, so I'm still able to watch her. Because we both know I'll never be able to leave her alone.

But maybe this means Drew will be out of the picture, since he may not be as pushy as me. That's a lie, he's just as pushy as me. He just hides it better.

I'm not sure why part of me hopes to see him appear on the camera and make me watch as he sneaks in and takes what he wants from her body. I'd be pissed, but she's so fucking pretty when she struggles.

"Where's your head?" Adam asks, pulling me from my thoughts as the fighters before me are still going.

"Right here," I grunt.

He looks at me like he doesn't believe me. It reminds me how he offered Max extra training lessons and how I wanted to talk to him about that. Because if he tries to move in on my girl, too, then we're going to have a real fucking problem.

"Remember what we talked about with your opponent. He's a guy that comes out swinging from the start to try and throw you off. Wear him out. You'll gain the advantage and take him down easily once he's exerted some energy," Adam instructs and I'm half listening because we've been over this already and I know how to fucking fight.

"Got it." I nod robotically, just waiting for my turn to go up there. I need to let out some of this aggression building inside me.

I need to fuck Max again, that's what this is. But fighting will have to do for now.

The fight before me is called and the winner gets his arm raised in the air, announcing him before they reset for my fight.

"Remember what I said," Adam says, and I just nod because I don't need another pep talk from him right now.

When it's time, I make my way to the cage, entering and locating my opponent on the opposite side. He's not as tall as me, but he's bulky. I watch him size me up as well. Some guys shit talk before a fight, some fist bump. I do neither. I ignore them and focus on myself and the fight I'm about to have.

They don't matter. Nothing matters except me and winning, so I don't care about niceties or sparring with words. We are about to fight each other. I don't give a fuck what anyone would have to say to me.

The start of the fight is signaled and just like Adam said, this guy—I didn't even catch his name—is coming toward me at full speed, fists swinging. He's sloppy in everything he's doing, and I want to laugh. I easily dodge every move he attempts to make, not even needing to throw any punches or pull any moves myself. He's over-throwing, sending himself off balance and wearing out his energy easily.

Honestly, I'm pretty pissed this guy isn't giving me a better fight. If I don't have a challenge, I'll never get better.

It doesn't take long for the perfect opening to come for me to take him down, wrangling his body easily into a submission with a choke. He taps almost immediately, and I tighten my grip slightly, choking him a little more before letting go. Annoyed I'm not getting a knockout and that it was over so quickly.

After I'm declared the winner, I meet back up with Adam who gives me a small, "Good job."

"That shit was too easy," I complain.

"Not every fight will push you to your limit and that's okay."

I shake my head, pushing past him back into the locker room to rinse off and get dressed. I want to be pushed to my limit—it's the only way to get better. I'm glad I won, but it doesn't feel earned since it wasn't difficult.

My dad used to tell us—my brother and I—that we had to work hard to get what we want in life.

"Easy doesn't get you anywhere. If it's easy, it's not worth it."

His words echo in my head, and it pisses me off even more. *This win wasn't worth it.*

The rage washes through me again and I want nothing more than to send my fist into the wall, but the smallest restraint stops me. Because I know if I break my knuckles, Adam won't let me train.

Shit, look at Drew, the guy got his knee kicked out in a dirty fight and even though it's been months and he's more than healed, Adam doesn't even let him spar.

Even though the last thing I want to do is go back out there and watch the rest of the fights, I do it. Adam tries to talk to me, but I don't give a shit about what he's saying. The only thing I'm able to think about now that the fight is over, is that he's been having alone time with Max.

"Since when did you start offering private lessons after hours?" I ask without even looking at him.

He doesn't respond right away and for a second, I don't think he even will.

"Just trying to give her a fair shot," he responds, and it's hard to hear him over all the noise around us.

"What the fuck is that supposed to mean?" I snap, turning toward him, wondering if I'm about to start a fight with my own coach right here and now. That'll be a way to make sure I never fight in the UFC, I'm sure.

He scoffs. "Come on, Caine. You've had your eyes on her since that first night at the bar and we all know that doesn't mean you're wining and dining the girl."

"You don't know shit about me or my life. It's not my fault that a girl like her would rather be chased and fucked than given roses and a nice dinner. I'm just giving her what she wants." I smirk when I see his jaw clench. "Not like it should matter to you anyway. Except, apparently, she may want Drew involved, too."

"All the more reason she should have the tools to deal with you both."

I narrow my eyes at him.

"Don't act like I don't know shit about you and your life. We both know you work so hard just so you can distance yourself from your family even more. You hate them, but still need them and their money, even though you hate it."

I hate that he knows that about me, and that it's true. I use my trust fund to live, but it means my family keeps control over my life. I can't work and train like I do, though and that pisses me off even more.

I get in his face. "Shut the fuck up."

Now it's him smirking. I may have a couple inches on him,

but he's one of the few people I could fight that actually makes me work hard for it and against him, I may not win.

"Yeah, you should just be glad I don't want your girl too because you're not the only one who could give her what it is that she wants."

I ball my fists, ready to swing at him, but he walks away and I'm not going to fight a man with his back to me. What he just said pisses me off even more, which I'm sure was his intention. I may have told her I was going to leave her alone, but when I get back, I'm going to make sure the only person she runs to is me. Me leaving her alone was a lie anyway.

§

BACK IN MY HOTEL ROOM, I pull up the camera in her room and see she's not there. Immediately, I'm frustrated and wondering where she could be. When I look at the time I realize she's probably still at work and manage to calm down a fraction.

Just to confirm, I text Drew even if I would rather chew on barbed wire than have him involved with my girl. I don't have anyone else I can ask.

She did want us both to fuck her. The thought of both our cocks filling her, one in her pussy, the other in her mouth while she struggles and gags while being forced to take us both. Shit, the thought makes me so hard for her.

Or one of us in her pussy and the other in her ass, the way she would scream. I bet she'd love it, though, God. Fucking. Dammit.

> Caine: Max at work?

> Drew: Yeah.
>
> Caine: You better not touch her while I'm gone.
>
> Drew: Maybe you shouldn't leave her, then.
>
> Caine: I'll fucking kill you.
>
> Drew: You can try.

I toss my phone onto the bed, and I know she won't be off work for a couple of hours, so I get in the shower and try to waste some time. Plus, I still smell like sweat and another dude and fuck that. I can't have a hard on and be smelling like anyone other than Max and her sweet cunt.

I hate that I have to wait for her to come back home to be able to watch her. Next time, I need to make sure to take some videos of us. Record the way her pussy sucks in my cock so well, squeezing around me while her wetness coats my shaft. Immortalize the way she screams and scratches me.

My hand is now around my erection because I can't help myself while thinking of her like that. I need her mouth on me. I'll record that too. I'd thrust into her greedy little throat, make her swallow me down and take everything I'd give her. I'd have her begging in no time for me.

She'll be conditioned to want me, and only me eventually. Every smell, every taste, and every sound, it'll all remind her of *me*.

"*Caine*," she'll moan my name as I fill her while she draws blood raking her nails down my back.

I strangle my dick in my fist, furiously fucking myself as the hot water beats down on my skin while thoughts of Max consume me. All the things I'm going to do with her and how well she's going to take them all flooding my brain.

"Such a pretty slut," I grit out, my balls drawing up right before I squeeze even harder, making ropes of cum shoot out onto the tile floor as my release finds me, and I'm unable to stop it. I groan, thinking about it covering Max instead of this fucking shower.

Once I'm out, I dry myself briefly before pulling on a pair of boxers. I don't even bother rubbing the towel over my head since my hair is buzzed so short, though it's almost time for another haircut. The curls that grow are starting to make an appearance and I don't like it. It makes me look like my older brother and dad. Just slap a suit on me and call me Mr. Aldridge, and it works for either of them.

Fuck that. I'm nothing like them.

I grab my phone again, and since I can't see my girl or watch what she does while she thinks no one is around for the night, I decide to text her.

> Caine: How's work?

Max: Who is this?

I let out a low chuckle, I guess she never *actually* gave me her number.

> Caine: Bet you'd look really good bent over the bar you're behind right now.

Max: You're supposed to be leaving me alone.

> Caine: Guess we're both liars.

> Caine: And I am. Leaving you alone means not touching you until you beg me to. I never said anything else.

> Max: That was definitely not clarified…

> Caine: Hm…too bad.

> Max: How'd you get my number?

> Caine: How many times have you thought about me tonight?

> Max: Negative a million.

> Caine: I thought about you when I took a shower earlier. I was thinking about your mouth and how good it would look wrapped around my dick.

> Max: I'm working.

> Caine: Glad I can distract you.

She doesn't respond again, and I wish I could see the look on her face right now. I bet she squeezed her thighs together, hiding the fact that the thought affected her, too. Now, I'll just wait for her to get home so I can see if she'll take care of that little problem herself.

CHAPTER 28
DREW

Caine and Adam are gone for two days to a fight and the fact that I'm here with Max alone has me being a bit reckless. I know Caine breaks into her house more often than he should, and it's something I've thought about, but I've stopped myself, because I swear I'm not a psychopath like him.

I refuse to be like that even if I was raised by one.

My dad bangs at my door, his fist sounds so strong against the wood, I'm sure it's going to bust open any second. He's yelling and I feel like I can smell the alcohol on his breath even through the splintering door.

"Open this fucking door and face me like the man you claim to be!" he screams.

I keep my back on the door as it vibrates with each pound. I put my hands over my ears like it'll help. I didn't claim to be a man. I don't want to face him. I'm only thirteen and just asked him if he could help me fix the garbage disposal because I accidentally dropped a rock that I *was cleaning down into it.*

He started screaming about how stupid I am, and I just ran into my room because I'm tired of being hit.

"Get out here, boy!" His voice pierces through my sad excuse for earmuffs.

I hold my hands over my ears even tighter like it'll suddenly start drowning out the sound of his voice. I want to get out of here, I want to be bigger and maybe then I could face him. Maybe one day.

Fuck that. I'll never be like my dad. And I'm not like Caine either because *she* has come to *me*. She makes it known she doesn't want Caine, but everything she's done to me has shown that she wants me.

The one thing I can't deny is that I still want Adam, too. His nonchalance is pissing me off, and I wonder if him offering Max extra gym time is his way of trying to see if I would be jealous, which I wouldn't be. But if he has any interest in her then maybe we could both have some fun. Doesn't matter if we've barely spoken and things are still tense between us. I know with a woman between us, we would get along just fine.

Knowing there won't be any interruptions, I pull up to Max's house a little over an hour after the bar has closed, knowing she's home by now. Her house is dark, and I'm hoping that means she's asleep already. Unlike Caine, I don't want her to fight me. I want her underneath me willingly, and unaware of it, too lost in her own dreams.

I get into her house easily and I guess this is how Caine does it so often, but I'm careful to not make myself known. Even as I make my way to her bedroom and open the door, she's there, covered by a thick comforter with one bare leg kicked out.

Biting back a groan, I approach her, pulling the blanket away from her body. She rolls from her side onto her back, and I can see that the large T-shirt she's wearing is tugged up slightly, revealing her bare pussy. She's so fucking pretty. So fucking *perfect*.

"Fuck," I mutter quietly.

She moans slightly, rubbing her thighs together, and if there was ever any question about me not touching her, that's out the window.

I trace the tips of my fingers up her inner thighs, and they part so easily for me as I get closer to their apex. Ghosting my fingers over the spot I'm dying to touch, she shifts slightly, almost like she's trying to guide my hand where she wants it.

With a low chuckle, I remove my hand, and she squirms slightly. I take that as enough permission to keep going. Placing my knee next to her inner thigh on the bed and swinging my other leg over her, I push her legs further apart and settle in between them. She doesn't wake up even as I lean over her, holding my weight off her with my elbow by her head.

Dipping my hand back between her legs, I swipe through her slit to find her soaking already.

"Already so wet for me, little one, and you aren't even awake," I growl quietly.

Using her wetness, I rub her clit with just enough pressure to ensure that she feels it, but not hard enough to jolt her awake yet. I want to make her come while she's asleep. I want her body to feel how badly it wants me without her mind in the way.

She moans again as I continue to play her body, but I want more. I want to push her limits. I want to feel her, to take things further. When she hitches a leg higher, spreading herself even more for me, even while her eyes remain closed, I decide to do just that.

Working my pants low enough to free my cock, I swipe her wetness on my hand and rub it along my rock hard dick. Using the evidence of her arousal to guide my fist along my length. I drop back down over her once again, this time swiping the crown of my dick through her center to get the sweet essence right from the source.

"*Fuck,*" I grind out, running the length of myself through her weeping center.

She's so warm, so wet, so pliant in my arms, and as I thrust, the worry about her waking up starts to fade. Especially with every sleepy little moan she lets out when my dick rubs against her clit.

The pace of my hips picks up as I fuck against her, fighting every urge I have to just pull back enough to push forward and fully sheathe myself inside her. She'd be even warmer, even wetter, and I want nothing more than to feel her for real. The way the bars on my ladder would rub against her, the way they would feel inside her.

I know how her mouth is—it's dangerously perfect. I bet her cunt is even better.

"Mmm," she moans, shifting underneath me, moving her hips against me like she wants more, too.

"You like that? You like how my cock feels, baby?" I moan much louder than I probably should, but I'm getting close to coming, even though I don't want this to end yet.

"Mm, *Drew*," she moans, and I freeze, looking down at her face, which still looks peaceful. Eyes closed. I wait to see if she's going to open them and kick me out, but she doesn't.

To my surprise, she brings one of her legs up around my hip. I don't move because I'm still waiting for her to catch me and freak out.

Instead, Max uses her leg's grip on me to move her hips up toward me, seeking friction and with my pulsing shaft nestled between her lips, begging for me to move. I wait.

She moans again, rubbing herself against me and I let out a hiss through my teeth.

"*Drew*," she moans once again, rubbing herself harder.

"You want me, little one? Tell me you want my cock," I groan, not caring if she's awake or not at this point because it's the second time she's said my name and I'm hanging on by a thread.

"Fuck me," she moans, arching up against me while her other leg wraps around me as well and I don't have it in me anymore to question whether she's awake or asleep.

I heard the two words I needed to hear, and nothing could stop me at this point.

Without hesitating anymore, my hips pull back slightly before easily lining up at her entrance and pushing into her with a single hard thrust. I groan loudly, dropping my head onto her shoulder and as she cries out, there's no doubt that she's awake now.

"What the—" She squirms, and my hips pull back again before thrusting forward even harder and she squeals.

Her arms fly up and I don't give her a chance to hit me or push me away. Instead, I grab them, shoving them above her head as I piston my hips forward once again and she screams.

"You asked me to fuck you. I'm just giving you want you want," I grunt with another thrust.

"How did you—*ah, fuck.*" She arches her back, while also pulling me down with the grip she has on me with her legs.

I'm proud of how worked up she was because I feel her tight heat pulsing around me already.

"How did I get in here? How did I sneak into your bed and touch you while you slept? How did I make you so desperate for me that your pussy was soaking before you even woke up? How did I make you beg for me even in your sleep?" I ask each question with a punishing thrust into her that has her barreling toward release, while I fight mine off for as long as I can.

"*Yes,*" she moans, and I don't think she wants any answers right now, not when I can tell she's so close.

I let go of my grip on her wrists, hoping she doesn't start using them to punch me in the face, and move that hand to rub at her clit as I continue to fuck into her. She tests the freedom of her arms and surprisingly, wraps them around my back and digs her nails into my skin, but it doesn't stop me. It only spurs me on even more.

Dropping my forehead to hers, our lips are less than an inch apart as we breathe in each other's air while both chasing our orgasms.

"Give it to me, little one. Come all over my cock and show me how desperate you've been for it," I demand, rubbing her harder while our hips slap together loudly.

She tightens around me to the point I know I'm not going to be able to hold off any longer.

"Yes, baby, that's it," I groan and that sets her off as she comes around me with a scream, tightening not only her pussy, but all her limbs around me.

I'm not able to do anything to stop my own release from taking over as my balls tighten and I bite her shoulder, muffling my groan as I thrust as deep as possible into her. My cum coats her inner walls and the thought makes me push in even deeper to make sure she's completely filled with *me*.

We're both breathing heavily as we come down, and I have yet to leave her body, or lift my head. But she also hasn't made a move to get me off of her, which is something I'm feeling triumphant about.

Finally, I pull away, looking down between us. My wet dick is almost fully hard again, and clearly not happy that I've removed him from the hot sweet place he just was.

I look up at Max, and see conflict in her tired eyes, but she still hasn't moved. I swipe a piece of her red hair away from her face and smirk.

"What're you thinking?" I can't help but ask, which is weird because I normally would never care what a hookup is thinking. Truly, I'm not sure why I'm even still here.

"I don't know." She shakes her head.

I nod once, lifting off her, watching as her eyes track my cock before I tuck it back into my pants. "Well, don't deny that you wanted it, because we both know you did. You were even begging for it in your sleep."

She doesn't say anything, and for a second, I'm wondering if she even did wake up because this isn't the spitfire Max I'm used to. I don't know what the feeling in my chest is right now. It's foreign and burns like an ache where my heart is. Whatever it is, I don't like it.

She grabs the blankets and pulls them over herself again. I look at her for a second, the ache intensifying and I'm wondering if maybe I'm having a heart attack. She doesn't move and I don't think I can leave her like this.

I go into the bathroom and wet a washcloth with warm water, coming back to her bedside and pull the blankets off her again, which earns me a scowl on her pretty face.

"What the fuck?" she snaps when I push her to her back, and she fights me until I press the damp fabric against her used core. She lets out a gasp before leaning into it as I reluctantly wipe my cum that's dripping out of her before tossing the cloth into her laundry basket and pulling the blanket back over her.

She looks up at me, her green eyes practically glowing in the dark and I wonder if it's because there are tears welling there.

The ache is back and makes me rub at my chest to try and ease it. I'm not going to dwell on this—she wanted this. She wanted me.

Yet, for some reason, I lean down and press a light kiss to her forehead before whispering, "I'll see you soon."

Then without looking back, I leave her house, making sure to lock her door once I'm gone. Before I drive away, I glance up at her bedroom window to see if she gets up, but after several minutes there's no movement. And with that, I head home, for some reason feeling like I should've stayed. Even once I'm home, the ache in my chest doesn't subside, and all I can do is just hope it's gone by the time I wake up.

CHAPTER 29
MAX

After last night with Drew, I knew I needed to find another outlet for myself. It used to be dancing, but I need something new. I need something different. Something that isn't at the gym since being around the men there is only making me crazier.

I've never done this before. Looking at the newly installed pole in my living room, I'm thinking I'm in over my head. The only dancing that's ever mattered has been ballet. That's the only "real" dancing, according to my family. And it's the one thing I was allowed to do for myself.

Until it was taken away from me and was no longer for myself anymore. It was for someone else. Someone else's pleasure. His desires, his needs. Dancing, the one thing I loved in this world that made me feel like myself was taken too.

I've never considered pole dancing before now. It's for strippers and gogo dancers, neither of which I could ever be.

I never considered trying MMA fighting either, though. And

yet, here I am. So, I bought the pole, installed it myself and swore to try it. I've seen videos, it looks difficult and I'm sure I'm going to end up covered in bruises.

But they will be bruises that I caused. No one else. And I'll wear them like a badge of honor. As I start the music, the sultry sounds play from my speakers before the singer begins and it's nothing like the ballet music I was forced to dance to. This is sexy, it flows through me, making me feel like I need to move.

So, without thinking about it too much I strip off my oversized shirt, leaving me in just a sports bra and leggings, I start to move the way the music demands. Rolling my body, grabbing the pole, swinging around it, holding it behind one knee as I spin.

I don't think about what I'm doing or how it looks. I just let the music flow through me. I feel it all without any concern for anyone or anything in this moment. It's only about me right now, as it should have always been.

I'm not sure how much time passes as I try and fail to do some moves that are pretty advanced on the pole. I also feel like I get some down pretty well, and for the little bit of time that I'm moving, I forget about everything else going on. I forget my past, and what's currently going on in the present.

I'm able to just forget.

As soon as the music reaches the end of my playlist, it stops. The silence surrounds me once again, and everything floods back like a tidal wave. Including everything I've been trying not to think about.

The texts with Caine.

Drew sneaking in and fucking me while I slept.

Me asking him to.

I was half awake and all I knew was that I felt good, being touched felt good, the weight on me felt good and I wanted more. More friction, more pressure, more pleasure. I wanted more. I always want more apparently, because that's what has caused my desire for things I've been told "aren't normal."

But they've seemed pretty normal recently. Especially from Caine, since he's made it his life's mission to push my boundaries. Including fulfilling the fantasies I've only spoken about to one person and was shamed for them.

Drew added to my fantasies last night, though. I don't know how long he spent touching me while I slept, but when I slowly became aware, I could feel his hard, pierced cock sliding between my lower lips. My body was grinding against him already, and when he pushed his thickness inside me, I was awake and the only thing I could think about was that I didn't want him to stop.

Unfortunately, it's not just the good memories that flood in. The bad ones are right there, rippling across the surface of my mind.

"Sloppy," Carson spits before the last beat of the music even plays.

I hide my heavy breathing from being forced to perform the number at least seven times at this point. Sweat dots my brow, the blisters on my feet are definitely bleeding. My muscles are aching, and I just want to take a break.

"Again," he demands into his glass of bourbon.

"Can I just take a break for ten minutes? I need water and I'm really sore—"

"That's probably why you're so fucking sloppy, you're taking breaks all the fucking time."

I shake my head. "No, I've been training just as much as always, but I'm tired and I really just want to get some water."

"Your mother told me how useless you are, but I didn't want to believe her. Your pussy is mediocre at best and that's your best quality. Do it again and prove why I'm agreeing to marry you in the first place."

I get back into position as the music starts over, this time when I dance for him, I can't stop the tears from falling down my cheeks and he just laughs. Drinks. Laughs. And I cry, wondering what I did to deserve this life.

I push myself off the floor and go to the kitchen, gulping down a full glass of water. Because I'm thirsty and want a break.

Because I can.

There are more messages from Caine on my phone that I left unread this morning. I'm annoyed that he said he'd leave me alone and yet, he can't seem to keep his word. Not that I should expect any less, he's delusional and a liar.

They both are.

And then there's Adam, who I can't quite figure out. One minute, he's touching me in a way that feels like it's more than helping me train. The next, he's just as cold and distant as he has been. And still, I'm intrigued. Which I feel will only get me into even more trouble. I need to keep my head down and stop letting these men do these things to me.

That's when I remember the distraction offer Danner made to have a slumber party. It's something I've never done before, and it sounds kind of fun. It also sounds like the perfect thing, with its lack of testosterone, and that's exactly what I need.

I send Danner a text, hoping that the offer still stands.

> Max: So…how about that slumber party?

Danner: Fuck yes!

I END up going to her house, and I wasn't sure what to bring, so I stopped at the store and got some snacks that looked good and some white wine. She told me to bring comfortable pajamas and a really soft blanket if I had one. I didn't, so I got one of those as well.

Danner answers the door in some pink pajama shorts and a matching pink button-down pajama shirt that both look really soft. I give her my best smile, trying not to show how out of my element I am.

She looks down at my hands and lets out a "whoop" noise. "You brought wine! This is perfect, come on in."

Her house is like a little cottage and it's cute, with the little pink accents helping break up the white of the space. She's clearly spent time decorating it, and it makes me wish that I had the ability to turn a space into something that feels like this—homey and comfortable.

"I really like your house," I compliment.

"Thanks. I used to want to be an interior designer, but…" She shrugs and I have a feeling she doesn't want to talk about it. Something I'm very familiar with, so I'm happy to let it go.

"So," I set the snacks and wine on the kitchen counter, "What does this night entail?"

"Well," she starts, ticking her fingers as she lists things off, "First, we get full on junk food and a little tipsy on drinks. Then we share all our secrets, and finally we end the night watching a cheesy rom com before we pass out."

I chuckle. "Okay, count me in."

"Great, but first, go get changed because none of this can happen until you're on the same level of comfort as me."

Laughing, I grab my bag and go to the bathroom to change, already feeling good about my decision to hang out with her. Maybe having friends is a good thing. It only irritates me further that I was robbed of this experience up until now.

After I change, I find Danner, and she has a collection of food spread out, including what I brought. It looks like she has enough to feed an army. She presents it all with an arm extending out in front of her, showcasing the spread. "Ta da."

"There's no way we're eating all of that," I tell her lightly.

She waves me off. "I know, but we need options." She hands

me a glass of wine and holds hers up to toast, "To your first sleepover."

We clink our glasses together and take our first sips. It's the first time since coming here that I don't feel the weight of anything on my shoulders. I can just…be me.

Once the first bottle of wine is gone, I realize I've laughed more in the span of a couple hours than I feel like I have in my entire life. Danner's told me all the gossip from around town, which is mostly small, petty things like who doesn't get along with who. Also, apparently my boss—George—is sleeping with a woman named Jennifer who owns a boutique just down the road from The Tavern.

I've avoided all talk about Uncaged, and the guys that go there, but of course, it was bound to come up.

"So, now it's your turn to share," she prods.

I take a healthy gulp of my wine to delay my response. "Nothing to share."

She sighs. "If you say so. You're training at the gym now, right?"

I nod. "Yeah, I wanted to learn some self-defense."

"That's badass. Do you like it?"

"I do, actually," I answer honestly.

"I've thought about going, just for the eye candy, but I don't think I'd like the actual training part." She shakes her head.

"The training part is fun, once you figure out the logistics."

"And the eye candy," she goads with a wiggle of her eyebrows.

I look down into my glass with a small laugh. "That, too."

"Fuck yeah it is. I won't lie Cal and Xander have tempted me before, but..." She shakes her head.

"Xander?" I question, not sure I've heard of anyone there with that name.

"Oh, yeah, Alexander, whatever."

"They've *tempted* you?" I attempt to tease.

"I mean yeah, you've seen them, and they have reputations. One I'm not wanting to add to."

I should feel the same, yet I've found myself lost in my current situation and it feels like I'm on a high-speed train going straight for disaster. Though, I'm also not doing very much to stop it. Or if I really want to.

"I get that," I say softly.

"Bet ya do." She winks at me. "Now, let's pick a movie."

CHAPTER 30
MAX

I head home after breakfast the next morning, but before going to work, I decide to walk down to the beach. It's cold today, but I don't care. Tossing on a hoodie, jeans, and some boots, I brave the cold to walk the short distance to the sand. It's not as foggy today, so I'm able to make out the mountains in the distance that are covered in trees.

One side of the town is forest, the other is the ocean, and it almost makes it feel secluded. Like no one could get in or out because they would have to navigate the forest or cross the ocean. Maybe that's why I feel safe here.

It's not reality, obviously, anyone can drive in or out of here, but the illusion makes me feel better. Even when I consider the fact that I'm still here with the danger prowling all around me.

I sit on the sand, not caring that I'm going to have to take a shower before going into work. I stretch my legs out in front of me, and lean back on my hands. Running my fingers through the cool sand, I let it ground me as the waves break against the shore. I let it all soak in. The smell, the feeling, the freedom.

When I let out a breath I didn't realize I had been holding, it feels like I'm letting go of so much.

"What're you doing?" a deep, familiar voice asks and my heart rate kicks up.

I turn slightly and see Adam standing about a foot away from me, all dark and broody against the beautiful scene behind him.

"Enjoying the beach. What're you doing? I didn't think you guys were back yet." I take in his T-shirt with its sleeves ripped off and shorts, knowing it's way too cold to be wearing that.

"We came back early this morning, and I always run out here before heading to the gym," he answers flatly.

I nod, wondering if Caine is going to pop out of nowhere, because I'm sure it'll only be a matter of time. I'm unsure of what to say—something that seems to happen when I'm around him—and the words that come out are, "Cardio is good."

"It is, and it's important when it comes to MMA. Your stamina has to stay up."

I don't think it's his intention, but for some reason the way he says that feels like an innuendo. Or it's because I'm still stuck on how Drew fucked me until I woke up. But hearing him talk about stamina makes me think of *his*. And that's when I really look at him.

Obviously, I find Adam attractive. He has a body that's honed by years of fighting and working out. The salt and pepper in his dark hair makes him look mature, but not old. His tattoos are on full display, and they seem to go on forever. The more I look, the more I find in the artwork covering every inch of available skin that shows.

My eyes are drawn to the snake on his neck again, still fascinated by the way it looks when he speaks and when he swallows. I don't have any tattoos, but maybe I should get some, as a part of my new life. Something small, something that represents me.

"If you ever want to join me on a run, let me know," he offers, pulling my eyes back to his. I realize I never said anything and have just been staring at him. My cheeks heat, but I hope he thinks that the pink tinge is just from the cold.

"I like different activities for cardio," I respond and immediately realize how that sounded. Clearly, so does he because the side of his mouth kicks up in a smirk.

"Anything you'd like to share?" The humor is evident in his tone, and it takes me back a bit. I don't think I've ever seen him joke around. He's been serious, stoic, and kind of scary, and seeing him like this throws me off.

"I, um, dance. Well, I used to. Sometimes I still do. And I used to run a little bit." I don't tell him that it was running away from my ex. Or that I would be forced to run on a treadmill by my mom, and that even when I would beg and plead for her to let me stop, she would just turn it up and tell me how much weight I've gained.

I don't think I ever gained even a pound while living with her. If she could see me now, she would lose her shit. I've filled out in a way I'm really enjoying, and I can feel my strength increasing from all the training.

Adding in pole dancing will only make me stronger.

"Well, if you ever want to start again, we can add it in as a part of your training," he offers, the serious aura back.

"Maybe, but I don't think I can handle running on this." I pick up a fistful of sand, letting it run through my fingers.

"You'll get used to it."

"I think I'd rather run on the sidewalk, or like normal dirt." I shrug.

And for some reason that makes his eyes darken slightly, his eyes run over me, and I suppress the shiver that wants to take over. I don't know what he's thinking, but clearly, it's something that should make me worried or afraid. Yet, my thighs are clenching together, reminding me of the soreness that's still there from Drew.

"The offer stands, wherever you want to run." He lets the words linger between us. I can't help where my mind goes once again, even as he continues his jog along the beach and I'm left here, staring after him.

Why does my mind wander to what it would be like to be chased by a man like him? Being trapped underneath him, the dirt, sticks, and leaves would press into my face while he dug his fingers into my hair, fucking it up while I struggled. But he wouldn't let me get away. Once I was caught, I'd be helpless, and he would growl how much he wanted me into my ear.

Fuck, Caine has ruined me.

That's what this is—he's altered what I feel like I want, what I need for sex, because he hasn't given me a choice, and now? Now, I'm fantasizing about the fucking coach that's training me to defend myself against a man like Caine, doing the same things to me.

I know I've lost my mind, but maybe I don't want to find it again. Maybe this is exactly what I want, and I just shouldn't fight my desires anymore.

Maybe I should take my power back and let it happen under my terms. Even if it includes fighting back.

CHAPTER 31
CAINE

We came back as early as possible. After I was forced to watch Drew sneak into Max's house and fuck her while I wasn't able to do a fucking thing about it, I snapped. I almost broke down Adam's hotel room door insisting that we needed to head back immediately.

If he had told me no, I would've left without him.

The drive back gave me time to plan. I told her I would leave her alone and wouldn't touch her until she wanted me to, until she begged me. While part of me is thinking of going back on my word, the other part wants to see this through. To watch the defeat in her face as she begs for my cock to fill her.

I show up to her house, but she's not there and a spike of annoyance runs through me, wondering where the fuck she could be. My first thought is that she's with the man I was forced to watch her with. I decide I need to pay Drew a visit, because we may have had somewhat of an agreement the night we both were there, but the bastard took it too far. That's why when he opens his front door,

I can't stop my fist from flying into his face. I look around for Max, but I don't see her anywhere. She doesn't come running out, and knowing she isn't here doesn't make my anger lessen.

"Fuck you!" he yells, his hand cupping his bleeding nose.

"You're a fucking asshole. You took advantage of me being gone and fucked her." I go to hit him again, but he manages to fight back, narrowly avoiding the blow.

I smile at the impromptu fight between us, and it feels better than the supposed competition I was in yesterday. Several minutes go by with neither of us submitting. I get close after getting a solid arm bar around him, but he's able to maneuver his way out of my grip, pissing me off.

"Fuck off and talk to me for a second." Drew shoves my chest when I try to come at him again.

My chest is heaving with heavy breaths, but not because I'm tired. It's from the adrenaline flooding my system, leaving me wondering if maybe this will be the day I commit my first murder. I wouldn't say Drew and I are necessarily friends, but we haven't hated each other. That may change now, because I really feel like I could kill him.

"What the fuck is your deal?" He wipes his nose, the bleeding easing slightly, but his hands are covered in it.

"You should already know what my deal is. I know what you were busy doing with Max."

The slow smile that spreads across his face has me ready to punch him again. Maybe this time I'll try and knock out some of his teeth. I'm sure Max wouldn't be interested in him with his front teeth missing.

"Oh, you saw that, did you? Did you hear the way she *asked* me to fuck her? Even while she was unconscious," he teases.

"And you try to say I'm fucked up. At least I fuck her awake and give her a chance to fight back." I move my head from side to side, stretching my neck to try to relieve some of the tension that's been there since I watched the live feed of them last night.

"She woke up, don't worry about that. And even then, she didn't do much fighting. She was too busy coming and covering my cock in her hot, sweet cunt."

I clench my fist tighter, the rage building inside me—I'm going to lose it. This is all so new for me, feeling so strongly about a woman, the urge to kill for her. The urge to do fucking anything for her. The fact that she doesn't feel the same and is letting someone else take what's mine is fucking me up even more.

"You think she wants you then? Think you'll be enough for her even after she asked for us *both* to fuck her?" I have an idea that makes me slightly less murderous. Mostly because it's a competition, and I always win.

"I think she wants me more than you, and that *you* will never be enough for her," he retorts. I want to deny it because I know I could be enough for her.

I could be more than enough. I could give her everything she never knew she needed, and she would learn to love it all. I'm obsessed with her. I can make sure she's just as obsessed with me. I could kidnap her, hold her hostage and make her see that.

But I won't because this may be more fun, a way to prove that I'm enough and prove that she wants me just as much.

"What if we make her choose? What if we show her what it's *really* like with each of us, then leave it up to her," I suggest.

"We have, and she still says she doesn't want you, but she shows me that she wants me." He can't keep the smug as shit smile off his face.

"No. She won't know who is who." I smirk at the confused expression on his face.

Yeah, this may only make me seem like more of a psychopath, but I don't care. I know Max wants me. I know I can give her what she needs, what she craves. And I know that she said she wanted us both to fuck her, but I can give her that too… sex toys exist for a reason.

I'm going to prove it to her and prove it to Drew. And I know one thing for sure—I'm going to fucking win.

CHAPTER 32
ADAM

I'm just finishing cleaning up the gym after classes are done for the day when Drew comes over, folding his arms across his chest. Things have still been tense, but we aren't ignoring each other as much.

I did try to ask why he came in here with a fresh black eye and a busted nose, though. He wouldn't answer me. I was tempted to chew his ass out about getting hurt again, but I need to let it go. He's a grown man who can make his own decisions. If he wants to ruin his body, then that's on him. It's why I gave him the green light to ease back into training again.

All that got me was a grunt and nod in response. Which is fine. I didn't expect a big thanks or anything dramatic.

"Can I talk to you?" he asks, breaking the silence of the gym.

I finish stacking the last mat and turn toward him with a nod.

"What do you think of Max?" he asks easily. I furrow my brow at him, curious why he's asking about her.

"She's improving, seems like a cool girl I guess." I shrug. But my mind wanders back to running into her on the beach and the way she looked at me. I could tell she liked what she saw, and I couldn't help my stamina comment. Her mind seemed to go to the same place mine did, but I couldn't show it.

Then I think back to our private training sessions. The way I can feel her hot cunt through her leggings when she's on top of me. The fact that I'm fighting a raging hard on every time she touches me because I don't want her to think I'm some creepy coach trying to take advantage of her.

I shouldn't want her, there are too many things working against us—our age and the man standing in front of me being two of the biggest.

"She's hot, you can say it," he encourages, and I feel like I'm walking into a trap.

"I mean, I have eyes," I answer, noncommittally.

"And your eyes have seen how obsessed Caine is with her, obviously."

I nod again because no shit, everyone here has. He hasn't tried to hide it, and if he has, then he's failed.

"What if I told you she has said she wants to fuck more than one of us." My heart almost stops beating in my chest at the thought of her saying that.

Of her *begging* for that.

"So, you and Caine are sharing her then?" I ask because

that's the only reason I can think of as to why he would be telling me this. I'm not sure why he would even bother. Another attempt to make me jealous, maybe?

"Remember how we talked about maybe bringing a girl in sometime?"

I swallow roughly. Of course, I remember—we talked about it a few times and I wanted to so badly. The thought of fucking him while he fucks her makes me hard as a fucking stone.

"Yeah."

"She could be it. If you're down."

If I'm down? Like I would say no, like I would deny this? Not when just the mention of it has me ready to tackle him right now. Ready to fuck him hard and fast while, imagining she's here, too.

But then the reality hits, "And what about Caine? There's no way he would be okay with that."

With a smirk, Drew lets me know about what happened. I had wondered why Caine appeared at my door, demanding we leave earlier than anticipated. I thought it was just him being him to be honest. I had almost sent him on his way while I did something else, but decided I might as well go with him.

Drew smiles, and it's the one that looks almost sinister. It doesn't happen often, but when he looks like that, I know there's a reason. He finishes telling me about the deal they agreed to and I can't deny the way it excites me. The thought of her not knowing which one of us it is. The way she'll love it and want to know who it is by the end of it all.

It reminds me of the brief conversation I had with her, and it's the icing on the cake.

"Have you thought of where you're going to have your little competition?" I ask.

"I mean, I kind of thought we could tie her to her bed and keep the lights off."

"What if we made it a little more my speed," I suggest. Drew knows exactly what I'm getting at. He knows what I'm into. He knows what it is I like and what I need when it comes to sex.

He knows it's going to be rough, dirty, and primal.

"I think she'd love it," he responds with that same sinister smile plastered on his face.

And any lingering thoughts I've had for a reason to not touch Max have evaporated into thin air. The thought of chasing her down and doing what I want with her, while Drew and Caine are also chasing her, has all my blood racing to my dick.

"I'm in."

※

FOR THE NEXT COUPLE DAYS, I've had to act normally. Like I'm not borderline losing my mind at the thought of getting to chase Max through the forest while Caine and Drew do the same, all hoping to get to her first.

Max was in one of my classes, and I was hard the entire time. I had to hide it, which resulted in me basically ignoring her. I also didn't have any extra training sessions with her because if we did, I would have submitted her, but not for the sake of training.

She would've found herself submitted with my cock buried deep in her throat. But I had to be patient while I waited for today—the day Drew told me it was going to happen. The day he and Caine agreed to for the competition. I'm still not sure if Caine knows that I'm involved, but I don't give a shit.

He's always gotten what he wants. His entire life has been privileged, and it's time for him to learn a lesson or two.

§

I'M WAITING at the spot we agreed on, off the side of the road and just under the cover of trees at the opening of the forest. It goes on for miles, and it's the perfect spot to show Max how much she's going to enjoy running from us like prey.

It'll be even better when I'm the one that catches her.

I'm straddling my bike, the engine rumbling lowly beneath me while I wait. We're all wearing black hoodies, jeans, and our helmets. The agreement is we don't take them off because she can't know who's fucking her.

Pretty sure she'll figure it out pretty quickly, especially with Drew and his pierced dick. But I wasn't putting up any arguments about the plan. I would have argued if Caine was the one that was supposed to bring her here because I don't trust him.

But it's Drew who should be getting her right now, and I'm sure she'll put up a fight. That's fine though, because whatever she thinks is about to happen, this is going to be even more.

Caine pulls up and looks at me, but I can't see the look on his face, it's just my reflection gleaming back at me in his visor. He doesn't say anything, but I can feel the pissed off energy radiating off of him from here. I refuse to move or acknowledge him.

It isn't long before Drew pulls up with Max behind him. Her arms are wrapped around his middle and the feeling it gives me isn't exactly jealousy, but it does make me want to rip them off him so they can be wrapped around me instead. Or pinned down underneath me.

She stumbles off the bike, pulling off the helmet I'm sure Drew forced her to wear as she looks between the three of us. Her eyes are bouncing around and I see the questions, intrigue, and most of all, fear swirling in her green eyes.

"Will someone tell me what the fuck is going on?" She throws her arms up then drops them down against her legging covered thighs with a slap.

I can't wait to rip those off.

"Who the fuck—" she cuts herself off, looking between the three of us again. I'm sure she can guess Drew and Caine, but it's me that she lingers on the most, unsure who I am, wondering who I could be. It makes me even more motivated to be the first one to catch her.

"Run," Caine's low voice commands.

She looks at him, her eyes narrowing but he revs his engine, and she stumbles back slightly, startled by the sudden noise.

"Whoever catches you gets to use you however they want," I

can't help but speak and she looks back toward me. I'm not sure if she recognizes my voice or not.

"Run," Drew repeats the same single word Caine said, but this time she doesn't question it.

This time she turns, running as fast as she can, heading deeper into the forest. I glance over at the two of them, waiting to see who will move first. We can't ride through the forest for long, but the bikes do give us an advantage.

Drew and Caine both look at me, then each other, right before Caine takes off first, because of fucking course he does.

Drew and I don't waste any time, each going in a different direction, trying to be the one to find which way she ended up going.

It doesn't take long before I'm not hearing the roar of the other bikes, and I know we're far enough away from each other. I stop to listen, killing the engine and waiting.

Silence.

The wind ruffles the leaves in the trees slightly, but there's nothing else. So, I wait, I don't know what it is, but I know she's close by. Instinct had me guessing which direction she went, and I can feel her close by.

There's a crack of a stick breaking behind a large tree, and I start making my way toward the noise. When I'm close, there's a gasp, and that's when I see her. She takes off, running deeper into the forest, and it sets me off again as I take off after her.

She may have said she doesn't run, but she is right now

and she's fast. But I'm faster. I gain on her, and despite the large helmet on my head, I'm not even out of breath as I get closer.

When Max looks back and sees how close I am, she squeals. She tries to increase her speed, and feet are pounding against the crunchy leaves and sticks. She slips on some mud and the small set back is all it takes for me to reach her.

Wrapping my arm around her middle, I yank her back to me and she starts flailing. All of her training is seemingly forgotten with the way her limbs fly around, trying to hit me as she screams.

I cover her mouth with my hand as I wrestle her to the ground. She screams again, but it's muffled by my palm as I flip her over just before she hits the ground. I groan at how pretty she looks, sweaty and lying on the forest floor. Her hair already has leaves and sticks stuck in it and I want to dirty her up even more. I want to get her nice and filthy.

"Let go of me," she cries, as she continues to fight against me.

"Make me," I practically growl, wanting her to use some of what she's learned.

She attempts to get a grip on me, but I'm able to get out of it easily, and I pin her arms above her head by her wrists.

She bucks up against me and I know she can feel how hard I am for her already. She tries to hide her gasp, but I push my hips down against her so she can feel it. So she can feel *me*.

"Fuck you! Get off of me!" she yells and is finally able to wiggle out of my grip. I don't let her get far as she tries to scramble away from me. I tackle her back down with her stomach on the ground while I cover her back.

"Such a naughty girl, running like the prey you are. You were just dying to be caught and fucked, weren't you?" I groan, thrusting my still confined cock against her ass, pushing her deeper into the dirt.

"Don't you dare fucking touch me," she cries, trying to get away from me. I keep her trapped underneath me and do what I imagined doing the moment I saw her get off the back of Drew's bike and rip the fucking leggings off her body.

When I shred the thin fabric, I'm met with her bare creamy skin. She screams as the first cool breeze hits her exposed skin, making it pebble. She wrestles underneath me, but I keep her pinned, not wasting any time going slow. I'm not sure how much time we're going to have until one of the other guys finds us and we're interrupted.

I grab a handful of her tangled locks in one fist, while the other grasps at the tiny thong she's wearing, snapping it against her skin once before ripping it off completely.

"Fuck you! Don't you fucking dare," she threatens. I yank her up a little further with my grip on her hair, so I can make sure she hears me.

"We told you what would happen. I caught you. I get to use you, and when you find out who I am, you'll want even more from me."

"I'll never want anything from *any* of you," she spits, and I push her head down, the side of her face smashing into the forest floor—she's going to be such a beautiful mess.

"Don't worry, baby girl. You will." I undo my pants easily, freeing my rock-hard cock from its confines, precum pooling at the tip. I use the liquid to run my fist up and down my shaft a couple times as lube because I'm not going to prep her like I should.

Instead, I slap my hand down on her bare ass, and she squeals, her skin immediately turning pink. I run my hand down to her entrance, swiping through her core to find her soaking wet already.

"You don't want this?" I let out a low moan. "You're fucking soaked. You love to be used like a whore, right here in the dirt."

"I'm not wet for you, I don't even know who you are," she insists.

I chuckle, running the tip of my cock through her wetness, coating myself with it. I put even more pressure on her clit when I run my dick over it. "I think not knowing who I am is what makes you even wetter. You love being chased and used by a stranger—that's why you hardly fought me."

She bucks again, but it's almost like she's bucking for more instead of trying to get away this time. Especially as I thrust against her again and she cuts off her own moan.

"You don't know me."

I pull back, lining up at her weeping pussy. "I know you better than you realize." I thrust inside her, completely enveloped in the tightest, wettest cunt I've ever felt, and I can't help the groan I let out.

I want to drop my head to her shoulder, but my helmet is still on and it's in my way. I know I shouldn't, but I pull it off, tossing it in front of her.

Immediately, she tries to turn and look at me, but I hold her head down with my fingers still tangled in her hair. There are leaves and sticks stuck in her red locks. I pull back, pushing my cock into her again and I see fucking stars at how good she feels.

"Your fucking cunt was made for me, wasn't it, baby girl? You look so desperate for it right now, and I'm going to give you what you need," I speak directly into her ear, making sure she can't get a good look at me, despite her best efforts.

"Fuck. You," she cries, but the cry turns into a moan when I tilt my hips slightly, my cock hitting a spot on her inner walls that I know she likes because she starts to move underneath me.

"Yeah, next time you can fuck me. Maybe you'll chase me before bouncing on my dick. I know how much you're going to want it," I taunt.

"I won't," she insists, all while continuing to moan and push back. It's like she's trying to get me to fuck into her more, to fuck her harder.

I feel myself nearing the edge, so I pull out of her, and she whimpers at the loss which makes me smirk. Pulling her all the way up, I don't let her turn to look back at me before pushing her front against a tree, trapping her body there with mine, and shoving inside her again.

We both moan at the feeling, and she can keep denying this all she wants, but her body is telling me something different than her mouth. My body is refusing to leave hers. The tree is scraping against her with the power of each thrust. I have control as I fuck her like a man possessed because that's exactly what I am.

I shouldn't have this woman, shouldn't want her. But I have her now, and I don't care what Caine or Drew say or think—she's mine.

She tightens around me, and I reach between her body and the tree and touch her clit, the back of my hand scraping the rough bark of the tree as I start to rub the sensitive nub and piston my hips roughly.

"You going to prove how much you don't want this by coming all over my cock? Do it. Give it to me. Claim this fucking dick as yours, just like I'm going to claim your cunt as mine," I demand, rubbing harder and tighter circles.

She's crying out, pushing herself back against me and I feel how close she is. She's on the edge, teetering right there. When I pinch her clit between my fingers, she detonates. Her pussy tightens around me so much that it's almost painful, and I can't hold back anymore. She screams a mixture of "yeses" and "nos." I groan, burying my head in her shoulder as my own release explodes and I push as deep into her as I can as my cum fills her. I don't think I've ever come this much or this hard in my life. All I can do is push it deeper and deeper. Part of me hopes she's on birth control. But knowing she's so full of me and would be stuck growing my baby makes a new type of possessiveness surface, and it's one I've never felt before.

I push even deeper into her making sure she takes all of it while I growl into her ear, my lips grazing against her skin. "Any time either of the other two touch you, I want you to remember what it felt like to be full of my cum and how much you screamed for me."

I want her to know it's me. It might be against the rules we set but fuck the rules. At this point, they're all out the window. The way I'm feeling right now is so different than anything I ever expected. I thought maybe this would be fun once, but there's not a chance in hell this will be the only time I have her.

She's going to be mine; I just can't decide if I'm willing to share or not either.

I back away from her, and it takes her a second before she realizes she's free. The second she does, she's whirling around, eyes locking on me. The shock is evident before she speaks.

"Adam?" she gasps. Part of me had wondered if she would freak out, be angry or regret that it's me, but she doesn't. Her eyes look me up and down, even though I've tucked my cock away; seeing her so dirty and marked is making it hard again.

I smirk, and before I'm able to say anything else I hear the rumbling of another engine in the distance, getting louder. She looks at me, panicked, but I'm not going to help her.

"Guess you should run again," I command. She tries to pull on her ripped leggings, which are just going to slow her down. Along with my cum leaking from her pussy.

But she doesn't let it stop her. She does what she's told and turns to run.

I watch her, knowing this isn't going to be the last time I have her. But I also hope the other two don't get to her either.

CHAPTER 33
DREW

She's not running as fast now. Her leggings are ripped, and she's limping slightly, which tells me she was already taken by someone. I know it had to be Adam. If it was Caine, he would've kidnapped her and left us here to figure out that they're long gone.

Adam set his prey loose for us to continue to play with, but he left his mark. He wanted whoever found her next to know that he was there first. And that only makes me more excited.

I rev my bike, and she looks back. The headlight shines on the terrified look on her face, and she picks up her speed a little bit more. But it's not enough. I hop off the bike with ease, catching up to her without even running.

My arms wrap around her frame, I pick her up, tossing her over my shoulder, and exposing her bare ass. I can't help but grab it. Squeezing it, letting my fingers graze her seam while she squirms and demands to be put down. I feel the wetness there, and I push my hand further in, knowing exactly what it is that's dripping out of her. It's not just her arousal. Pulling my hand back from between her legs, I taste my fingers and make a low sound in the back of my throat as I find exactly what I thought I would.

It's Max—sweet and musky—mixed with the salty taste of cum. And I know exactly whose it is. I hadn't thought my erection could get any harder after seeing her, her clothes ripped and body used, but it has.

I don't say anything as I bring her back to my bike and start prepping her for what I'm about to do. I didn't plan this, but seeing her looking so wild makes me want to tame her. At least for now, because I like her wild, too.

Her protests continue as I sit her on the seat of my bike with her back to the handlebars. She doesn't make it easy for me. I use some bungee cords that I've got and anchor her wrists to the handlebars. It keeps her arms spread and most of all, secure.

I straddle the seat in front of her, and don't waste any time ripping her shirt open. She gasps in yet another protest I don't listen to. Her pink nipples are puckered and begging for my mouth that's watering at the sight. Her soaking pussy, still dripping with another man's cum is tempting beyond belief. And even though she's not supposed to know who's who, I don't give a fuck.

Ripping off the helmet, I toss it onto the ground a moment before my mouth latches onto one of her tight nipples, sucking it hard into my mouth.

"*Drew,*" she gasps, her body tensing while she pulls at the wrist restraints. The stretchy cord allows her some movement, but not enough to free her.

I lap at her nipple, licking around the peak before sucking it into my mouth roughly, then moving onto the next one. When she lets out a low "fuck" I sink my teeth into her flesh, and she screams for me. I pull back, smirking at her.

"Why the fuck are you guys doing this?" She pants.

"We're proving to you that you want us. Or at least one of us," I tell her, while I work off the remainder of her torn leggings.

"Why can't you all just leave me alone?" She complains and I'm staring at the most beautiful sight, so I can barely hear her.

"You expect me to leave you alone when your pussy looks like this? Wet and dripping with Adam's cum?"

I lift her hips, throwing her legs over my shoulders so she's forced to arch her back and then, I'm face to face with my next meal.

"Ah, fuck Drew, I can't!" she screams, trying to squirm away, but she's unable to do much in the position I have her in.

"You can, and you're going to."

I run my tongue along her entire slit, collecting every drop that has seeped out of her. The taste explodes on my tongue. The mixture is the perfect blend of Max and Adam, and I groan. Spreading her open with my thumb I take in her and used cunt that's just begging for more.

Begging for *me*.

My thumb grazes her clit as I hold her open for my mouth

and she bucks up against me, making a sound that sounds both pleasured and tortured. My tongue licks her core, tasting everything and it's driving me insane. I moan, letting her feel the vibration from my mouth as I devour her. Licking and sucking the cum from her has me needing to use my free hand to undo my own pants and fist my cock.

I groan the second my fist squeezes around my dick and when I feel the drip of precum, I take it and shove the coated finger into her tight entrance, mixing the three of us together. My eyes look up, spotting a lone figure in the distance, standing there watching. And I know who it is, so I smirk.

She gasps at the intrusion while I work my finger into her, curling it up to rub her inner walls before replacing it with my mouth on her once again. I need more of this taste on my tongue. I need more of *her*.

"Drew, oh my God, I can't. It's too much. I, please! *Ah fuck*," she cries and begs, and I can't help but smile against her. I use my finger that's coated in a mixture of *us* to press against her back entrance, and she tenses in my hold, her legs squeezing the sides of my neck.

"Yes, you can," I encourage, pressing the tip of my finger into her ass just barely while I suck her clit, and she comes with a scream. She tries to rub herself against my mouth as she works herself through the orgasm.

I tug on my cock roughly, needing to be inside her as soon as possible. Moaning against her as I make sure her release continues for as long as possible, until she's squirming in my arms trying to get away.

Sucking at her clit one more time, she cries out again before I finally let go, and I revel at the sight in front of me. Dropping her back down on the seat facing me, I work my pants down a bit more. Once I'm able to completely pull my cock out fully, my hands stroking over the bars on the underside as I look at Max. Her clothes are ripped, her skin flushed, and hints of the bruises and scrape marks mar her perfect body.

I grab her hips, and I lift her up to straddle my lap. Her arms are attached to the handlebars so she can't touch me. No matter how badly I want to feel the burn of her nails scratching down my chest, or the feel of her mouth enveloping my dick again, I need her pussy. It's all I've been able to think about.

Without hesitation, I pull her down onto my erection, and she cries out as the first bar slips inside.

"Please Drew, it hurts. It's too much, I'm so sensitive," she whimpers.

"I know, little one. I'm going to make it all better and you're going to swallow my dick in that tight little cunt, aren't you? Going to show me what a good slut you are for us?"

She bites her bottom lip, shaking her head in protest as I pull her down farther and her pussy takes another one of my bars. She can deny it all she wants, but I feel the way her hips are rocking, desperate for more. And I plan to give her exactly what she wants. It's killing me not to slam her all the way down immediately, but I let her take it inch by inch until she's fully seated on my lap.

Her body shakes and it may be from the cold, or it may be from being overstimulated, but I don't stop. And neither does she. Rocking against me, the little sighs and moans coming from her mouth aren't from pain like she wanted me to think. She wants this.

And I want to tease her.

Pulling back slightly, I scoot back on the seat so only the tip remains notched inside of her. She lets out a little mewl of frustration.

"What the fuck are you doing?" she asks, trying to push down further on me, but I'm too far away.

I'm only giving her shallow thrusts, pushing just a couple inches in, and I never fully retreat. It's just as much torture for me, but I want to hear her beg. I need it. I know that Caine is still watching, and I want him to hear how she begs for me.

Max tries to force herself further onto me again, but it doesn't work. She whimpers and complains, while I just chuckle.

"Come on, little one, how badly do you want my dick to fill you? Tell me how badly you want it," I demand with another shallow thrust.

She's dripping, coating my bike seat with her wetness and I'm half tempted to lick it up once when we're done.

"Fuck! Please, yes, I want it. Fuck me! I just—please." She can't get any purchase from the way she's strapped down and I smile at her begging.

Grabbing her waist, I move forward the same time I'm slamming her down onto my cock, filling her in one thrust. She cries out a loud and needy, "yes."

"Yeah, thatta girl," I praise. Her noises don't let up as she squeezes around me. A couple swipes to her clit with the way I'm thrusting up into her with wild abandon has her pussy quivering around me again. Pleasure filled sounds are tearing from her throat.

She's so loud, I'm sure all the animals have headed in the opposite direction. We're probably going to be caught by more than just Caine, who's still focused on us. I expect for him to interrupt us at any time, but he doesn't. He just watches.

"You can give me one more," I tell her, rubbing her clit even harder as my thrusts grow stronger, our skin slapping together roughly and she's coming with another scream. This time I feel the way she coats my skin as she squirts all over my dick and it's enough to send me over the edge. Pushing up into her, I grab her shoulders and shove her down onto me as I come. Knowing my cum is mixing with Adam's inside her has a low growl working loose from my throat.

Max slumps as much as she can with her arms still restrained and I reluctantly remove myself from her body, pulling my pants back up.

Before I'm able to release her, Caine is standing in front of my bike. The look in his eyes is murderous, but he just removes the restraints from Max's wrists, and she lets him without protest.

"My turn," he says darkly, and I'm not about to stop him. As bad as I want Max to myself, I think I may want to share her even more.

CHAPTER 34
CAINE

Max is limp in my arms as I lift her off Drew's bike and over my shoulder. I'm both pissed off and more turned on than I've ever been in my fucking life. I was pissed that I didn't find her first, and if I would have these other two fuckers wouldn't have touched her ever again.

But when I caught Drew with his mouth buried in her cunt as she writhed against the restraints on his bike, I wanted to rip her away and take her for myself. But I didn't. I stayed rooted right where I was while I watched them.

It brought me back to the other night when I was forced to watch them through the camera. I've wanted her all to myself. I've wanted to be the only one that touches her, but for some reason watching how she reacts with someone else is just as fucking hot as when she's with me.

That doesn't mean I'm going to let her off easy now, though. Because she deserves to be punished for what she's been doing to me. She jostles on my shoulder slightly, like she just now realized she's being carried somewhere. Her clothes are barely hanging onto her frame and I don't bother trying to cover her up.

"Wha—" I cut off anything she was about to say with a sharp smack on her ass.

"Don't say a fucking word, killer. Or I'll fuck you right here in the dirt instead of bending you over my bike."

She lets out a little huff, and I hear, "Too late."

I just smack her ass once more as we get closer to where I left my Ducati. I already know it's too late. She's covered in mud, leaves and sticks plastered to her face and hair, her skin is red and scratched. I'm sure that Adam, our uninvited guest, has already shown her what it's like to be fucked into the dirt.

And *that* is something I'm not okay with.

I maneuver her easily so she's laying across the seat of my motorcycle, bent in half and her toes barely graze the ground. I keep her trapped with my body against her because I know she's going to try and escape the first chance she gets.

"Please Caine, I can't anymore," she sobs weakly.

"Aw, can't what? Can't take anymore in your sensitive little pussy?"

"No. Yes. Just let me go."

I huff out a breath, leaning over her back to speak directly into her ear, "Good thing I wasn't planning on using your pussy, then."

She gasps, immediately trying to get away from me, but I don't let her. Using one hand, I hold the back of her neck, forcing her head down while I use the other one to push my pants down. Freeing my dick, I pump it in my hand a couple of times, not that I need to because I'm hard as steel.

I let a trail of spit run from my mouth into the space between her plump ass cheeks. I spread them apart to see the tight bud there, just dying to be taken by me.

"Don't you fucking dare," she seethes, squirming even more when I rub the tip of my cock through her folds, up to her ass, applying the smallest amount of pressure.

"Drew started prepping you, didn't he, killer? You liked it when he put his finger back here, so you can take my cock."

She shakes her head against my hold, but I just apply more pressure to her back end in response.

"Caine, I can't. Let me go, please." she grits out weakly when I use the head of my dick to rub my spit and precum against her back entrance.

"You can, and you fucking will," I growl, pushing the head in just barely and she lets out a loud scream that quickly morphs into a moan.

I'm not even an inch inside her and she's already so tight around my crown I may lose circulation.

"Too much, Caine, it doesn't fit." she cries as I rock slightly against her, gritting my teeth.

"You need to let me in. Relax for me," I reach out, shoving

my hand between the seat and her body to rub her clit to help her unclench every muscle in her fucking body.

"I can't fucking relax when you're trying to jam your massive dick in my ass," she screeches and I can't help the low laugh I let out.

"God, I love it when you fight me." I rub her clit even more. She moans, relaxing just enough that I'm able to push in another inch.

"There you go. Good little whore taking my *massive dick in your ass*," I mock her words, continuing to rub her bundle of nerves while she lets me in.

I feel the tight stretch around me as her whimpers and cries fill my ears. They seem to be a battle between pleasure and pain, which is exactly how I like it. Especially with her.

"Yeah, open up for me," I groan, pulling back to push in even more.

"Fuck, I can't anymore, I really can't." she protests, while also moving her hips just slightly, contradicting her words. Always fighting me with her words, while her body tells a different story.

I push her head down further. I'm sure any creature within a three mile radius can hear her and I hope that includes Drew and Adam.

I want them to hear what I'm doing to her, what she sounds like for me. I want them to be forced to watch me and watch how her tight little ass stretches around my cock as I pound into her.

"You can, and you're going to come for me, going to show me how much you love this. I know what you really want." I prove that by pushing into her ass almost all the way, then pressing a finger inside her pussy.

The cry she lets out has me close to bursting. I take in the vision in front of me, and it's so fucking pretty. So perfect, just like her. Especially as she clamps down on my cock and my finger, filling both her holes.

"You wish it was two dicks inside you like this, don't you?" I taunt.

"I don't—Caine, please," she begs and it is the best sound I've ever fucking heard.

"Please what?" I taunt.

"Please, *ah*, more." She cries

"You want more? You need more?"

"Yes, *fuck*."

I can't help the way my hips piston against her as we both are close to our releases. She's squeezing both my finger and my dick while screaming my name, pleading, and I can't take it anymore.

"Give it to me right now, killer." I grind out, filling her completely while my finger rubs her inner walls while the palm of my hand rubs against her clit.

Even though she whimpers and continues to cry about how

she can't. I can only imagine the pretty tears running down her cheeks, making her even more of a mess than she already was. Such a pretty mess for me.

"You're mine." I come with a roar as she clamps down on me so hard I'm unable to move as she comes. She's screaming so loud that my ears are ringing with the sound of her pleasure and I'm consumed by mine. I shoot ropes of cum into her ass while my hand is flooded with her orgasm coating us both.

Max sags over the seat and I can tell she really has had enough. Not that it would stop me, but I want to take her home so the next time I make her scream it's not where these other two assholes could be around listening.

Or maybe I do. I don't fucking know, because the way my cock is still buried in her ass has me unable to think clearly. I pull out slowly, tucking myself back in my pants before hauling her into my arms. She goes easily, and I know that's how exhausted she is. She would put up a fight if she had any left inside her.

I wrap my leather jacket around her so I can speed back home with her and not worry about her being a solid block of ice by the time we get there. I help her straddle the bike in front of me, and she whimpers. I don't trust her muscles to not give out while trying to hold onto me, so I keep her plastered against my front as I navigate us out of the forest and back to her house. I don't catch a glimpse of Drew or Adam on the way, and I hope that they decided to go their own way. Maybe forget about her.

Yeah, right.

When we get to her house, I carry her inside and immediately take her into the bathroom. I start the shower so she can get warm. I may be a monster, but I don't want her getting frostbite.

I strip off my jacket and what remains of her clothes while she sits on her bathroom sink. In the light, I'm able to see how marked up her body really is. The way mine reacts should probably have me committed. Her red hair is so caked with mud that her red locks are now brown, and the mud is smeared everywhere. Scratches and scrapes are raised and bleeding all over her chest and stomach. There are red splotches and bite marks marring her tits from where Drew feasted on her perky little nipples.

It makes me even more feral for her and I want to take her again right here. But she looks like she's ready to pass out any second with how her head is bowed. I know that I need to wait, even if it kills me.

Once the water is warm enough, I frame her face with my hands, and force her to look up at me. Her eyes are bloodshot, eyelids hooded as she seems to look past me and not at me.

"If I get you in the shower can you stand by yourself?" I ask, rubbing my thumbs across her cheeks, taking in the beautiful mess in front of me. And *fuck* is she beautiful. I've known it since the first time I saw her. She's the source of my obsession, this woman who has me so fucked in the head, someone so fucking perfect that it has me doing things I'd never do for anyone.

Like the temptation to kiss her, which is back right now. She nods weakly and I don't believe her, but she hops down from the counter in front of me and wobbles for a moment before I steady her.

She doesn't protest when I help her get into the shower. Once the hot water hits her skin it seems to help rejuvenate her a bit.

"Are you going to fall?" I ask, preparing to catch her.

"No," she replies weakly.

I still think about shedding my clothes and joining her, but decide against it, leaving her to shower while I get clothes for her.

Once I step into her room, I'm not expecting the two figures to be standing there, waiting. I throw my head back with an annoyed groan. I knew I wouldn't get rid of them that easily.

CHAPTER 35
MAX

I feel like I've died and the scalding water pounding against my skin is reviving me. My entire body is sore, every muscle aching, including ones I didn't even know I had. Don't even get me started on the parts of me that were used by three different men tonight.

Oh fuck.

Three. Different. Men.

I groan, dropping my head against the side of the shower, fighting back the internal slut shaming comments about myself. The problem is that I liked it. I enjoyed every single painful second as they each used me in their own way. They gave me everything I've ever fantasized about in the privacy of my own mind and yet I still can't help but feel shitty about it.

The hateful words from my family and Carson start to play in my head, making it pound as I imagine everything they would say to me. My heart rate kicks up and the steam around me makes it difficult to breathe. I'm worried I'm about to pass out. I think about calling out for Caine, but then I hear voices, and it pulls me back to reality.

I stick my head out of the shower to hear a little better.

"You don't get to have her all to yourself."

"You should've taken her then."

"What about what she wants?"

What *I* want.

I duck my head back into the shower, letting the water run over me. I pull out the leaves and sticks that are stuck in my hair while I think about that. What is it that I want?

What I want is for the three of them to do that again if I'm honest. But I know that's an insane thought and try to shake it away knowing that it could never happen.

I scrub my body, the exhaustion taking over, and I just want to lay down. Hoping I'm alone once I leave the confines of my bathroom, I dry myself off and slowly open the door to my bedroom. To my surprise, no one is standing there, and I breathe out a sigh of relief. All I want to do is crawl into my bed, curl up under the blankets, sleep for at least twelve hours and hope the ache between my legs is better by tomorrow.

My eyes catch on the clothes laid out on my bed and I do a double take. It's just a long sleeve oversized T-shirt, but the fact that Caine would even consider doing this has my heart swooping in my chest. Of course, there aren't any panties, but he knows I don't sleep in them anyway, so in a way it's sweet because he knows that.

No, I don't like him. This isn't sweet and he's still a psycho.

But he's a psycho who did a nice thing, so I pull on the shirt and start to climb into bed. When I hear the voices again I narrow my eyes at my closed door, waiting to see if the voices are coming from inside my house, or if they're somehow carrying in from outside.

I really should know better, this street is extremely quiet but still, I wait. It doesn't take long to confirm that the voices are in fact coming from inside my house and they definitely belong to men I am intimately familiar with.

But unfortunately for all four of us, I'm tired and don't want to deal with any of this until the morning. So, I go out into the living room, where all three of the large men are arguing. The way they're all taking up space makes my living room look tiny.

"You should be sleeping," Drew comments, drawing Caine and Adam's attention to me. I suddenly feel even more exposed than I ever have, despite the fact that all three of them have now seen more of me than I'm currently showing. All three of them have been inside of me in various ways. Yet, standing here in just a T-shirt that hits mid-thigh and having all of their eyes trained on me has me feeling like I should drop to my knees or something.

"I would be, if you guys would leave my fucking house," I snap, folding my arms across my chest with some false bravado.

"Just go to bed, we'll be quiet," Adam says calmly. I narrow my gaze at him. I have so many questions. Like how he became involved in this and what that means. I don't want to stop training, but I don't know if I'm going to be able to continue now.

"Perfect, be quiet out of my house." I extend my arm and point toward the front door.

Caine scoffs, "Go to bed, killer, or I'm putting you in it myself."

I roll my eyes at him, turning on my heel and walk back to my room. Even though I doubt it'll do anything to deter any of them, I lock the door. It'll at least give me a warning if any of them try coming in here.

Once I climb into the cool sheets, resting my head on my pillow, the exhaustion hits me and I'm asleep within seconds.

𝄞

I DON'T KNOW what time it is when I wake up, but my room isn't bright, and I slept so hard that for a moment I forget where I am. I didn't have any nightmares and as I open my eyes, I'm expecting to see the room I shared with Carson. My ballet slippers resting neatly by the leotard I laid out the night before.

But instead, I see my new house. There are no ballet slippers, and the sun isn't shining through the window, just the glow of it behind clouds that's when I remember where I am. That I escaped and that I now have three men vying for my attention.

And taking full advantage of my body whenever they feel like it.

Remembering last night, I listen for their voices. Waiting for one, or all three of them, to burst in here. That's when I hear them. They're faint, clearly trying to be quiet and I turn my head and scream into a pillow.

I drag myself out of bed, silently cursing them all for their big dicks that have caused the current soreness between my legs. But, like the strong woman I am, I pull myself up and prepare to face whatever is waiting for me in my living room.

Except, I pull on a pair of shorts first because I'm sure as shit not going out there without pants on.

I'm greeted by Caine leaning over my kitchen counter, bright eyes staring daggers across the room at the other two men. Adam is sprawled out on my couch like he's trying to take up as much space as possible. And Drew is sitting in a dining chair, man spreading while leaning back slightly.

"Good morning," Drew greets with a small smile, reaching behind himself he grabs the to go cup of coffee, holding it toward me.

I look between him and the cup, skeptically. I'm not sure that I should trust a drink from any one of them.

"How'd you sleep?" Caine asks with a tone that suggests he knows something I don't, and I immediately take inventory of myself. But honestly, with how sore I'm feeling I wouldn't know if he did anything to me in my sleep or not.

Though, it turns out that's more Drew's forte anyway.

"Why are you all here?" I ask, looking at each of them.

"We didn't want to leave you alone," Adam answers easily.

"Okay, cut the shit," I announce. "What the fuck was yesterday and why the fuck are you three here now?"

They glance at each other, like they are waiting to see who will speak up.

"Someone fucking tell me, or you can all get the fuck out of my house," I demand.

Again, they don't say anything. I throw my hands up with an annoyed grumble, bypassing the coffee offering from Drew, and avoiding Caine virtually standing in my way of making my own.

"We wanted to make it easy for you, to choose," Drew finally says, and I spin around to glare at him.

"Choose? After yesterday you three want me to *choose?* What am I choosing? What brand of torture I prefer?"

"Don't act like you hated it. You loved every second of what we did," Caine scoffs.

I ignore him, turning to Adam. "Since when have you been involved in their shit anyway? What happened to helping me defend myself."

"We can call yesterday part of your training. And you failed," he responds.

"Please, sir, next time show me how to defend myself when I'm being rammed against a tree by a professional fighter," I retort sarcastically.

"Retired professional fighter." Adam shrugs.

I roll my eyes. "Don't you three have places to be? Jobs to get to? Lives to ruin?"

Adam looks at the time. "The gym doesn't open for another two hours."

I look between Drew and Caine. "And you two don't have other jobs to go to or anything?"

They both shake their head, and I'm realizing how little I know about these men that have done unspeakable things to my body. It registers that I don't even know their last names.

"I'm a coach at the gym," Drew says in defense, and I look at Caine for his response.

"I fight." He shrugs, but I can tell there's more that he's not saying, but he doesn't offer anything else.

"Okay, well, I want to be alone now, so you all can leave."

"When'd you put this in? I like it," Caine says, looking toward the pole in my living room instead of acknowledging my request.

"If you all won't leave then I'm locking myself in my room until you do," I threaten.

"Cute you think that we won't join you," Drew jokes and I glare at him.

"Alright." Adam sighs, standing up. "Let's leave her alone."

I look over at him, surprised that he's giving me what I want. Or what I think I want.

No, it's definitely what I want.

I nod, looking between Caine and Drew. "Yeah, listen to your coach and leave me alone."

Caine crowds me against the counter and I immediately put my hands up on his chest in a weak attempt to stop him. He speaks low, leaning down so our foreheads are almost touching, "He doesn't tell me what the fuck to do."

I stand my ground, looking up to meet his eyes, which only brings our faces closer. "But I do."

He lets me push him back slightly, but I'm not delusional enough to think my strength did that. The smirk he gives me only proves that he allowed the move.

Drew steps between us, his hand threading into my hair as he starts to dip his head down like he's going to kiss me. I easily dodge his mouth, and he chuckles against my ear. "You're going to drive us all crazy, aren't you, little one?"

He walks away, clapping his hand on Caine's shoulder as they walk toward my front door. Adam glances back at me. "You're still coming to class later. And we're talking about this."

His tone boasts no argument and for once, I have nothing to say. My body protests any training, but I'm unable to say anything as the three of them walk out of my house.

The weirdest feeling washes over me once they're gone. The coldness. Loneliness. The feeling that takes over is foreign and I shake it away, turning to the one thing that never hurts me.

Music.

CHAPTER 36
ADAM

We all go our separate ways after leaving Max's house. I wanted to talk to Drew since we really didn't get to after everything happened. Even though we all stayed at Max's while she slept, we didn't say much to each other. Mostly because Caine was there, and I don't know where any of us stand now.

I get why Caine didn't want to share.

I get why Drew does.

And here I am, somewhere in the middle. But one thing has me drawing up short. I wish I had seen Drew and Max together. The way that I want her between us.

But first, we all need to talk about things. We need to figure this out because the point of last night was to get Max to choose, and I'm not sure that's going to be possible. Even if she chooses, I don't think any of us are going to give her up.

I turn on the lights and see Athena slithering around her

enclosure. I pick her up and let her have some freedom after being cooped up since yesterday. She slides up my hand and up onto my arm, settling around my shoulders.

"Sorry, girl, I had some stuff to do last night," I tell her, heading into my kitchen to make a protein shake as she settles onto me a bit more. Being wound around my neck is her favorite place to be.

I'll be honest, the weight of her is comforting around my shoulders. She has the ability to take my stress away and helps me relax. It doesn't matter that people would think I'm crazy talking to my snake, she's the biggest constant in my life and I know that she understands what I'm telling her. She understands what I need.

"That girl, the new one, Max," I tell her, feeling good to say things out loud when I don't have anyone else to tell. "She's amazing. I've never met someone like her before. I get why Caine is obsessed with her. Shit, now I understand why she has him and Drew wrapped around her finger."

I shake my head, thinking about how she's turned all our worlds upside down and I don't think she even knows it. Probably because we've done the same to her. I want to know more about her. I want to experience her again, but I want her to know it's me from the start.

"I think you should meet her at some point," I say, taking a big sip from my shake. And when Athena starts to wrap herself around my neck like a scarf in the way she does, an idea clicks. A way for me to get more from Max. I know some of what she likes and how dark her desires go, but I know how to give her more.

I could expand her horizons in so many ways and give her

things she's never imagined before. Even if that means sharing her, because I think I would give her anything she wanted.

⸸

I'M the first one at the gym, which isn't unusual, but what is unusual is that Drew and Caine aren't far behind me. I can't help but think that it has to do with knowing Max is going to be showing up here. None of us want anyone to be alone with her. We're going to end up smothering her and I can't find it in me to even care.

Caine doesn't say anything, immediately starting his workout, which isn't a surprise. Drew ends up walking over to me at the front desk, and I just glance up, waiting to see if he'll talk to me.

"Hey," he finally speaks and that's when I give him my full attention and nod my head at him in greeting.

"I think we all need to talk about this shit," he says exactly what I've been thinking.

"I'm not going to back off, just so you know." I want to make it clear, to both of them, that this isn't ending today.

"Neither am I," he agrees.

"We know he's not." I gesture toward Caine who's lifting probably more than he should be as a warmup.

"What about what Max wants?" he asks with a smirk.

"You think she's going to choose?" I wonder.

Drew looks at Caine, then back to me. I can't deny the heat in his eyes that used to be there when we were hooking up, is back. I also can't deny that I've missed it. It's the same look he'd have with my dick in his mouth, looking up at me. Or right before we would fuck.

"Do you want her to?" he asks, pulling me from my memories of us.

"Do you?" I fire back.

He stands up straighter, not breaking our gaze. "No, I don't."

I'm not surprised by his response, but hearing it out loud does make me feel better about whatever is going to happen. Maybe the two of us will be able to convince Caine that he doesn't get to have her all to himself.

"Caine," I snap, getting his attention, because I don't want to put this off any longer. The three of us need to be on the same page before Max gets here.

He drops the weights with a loud thud. "What?"

I nod my head to the side, signaling him to come over to where we are. He gets up from the machine, grumbling to himself. I'm going to ignore that for now.

"Where do we all stand with Max?" I ask seriously, and Caine just scoffs.

"Same place we stood before. She's mine, and you two need to back off. You've had your fun, but it's over now." He shrugs.

"We're past that shit, she wants all of us, and wasn't that the deal? That we let her choose?" Drew argues.

"Since when did she say that?"

"Uh, yesterday, she didn't need to say it. It's pretty fucking obvious."

They continue to bicker, and I stop it with a strong, "Enough."

They both look at me, and I don't let the fighting continue before speaking again. "Did either of you know she was engaged?" Neither of them say anything, but the surprised look on their faces is my answer.

"Yeah, didn't think so. I looked her up, she's from a really wealthy family in Texas, supposed to marry some douche in January, but clearly didn't. Now she's here with us and she clearly wants all of us. Caine, you need to get over your possessive bullshit and see that. We *all* can give her what she wants. What I think it is she *needs*."

He looks horrified at the thought, immediately shaking his head. "No, I don't share. And there's no fucking way I'm sharing with the two of you."

"Either you share, or you'll constantly be competing with us. Which would you prefer?" Drew challenges.

"No more competitions. No more bullshit arguments and fights. We are going to be *adults* about this," I explain.

"Oh, I forgot you were in charge, *dad*," Caine retorts.

"Not your fucking dad, but yeah. I'll be in charge if you're going to be an immature dick about this."

The front door of the gym opens, and we all swing our heads over to see Max walking in. She stops dead in her tracks when she notices all of us looking at her.

"I feel like I just interrupted something," she says skeptically.

"Not at all, we were just talking about you." Caine walks over to her, draping his arm across her shoulders, which she shrugs off with a glare.

"That's not helping," she tells him.

"We were talking about how we don't want you to choose. We want all of us to have a chance with you," I say, cutting to the chase. Like I said before, I'm done with these games that they've been playing with her, and she should know it.

Her head swings between all of us before shaking it in disbelief. "You're wanting me to, what, date all of you? After *yesterday?*"

"We don't need to put a label on it. But yeah, we all want you," Drew chimes in.

"I—" She pauses with her mouth wide open. It makes me want to shove her onto her knees and feel that mouth wrap around my dick. "I don't know what's happening right now."

I step closer to her, and she doesn't back away, not even when I gently cup her cheeks, sliding my fingers into her hair and forcing her to look up at me. "Give us a chance," I request quietly.

"Adam, you don't understand. This isn't normal, I can't—"

"Who gives a fuck what's normal? Did you like yesterday? Do you want more like it? Do you want *more?*"

Her mouth snaps shut, and she swallows roughly.

"You don't have to answer now, just don't kick us out the next time we want a taste of you." I wink, stepping back from her and she sways on her feet slightly at the loss of my touch.

"Now, let's get to work. You're at the gym, it's time to train," I announce, hoping it'll be enough of a distraction.

I don't miss the looks I get from everyone, trepidation rolling off them in waves. Except Caine, he just looks pissed, but I think he always looks like that. Good thing he gets to take out some of that aggression during training—we have a lot to do today.

CHAPTER 37
DREW

Max leaves immediately after her training is over, and it's impressive how fast she's able to move for how tired she clearly is. Yet, as I watch her, I notice she isn't going toward her house. She pauses before choosing to walk in the direction toward the beach. I don't know why, but what I do know is I want to be around her.

I glance at where Adam is cleaning up and call out his name. "I'm heading out."

"You're not gonna help clean up?"

"Rain check."

I feel his glare from across the gym, but I don't care right now. We have a shit load of issues to work through, and I'm sure that's about to explode soon enough with the addition of Max into everything. But right now, my mind is screaming at me to go to her. I need to take advantage of time with just the two of us for once. Because I doubt it'll last long.

I head out, and she's already far enough away that I can't see her. I know where she was going though, so I hop on my motorcycle and drive down to the promenade. I park on the street before making my way onto the sand.

Her red hair is blowing behind her as she walks closer to the ocean, and it's like a beacon for me. I give in to the pull and follow after her.

She's sitting down in the dry sand that the ocean hasn't reached yet. I sit down next to her, not saying anything right away. She doesn't look at me, but I know she knows I'm here.

I haven't been to the beach in several months. Adam tried to get me to jog with him down here before my injury, but since then, he stopped. I also prefer to run on solid ground, not with my feet kicking up sand constantly.

We just sit in silence, the only sound coming from the waves breaking onto the shore. I realize how peaceful it is, and I wonder why I haven't come here more often. Especially when the noise in my mind gets too loud, when the memories are unbearable and I feel like I want to jump out of my skin.

I notice the shine of a tear sliding down Max's face, but she wipes it as I turn my head to look at her.

"What's wrong?" I ask, breaking the silence.

"Nothing, I just got some sand in my eye or something." She shrugs me off, but I don't believe her.

Instead of calling her out, I go back to facing forward and

settling into the silence. Even though there are things to talk about and even more to figure out. I just sit here with her, and that pull I've felt since I first saw her is stronger than ever.

"Why are you here?" Max finally asks.

"I saw you go this way, and I wanted to join you."

"Why?"

"I wanted to be around you." I surprise myself with how easily the truth stumbles out.

"You mean you want another chance to fuck me when I'm most vulnerable, right?"

I shake my head. "No. I'm not really a fan of sand getting near my dick."

She huffs out a small laugh.

After another couple minutes of silence between us, I let another truth stumble out. "I like it out here."

"Good thing you live so close to it, then." She pauses, furrowing her brows before looking at me. "How long have you lived here?"

I think for a second before answering. "Five years."

"Really?"

"Yeah? Why is that surprising?"

She shrugs, "Just seems like all of you are from here considering how I was treated when I first showed up here."

"Well, we all moved here at one point. It wasn't easy at first for any of us."

"Where are you from?"

I hide the shudder that threatens to take over when it comes to talking about my past. "California."

"That's also near the ocean, you know?"

"Sacramento isn't, but I'm glad you're familiar with your state geography."

She shoves at my arm. I hardly move from the force, but let out a laugh at the attempt.

"Why did you decide to move here?" I ask and notice the second the last word leaves my mouth, she shuts down again. I think about what Adam told us, but I want to hear about it from her. I want the full story.

I want to take it back, but don't because I want to know more about her. Which is fucking weird.

"Why'd Caine say you practically killed your dad?" she asks suddenly and I don't think I'm able to hide the shock on my face this time.

That dude has a fucking death wish.

"You answer my question first," I challenge.

"It looked nice." She shrugs.

"That's not it." I know there's more to it than that.

"I was supposed to get married." She starts moving her finger through the sand, drawing designs in it. "But I didn't want to, so I left."

She's still hiding things. I knew that part already, but there's more to it. I'll get the full story out of her eventually. Which is why I decide to give her a portion of my truth as well.

"My dad used to beat me after my mom left us. A lot. When I was big enough to fight back, I did. And I didn't stop."

She sucks in a sharp breath but doesn't run. She's seen some of the darker parts of me already. She heard what Caine told her and still didn't run, just like she's not running now.

Instead, she surprises me even more by nodding and saying, "He probably deserved worse than he got."

"You have no idea," I agree quietly. Then, I decide to tell her a little more. "I ran away and was homeless for a couple years after that happened. Once I found MMA, I never looked back. Eventually, I heard about Adam and Uncaged and ended up here."

She looks at me, her green eyes meeting mine, and the pull is more potent than ever. The look I see in them shows me that we have more in common than I thought. I know this even without her telling me. I know she's been through shit she doesn't want to talk about. But the demons are there, and they are the type that could play well with mine.

"Seems like this is the place to run away to then, isn't it?" she practically whispers.

I shake my head. "No, this is the place to find yourself. I think you're starting to do just that."

CHAPTER 38
MAX

After my conversation with Drew at the beach, I went home, and I'm surprised he didn't try to follow me. I was even more shocked to not find Caine there waiting for me either.

The worst part of it is that instead of feeling relieved like I should, I feel cold. And alone.

I don't like it.

Maybe it's because when I went to go to sleep, I imagined Carson was breaking in. And I was alone and vulnerable like I always was, just waiting for his wrath.

Despite what these men have done to my body and how much I've denied it, I'm starting to crave it. The fact that they always seem to be around makes me feel oddly safe, too. Which is only adding to my concern about the status of my mental health.

I'm wiping out glasses at work, clearly lost in a mental tailspin, when Danner practically screams my name to get my attention.

"What?" I snap, putting the extremely dry glass away.

"You were just staring at nothing while you dried that glass so hard I was worried it was going to break."

I roll my eyes. "I don't think that's possible."

It's another slow night, and I'm thankful for it because I don't think I could handle being treated like shit today. I might actually lose it, and I do need this job.

"Is it Caine? Or maybe Drew, that has you acting all spacey?"

I scoff and add under my breath, "or Adam."

"What was that?"

"You're hearing things," I divert, and she gives me an unimpressed look that I shrug off.

The door opens, and I look up to see if the person walking in is going to be a problem. When I see that it's that Officer again, I roll my eyes, finding something else to be busy with.

Danner, on the other hand, is choosing violence tonight. She spins around on the stool, facing the overweight older man, resting her elbows on the bar behind her when she calls out, "How can we help you tonight, Officer Doogie?"

He looks over at her, and I don't like the look in his eyes. It's angry and evil. I've seen it. I've lived with it. I know the type of man that has those eyes.

"I actually am here to check in on our newbie." He nods in my direction. I stand up taller, folding my arms across my chest.

"Hardly a newbie anymore since I've been here over a month and haven't caused any problems." Partly a lie, but I haven't broken any laws, so there's that.

"Been a bit busy but figured I should know your name."

"Why?" I don't want to answer him. I don't need him knowing anything about me.

"Just trying to be friendly." He tries to smile in a way that conveys that, but the way his gnarled teeth are showing is anything but friendly. It only makes the gleam in his eye worse.

"Well, I haven't done anything that warrants a cop to know my name, but if I do, then you can learn it."

"If I said you're in contempt of a cop, then you'll tell me."

Danner scoffs, "She also has the right to not tell you shit, Doogie."

The side of my lips quirk up and I have to hold back the laughter that's about to break loose.

"We'll see," he says ominously, looking over Danner in a way that has my skin crawling before he turns and leaves.

Danner faces me once again and makes a retching noise. "I hate that asshole."

"Talk about abuse of power." I shake my head, picking up another glass to start drying.

"Keep hanging out with the guys from Uncaged, and you'll see how true that really is."

I have a feeling she's right about that.

※

AFTER ANOTHER NIGHT of no one appearing in my house, I'm feeling weirdly on edge. So, I show up early to the gym—I can make some sort of excuse as to why I'm here later, but I just need to be around them.

Fuck, it feels weird to even *think* that.

No one is around when I walk in and the disappointment that washes over me is like a slap to the face. Turning around, trying to figure out where they are, I start to hear loud familiar voices coming from the office.

"I didn't say no, I just said to fucking wait."

"That's a no from you and I'm fucking sick of it. You don't get to control everything."

"No, but I do get to control what happens in my gym."

"You can't help yourself, can you? You just have to be in control of everything all the time."

"You didn't mind that before, did you?"

"Oh, now you want to bring that up? Fuck off."

I find myself pushing the door open to reveal Drew and Adam, both standing tall and *very* close to each other. Closer than you'd expect for a normal argument. Seeing them together makes my thighs squeeze together while memories of the forest—the last time they touched me—flood my mind. I let out a soft whimper that has both of their heads swinging in my direction.

"Sorry, I'm early. I just—"

"It's fine. We're done," Adam says sternly, and I can see the look on Drew's face, which tells me they are, in fact, not done.

I remember Caine saying that they were involved, and I know just from standing here that things aren't resolved, not by a long shot. Maybe I complicate things, but maybe I can make things better.

I *want* to make things better.

So, I steel my spine, finding the confidence I've been working so hard to strengthen and also tuning into the woman that holds so much power over these men.

"You didn't sound done. After work today, you're figuring your shit out once and for all," I command, and they both look at me with different levels of surprise.

"You don't understand, Max—" Adam starts, but I hold my hand up stopping him. I see a flare of anger pass over his face, and it makes me smirk.

"I don't care. We're all meeting at your house after the gym closes today."

"All of us?" he questions.

"Yes, the three of us. Clearly, I need to make sure you two don't kill each other."

"Sounds like you care about us, little one," Drew comments, moving past Adam to leave the office. He makes sure to rub his chest against me on the way and I hate how the simple touch has my knees close to buckling.

They've conditioned me. Or broken me. Either way, I can't find it in myself to hate it.

I look back up at Adam who hasn't broken eye contact with me. I don't back down and he says, "Fine."

Even though I'm pretty sure he's mad, I can't help but feel like I won.

Considering the stupid competitions and fights they've had over me—over my body and my attention—I can't help but be proud of the fact that the tables are about to turn.

※

Throughout training, Caine never strayed too far away from me, and I can't deny how weird it's been that he hasn't tried anything. Maybe he got enough. Or maybe sharing me in the forest was too much for him.

Deep down, I know that's not the case. Just like I know he's about to bust back into my life like a wrecking ball again. He's like a time bomb, always simmering, just waiting as the clock counts down before he explodes.

And I've grown to like his brand of explosion.

I've missed it.

But tonight, my mission doesn't have to do with him. Tonight, it's about Adam and Drew and helping them get their shit figured out. Then, maybe I'll figure out if it's possible for Caine to get his shit figured out.

Drew told me where Adam's house is, and even though he insisted he bring me himself; I make the drive myself. It's not far from town, but it is further away from the ocean than my house is. After I park, I hear the familiar rumble of a motorcycle before I see it pull up next to me in Adam's driveway.

Drew takes his helmet off, and my eyes dart from him and the way he's sitting there, to the handlebars that I was tied to while he fucked me. *Shit,* I should not be this wet from a memory. Especially a memory of something so depraved. The wildest thing I've ever done. Even wilder than enjoying being woken up with him between my legs. Or enjoying the way Caine took from me when I fought back.

"Are you getting out, or are you going to sit in your car daydreaming?" Drew jokes and I open the door, trying to hide the way my face reddens. Because of *course* he knows exactly what I was thinking about.

It feels weird to be approaching Adam's front door with Drew next to me because I'm not here to pick sides in their situation. I'm here to make sure they fix whatever this is that they need to fix between them.

However, that needs to be done.

Adam opens the door, but his greeting is less than welcoming. Even as he gestures us inside, he doesn't seem thrilled about this.

I take in the space. It's dark with a lot of browns and blacks, which doesn't entirely surprise me. I notice the large tank on one wall and I try to see what's inside from a comfortable distance. Drew notices, stepping close behind me, leaning down to speak directly in my ear when he says, "That's Adam's ball python, Athena."

I shiver thinking of being near a snake. I don't have a fear of them I don't think. But the thought of them doesn't exactly make me feel warm and fuzzy inside like cats or dogs, or fucking bunnies.

"Okay, we're all here, what are you wanting from us?" Adam asks, sitting on his couch, spreading his legs to get comfortable. I have to bite my tongue to keep from saying what I'm really wanting from them right now.

"Right." I nod, regaining my composure. I step away from Drew, sitting on the large ottoman in front of Adam's couch while Drew takes a seat, keeping his distance from Adam. "So, you two used to be involved?" I decide to just go for it.

"Caine told you too much," Drew comments under his breath.

"What happened? Why are we here?" I ask them, but they both refuse to answer. "Is it because of me?"

"No," they both answer instantly, and I smirk.

"It's because of my injury." Drew sounds reluctant.

"And you two stopped fucking because of it?" I'm confused.

Adam groans, scrubbing his hand down his face. "Max, what're you doing?"

"Fixing this."

"Well, I don't think you can. It's cute that you want to try, but you don't get it." Drew shakes his head.

Plan B it is. Maybe it's from the level of turned on I am just being in their presence, thinking about the last time we were together. Or thinking about what could happen if we were *together*.

So, without thinking too much about it, I stand up, closing the short distance to Adam, and straddle his lap on the couch. His hands immediately find my waist when I settle my weight on him, running my hands up his chest. He stops the movement instantly, snatching my hands in one of his.

"What're you doing?" His deep voice goes straight to my core.

"Helping." I lean in, pressing our foreheads together, I rock myself just barely over him, which has his grip on my hip and wrists tightening.

"Helping what?" he grits out.

I pull at my wrists, and he lets go, but I make sure to be careful about where I touch him, since that seemed to cause a reaction. I wrap my arms around the back of his neck, moving closer so our lips are less than an inch apart.

I realize I haven't kissed any of them. They've all fucked me, but we've skipped the simple step of a kiss. And I want to change that.

"Helping fix this." I close the distance between our mouths, grazing our lips together just slightly.

The barely there touch of our mouths causes Adam to make a noise in the back of his throat before closing the distance roughly. I gasp and it gives him the opportunity to shove his tongue into my mouth, finding mine easily.

I rub against him again, and he groans into my mouth, sinking his teeth into my bottom lip. I swear I almost combust just from that. But that's not the plan, this isn't fixing anything. This needs to be about *them*.

Reluctantly, I pull away and look over at Drew who has his gaze fixed on us. The obvious erection in his pants has me bringing my bottom lip between my teeth. And I climb off Adam's lap and onto Drew's. He immediately pulls me tighter against him, making sure I feel him.

Without giving me a chance to tease him, his hand is in the hair on the back of my head, gripping it tightly as he yanks me down to him in a feral, searing kiss. There's no softness or playing. With the way Drew's lips are on mine it's like he's been starved for me and I'm everything he's wanted.

His tongue delves into my mouth, tangling with mine while he thrusts up underneath me like he wants to fuck me through our clothes. I'm throbbing for him already, I would let him if I could.

But again, I pull away, even as he tries to chase my mouth with his. He tries to keep me held onto his lap, but I manage to sit between them, looking at each of them.

"Your turn," I tell them.

I'm met with confused looks before Adam seems to understand what I'm saying.

"Max, this isn't going to solve anything."

"I think it will. You guys need to work it out, and if that's fucking it out, then that's what you should do."

Drew drops his lips to my neck and starts tracing them along the area below my ear and I fight the urge to lean into him. "What if we want to fuck it out with you?"

"Maybe, I'll let you." I moan when his teeth graze along my ear lobe. "Afterward."

He hums, and I see him look at Adam. I crook my finger at Adam, beckoning him closer, and I watch as he does it reluctantly.

They each close the distance, right in front of me. I'm nervous, excited, and unbelievably turned on. Especially as they get closer, their lips are so close to brushing while they're still so close to mine.

"This means nothing," Adam states.

"Never has," Drew agrees.

I want to argue with them, but then they're kissing right here in front of me. It's rough like they hate each other, and it's also the hottest thing I've ever witnessed. If I wasn't soaking before, my panties are completely drenched now.

Their tongues battle, teeth biting hard enough to be painful. I can't help myself and I reach into Drew's pants, fisting his cock, and he groans into Adam's mouth as I move my hand over him.

"I want you both to touch each other like this," I tell them both, causing them to break apart to look at me.

Instead of giving them the opportunity to argue or stop this, I go back to sitting on the ottoman. I lean back on my hands so I can look at them.

"You think you can just boss us around, baby girl?" Adam asks.

"Yeah, I do. Now, show me what I want to see."

CHAPTER 39
ADAM

F*uck.* The taste of Max on my mouth, mixed with the taste of Drew, has me ready to blow. It makes me want to have him fuck her just so I can taste her pussy on his cock. Especially when she's sitting there, reclined in front of us, eyes heavy, lips red from both of our kisses. I want to force her back over here, but I'm also curious to see what she's about to do.

"What are you wanting to see?" I challenge, wanting her to be specific in what she wants us to do.

I'll let her play for a little bit, but I'll end up taking control like I always do.

Max looks between the two of us, and I don't miss the subtle way she presses her thighs together, thinking we won't notice. I don't even need to look at Drew to know that he saw it, too.

"Kiss again," she commands softly.

I don't need her to tell us twice. Turning toward Drew, I grab the back of his head and slam our mouths together. Kissing Drew has always been on my terms and the way I like it. Rough, messy, and easy. He takes what I give, and he gives as good as he takes. We balance each other out in the best way sexually and it's been too long.

Nothing about this is sweet or slow—it never has been. We've always had one intention when we're together and it's to find the best way to get each other off. Right now, we're falling into old habits, which is even more obvious when Drew starts to pull at my shirt. I let him, even though Max hasn't said anything.

If she's not going to instruct us to do what she wants, then we're going to do whatever we want and she's just going to be here for the show. The thought of her watching us makes me even harder. I bet she'll touch her tight little pussy while she does. I want her to join in so badly.

"Touch each other," she finally says, her voice barely above a whisper and I hear the breathy tone of it like she's struggling to breathe.

I break away from Drew's kiss to look over at her while he continues to kiss and nip the skin of my throat. "Touch each other how? You need to be specific, baby girl."

Max's jaw drops slightly like she's unsure of what to say and I smirk. Unable to stop myself, I yank at Drew's pants, and he groans as his dick bobs free. And again, when I wrap my hand around him, feeling the piercings on the underside against my palm.

"Like this?" I ask her, while stroking my hand along him.

Max nods. "Yes, both of you."

Drew doesn't waste any time, freeing my own cock from my pants and wrapping his hand around me so tightly, I grunt. He knows what I want, he knows the bite of pain I need. He also knows this is one of the only touches I won't deny.

"Fuck," I groan when he runs his thumb along the sensitive area right below the crown.

His lips are on mine again as we fuck each other's hands. It feels so good, and yet isn't enough at the same time. Our tongues thrash against each other, hips thrusting into each other's hands and I think I hear Max make a small noise of pleasure.

Drew moans, breaking our kiss and I work him harder, pressing our forehead together as I say, "You think Max should touch herself while she watches?"

Drew nods. "Yeah, she fucking should. Or she could come over here and help us."

"Hm," I hum, looking at her.

Her eyes are hooded, and I see her conflict as she thinks about it. I make sure to tighten my grip on Drew's cock, rubbing my thumb along a piercing in the way I know makes him moan loudly and it works as it always does.

Max's eyes flare with desire and I want nothing more than for her own hands to take over, or for her to join in some way. Instead, she stands, and I think she's about to close the small distance between us. Instead, she hooks her thumbs in her pants and pushes them down to reveal the white thong she's wearing.

Both Drew and I are fixated on her, hardly moving as we wait to see what she's going to do. When she sits back down on the ottoman, I almost lose it. But then she draws her feet up there with her, spreading her legs to show the drenched fabric resting between her thighs and my mouth waters.

"Keep going," she demands at the same time her hand slides along the wet fabric, pulling it aside to reveal a glimpse of her glistening pink pussy. "Keep. Going," she repeats.

"Shit," Drew mutters, his hand working my cock even harder. I need more, and I want her to still feel like she's in control to some extent, but I need her to know that I am, too.

Which is why I move away from Drew slightly, sitting back on the couch, and guiding his head down to my lap. He goes so easily, his mouth enveloping my dick, instantly taking me to the back of his throat. My eyes remain locked on Max. Her hand stilled as she watches us, completely transfixed. Particularly on Drew as he swallows me.

"Keep going," I repeat her words back to her and she looks up at me.

I stretch my arms out on the back of my couch, watching Max rub her clit with the pads of her fingers before she pushes a single digit inside her soaking pussy while Drew licks and sucks my cock. I want this to keep going forever. Both of them just like this, but my hips start to thrust up further into Drew's throat and he takes it like a fucking champ. While Max uses her hand to fuck herself even harder, watching us.

She bites back a moan, and I can tell she's getting close.

"Don't come," I tell her, not caring if I'm taking control now.

She whimpers, "Why?"

"Because you're not wasting something so perfect on your fingers. You're going to come on one of our mouths or cocks tonight. Maybe both."

I feel Drew's hum of agreement around me, and it causes me to thrust up even harder and he swallows around me, not even gagging.

I'm getting too close; I can't take this much longer, and so is she. I pull Drew off me and stand up. He looks up at me, lips red and swollen while Max pauses, but keeps a finger buried inside herself, though she's looking at me like she's waiting for whatever's about to come next.

To Drew I say, "Lay down." And he does, lying on the couch, his large frame taking up the entire space.

Then To Max, I say, "straddle his face."

She looks at me, shocked and I wonder if she's about to fight the order. But like the good fucking girl she is, she stands up and pushes off her useless panties, stepping up to the couch. Drew gives her a heat-filled look that I know extremely well. Before she has a chance to do it herself, he's pulling her onto him. She squeals, trying to lift off slightly, but doesn't let her. Instead, he wraps his arms around her thighs and pulls her down to his mouth.

"Coach said to straddle my face, little one, so you better suffocate me with this sweet cunt," he growls, right before burying his face in her. I can tell when she cries out that he's using his talented mouth on her and that she's not going to last long.

So, I drop to my knees on the side of the couch, gripping his cock before sucking him into my mouth. He groans, and I know Max feels it because of the sweet sound of pleasure she lets out. It only makes me suck harder because I know exactly what he needs, just like he knows what I like. I run my tongue along the underside of him before sucking him into my throat again, and he groans.

"Wha—fuck." Max turns to look over her shoulder to see me and lets out a loud moan the second she does. "Let me turn around."

Drew lets go for a second, allowing her to turn before yanking her back down onto his mouth. She leans forward, bracing her hands on his abdomen, and watches me.

"You wanted to watch?" I ask with a smirk.

"I wanted a front row seat." She smirks right before Drew does something that has her dropping her head in a loud moan. The curtain of red hair falls around her and I can't help but try to make her front row seat worth it.

I take Drew into the back of my throat once again and can hear him groan his answer against Max's pussy. She grinds down onto his face, and I watch, entranced while I work to try and get Drew to come. Hard.

I'm practically humping the side of the couch at everything that's going on. The mixture of all our moans, the wet sounds coming from our mouths and then Max starts chanting some variation of "yes, more, fuck, please." I suck Drew in further and swallow around him.

They're both close, and it doesn't take long before Max is screaming out her release, which triggers Drew to come down my throat. I take everything he gives me, swallowing every drop.

As soon as he's done, I sit up, grab the back of Max's head, smashing our mouths together. Her tongue immediately tangles with mine and I pull her off Drew, and onto my lap on the floor. My dick is begging to feel her again, especially as her bare pussy drips onto it.

I hear Drew, who has come closer, speaking close to Max, "You want to fuck him? Want to feel him fill your tight little pussy again?"

I suck her bottom lip into my mouth, when she gives her answering moan, "*Yes.*"

"You heard her, then, Coach. Give the girl what she wants."

"You want to watch me fuck her?" I ask with a smirk.

"Fuck yeah I do."

I rub my cock through her slick folds and feel how wet she is from Drew's mouth and her orgasm. She lifts slightly and I hold her hips slamming her down onto me. She cries out at the intrusion but starts rubbing herself against me almost instantly.

Drew is right behind her, he's moved her hair over her shoulder while he kisses, licks and bites her neck, pulling the collar of her shirt to the side before lifting it off her easily.

My mouth finds one of her peaked nipples, sucking it into my mouth while guiding her hips as mine meet hers with even thrusts. Her head drops back against Drew as both of our mouths are on her and my dick is buried inside her.

"Gonna need you to come for us again," I groan, moving her so she rubs her clit against my groin while I fuck up into her. Moving my mouth to her other nipple and sucking hard, grazing my teeth around the peak.

"I'm close, fuck, how—" She moans, rubbing even harder and I can't help it—I need more.

"Drew, move," I tell him roughly, and he listens easily, moving to the other side of the couch so I'm able to lift Max up and lay her back on the couch, wrapping her legs around my waist as I pound into her.

Max reaches up behind her, searching for something to hold onto as I feel her get closer, squeezing around me. Drew grabs her hands in one of his and she arches her back.

"Come on, little one, come all over him. Soak his cock, then we can clean him up."

"Oh fuck," I groan, my hips stuttering as my balls tighten and I feel my orgasm closing in.

I rub Max's overstimulated bundle of nerves, because I need her to get there before me. She comes with a scream as Drew continues to hold her down while I fuck her so hard I think the couch has scooted across the floor.

Once my orgasm hits, I lean over, catching myself on the

couch, barely keeping my weight off her as I come harder than I ever have \while she writhes against me, quivering with the aftershocks. I don't want to pull out of her. I want to stay right here, but I'm sure she's done. For now.

I pull out slowly and she lets out a small whimper at the loss. That's when Drew leans down, licking her orgasm from my cock with a single swipe of his tongue that has me almost ready to go again. She watches Drew with so much heat in her eyes it makes me think she may not be done.

She manages to sit up slightly, looking between Drew and me. I may not know what's going to happen after this, but it solidified one thing—and that's the fact that none of us are going to give her up.

She'd better understand what this means, because we all want her. We're all going to have her and there's nothing that could take her away from all of us now.

CHAPTER 40
CAINE

I fidget with my phone while sitting on Max's bed in the dark, waiting for her. I've shown as much restraint as I have since the other day, and I'm done.

It was only made worse by the phone call I got earlier from my family. I knew it would piss me off before I even answered. Since I still need their money, I have to play by their rules for a little while longer.

I knew I would need a hit from my addiction afterwards, only to find she isn't even here. The longer I wait, the longer I think about my conversation with my dad and the more pissed off I get.

"It's time to come home," my dad says sternly. No hello, nothing first.

"Is that what time it is? Our clocks must say different things."

"Goddammit, Caine. Your play time is over. You're twenty-six years old. You had your fun, now you need to go back to school so you can join your brother and I at the firm."

I'd rather fucking die.

"Yeah, I'm not doing that. I'm close to making it, I'm really good, you know?"

"Good at punching guys in the face is not the accomplishment you think it is, son."

"That's not all MMA is," I say for probably the millionth time.

"Well, it's also not paying your bills. That's still me."

I fume at the reminder. I want nothing more than to stop needing his money, because as long as I do, he's going to hold it over my head.

"Cut me off, then," I threaten, knowing it would suck because I would have to get a job for the first time in my life, but maybe I should anyway. Though, I know he won't follow through, because if he does, he loses the leverage.

"You have six more months. Then you're coming home, going to school, and courting Amelia."

I grimace at the thought of all of that. Amelia is a woman they've wanted me to be with since I was a teenager. The most boring, frigid bitch I've ever met. She would never be able to handle me. Not like my little killer. No, nothing like Max. No woman can compare to her. Which is why I remember her last name, the well-known family she comes from, and I can't help myself.

"I'm not doing anything with Amelia. I'm seeing someone."

"Who?"

"Someone from a family you'd approve of."

"Who?" His voice has more of an edge to it this time.

"She's a Barclay," I answer confidently. I feel even better about it when my dad doesn't say anything in response right away.

"Well, does her family know she's dating the failure Aldridge?"

I ball my fists, wishing he was in front of me right now so I could drive it through his face.

"She knows she's with a future UFC champion."

He laughs. "Six months, Caine. Maybe you'll get to keep your play time with the Barclay girl, but I doubt she'd stick around if she really knew you."

"She knows more about me than you ever will."

I hang up before I completely lose my shit. I need to see Max. I can't stay away any longer, I need to remind us both that she's mine.

I hear the front door open and stop tossing my phone between my hands as I wait for her to come in here. Resting my elbows on my knees, I lean forward slightly, facing the bedroom door as I listen to her footsteps approach.

She doesn't notice me right away when she steps into her room, not bothering to turn on the light before she starts kicking her shoes off.

"If you're going to get naked, do it with the lights on," I say.

She screams, slapping the light switch on before narrowing her eyes at me.

That's when I see it. I know what my girl looks like after she's come. I know what she looks like when she's been fucked, and I know instantly that she was with one of them.

"Who were you with?" I demand, standing, stepping closer to her, taking in her flushed skin, red swollen lips. Her red hair is pulled up in a messy bun, but it doesn't hide the fact that I know hands have been raked through it.

She looks up at me, defiance in her eyes. "Wouldn't you like to know?"

"Yeah, I do. Which one do I need to kill?" We both know who else she would've been with.

She smirks, the devious look makes my cock throb. "What if I was with both of them?"

"Then you're going to have to help me, because hiding two bodies is going to take a lot more work." I stalk closer to her, backing her up to the wall and caging her in.

"You're not killing them." Her voice is firm, definitive, and it's fucking sexy.

"No? Why's that?"

"Because I want them."

I tilt my head to the side. "Oh do you?"

She nods.

"And you think I should just be okay with that?"

"You didn't seem to mind before."

I have her completely pinned to the wall now, my hips pushing into hers as I look down at her. Her lips are so red and puffy, and I'm tempted to sink my teeth into them. The way that she's pushing the boundaries, talking about being shared isn't helping either. I want to claim and possess her in every single way possible. I've done it with most of her body, but I've yet to have her mouth in any way.

What would she do if I closed the distance between us and pressed my lips against hers. I wouldn't be soft or gentle. It would be my first kiss, but I already know it would feel like claiming her in yet another way.

"I do mind," I tell her sternly.

"That's too bad." Her voice is throaty and breathy, showing me how affected she is by me. "Because if you want me like you claim you do, then this is my condition."

My forehead drops down to hers. "Your condition?"

"Mhmm." She shifts slightly, and I know she can feel my cock poking her stomach.

"What if I don't accept your condition?"

Her eyes lock on mine, the green mixed with gold is bright, and I see a difference from when she first got here. She's more confident, more sure of herself. She's also stronger from the training. I remember the pole in her living room and I'm sure that she's been using that to get gain muscle as well.

It only makes me want her more. And I won't say it out loud, but I would give her whatever she wanted. I just hate that what she wants is for me to share because I want her. I want all of her all to myself.

"Then you don't get to have me."

"Telling me no doesn't stop me. You know that, killer."

"It should." She shifts again, her breath hitching, and I know she feels me.

"Why? You want sweet?" I bring my lips to her cheek, ghosting them over her skin as I continue, "You want someone to treat you like you're fragile?" I move down her neck, barely touching her.

She hums, her head falling back against the wall as I continue.

"You want someone to take you to dinner? Someone who will ask permission to kiss you? Someone who asks before they touch your greedy cunt? Tell me that's what you want. That it's what gets you so wet that I can smell your arousal."

She rubs herself against me with another soft noise as I move my mouth to trail the other side of her neck. "That's not what you want."

"It's what I should want."

"You want to be chased through the forest by three different men. You want them to take what they want from you while you act like you don't want it. You want to be forced to take cocks in every hole you have. You want to be a drooling, crying, wet beautiful mess."

She moans, her hands finding my shirt, fisting the fabric and anchoring herself to me.

"So, it doesn't matter what you ask for. Doesn't matter if you tell me no, because you're mine. Mine to do with as I want. Mine to take." I bite the spot where her neck meets her shoulder. "Mine to fuck." I bite her jaw. "Mine to share." My lips linger above her mouth, and she closes the minuscule distance between us, crashing our lips together.

It's everything I never knew I needed, but it's because it's her. Just like I knew would happen, I turn completely feral, claiming her mouth with mine. I force my tongue inside to taste every inch of her mouth.

She moans against me, lifting up to wrap her arms around my neck as we kiss fiercely. She doesn't want sweet; she would never want sweet. Not with me or anyone else. Max meets every deranged and fucked up part of me, and this only brings it out even more.

I grab her ass and lift her up, forcing her legs to wrap around my waist as our mouths stay sealed together. I bite her bottom lip, and she moans. Rubbing herself against me as I thrust my hips against her and into the wall. I want to bury myself in her right now. To take like I always do.

I also want to punish her for being with them without me being involved.

Carrying her over to the bed, I drop her onto it. I descend onto her body and force her hands above her head, holding them still while keeping my mouth just barely out of reach.

She lets out that cute growl that I love, and I chuckle. "Wanting something, killer?"

She squirms slightly, but doesn't get far when she pants, "I don't want you to stop."

"Hm," I drop even more, my lips grazing hers just barely. "Guess you should've thought about that before you fucked them."

I lift off her, leaving her shocked, and clearly frustrated.

"What're you doing?" Her chest heaves with heavy breaths as I get closer to the door.

"Leaving."

"What?"

"You got off already today. Maybe next time, you'll make sure I'm there to help if you're wanting me to share so badly."

It takes an insane amount of control to walk out of her house without sinking my cock so deep inside her she feels me for the next week. But proving a point feels just as good. I want her just as desperate for me as I am for her.

Plus, I have two dickheads I have to deal with that think they can take my girl for themselves.

CHAPTER 41
MAX

I shouldn't be this wet and angry watching Caine leave my bedroom. I think he may turn around and come back. He'll say he's kidding and then do what he does best, which is take complete control of my body. But when I hear the front door close, I know he really left.

Collapsing back on my bed I cry out, "What the fuck?!"

Adam and Drew may have made me come enough that I should be completely sated. Then Caine just had to go and get me worked up again and then had the audacity to leave. For a man completely obsessed with me, he sure likes to leave me desperate.

It's probably because he knows that will only make me want him more.

And the fucker is right.

Because here I am, ready to call him back and beg him to fuck me. But I can't—I'm too proud to give in yet. Plus, the exhaustion is taking over, and I sink into my soft bed, feeling how heavy my eyelids are. I want to shower first, but maybe if I just lay here for a couple more seconds, then I'll get up. Except sleep ends up winning.

♦

MAYBE I WAS NAÏVE to think that after everything that has happened, that the awkwardness would be gone between the four of us. But when I get to the gym for BJJ the next day, I find out that's not the case. Everything feels tense.

Adam and Drew are short with each other. Caine is across the gym staring daggers at them. I'm just here trying to learn a new sport and how to feel comfortable defending myself.

After class is finished, I'm a sweaty mess as always. I try to say something to them, but the next group of students is coming in and I feel like I can't. Caine is in the cage, prepping for his own practice and I know better than to get involved there.

As I collect my things, I look up to see him already watching me while he warms up. I watch him trail my body with his eyes, and he gives me a knowing look—one I don't reciprocate. Next, I see Adam, who looks at me like he wants to tackle me. Then, Drew gives me that smile of his that sends a chill down my spine.

I leave before I can say anything, but I know this won't be the last I see of them today. If there's anything I've learned when it comes to these men, it's that I'm clearly never getting rid of them. Good thing that I don't want to.

I'm at work when I see the group of guys from Uncaged come in, just like my first shift, and it feels so weirdly different now than it did that first time. I never would have expected for things to be how they are, but I can't find it in me to worry about it like I have been.

I'm not wanting to care about what I should do, how I should feel, or how things should be. No, the only thing that matters right now is what I *want*. Who I *want*. Things I *want*. For the first time in my life, the only thing that matters is myself.

And it feels so fucking amazing.

And freeing.

"Your fan club is here," Danner teases.

I roll my eyes. "Why are you here so often? Did you get a job here that I don't know about?"

"Hah! Hilarious. Someone has to keep you company."

Danner isn't here every night, it really is only once or twice a week, but I can't help but give her some shit for it. Even after our slumber party, I'm still trying to work up the courage to hang out with her more outside of the bar. To be friends with someone. It's weird, but I figure if I'm willing to open myself up to being involved with three guys, I can be open to having a friend for the first time.

"Is that what you're doing?" I joke and she barks out a laugh which has me smiling.

"You're in a good mood, any particular reason why?" she asks knowingly, leaning her head toward the table where the guys are sitting.

"I don't know what you're talking about." I smile innocently as I serve one of the other customers.

"Oh, yeah you do, you little liar," she says a bit too loudly. I don't care, I laugh anyway, knowing the guys can likely hear.

By the time I'm done with a set of customers that came up to the bar, I turn and see Drew leaning against the bar talking to Danner which shocks me a little bit. I approach slowly, looking skeptically between them because I'm not sure what Danner would be saying to him or vice versa.

"Can I help you?" I ask Drew and ignore the way my body reacts when his green eyes lock onto me. Even more so when they rake over my entire body in a slow, deliberate way. The air around us has shifted lately, and it makes me so reactive to him. To all of them.

"We'll take a round at our table, you know what we like." He winks before walking back over to the other guys.

Danner turns toward me slowly with the most shit eating grin on her face.

"Don't," I tell her.

"I'm not saying anything."

I get several glasses of water to bring to the table. It doesn't matter that some of them drink, I want to do what I did that first day just to fuck with them. And maybe it'll result in a punishment for me. Either way I win.

When I approach the table with the platter full of water, I notice a different sort of tension between the three of them.

Alexander and Cal talk to each other, clearly not entirely aware of whatever is happening on the other side of the table.

"Here you go," I announce tightly.

"I thought you knew what we like." Drew smirks, sitting back, kicking his ankle onto his knee.

"I do." I look at Adam, then Caine and see the tension still evident on their faces. "And I know you guys need to be hydrated after training. Enjoy."

Looking over my shoulder as I walk away, I notice the three of them are back to being tense with whatever they were talking about before.

Throughout the night, I keep looking at their table. Alexander and Cal eventually do what they always do, which is talk to anyone who will listen. Sometimes that includes Danner. But what doesn't change is the obvious quiet arguing between the three men that claim to want me.

At around midnight, Adam gets up and storms out. I look at Drew and Caine, who don't stick around much longer. Unlike Adam, they stop by the bar before leaving. No one else is around, even Danner went home about thirty minutes ago.

"What's going on?" I ask either of them.

"Nothing, I'll see you later." Drew still sounds tense.

"*I'll* see you later," Caine counters, and it clicks.

They were fighting over me. Again. Even after everything.

"You both will, and make sure Adam is there too," I say, turning around to work on stocking the bar before closing, hoping that they're gone by the time I turn back around.

When I get home, I go about my normal routine while anticipating one or all of them to show up eventually. If they don't, I know the hit of disappointment will come over me. It's weird to think about that, considering my reaction has always been the opposite.

Just as I'm about to take a shower, I hear them. They aren't even trying to be quiet or sneaky now. I did leave the door unlocked—if they weren't here before I went to bed, I'd lock it, but I figured that wouldn't happen.

They're arguing the second they clear the door, and I can't even tell what they're fighting about. When I reach my living room, the three of them are standing there with various looks of anger and frustration on their faces as they continue to argue.

I need to do something. We're all involved now and it's about time they fucking deal with it. I want them all, for some reason, and they all want me. So, why shouldn't this work out?

"All three of you sit down and shut up," I demand resulting in a variety of looks. Caine looks like he's about to take me over his knee. Drew looks like he is going to laugh. Adam looks like he wants me to run, but I'm not going to.

I stand my ground, folding my arms across my chest while I wait. Slowly, the three of them sit, keeping their distance from each other and I want to roll my eyes because my couch isn't very big, and they are all huge.

"You three want me," I state as a fact because there's no question—they've made it known. Each in their own psychotic way, and now we all need to get along. "So, right now you three are going to sit there like the good boys I know you can be and watch me."

They all react once again, and I see Drew about to argue about the good boy comment. I hold my hand up to stop him, surprised when he actually listens.

"Afterwards, you three are going to show me how you play nice together." I pull off my shirt, revealing the lace bralette underneath. "With my body as your playground."

I wait for any protests, but they're all at different stages of scanning my body.

Except Adam.

His eyes are locked on mine, intently. So focused. So...*primal*. I fight the shiver that wants to run through me.

"If you don't agree then walk out now, because I'm done being fought over. It's all or nothing. That's my decision."

None of them move a single muscle. So, I nod in response.

"Good, now control yourselves until I'm done with my show."

I worry that this may be a bad idea. I've only danced for others when I was forced to. But right now, at this moment, I want to do this. I want to show them this piece of me. Most of all, I want to tease them with my body. I want them to look and not touch.

With that, I turn on the music and let it flow through me. This time, instead of doing this for someone else or out of fear, I'm doing it for me. When I start moving along the pole, these moves are for me. It doesn't matter that they're watching, and it doesn't matter that they think this is for them. It's not—I have all the power here.

It doesn't matter if they chase me through the woods, hold me down, and fuck me to the point of madness. I'm the one in control. It may not have been obvious, especially when this all started, but I've always had all the power here. It's about time I took a hold of it and used it to my advantage.

They all sit, eyes transfixed on me as I move, practicing what I've taught myself. Using my newfound strength from training to be able to lift myself up on the pole.

By the time the song is done, I twirl around one more time before sinking onto the floor, breathing heavily as I watch the guys. They're all watching intently, waiting for what I'm going to say next.

I stand up, the pole at my back, holding onto it with both hands.

"If you're all going to play nice with each other, then you can have me."

CHAPTER 42
DREW

Caine is the first to jump up, grabbing the back of Max's thighs and lifting her into his arms, holding her up against the pole as he attacks her mouth. I know that he's still not happy about sharing her with us and that her asking us to play nice won't happen, but she's going to enjoy everything we do to her body.

Using her like a playground is what she wants and that's what she's going to get. I'm going to enjoy watching it first. So, when Adam gets up and stands on the other side of the pole, behind Max, I sit back, stretching my arms out on the back of the couch.

Adam starts kissing along Max's neck and she arches back, breaking her kiss with Caine, but he doesn't move to let her go. He moves down to her chest, and it looks like he bites her nipple through the little bra thing she's wearing, which only makes her arch back further into Adam.

"More," she gasps.

"Oh, you'll get more, killer," Caine growls, yanking at her bra to pull it off as quickly as possible.

As soon as he does, it gives me a glimpse of one of her perfect pink nipples before he sucks it into his mouth. I bite back a groan, shifting slightly because my dick is already hard enough that the restraint of my jeans is pissing me off.

Adam has his hands on her hips, even though Caine is still holding her up. He continues to kiss, lick, and bite her shoulders and neck. The sight of them touching her like this, and the little sounds she makes as she tries to rub against Caine, has me edging myself, which is exactly what I want.

"You guys should feel the way she's rubbing this needy pussy on me right now," Caine teases, moving to her other breast, and latching his mouth onto her again. "You're so desperate to be filled, aren't you?"

Max moans, and as it turns into a squeal, I'm fighting the urge to jump off the couch and join in. But I wait, wanting to make myself just as desperate as they're making her.

"Fuck, please," she squeaks.

"Please what, baby girl?" Adam groans against her neck.

"I need more."

"Let us give you more then," Adam agrees.

I can tell that Caine wants to argue, to fight against this, but instead, he pulls back from her chest with a pop from the suction he had on her nipple. Then, he pulls her away from the pole and tosses her over his shoulder which makes her gasp.

"Let's go," Caine grunts, walking toward her bedroom.

Adam and I look at each other before following.

By the time we enter the room, Caine has Max seated on the edge of her bed, while he kneels in front of her, pulling off her shorts. She looks from him, up to us, a small smile pulling at her lips. Leaning back slightly, she helps Caine remove the last piece of her clothing.

"I hope you both aren't planning on just watching," she taunts.

"Fuck no," Adam shakes his head. "Lay back, baby girl."

She doesn't have much of a choice because as soon as Caine buries his face between her legs, she falls back with a moan. That has Adam tapping my chest with the back of his hand before he steps up to the side of the bed.

And with that, I'm done waiting, done edging myself for no reason. She wants more, and I'm not about to be left behind during any of this. I go to the other side of the bed, opposite of Adam, and as soon as we're both within reach, Max is grabbing at our pants. All the while, she's writhing on the bed, moaning from the pleasure Caine's mouth is giving.

She struggles to work each of our pants with one hand, so I help her with mine. As soon as my cock springs free, I moan in relief from how good it feels already to not be confined. Adam makes her work a little harder, and it only proves to be more difficult as she gets closer to her release.

I kneel on the mattress by her head, stroking myself slowly

while she finally gets Adam's pants undone. She works them low enough that she can wrap a fist around his dick, but ends up dropping her hand, gripping the blanket underneath her with a loud moan.

"Fuck yeah, killer," Caine groans from between her legs. I look and see him lapping at her release and it makes precum drip from the tip of my dick. I want to feel her, to taste her—something.

Once she comes down from the high of her orgasm, her chest is heaving. She looks up at me and then over at Adam before getting a gleam in her eyes. It's a wicked look and it only turns me on more. Caine lets go of her long enough that she scoots back on the bed, kneeling while looking between the three of us.

Adam and I move so we're next to each other in front of her. The way she looks up at us with her big hazel eyes has me ready to unravel.

"You want to touch?" Adam asks her and she nods easily. "Show us."

Without hesitation, she reaches out, taking each of us in her hands, but she isn't squeezing tightly enough. It feels so fucking good, and my hips involuntarily push into her hand.

"Use that pretty mouth on us, baby," I demand roughly, needing to feel her tongue wrap around me.

She listens, leaning down to swallow my cock into her throat. I throw my head back on a groan at the feeling of her warm mouth enveloping me. When she rubs her tongue up along my piercings, I about lose it.

"Think you can take us both in your mouth?" Adam taunts, and she pops off me, which makes me want to grab the back of her head and shove her down again.

Max looks between my dick, then Adam's. "No fucking way."

He breathes out a small laugh. "No? Think we both could fit in your cunt?"

Her jaw drops. "Definitely not."

"Hm," Adam hums, moving closer to me, turning so he's able to take both our cocks in one of his hands. He squeezes hard enough that I grunt, especially when I see him use the spit Max left on my dick to move his fist along both of us. "I think you should try."

She watches the movement before leaning down and trailing her tongue up my dick, teasing my piercings before licking Adam the same way. Wrapping her hands around us both, she tries to do what Adam was doing, but her hands are so small that she has to use both, and still can't completely wrap around us.

But she's trying, and when she dips her head down, attempting to take us into her mouth, she groans in frustration that we don't fit. Our girl isn't a quitter, though, and takes me back into her mouth again, sucking and bobbing her head while keeping her hands around both of us before she moves her mouth to Adam.

My hips involuntarily thrust forward, seeking more from her, and I can't get the thought of both Adam, and I squeezed inside her pussy out of my mind.

Caine is standing on the side of the bed, watching. His own hand wrapped around his cock with his eyes glued to Max as she does everything she can to work both Adam and I at the same time.

"You like that, killer? Like struggling to take two cocks?" Caine grits out.

She hums around me, and I see stars at how good the vibration feels.

"Bet she'll like it more when two of us are trying to squeeze into her desperate pussy," Adam says.

Max whimpers, moving to take him into her mouth while pumping me in her fist.

"Yeah, I bet it's really desperate right now. You fucking soaked my mouth, and I know how badly you wanted to be shared. You must be dripping."

"You should check," I add, struggling to talk with the way I'm holding off an orgasm. "See how wet she gets trying to fit both our cocks in her mouth."

Caine does just that, his free hand sliding from her back, over her ass, and to the spot between her thighs. I can't see what he's doing, but the way she moans around me again has me taking a pretty good guess.

"Fuck, you're so wet, you love sucking their cocks, don't you?"

"Mhmm," she moans, moving back to Adam again.

"Get on Caine's lap, baby," Adam demands and Caine climbs on the bed behind her, leaning against the headboard. He doesn't give her a choice, forcing her to straddle his lap reverse cowgirl style so she's still able to touch us. "Should we see how much you can take?"

"What do you mean?" she asks with a hint of fear lacing her tone.

"Do you trust us?" I ask, unsure of what Adam's planning right now. But also wanting to be involved in whatever it is.

She looks between the two of us, then over her shoulder at Caine. And with a hesitant nod, Adam smirks, "'atta girl."

Caine grips her hips, lifting her up slightly so he can angle his cock at her entrance. "You going to keep sucking them while I fill this pretty pussy?"

"Yes," she answers confidently right before he pushes her down onto him. She gasps at the sudden intrusion, and without missing a beat I fill her mouth with my cock not giving her a chance to breathe first.

I grip the hair on the back of her head, pushing her down onto my dick. The way she feels is too fucking good and the moan she lets out feels even better. I can tell when Caine starts to fuck up into her because she fights to keep pace with the thrusts.

The back of my neck is grabbed by a strong hand, and I'm pulled into a rough kiss with Adam, his tongue invading my mouth while Max's dances along my dick. I use my free hand to wrap around Adam's cock that's stabbing into me because it's all too much. Too much feeling, too much pleasure. I'm fighting an orgasm that's sure to send me spiraling into madness.

And I never want it to end.

"Fuck, just like that," Adam growls into my mouth when I tighten my grip on him even more. He bites my bottom lip so hard he draws blood and Max's mouth creates the best suction around my dick that I can't help the loud groan I let out.

I faintly hear Caine's grunting while he fucks our girl as she struggles to breathe around my dick lodged down her throat. I'm so close, I don't know if I'm going to be able to hold off much longer. It's like Adam can tell because he breaks our kiss, taking my hand off his dick, then pulls Max's mouth off mine.

"You're going to take two of our cocks. Are you ready for that, baby girl?" Adam asks her while she pants, Caine having paused his movements, buried inside her.

"How?" she asks weakly.

"Still trust us?" he asks instead of answering.

She nods, just barely and he smirks.

"Drew, you want her ass or her pussy?" Adam asks me.

Before I can answer Max gasps, "No way your piercings are going in my ass."

Adam chuckles. "You can handle it."

"I get her ass," Caine insists, already shifting her in his lap, pulling out of her, and rubbing her wetness from his dick, and using it to prep her with his fingers.

Adam shifts to the side, making room for me in front of Max. Her legs being held open by Caine's as she leans back slightly, spread out like she's waiting for me. Just like how she is when she's sleeping. Glistening, dripping, just begging for me to fuck her. I need her and any sort of restraint I've had is gone.

Pressing my hands on the inside of her thighs, I push her open a bit more as I line up, pressing the blunt tip of my dick against her cunt and she whimpers my name.

"You going to take both of us, little one?" I ask, pushing in just an inch.

"I don't—" Her words are cut off with a cry when Caine starts pushing inside her ass.

"Yeah, you are. And you're going to do it. So. Fucking. Well," he grits out.

Adam slides his hand along Max's cheek, into her hair, guiding her to look at him. "Keep your eyes on me while they fill you."

The way she melts has me pushing into her a little more. It's almost like she sucks me into her, because she's that desperate for me.

"Oh fuck," Max groans, grabbing my forearm and digging her nails in.

I can't be slow anymore, I push my hips forward, filling her completely with a groan. The way she clamps around me has me struggling to keep it together.

"You feel so fucking good," I tell her quietly as she keeps her eyes on Adam.

I feel when Caine finally pushes the rest of the way into her ass, making her channel even tighter than before. She makes a strangled noise as she struggles to breathe.

"How does it feel?" Adam asks.

"Too much," she whispers.

Adam just chuckles. "No, I don't think it's enough. You can take it."

I pull back before pushing in again roughly and she cries out.

"So fucking pretty," Adam praises.

Caine lifts Max slightly before dropping her back down, making her ride both of us.

"Fuck, I didn't think you could be any tighter," I grind out.

"God, and her fucking ass," Caine groans behind her as we both move in and out of her.

"Open up for me, baby girl," Adam instructs, and Max starts to protest, but he doesn't let her, shoving his dick into her mouth while Caine and I continue to fuck her.

Max takes everything we give her like she was fucking made for it. I watch the way Adam fucks her mouth and feel the way

Caine fucks her ass while I fill her cunt. It doesn't take long before I feel the signs of release, the tingling at the base of my spine.

"Fuck, I'm close," I groan.

Max listens and makes a noise around Adam, shifting her hips slightly like she wants to drive me to the edge even sooner.

"Goddammit, killer, I'm gonna—*fuck*," Caine groans.

I'm not able to hold out any longer, slamming as deep as I can go before my orgasm takes over and I'm coming with a moan that has Max spasming around me crying around Adam. Her release triggers Caine and Adam as they both fuck into her even harder before filling her, too.

She collapses when Adam removes himself from her mouth, gasping for air. She looks up at me—her eyes filled with tears, lips swollen—and before I'm able to slip out of her pussy, she gives me a small smile. It says more than words in this moment. This just solidified that everything going on between all of us isn't going to be ending any time soon.

CHAPTER 43
CAINE

Never in my life did I think I would be okay sharing my woman. Especially not when I'm as obsessed as I am with Max. But I hate that I didn't mind it. The way she looked so helpless against all three of us is everything I didn't know I wanted. I didn't know I needed.

We helped her clean up, but she insisted that she shower alone. Only because she claimed we wouldn't be able to keep our hands off her again.

She's right.

She ended up falling asleep almost immediately. Now the three of us are in Max's living room and kitchen while she sleeps. I want to join her, but I also want these two to leave. I may accept sharing her, but I still want her to myself at times.

Most of the time.

"You guys can go home, you know," I end up announcing, which is only met with glares.

"So can you," Drew retorts.

"Do you guys think she's going to stick around or go back to her fancy old life?" Adam asks out of the blue.

"Why the fuck would she do that?" I snap defensively.

"Because she came from a bunch of money and has a family." Adam stops himself at the mention of family, just like he always does. He doesn't talk about his history much, but I know that he grew up in the system and has never known his real family.

"Just because they're family doesn't mean she wants to be around them," I defend. I would know that better than anyone.

Well, Drew too, considering his only family was his dad and he fucking hates him. So, he remains silent, sitting with his elbows on his knees and his hands clasped together.

"What if she does? This could just be some temporary life for her, you know?" Adam says seriously.

I shake my head. "It's not."

"Maybe she will, and then we'll have an excuse to kick the ass of whoever she was engaged to." Drew's tone is sinister, and I know he would love nothing more. I wouldn't mind it either.

"If she chooses to go back to anyone, that's her choice and we have to respect it," Adam says sternly. I roll my eyes at his parental tone. He thinks he can be in charge of everything and it's fucking annoying.

"Yeah." I push up on my thighs as I stand up. "You can respect whatever the fuck you want, but if she thinks she can leave, I'll find her and remind her that she's not getting rid of me."

"If you go, I go," Drew agrees.

I want to argue, but then I remember that I have to share her like she wants, so I have to agree. But I know she won't go back. There's just something about her that tells me the reason she's here is the same reason she won't leave.

"I'm going to bed, then," I announce.

"Here?" Drew questions.

"Yeah. With Max. In her bed."

"The fuck you are." He stands up and I really don't want to wake her up by fighting with him right now.

"Whatever." I continue to walk toward Max's room, and I feel Drew following, so I turn to glare at him. "What're you doing?"

"Joining. I need to sleep, too."

"We aren't all fitting in her bed." I look at Adam who's still on the couch.

"I guess we're going to try."

"I'm sleeping out here," Adam calls out, and right now he's my only friend.

"I don't even want to know you're there," I tell Drew as we make our way into Max's room as quietly as possible.

I reach behind my neck and pull off my shirt, then push off my pants so I'm only in my boxers before I climb into bed next to Max. I pull her body into mine before Drew has the chance to. I don't usually cuddle, but I'm a selfish bastard and I want to feel her pressed against me while I sleep.

Drew grumbles something, but it's quiet enough I can't really hear him, and Max doesn't stir. I'm proud of that and I'm pretty sure I'll fall asleep with a self-satisfied smirk on my face.

§

I WAKE up to a thumping sound and then a quiet but frustrated, "shit." The weight that was in my arms is now gone, and that has me shooting my eyes open to see Max holding her foot at the end of her bed that she clearly just kicked.

"What're you doing, killer?" I sit up, not giving a fuck if Drew wakes up.

"Trying to sneak away from the human heaters that took over my bed." She grimaces, letting go of her foot.

"And where were you going to go?"

"The couch."

"Adam's out there."

She groans. "Don't you all have your own houses?"

I nod.

"Then why don't you stay there?"

"Because you're here."

"For the love of—"

"Come back to bed, killer." She shakes her head. "It wasn't a request."

She folds her arms across her chest. I accept her silent challenge, getting out of bed, and grabbing her around the waist before she has a chance to get away from me. I pull her back into bed and Drew grumbles something before wrapping an arm around her and trying to pull her into him.

With a smile, she goes willingly to him, and I lean down to speak directly into her ear, "We'll see whose face is between your legs when you get up."

"We'll see who's dick I'm riding when *you* get up," she retorts, giving me her back, and I slap my hand on her ass.

"Get some more sleep, you're going to need it."

※

I'M DEADLIFTING, working on getting my strength up. Even though Adam insists that I need to train my technique more than strength, but I don't give a shit. I train what I want to train. When I see Max come in, I keep my eyes on her as I lift once more. When she looks over at me, I drop the weights, finishing my set and flick the latch on my weightlifting belt, catching it in my hand as it falls. I don't miss the way her mouth drops just slightly before turning away.

I let out a silent chuckle, grabbing my hand wraps and walking over to where she's stretching. Stepping up behind her, I take the wrap I have in a half loop and bring it around the front of her neck, under her chin and pulling up so she's forced to look at me.

"Ignoring me today?" I ask.

"Seems like every time I try to, you don't let me."

I lean down, tightening the wrap around her neck a little as I get closer. "And I never will."

"Caine," Adam's voice across the gym ruins my moment with Max and I scowl.

"Daddy's calling," she teases with a smirk, but gasps as I tighten the wrap even more for a second before loosening it and taking it with me to see what Adam wants.

I start wrapping my hands as I approach, waiting to see what he's going to give me shit for today.

"We're going to Vegas," he says instantly.

"Why?" I don't really want to go there just to fuck around. I don't drink or party and Vegas sounds like a crowded nightmare.

"You got into a fight, a big one. Some UFC guys are gonna be there, and it may be the shot you need to really get noticed. Especially if you win."

"When I win," I correct. "When is it?"

"Next weekend, we leave on Friday."

I glance over at Max, nodding my head in her direction. "She's coming."

"You sure about that?"

"She's coming," I repeat sternly. I want her to be there, I want her to watch my fight.

I also don't want her here alone with Drew again, forcing me to watch on the cameras. He can come too for all I care; I just know I don't want to be left out of the fun again.

Adam gives me a look that tells me he doesn't think it's a good idea. I know he won't argue, because while he may not admit it, I know he wants her to be there, too.

"We're upping your training until then. This isn't an amateur fight."

"And I'm not an amateur fighter."

He nods. "Prove it."

I wrap my hands, looking back at Max, who's pretending like she didn't just watch our entire interaction. Just for fun, I take my shirt off with my eyes locked on her before heading to warm up on the bag.

She tries and fails to look unaffected by me. She can pretend all she wants, but I know my killer likes the games we play. And I'll drag her kicking and screaming to Vegas with me if I have to.

CHAPTER 44
ADAM

Everything has been calm since the night Max made us all play nice together. Surprisingly, it helped ease some of the tension around the gym, too. Of course, Caine is still Caine, but Drew and I aren't at each other's throats anymore, or ignoring each other, either.

And then there's Max.

Her confidence has increased, both during training and outside of it. She's been sure of herself since we met, but there's more to her now. It makes me crave her more than I ever have, and every time I'm around her, it's a constant battle with my self control to not take her, even when we're in front of people.

I'll help her during class, and every position feels sexual with her. Especially when she shifts her hips a little more than necessary or pushes her ass back against me. I may have written it off before as an accident but seeing the little smirk on her face when she does it tells me she knows exactly what she's doing. It makes me want to shove her down and show her what she does to me.

That's exactly what's happening right now as I'm showing her the new choke she asked about. I have a feeling that the real reason she did it was to drive me crazy. Especially since she's currently between my legs while I show her the triangle choke, and she's giving me that little smirk.

"Ready to try?" I ask before letting her go.

She nods, and we stand to get into position when Drew walks up with an amused expression. "You know if you're wanting to practice BJJ moves, you really should talk to me instead of the ex-pro boxer."

We stand up, and I shake my head at him. "You know I've got a black belt, too."

Drew shrugs. "I'm better. More youthful which helps."

Max stands between us, a hand planted firmly on each of our chests. "Stop it, I'm trying to learn."

Drew leans down. "Oh we'll teach you lots of things, little one."

A shiver runs up and down her body and I scoff, gripping her hip and guiding her away from Drew to be in position for practice while he laughs to himself.

"Focus, and remember what I showed you," I tell her as we begin. I let her work through the steps to get me into the choke.

The first couple of times she struggles and proceeds slowly through the moves, but she gets there. After a few practice rounds, she manages to get it down.

"I'm next," Caine states seriously.

We stand up and he's staring at Max, that way that he always does. Like he's seconds away from grabbing her and hauling her off somewhere. Intense and hungry. But she doesn't run from him anymore.

I like her fear, though. I like it when she runs, and I want more of it. That day in the forest plays on repeat in my mind more often than it should.

"You excited for Vegas?" Caine asks, pulling her into his body and I notice how she doesn't fight it.

"Getting to watch you get your ass kicked? Can't wait." She smiles.

"Oh, killer, I don't get my ass kicked."

"Speaking of," I interrupt. "You have some training to do before we leave and yet you're here harassing a girl."

He scowls at me, then grabs the back of Max's head, yanking her hair roughly so she's forced to look up at him with a gasp. He slams his mouth onto hers, and I can see the way his tongue invades her mouth. She lets out a small moan before he lets go of her, looking up at me with a wink.

"Harassing *my* girl," Caine corrects, letting go of her and slapping his hand on her ass before going back to his training.

Max rolls her eyes, facing me again. "This feels weird."

"Why?"

"Because of that, and then you, and—" She gestures over to the side of the gym where Drew is.

I shake my head, stepping closer to her, but not touching her. Her breath hitches, looking up at me. "If we don't feel weird about it, why should you?"

She shrugs. "Because it's not…" Her voice trails off.

I hook my finger under her chin and tilt her head up to look at me. "Baby girl, if we didn't want this, we wouldn't be involved. But we want *you*."

Max takes her bottom lip between her teeth, and I can't help but lean down and pull it out with mine before running my tongue along it lightly. I pull back before really kissing her and she makes a small noise of protest. "Come over later," I tell her quietly, not wanting the other two to hear. I want her to myself before we all go to Vegas.

I expect her to question me or say no, but she doesn't. Instead, she smiles with a small nod, and we go our separate ways—her to go to work and me to work on whipping Caine's ass into the best fighter he can be.

I TAKE my time cleaning up the gym after we close, and I turn down the invitation from the guys to go to The Tavern. I know Drew and Caine are going there to see Max, and that's fine. She agreed to come over to my house. Even though those two may do their best to get her plans to change, I know they won't succeed.

When I get home, I shower and clean up a little bit. Finally turning on the fights for some of the guys that are going to be in Vegas while I wait for Max to show up.

I end up taking some notes about things for Caine to focus on these last couple days before we leave and end up losing track of time before I hear the subtle knock on my front door. Turning the TV off, I open the door for Max, who stands on the other side looking fucking perfect as always.

Her long hair is pulled up in a messy ponytail, a large zip up covering her chest. Her jeans fit her like a second skin, and for some reason the Converse on her feet make me think about her keeping them on while she wraps her legs around me. I can't believe that she has me thinking like a teenager, instantly stuck in a fantasy with my dick already getting hard for her.

"Come on in," I say, opening the door wider for her, and even though this isn't her first time here, I watch her take it all in. I guess it's a little different not being here with both Drew and me.

Especially because her focus was on *our* issues that day rather than just me.

She walks up to Athena's tank, and shudders before moving away from it. That's when I decide that they should meet. My number one girl should become familiar with the new girl in my life. Especially considering the fact that I don't see her going anywhere any time soon.

I open the enclosure and hear Max's small gasp from behind me. She lets out a squeak when I put my hand in and allow Athena to slide up my arm. The white section of scales shine against the heat lamps as she climbs further up my arm.

"What are you doing?" Max's shaky voice asks.

When I turn around, she backs up slightly but isn't able to get very far because of the wall she runs into. Athena is around my shoulders now like she usually is when I hold her.

"This is Athena," I tell her, instead of answering her question.

"Great, why is Athena out of her cage?"

"Because I want you to meet her."

"I could meet her behind the glass of safety."

I smirk, moving my snake from behind my neck and holding her in front of me. She curls around my forearm like ball pythons do, and I see the panic shine in Max's eyes as she watches me bring Athena closer.

"Why don't you think you're safe with her?" I taunt, moving my hand around to watch how she wraps around me.

"Because she's a *snake*."

"Put your hand out," I command.

Max shakes her head.

"Put your hand out or I'll tie you up and not let you say no to me."

With a grimace, she puts her shaky hand out slightly, but not enough. I grab her wrist and pull it out more so it's straight in front of her. I can tell she's trying to hide how scared she is, but she's doing a horrible job. I also know that being scared turns her on, which is how I know she's going to hate this, but also be dripping for me.

Athena starts to slither off my arm and onto Max's, and she flinches at the first touch.

"No, Adam. I hate this, please," she begs, and it makes my dick twitch in my shorts. She's so scared. And I fucking love how she sounds like this. When she's being chased through a forest, fucked into the dirt, or right now when she has my snake climbing up her body and closer to her neck.

"Tell me something, though, baby girl." I guide Athena around Max's throat, and she goes easily. "How wet is your cunt right now?"

"As wet as a desert, get her off of me." I can see her chest rising and falling quickly. With the movement, Athena slides around Max's shoulders and down around her chest, too.

"No, she likes you."

"Well, the feeling isn't mutual." She shakes her head, and Athena is starting to wrap loosely around her throat just like I want.

"Hm," I hum, pressing my body into hers, trapping her against the wall and she gasps. I know she can feel how hard my dick is for her already, knowing how scared she is right now and knowing what I'm about to do only makes me harder. "She can tell that you're scared."

"And I can tell that she's evil."

"That's not very nice, she won't hurt you."

"The way she's trying to kill me, is saying something different." She reaches up to try and remove her, but I grab her wrists in one hand and push them above her head. The move makes Athena wrap even tighter around her neck and I see the panic in Max's eyes.

I unzip her jacket, opening it to reveal the tight tank top she's wearing underneath, pushing the jacket off her shoulders onto the floor. "Do you know why I named her Athena?" I ask, moving my free hand to the waistband of her jeans, undoing them quickly, and then pushing them down so they're between her knees, keeping her trapped.

Max pushes against me trying to get free, or maybe she's trying to make sure I don't get to touch her pussy and discover how wet I know she already is. I lean down, using my free hand and my teeth to rip the flimsy tank top apart, exposing her bra covered chest to me and I groan.

"No, but she's going to kill me and you're trying to fuck right now?"

I chuckle darkly, pushing my hand lower in between her thighs, grazing my fingers over her underwear that are soaked just as I knew they'd be.

Ignoring her comment, I continue while Athena continues to wrap herself tighter around Max's throat.

"I named her Athena, because Athena is the Goddess of wisdom and warfare and one of her symbols is a snake. But do you know what snakes symbolize?"

"Death. Venom. Evil. Gross," she gasps when I move her underwear to the side and shove a thick finger inside her tight channel.

"Rebirth. Temptation. Danger. Some cultures even say snakes represent sexual desire." I rub my palm against her clit, pumping my finger in slowly. "Seems like that last one is true for you."

"Adam," she gasps, "she's squeezing me."

"Guess she wants you to feel some danger, but don't worry, she won't kill you."

"You don't know that."

"Snakes shed their skin when they're done with it, when they've outgrown it. Humans should be able to do that."

"Adam," she cries softly, and I remove my hand from between her thighs, but not for long because I'm shoving her panties down and pushing into her again. She's fucking soaked for me—she loves this, and she knows it. The threat of danger and fear get her off more than anything else.

"Then there's temptation. That's what you are, Max. You came into town as a huge temptation for me—for *us*. You fuck us all up. You're the forbidden fruit we all want and shouldn't have. Too bad we're taking it anyway and you fucking *love it*. Don't you?"

She tries to shake her head, but she can't with the way Athena is wrapped around her and how I have her arms held up.

"Should I fuck you like this?" I ask, pushing two fingers into her and she moans, making Athena constrict even more.

"No, no I—I can't breathe."

"If you're talking, you're breathing. But let's see what it's like when you can't."

CHAPTER 45
MAX

I'm fully panicking. There's a fucking snake wrapped around my neck and she's slowly tightening which is making it harder to breathe. I'm sure my fear isn't helping that, but I can't help it. I also can't help the way my pussy floods from how turned on I am. Adam has his fingers shoved inside me, and an orgasm lingers nearby despite it all—I'm depraved.

I can't move because he's holding my arms above my head and his body is crowding mine while he fingers me. *Oh*, and while his fucking snake tries to choke the life out of me, all Adam cares about is talking about symbolism and finger fucking me to insanity while I slowly lose my life at the hands of him and his snake.

"Adam please," I plead, as he continues to work his fingers into me, and the pressure he's putting on my clit has me ready to see stars.

Or maybe it's the oxygen deprivation, I'm really not sure.

At this moment, I know I'm truly losing it because part of me wishes Caine were here so he could just put a stop to this. He doesn't stop when I tell him to, or actually do anything I say I want, but I feel like this would push him over the edge.

Or he would want to join.

Fuck, the thought makes me moan.

"You like this don't you? Like feeling scared and having to work for your air. You're going to come for me anyway, aren't you?" Adam grinds out.

My head feels light from Athena cutting off my air, and yet I moan because I'm thinking of these men using me at the same time. Especially right now when Adam continues to pump his fingers and rub me right where I need him to. When he curls his fingers to hit my G-spot, I push against the hand wrapped around my wrists, wanting to grab onto something because I can feel my knees buckling as the orgasm starts barreling toward me.

I'm gasping for air while Athena squeezes, and my pussy cries. As much as I hate to admit it, the feeling of air being constricted and the fear have me even more turned on. It doesn't take long before the release that's been teasing me since Adam's first touch slams into me.

As my body convulses with the orgasm, my vision blurs as I try to gasp for breath, but I can't. And before I can tell what's really happening, my arms are dropped, my pants are pushed completely off my body, my knee is grabbed to wrap around Adam's hip and the head of his cock is pressing against my entrance.

I still feel like I can't breathe, but when he pushes inside while his fucking snake is still wrapped around my throat, I feel like I'm going to pass out.

Reaching up, I try to pull her from my neck, but I'm stopped again when he grabs my hands, pinning them to the wall with his on the side of my head.

"Take her off," I beg, my voice is hoarse. I don't even know if he's listening to me because the way he's pistoning his hips against mine tells me he has a singular focus and apparently, it's to fuck me until I pass out.

"You're okay, baby girl. You can take it, I have you," he says, and my body relaxes slightly even though I really can't breathe. She's even tighter now and I think it's from the way Adam is fucking me into the wall. Still, I can't help but wrap my leg tighter around him, holding on while he stretches me perfectly.

"You feel so fucking good. *You* are the fucking temptation. *You* are the fucking danger, and *you* are going to be the fucking death of me." He moans and it only adds to the pleasure building once again, even stronger this time, but I feel like I may not even get there before I lose consciousness from the lack of blood and oxygen to my brain.

I try to say his name again, but nothing comes out. My vision begins to tunnel, the white spots appearing and yet the way he continues to fuck me only brings me closer and closer to the edge. The release building inside me only increases the closer I get to losing consciousness.

Just as I feel like I'm about to crumple to the ground, I'm able to take a deep breath and at the same time, my orgasm completely consumes me, and I scream without thinking about the fact that there's still a creature around my neck. My knees buckle, but Adam just picks me up easily, wrapping both of my legs around his waist as he fucks into me roughly. I'm being slammed against the wall with each thrust until he finds his own release with a loud groan, pushing himself as deep inside me as possible, filling me completely.

I still feel like I could pass out as Adam sets me down, holding me steady as he removes Athena from around my neck and cool air hits where she was coiled while I continue to gasp for air. I wonder if I'll have a mark from her.

"You're insane," I tell him when I finally find my voice after he puts her back into her cage.

"You must be too, because you loved that."

I want to deny it because no one in their right mind would love that, but even when I try to voice it, I can't. Because I did. And it only solidifies what I've been learning about myself lately—that I don't know who I am.

I think about one thing that Adam said about what snakes mean, about rebirth and shedding their skin. When I look over at Athena slithering around her cage once again, I get it. Maybe humans can do that because I feel like that's exactly what I've done.

"Come on, let's get you cleaned up. If you're still mad about what just happened, I'll kiss it all better." He winks, and starts walking back toward the bathroom.

I follow him, taking off the shredded remains of my shirt,

calling after him I say, "You guys really need to stop destroying my clothes."

"Maybe you should just always be naked around us, then."

"I don't think that'll go over very well at the gym, but I guess I could try."

Adam whirls around, scooping me up over his shoulder. I squeal as he carries me into the bathroom, dropping me onto the counter which sends a shock of cold through me as soon as I make contact with the stone.

He starts up the shower and takes his shirt off that hot way guys do with one hand behind his neck. I take him in. I've seen him in minimal clothes before, but this is the first time I'm getting to really enjoy it. He's big, but not as big as Caine. A light dusting of chest hair obscures some of the tattoos that completely cover him. From his neck down, he's one piece of art. A very sculpted, sexy piece of art.

"You like what you see?" he asks, pushing his pants and boxers off all at once.

"Mhm," I hum, spreading my legs apart and his eyes draw in between them, where I can feel his cum leaking out of me. "Do you?"

"*Fuck,*" he groans, wiping his hand down his face. I see the moment he snaps before giving in. He closes the small distance between us, dropping down to his knees and pulling me against his mouth, tossing my legs over his shoulders before lapping at both our releases.

I moan, leaning back and grabbing the edge of the sink,

trying to keep myself from slipping off and giving in to how good everything feels. "I don't think this is what you meant by clean up," I gasp.

He chuckles against me, spearing his tongue into my pussy while I writhe against him. One hand grabbing the back of his head, I try to push harder against his mouth, which only makes him hum against me and suck my clit into his mouth.

I already feel close to coming again, but he lifts up, and his mouth meets mine. The taste of both of us has me licking and sucking his lips while we kiss. My hips move on their own seeking him once again because I'm desperate for him.

Adam lifts me up, wrapping my legs around his waist as he carries me into the shower. The hot water pelts down on us as the steam invades my lungs. He pushes me against the tiled wall, and I gasp at how cold it is. He uses the opportunity, and his tongue invades my mouth as he grinds his cock against me. I want to make a smart-ass comment about how quickly he was able to get hard again. I'm unable to form any words as his shaft slides through my wetness and hits my overly sensitive clit while he pinches my nipple between two of his fingers.

"Adam, please," I beg into his mouth.

"Please what, baby girl?" he asks with one strong thrust against me.

"I need you, please. I want more."

"That wasn't enough for you? You need my cock filling this sweet cunt again?" He grinds against my sensitive core, and I moan, trying to get some leverage to get him inside me again.

"Yes, please."

"Need my hand around your delicate little throat too?" he asks, sliding it up, wrapping his fingers around my neck, but not tight enough to cut off my air supply—yet. "You like being a helpless little thing, don't you? You like when you're chased through the forest and held down. You like when I hold your life in my hands."

I moan, rubbing against him as he talks and the way he's tightening his hand just slightly around me. I gasp, sucking in as much air as I can before he takes the ability away completely.

"You want more than that, though. You want to be filled by all three of us because just one isn't enough for someone as greedy as you. You want to be used by all of us, and you know what, baby girl?"

"What?" I moan, holding onto him so hard, just dying for him to fuck me again.

"We want to give you all of that and more." He angles his hips, the tip of him just barely pressing into me. "And you're going to take it, because you're never getting away from us."

I'm not able to say anything because he's pushing into me once again, filling me so perfectly that I cry out, holding onto him as he fucks me with a punishing pace. The orgasm starts to come at me so suddenly, I'm worried if I'm going to be able to hang onto him when it finally hits me. Plus, his words are ringing in my ear and I can't tell if I should be afraid or comforted by them.

You're never getting away from us.

Right before the orgasm slams into me, I realize that I don't think I'd ever want to.

※

AFTER WE FINISH in the shower, it hits me how exhausted my body is and that I still have to go home. Adam got me one of his T-shirts that fits me like a dress and some of his boxers that I'm struggling to keep up on my hips.

While he's getting dressed, I'm picking up my clothes, including the tattered remains of my shirt. My eyes catch on Athena in her cage, and I bend down to look at her, shivering when I remember what it felt like to have her scaly body wrapped around my throat.

"Thank you for not killing me," I tell her.

"She wasn't going to kill you," Adam's deep voice says behind me, making me jump. He looks at my arms with the ripped clothes. "What're you doing?"

"I was going to go home."

"No, you're staying here. You need some sleep."

I know the shock is evident on my face. He takes the clothes from me and sets them down on the arm of the couch, pulling me into his body. My hands land on his still bare chest, and I trail them down, feeling the way his muscles tense under my gentle touch. I feel his struggle before he grabs my wrists stopping me from touching him anymore.

I look up into his eyes, my mouth opening to say something, but he just says, "Let's go to bed."

Even though I have so many questions, mostly about his aversion to touch, but also ending with why he wants me to stay. I can't seem to voice any of them as he leads me back into his bedroom, pulling back the blankets on his large bed. The exhaustion hits me as I start to sink into the mattress, and I fall asleep before I'm fully covered in the blankets.

CHAPTER 46
DREW

I'm excited to be going to Vegas for the fights. I haven't been able to go to any since my injury. I've had to stay back to teach classes or just take care of the gym. I'm ready to be back in the environment again, even if I'm not the one fighting.

Even though Caine has his flaws, I'll never deny that he's a good fighter. Also, there's something about watching Adam in his element, coaching during a real fight, that always made me hard for him. I've always been used to being more dominant in any sexual relationship I've had. Men or women, they've all known where I stand—I call the shots.

Except Adam.

He's been the first and only person I've been with that has turned me on with his authority in and outside the bedroom.

And when Max tries, I will fall to my knees for her. Even when she makes her "good boy" comments. Though, she'll still pay for them every time. If she wants to tell me how she wants me to fuck her, then I'm not going to deny her. I'll give her whatever she wants, whenever she wants it. I'll just make sure to do it even better.

I helped Adam clean up the gym after all the classes were done for the day before we leave for Vegas tomorrow. We're all driving to Portland early to fly out, so we decided to stay at Max's tonight. She may not know that the rest of us planned that, but she also won't fight us too hard, I'm sure of it.

Which is why I'm at her front door and knocking like a gentleman. She answers with a confused look, especially when she sees the duffel bag over my shoulder.

"What're you doing here?"

I don't answer, instead I lean down, pressing my lips to hers in a quick kiss and holding her waist as I walk by her into her house. "Good, I'm the first one here."

"First one? What?"

She shuts the door, and whirls around to me.

"We're staying here tonight. It'll make things easier."

"And no one thought to ask me?" She pouts, crossing her arms in front of her chest.

I smile, pulling her into me while I sit on the couch and set her on my lap. Even though she wants to pretend like she's upset about this, she goes willingly. As soon as her ass lands on my lap, my cock is at attention, trying to get inside of her.

"You want to fight about this, or do you want to take advantage of the fact that we're alone for now?" I ask, running my lips along her jaw and onto her neck.

Max arches into me automatically, any fight leaving her body. I love when she gets like this. When she's pliant for me. Maybe I'll sneak into her bed tonight and do what I want with her—what she loves.

Well, one of the things, since I've seen her get chased and held down. Our girl likes a little bit of everything.

"What're you wanting to do?" Max swivels her hips and I grip them tightly.

"I had another idea, but now I'm wanting to see if you could make yourself come just like this again." I guide her hips along me, rubbing against my erection.

"Or," she adjusts slightly, "we could see if I could make *you* come like this."

"Want to see if you can get me to come in my pants like a teenager, little one? Does that turn you on?"

"Mhm," she hums, rubbing even harder against me.

"What if I snuck into your bed tonight while you're sleeping?" My lips graze against her ear as I speak, and I feel her shudder while she continues to grind against me. "You wouldn't wake up as I started touching you, making your pussy weep for me even while you stay unconscious. Then, while you're searching for my dick in your sleep, I'd feed it to your desperate cunt inch by inch."

She moans lightly, scraping her nails down my scalp, gripping the hair at the nape of my neck tightly as she moves against me.

"You love the thought of that, I know you do. I'd go slow enough that you wouldn't wake up. The only evidence would be my cum dripping from you when you woke up and you'd know it was me."

"*Shit, Drew,*" she moans, dropping her forehead against mine. Her movements on my lap increase, and I keep going because she likes what I'm saying. She wants the fantasy just as much as I do. Especially because we've lived it before, and we both know exactly how much she enjoyed it.

"What if I did that while Caine was sleeping next to you? Just climbed on top of you, making you come on my cock while you slept. He would never even know."

"What if he caught us?" she breathes and I can tell she's already getting close. I want to reach down and feel how wet she is, help her get there with my fingers. Or throw her down and bury my tongue inside her pussy.

"I guess that would be up to you, then. Would you want him to join? Or should we make him watch?"

Max moans, and I reach around to cup her ass, pushing and pulling her against me even more. "He could watch. Make him see what it looks like when you fill me with your cum."

Now it's my turn to groan at her saying those words to me. "You drive me insane, little one. You're so fucking amazing." I sink my teeth into the skin of her neck. She gasps, tightening her hold on me and I can tell she's close, and I know I won't be far behind.

"Drew, I can't, *ah, fuck*," she cries, losing her pace as she comes, right here on my lap without me even really touching her. Watching it happen, knowing it's because of me. Knowing this beautiful, amazing woman used me to get herself off has me falling over the edge with her. I lose myself and do exactly what she said she wanted and coming in my pants like I'm a fucking teenager again.

Except I don't think I even did this as a teenager, but it's Max. She has this special ability to get me to do anything.

She looks down in between us, and a smirk pulls at her lips. "Why is that so hot?"

I bark out a laugh. "Coming in my pants is hot to you?"

She bites her bottom lip with a nod.

I stand up, carrying her toward her bedroom, scooping up my bag on the way to get myself cleaned up before Adam and Caine get here. She may think it's hot, but I don't need to hear their thoughts on it.

When we get into her room, I drop her onto her feet, and she immediately drops down to her knees, pulling my pants off while she looks up at me with a mischievous look.

"What're you doing, little one?"

"Cleaning up the mess I caused." Her tongue runs up my newly released dick, lapping up the cum coating it. She hums around me, and I groan.

I hear the sound of a door closing, and she looks up at me,

making sure to lick around the head one more time before standing up. "Guess our alone time is up."

She goes to walk away, but I reach out, grabbing a fistful of her hair, yanking her back against me. "This isn't over. Prepare to wake up with my cock buried deep in your throat later."

I let her go, and she gives me a lingering look before walking out to the living room. I hang back to change my pants and prepare for what's sure to be an extremely interesting weekend.

It'll be a whole weekend where I get to have our girl, mostly to myself while Adam and Caine are busy with the fight. Plus, now she gets to see what a real fight is like, and something tells me that all the violence is only going to turn her on more.

It's a good thing the three of us will be there to help make sure she's always taken care of.

CHAPTER 47
MAX

I'd never been to Vegas before, and I didn't exactly know what to expect. It's just…a lot. Riding in the car on the way to the hotel, a lot. Checking in, a lot. All the people, a lot. I'm trying not to feel overwhelmed, but once we're in our suite, that becomes even more difficult, because again it's…a lot.

"What's this?" I try to take it all in, but I'm failing. This isn't a normal hotel room. This is a penthouse, and it brings me back to when Carson would make me go with him to events. This is the type of place we would stay in. When it was the two of us, it was too much. But for the four of us it makes more sense.

"It's where we're staying, only the best," Caine insists, tugging me into him with a hand around my waist.

"No distractions for you until after the fight," Adam snaps.

I hear Caine's annoyed growl before he slips his hand lower, grazing me in between my legs. "killer isn't a distraction; in fact, I think I'll be more distracted if I don't get to feel her come before tomorrow."

I turn around, pushing him away, which only makes him smirk.

"Nope, no distractions because you need to win," I tell him, standing my ground even though with the way he's looking at me like he wants me to be his next meal, I would easily fold. Luckily, he steps back.

"You're right. I do need to win, and I know exactly what my prize is going to be." He looks me up and down, making it obvious what that's going to be.

Not wanting him to somehow turn this around and distract *me*, I take my bag into one of the bedrooms that I've decided to claim as mine. Then, I mentally prepare for whatever this weekend is going to hold.

As I stand here, I can't help but think back to all the things that led me here to this point. The memory of the day I left comes back full force as I remember everything that happened.

"You're not even ready yet? Honestly Maxine, what have you been doing?" My mom sounds exasperated, and I can't get my hands to stop shaking from the nerves.

"My hair took longer because you told them to do an updo instead." I do my best to hide any sign of distress right now. Though, I'm sure I could just blame it on the day, it's not the truth.

Today's the day I'm leaving.

I'm getting out of there and running away.

Finally.

After months of planning and being so careful not to let anyone find out, it's finally going to happen today. I just need to be alone. Once everyone is in the church waiting for me to meet my dad who will walk me down the aisle, I won't be there.

If it all works out, I should be on the road and heading to my new home before they even notice I'm gone. But I have to be quick. There can't be any second guessing, or any hiccups in my plan. Everything has to work out perfectly or I'm going to get caught. I know my punishment will be even worse than just being made to spend the rest of my life with Carson.

I don't want to be forced to spend one more night in his bed. Or to deal with the venom my mother spews at me on a daily basis. Or hear my dad tell me that marrying Carson is the only job I have for this family.

I can't deal with it anymore. I need to get out.

"Let's get you dressed, and hope you even fit into this still."

I bite my tongue to prevent myself from saying anything, even though I want to, but I'm just reminding myself it's almost over. I'm almost out of here. I just need to stick to the plan.

Stepping into the dress that was already at least a size too small when we bought it, my mom forcefully squeezes me into it and makes sure to express her disgust at how difficult it is to zip it up at the top.

"Thought you were on that diet, Maxine."

"I was," I grunt.

"Then you should be skinny enough to fit in this."

I don't say anything because if I do, it's going to come out harsher than it should and that'll only cause more problems.

I'm almost out.

"There," she announces. "Where's your veil?"

"I got it. I'll see you out there."

"I'll help you."

"I want it to be a surprise."

She looks at me skeptically, clearly wanting to argue more. But after looking me over one more time, and clearly approving of what she sees. She must determine that whatever I do won't fuck me up enough to drop below her standards, so she leaves.

And the timer starts now.

This is the last time I'm going to see any of these people again.

"Come on, Max, we're going to walk the strip while these two prep for tomorrow." Drew pulls me from the memory, and I paste on a smile I hope looks genuine while I agree.

§

I WISH I could shake the uneasiness as Drew leads me through the crowd at the arena while we get to our seats. There's just so many people, and the only thing keeping me grounded is Drew's hand in mine.

Once we get to our seats, I glance around and lean over to Drew. "Are all the fights this big of a deal?"

"No, the amateur ones aren't like this. This is a pro fight; it's recorded and televised and shit."

"Televised?" I look around, trying to find the cameras to make sure I'm not seen by any of them.

"Don't worry, it's not on any major stations or anything."

I don't know why that doesn't make me feel better, but it doesn't. I feel extremely exposed like this, and it may be irrational, but I can't seem to shake it.

"But it's online?" I try to keep the shakiness from my voice, so he doesn't catch it.

"Yeah, that's usually how the guys go back and watch their opponents, so they know how to train in the future."

I nod, focusing ahead on the fighting cage that's untouched for now. While we wait and the noise around us increases, I try to look around without seeming obvious as I try again to find the cameras to make sure to stay out of their line of sight.

Call me extra paranoid because I know Carson doesn't watch MMA fights; I don't think he's ever even heard of them. No one in my family would either, but I don't want there to be any trace of me anywhere that could lead to me being found. I'm just now starting to feel safe, and I'll be damned if anything ruins that.

When the fights start, Drew has to explain a lot to me. It's so fast paced and there's things that don't look like they should be allowed, but apparently, they are. I'm quickly learning that while

I train the moves extremely slowly, that's not how they're supposed to be done.

I'm also learning that I really like watching MMA.

When it's Caine's match, Drew lets me know so I prepare to pay even more attention. Just seeing Caine enter with his shirt off, showing off every glorious inch of his chiseled body while Adam stays close by has me clenching my thighs together. The determined look in his eyes, the way he's so focused as he bounces on his feet and shakes out his arms.

Then his eyes find mine, and he smiles around his mouth guard, and I almost collapse into Drew. I'm not a weak woman, even when I thought I was, but right now, seeing him like this has me ready to drop down to my knees and give this man whatever it is he wants.

That's a weird feeling to have, especially when it comes to Caine.

Adam's saying things to him that we can't hear, and the way he's so focused and in charge has my arousal pooling even more. Especially when I think about the way they both have played my body before.

Drew slides his hand around my lower back, pulling me into him, and I melt. Watching the two of them, while having Drew here next to me has me becoming a horny puddle for all three of them.

"You okay?" Drew asks against my ear.

I nod, still focused on the other two men straight ahead as the fight's about to start.

"Fucking hot to watch them, isn't it? With them in their element. I'll bet your pussy is soaked right now."

I squeak out a small noise I don't think he can hear over the crowd and squeeze my legs together even tighter.

"I bet you'd love it if I stuck my hand down your pants and took care of that needy cunt while we watched the fight."

I shake my head in denial, and it just makes him laugh. "The only reason I'm not going to do that is because I know how pissed Caine and Adam would be if he lost because he was too distracted watching you come all over my hand."

His words only make me want it to happen even more, and that probably says something about me. I'm not able to reply or do anything because the fight's starting, and my eyes are glued to the way Caine and his opponent go at each other.

This is different from anything I've seen from him at the gym. Of course he's fought in front of me, but this is more intense. This is aggressive and calculated. This is him in the zone. I dare a glance at Adam who's outside of the cage yelling out things that I can't hear, but I can see his focus and intensity from here.

This is where they thrive. The fact that I'm getting to be a part of it and see this from them has me feeling more things than I can even try to describe. My brain is misfiring, and it all leads to one thing—the fact that I can't wait to get them naked.

Caine's fight continues for several rounds, both of them bleeding, but neither submitting, even when it looks like one of them might, they manage to get out of the position and turn it around. I've noticed they're both slowing down, even though Caine is trying not to show it, which isn't surprising.

The way he's a bit slower to react, and his moves are less defined as the fight goes on, but it's when he gets the opportunity to strike that he takes it, winning with a knockout. His victory is announced and the crowd cheers, including Drew and myself. He looks down at his opponent, his chest heaving with heavy breaths and defined muscles bulging while his tan skin is completely slick with sweat.

Caine looks out at me immediately, and even through the blood and bruises forming on his face, I can tell everything I need to know about tonight by the look he's giving me. It's the look in his eyes, plus the way his body is coiled and delicious looking, I can't help my body's immediate reaction and how much I want him. How much I want *all* of them.

He and Adam leave while the next fight is prepared for, and Drew and I settle back into our seats after standing in celebration. He leans over, resting a large hand on my thigh. "I hope you're ready for a really *big* celebration tonight."

I shiver at his words, but I know for a fact that I'm more than ready.

CHAPTER 48
CAINE

I don't know if Max should come to my fights. I was distracted knowing she was there, seeing her look at me before and then fighting the urge to look at her during. I know that the violence turns her on, just like I knew I had to win.

Adam wasn't kidding about this being a tough fight, and I fucking loved it. I haven't had a real challenge in so long it felt good to have one again. The adrenaline, the bite of pain from each hit, the challenge of outsmarting him.

As soon as I won, I had to see what Max looked like. Seeing her cheering with Drew had me ready to jump out of the cage and make sure everyone in this place knew that she's mine. But I had to go back and get showered and changed before I could see her.

Adam protests as I leave the back area and go to her, but I ignore him. I know exactly where she is with Drew and I come up behind her, grabbing her face, squeezing her cheeks together to turn her head to look up at me. She goes to hit me, but I crash our mouths together, not giving a shit about how beat up my face is. I groan at the pain as I kiss her. When her tongue runs across a cut on my lip, I grip her face even harder, deepening the kiss, reveling in the pain.

She presses a hand against my chest and pushes. It only makes me kiss her harder before letting go. She pretends to scowl, but I can see her chest rising and falling in rapid heaves that give away how much she wants me.

"What're you doing? Shouldn't you still be backstage or something?"

I breathe out a laugh. "It's not backstage."

"Whatever, are you allowed to be out here?"

"I'm allowed to be wherever it is that my girl needs me to be." I get closer to her again. "And from the way you've been here practically humping the air tells me how badly you need me."

She gasps. "I have not."

I nip at her jaw before pulling back and smirking. "Whatever you say, killer. We're going out to celebrate. And then, *we* are celebrating."

I head back to where Adam is to watch the rest of the fights, but I'm antsy to leave. Nothing makes me more fired up than winning a fight. Add in the fact that my girl was here to see it, and any exhaustion I might have felt from the fight is long gone. It's going to be a long night, and I'm going to enjoy it.

I DON'T PARTY or drink, but it's Vegas. And celebrating in Vegas means both of those things. While I'm not drinking, we all decided to come to a club and I'm watching the way Max dances with Drew. He's the only one she was able to convince to dance with her.

That's fine by me because watching her dance is one of my favorite things. This is different than when she's at home, and the way she moves, like the music is truly running through her, is something I've never seen before.

Right now, it's different because she's smiling and laughing. Drew holds her against him, their bodies moving together while she throws her head back on a laugh. She's carefree and possibly a little drunk. Yet, she's never been more beautiful to me—I've been obsessed since I first saw her. But *this* Max is someone I could become more than obsessed with.

I've never fallen in love. I don't know what love feels like. I never had it with my family, never cared enough to have a relationship with anyone. Any girls that I fucked more than a handful of times never made me feel anything the way Max does. Like I want to have more with her. Like I don't want to ever give her up. Like I want to give her whatever she wants, even if that's sharing her.

"Good job today," Adam interrupts my insane thoughts.

"I knew I'd win," I grunt.

"You could *try* to be humble; you know."

"Why would I do that when I know I'm the best?"

He shakes his head but looks back at Max and Drew. We both get lost in watching them, and I get more impatient by the second. The music's loud, and the crowd is overwhelming, but I want her to have a good time. I wanted us all to celebrate, but the longer we're here the more I want to get back to the hotel with her.

She's sweaty and out of breath when she crashes into the table where Adam and I are standing. Drew cages his body behind hers, and they're both smiling and laughing.

"Having fun?" Adam asks.

She looks up at him with a giant smile and nods. "I need water." She eyes my glass, knowing exactly what's in it, and takes a big gulp before setting it back down. She looks at me seductively as she licks her lips.

"You ready to get out of here, killer?" I ask, my patience wearing thin.

"No, I want to *dance*," she whines dramatically, grinding herself against Drew, who's still standing behind her.

I yank her out from his grasp and into my body. Gripping her neck, I use my thumb to tilt her chin up. "You want to stay here and dance, or do you want to go back to the hotel and get fucked like the greedy little whore you are?"

Her sharp intake of breath tells me everything I need to know. So, even though she doesn't answer, I look up at Adam and Drew while wrapping an arm around her shoulders. "Let's go."

Without waiting for them to follow, I guide her out of the congested club. We head back to our hotel suite, where I plan to make her pass out from the number of times she's going to come tonight.

CHAPTER 49
MAX

I'm feeling light and I don't think it's from the drinks I've had because it hasn't been that many. Dancing out in the open in a hot, dim club with Drew up against me felt better than any performance I've ever done. Maybe it was Caine and Adam's eyes on me the entire time, and the fact that I actually *wanted* them watching. Or maybe it was the way Drew was gripping my hips and feeling how hard he was against my ass.

Whatever it was, I want more of it. So, I don't fight Caine as he pulls me out of the club or on the short walk back to the hotel. I stumble slightly, but he doesn't let me fall and the tipsy part of me swoons a little bit at that.

The rational part tells me I shouldn't and tries to remember all the fucked-up stuff he's done to me. Then I'm remembering how much I liked all of those things, and I can't seem to think straight.

Especially not when we're all in the elevator on our way up to our room and the three of them crowd me against the wall. I grip the railing digging into my ass, looking between the three of them. Unsure of what to say, I squeak out a weak, "Hi."

They all seem to have some sort of nonverbal agreement as they look between each other. Then the signal goes off, telling us we're at our floor. They take their time backing away from me. I'm worried the door may end up closing, but maybe it's all in my mind that everything is moving slowly, because the door stays open and then we're all entering the suite.

My nerves kick up—along with my arousal—once the door is kicked closed. I'm standing in the foyer of the suite, taking cautious steps backwards while they all stand by the door, looking like they just walked out of a wet dream—*my* wet dream.

"Strip," Adam commands, breaking the tension of silence around us.

I hesitate for just a second too long and Caine narrows his gaze on me. "Get naked, killer. I want my prize for winning my fight tonight."

My arms feel like they move on their own as I do what I'm told and remove my clothes. I think they're going to descend on me like vultures, but they don't. They remain rooted to the same spots, staring at me with looks that tell me they want to devour me. I'm not sure if I'm going to make it out of this room alive.

At least my pussy may not. That traitorous hoe clenches at the thought. When I hook my thumbs in my panties, the last barrier between me and them. The anticipation is amplified, and I feel the buzzing in my ears.

Although my panties hitting the floor doesn't actually make a noise, they may as well have had a "ding" from a timer with the way everything is set in motion the second they fall.

I can't keep track of who grabs me first. I'm tossed over a shoulder and before I'm able to figure out which burly body it is, I'm thrown onto the soft bed. While I try to scramble away to gain a semblance of control, I'm yanked back by my ankles. Caine cages my body with his, pinning me there while his face leans close to mine.

My chest is rising and falling with rapid breaths already, but not from exertion—it's from how turned on I already am by these men, *my* men, and whatever's about to happen.

"You ready for us, killer?" Caine's breaths ghosts across my lips and I want to arch up to capture them with my own. "We're going to do whatever we want to your body tonight, and you're going to let us."

I lift my chin, pulling every ounce of strength I have to sass back, "And if I don't?"

His lips pull into a smile I've never seen from him before. It's a challenge and a threat all at once.

"You will."

I'm instantly flipped onto my stomach and then pulled up onto my knees. I try to shove up on my hands, but I'm pushed back down with a hand between my shoulder blades.

"Stay like this, baby girl," Adam instructs calmly.

All I can do is melt into the mattress while a large set of hands hold me down, and another set touches me, rubbing my thighs and kneading into my ass. When my cheeks are pulled apart and I feel a drop of spit land between them I gasp. It quickly turns into a groan as one of them latches their mouth onto my core, sucking my lips into their mouth before pulling back, spreading them apart and licking at every sensitive part of me.

I moan into the mattress while Adam swipes my hair to the side, and I'm able to look up at him through my lashes.

"You're going to come on Caine's mouth like a good girl, because we need you ready for everything we're going to do to you tonight."

I whimper, and when Caine spears his tongue into my pussy. I moan again, loudly, trying to push back into him harder, but I can't with the way I'm being held down by both of them. I want to ask where Drew is, but the silent question is answered when Adam moves his grip to my hair, pulling tightly at my roots. He turns my head to the side so I can see him better.

I can also see a shirtless Drew standing next to him and see the way he grips the back of Adam's head pulling him in for a rough kiss. The way their tongues thrash against each other's while Caine's does sinister things with his in my pussy has me gasping and writhing against their holds.

They break apart, both looking down at me with their kiss swollen lips and Drew undoes his pants without ever taking his eyes off me. Adam's grip flexes in my hair, and Caine pulls back, the cool air hitting my drenched center and I'm about to protest when he shoves a thick finger inside me.

I cry out, trying to bury my face in the blanket, but I'm unable to with how Adam holds onto me. Drew pushes his pants down just enough to fist his cock and I watch the way his large hand works himself. The way he rubs the piercings of his ladder, and I clench.

"She likes that," Caine states roughly right before he buries his face against me again while he adds another finger, curling them to hit the spot that has me seeing stars already.

"Bet she does," Drew grunts.

Adam looks down at Drew's hand. "I think she would like it even more if she had your dick in her mouth."

I try to bite back my noise of pleasure, but the smirk Drew directs at me proves that I failed.

"Open up then, little one." His voice drops with the command. Adam gives me no choice with the way he lifts me up with a sharp tug on my hair, and I gasp, which Drew uses to his advantage, shoving his cock deep into my throat.

Caine takes advantage of my current situation by sucking my clit into his mouth while his fingers continue to fuck me, and I moan around Drew's cock. I run my tongue along one of the piercings and he groans. I smile around him, and Adam pushes my head down further on Drew, making me gag around him, and I hear someone let out a deep, "fuck."

My orgasm is coming, and Caine rubs my inner walls perfectly while flicking my clit. When I start to grind against him, he pulls back, and it fades. I let out a frustrated growl, which makes Drew groan with the vibrations. I try to pull back to tell Caine to make me come, but Adam won't let me. It only makes him push me further down on Drew and I look up wide-eyed.

"You're not getting off his cock until you come. Get him nice and wet while you're down there." Adam's instructing me like he does at the gym only makes the moment even hotter, which says something about me. But I don't care.

Especially as Caine brings me back to the brink again before pulling back just enough to let it diminish slightly. Keeping me on the cusp for far too long. I want to scream and yell. I want to hit him and force him to make me come. I reach out, pushing at Drew's thighs so I can scream at him, but he grabs my wrists, holding them with one of his hands and thrusting deeper into my throat.

There are tears streaming down my cheeks. Drool dripping out of my mouth. I'm gagging and doing everything I can to breathe through my nose. The panic is starting to set in as I start to wonder if I'm going to survive this.

As Caine brings me to the edge again, my release in the distance, I grind down, and groan, silently begging for him to let me have it this time. I feel like I'm going to go insane if he edges me one more time. That's when I feel it. Right there, I'm moaning, trying to grab for something, but I don't have access to my hands.

"Let go, baby girl, soak his face." Adam's words are what sends me over the edge, doing just that, while Drew pulls out of my mouth just in time for my orgasm to take over. I'm screaming and crying as I finally get the relief that's been held out of my reach for far too long.

I think I black out because I don't even register everything that's happening until I come down. Drew lets go of my hands,

Adam has let go of my hair, and Caine doesn't have his face buried between my thighs anymore.

The small amount of energy I have goes toward trying to scramble up the bed, but they don't let that happen. I'm flipped onto my back and moved so my head is hanging off the edge while I'm laying horizontally across the large bed.

Drew is on me, holding the back of my neck to devour my mouth. I'm slow to catch up to the kiss, but once I do, our tongues finally meet, and I groan against him.

"You ready to take my cock? Caine get your cunt nice and ready for me?" He runs said cock through my soaking core, getting himself wet with my arousal and Caine's spit.

I nod, but he's already notched himself at my entrance and is pushing in. "Let me in," he groans softly. The way I stretch around him and the way his piercings rub me is so much, even after an orgasm as powerful as the one I just had. He doesn't give me more time before shoving his hips forward, slamming into me so hard I cry out, wrapping my legs around him.

When I try to grab a hold of him, my hands are taken from me again, and I look up to see Caine holding them hostage. He's shed his shirt, revealing the bruises from his fight that don't seem to bother him, especially with the hungry look he's giving me right now.

He leans down, keeping hold of my hands. "I didn't think I could share you, but Goddamn do you look good with his cock inside you."

My jaw drops at his confession. Then, he follows it up, "Not as good as when you're screaming around mine, but I like seeing you be used."

I want to say something, but no words come out as Drew slams his hips into me again and all I can do is moan.

Adam leans down, brushing his lips against my cheek and jaw. I try to chase his mouth with mine, but I'm unable to reach him with the way I'm pinned down.

"You going to be able to handle how Drew fucks you, while I fuck him?" Adam asks, and I rear back, not sure if I heard him correctly.

"Wha—" Drew must have heard him because the way he groans with his next thrust cuts me off.

"That's right, baby girl. Think you can handle it?"

I nod, because I'll agree to anything right now. His lips find mine, kissing me like he's starved. I don't want to part from him because I like the added connection while Drew continues to fuck me like he hates me. He leaves me before I'm ready and I whimper at the loss.

Drew leans down over me, plastering our bare chests together while his thrusts slow to a hard steady pace, the angle and pressure has me shutting my eyes with how good it feels. And when Drew drops his head on a loud groan, I want to know what's happening. I want to be able to watch. I want to be a part of everything going on.

I strain my neck trying to look around Drew's large body on mine, but I can only see Adam behind him. The feral look in his eyes and his bare chest.

"You want to watch them, killer?" Caine's voice is next to me now, and I feel like I'm spiraling out of control with the way they all keep talking to me. I can hardly tell who's who.

"Yes, *ah*." Drew's hips slam into mine again, filling me so perfectly once again.

Caine's hand cups under my chin, tilting my head back even more so I'm looking at him upside down. "Too bad, you don't get to watch this time because you're going to be too busy with my dick in your throat."

Instead of fighting him this time, I open my mouth, sticking my tongue out, tears already forming in my eyes from the sensations Drew's causing in my body. With a silent dare in my eyes, I look to Caine. *Do your worst.*

CHAPTER 50
ADAM

Max is screaming and writhing underneath Drew while I use the lube I brought to prep him with one finger and then two. He keeps a steady pace fucking Max, but I know it's driving them both insane. Not quite enough and they're both greedy for more.

They're similar in that way, always wanting more. Greedy sluts wanting to be used, and tonight that's exactly what they're going to get. I'm rock hard watching them, and especially when Caine feeds his cock into Max's mouth.

Drew must be watching the same thing I am because he groans loudly as Caine doesn't take it easy thrusting into Max's needy mouth. I can't take waiting anymore, feeling how hard I am. I need to feel the tight warmth of Drew to relieve me.

I coat my dick in lube, fighting myself to make sure it's covering my entire erection. I spread Drew's cheeks apart, which makes him thrust into Max again.

I chuckle, pressing the tip of my dick to his back entrance. "You ready for me?"

He groans in response, and I think I hear Max mumble something around Caine, but I don't take the time to try and figure it out. I'm pressing against Drew, giving him time to adjust.

He pauses, dropping his head against Max's chest, and with the way she moves underneath him, I think he's pulled one of her nipples into his mouth. His hands fist the sheets next to her as I push further in.

"Oh fuck, that feels...*shit*," Drew groans.

Caine thrusts forward, burying himself deeper in Max's throat while letting out a guttural sound of pleasure. I can't help but bury more of myself into Drew as well.

We're all a pile of need and want as our moans mix together while finding our own paces. Max takes both Drew and Caine like she was made to. Drew takes me like he's never wanted anything more.

When I'm buried to the hilt, I let out a moan. I barely keep myself from collapsing on his back, and only because I don't want to crush Max. Especially since I'm not sure if she can even breathe with the way Caine is fucking her throat. The wet, sloppy sounds of her mouth around him while he looks down at her, watching her take it with feral need.

I grip Drew's hips, bracing myself against him before pulling back and slamming forward, which causes him to do the same into Max. I've shared partners before, but never like this and this is easily the hottest thing I've ever experienced. The way we all start to move together, noises blending, bodies moving.

It's all so natural, like we were meant to be like this and I'm not going to last long. Based on the sounds coming from Drew, I know he's not either.

Especially when he starts to beg, and I fucking love the sound of it.

"Fuck, I'm so close, I'm going to come. Max, I need you to get there." Drew grinds out.

She moans around Caine while Drew angles himself slightly and I know it's to get his pelvis to rub against her clit, and I use my grip on him as leverage and fuck into him harder. My thrusts into him make him thrust into her, and it's like I'm fucking them both at the same time. It only adds to the moment, I'm groaning and losing my pace as I'm lost in the entire moment.

Max cries out around Caine's cock, and I know she's coming from the way Drew loses himself, moving and moaning as he finds his own release, burying himself inside her while he comes. Caine isn't far behind, shouting while he fills up her throat, and that's what does it for me, my own release consuming me. My hips are flush against Drew's ass as I come, barely holding myself up above him and I feel like my orgasm goes on forever.

We all come down in a sweaty pile and I remove myself from Drew's body first. With the way he doesn't move from on top of Max, I'm wondering if they're just going to stay like that. Caine kneels next to the bed, turning Max's face toward him, kissing her so hard I can feel the intensity from here.

I tap Drew on the back, and he grumbles something with his face buried in Max's chest.

"Get up," I demand.

He doesn't move, and Caine separates from Max's mouth long enough to glare up at Drew. Clearly, he's thinking the same thing as me when it comes to Max.

I slap Drew a little harder on the back. "Up, we need to take care of our girl."

That gets him to move this time, rolling onto his back on the bed and I see her dazed, sated smile as she looks up at me.

"Come on, baby girl, let's get you cleaned up." I wrap an arm around her back and under her knees to carry her into the bathroom.

She hums in my arms, loosely wrapping hers around my neck as she nuzzles into my chest, and I swear I hear, "Yes Daddy."

That's never been a kink I thought I had before. But hearing the words come from her mouth have me ready to drop her onto the floor and fuck her again. It's going to have to wait, though, because she's exhausted and I need time to reset anyway.

Drew and Caine follow us into the large bathroom, and even though I want to do this part on my own, I don't fight it because aftercare isn't just for her, and I know that. I also know that I want to be selfish with her sometimes. Like right now.

Instead of starting an argument and ruining the moment, I turn the shower on, and it's large enough for all of us to fit in. Without paying much attention to Caine and Drew, I carry Max in and set her down gently. She sways on her feet, and I keep an arm wrapped around her as the hot water pelts our skin.

I can tell when Caine and Drew enter as well because the air seems thicker. Caine steps up behind her and doesn't pay me any attention while he guides Max's head back, letting the water run over her long red hair. She closes her eyes as he works his fingers into her scalp with the shampoo I didn't even see him grab.

She's still gripping my forearms but swaying back slightly toward Caine. I just watch the suds fall down her body, over her neck, down her chest, over the perfect pink puckered nipples. My mouth waters and my cock hardens, which I know she feels.

Drew steps up behind me, and I can feel the warmth of him without him even touching me because he knows not to. He's never asked the reason why, never tried because the first time we started hooking up I set the one rule in place. I always do. "Don't touch." And he listened.

But I didn't do that with Max.

She's the first person I haven't set the rule for initially, and I even tried to see if I would be okay with it when she tried.

Of course I wasn't, but didn't react like I usually do. I didn't freak out and take it out on her. But I also didn't let her continue to touch me. Maybe I'll tell her why one of these days. That's also new for me because I've never had the desire to tell anyone why.

Or to tell anyone about anything from my childhood beyond the fact that I didn't have one. But everything with her is different. Being here with her, sharing her with Caine and Drew. Wanting to keep seeing her. Wanting her this badly. Wanting to share things with her. It's all different. And I think they're feeling the same way.

I suspect that we all are.

I think it's time we stop trying to fight it, and accept that whatever this is, it isn't going to stop any time soon.

CHAPTER 51
MAX

Vegas feels like a dream and a nightmare all at once. The majority of the trip was easily the most fun I've ever had. But the entire time we were there, I couldn't shake the lingering fears dancing in the back of my mind.

There were so many people, too many to keep track of, and it would only take one person to recognize me. One person to ruin my entire life, all over again.

I just started feeling comfortable in my new life. I've accepted the realities of it and the fact that it's going to include three slightly unhinged men that are borderline obsessed with me. I'm accepting myself and the fact that I like that these three have pushed me so far past my limits that I can't even see them anymore.

My entire life view has changed in the couple of months I've lived in my new home, and I'll never go back. Never have to hear about all the things I've done wrong, and how anything I show interest in gets skewed and changed for someone else's pleasure. For the first time in my twenty-five years of life, I'm living for me and only me.

We got back from Vegas a couple days ago, and I've embraced my new routine. In the morning, I go to the beach and take it all in. Even when it's cloudy and so foggy that I can't see the ocean until it's only a few feet in front of me. I go and sit in the sand while looking out at the water that seems to go on forever.

If I have training, I go and drive the guys slightly crazy with my taunting because they don't dare touch me at Uncaged. Especially when class is going on. But fuck, is it fun.

I've gotten some looks from that bitch Karissa who always hits on the guys, but I don't say anything. She can try, I know they don't want her. They want me. There's a power in that, that I've never understood until now either.

Carson never was mine. I never wanted him to be, even though he thought I was his. Not that it stopped him from looking elsewhere. I know his bed wasn't empty on the nights we were apart, and whenever I told my mom, she just said that it's the realities of this life and that I'll get used to it.

I didn't want to get used to it. I wanted better for myself. I wanted *more* for myself. And that's exactly what I've found here.

If it's a day I don't have training then I'm at home dancing, practicing on the pole in my living room, or falling back in love with ballet because I'm doing it for me and only me.

I've never felt so strong, both physically and mentally.

Afterwards, I go to work, where I've become more accepted

than I was when I first started. I've even made plans to hang out with Danner again. I'm making friends.

Everything's been getting better.

Though the nightmares haven't stopped. They're less when the guys are around, but they never go away completely. They add to the lingering fear that hangs around, telling me that it could all be ripped away from me.

I try to shake it off, I'm trying to move on, to get comfortable and know that they aren't going to find me. I've been careful, and I continue to be careful. They'll give up eventually. Carson will find someone else, and my parents will accept that they've lost me for good. I don't know how long it'll take, but eventually, I'll be able to live my life without the worries plaguing me.

Unfortunately, that day is not today. After I get home from work, I can immediately tell something is off. That feeling is only compounded when I see my front door is cracked. My nerves kick up, but I rationalize that it could be one of the guys.

It wouldn't be the first time any of them have broken in. In fact, after work it's pretty common to find one, two, or even all three of them here waiting for me. This doesn't feel the same though, because they never leave my door cracked open.

But they're also completely unpredictable, which is why I walk in, despite the uneasiness in my stomach. I push open the door, and call out, "Hello?"

No one responds, and as I step inside, it doesn't take long for my stomach to bottom out at what I discover.

My house is trashed. Not just a little bit, but completely

ransacked. Cushions are tossed and look like they had a knife taken to them. The TV is smashed on the ground. Dishes are broken and thrown. It's utterly destroyed.

I should leave. I should do something, but I feel like I'm in a trance as I walk through the space, mentally cataloging everything that's broken. Even my pole is knocked over.

Not an inch of my house has been left untouched, and my fear morphs into anger. I don't know who could have done this, but I know who would have the access to. While I thought we were done with the mind games and fucking with me, apparently I was wrong.

I let the anger build. It starts as a simmer, but quickly turns into a raging inferno. I'm seeing red as I storm out of my house with one destination in mind. Pulling out my phone, I start to call my first suspect, but then put it away. No, I'm going to invade their space just like they did mine.

While I haven't been to Caine's house yet, I know where it is, and it's not far. I drive the short distance over and once I arrive, I attempt to walk in, but he has his door locked and I'm annoyed. Searching around, I find a rock that should work.

When it flies through the window by his front door, it does, in fact, work. I clear the glass, reaching in to unlock his door, and storm in. He's passed out on his large bed, and while I normally would take a second to enjoy seeing his muscular, shirtless back on full display for me, I'm too mad to care.

I go back to his kitchen, fill a glass of water and bring it back to his bedroom, dumping it on him.

He shoots up. "What the fuck?!"

I stand my ground, hands on my hips as he searches, then he narrows his eyes on me.

"What're you doing, killer? If you wanted to wake me up with something wet, I would've preferred your pussy on my face."

"I don't know how you were sleeping so peacefully after destroying my house, and for what? Fun?" I accuse, but instantly regret it once the words leave my mouth.

"Wait what?" His tone becomes serious as he stands up, not even caring about how soaked he is.

"You fucking heard me."

"Someone broke into your house?" His voice is dark, it reminds me of when I first met him. When he first took advantage of me in my kitchen.

"Like I said, you fucking heard me."

"Let's go. Show me." He grabs clothes, pulling them on, and I shake my head.

Even though his reaction is not what I would've expected for someone who actually did it, I stick by it. Because if it wasn't him, then the probability of it being someone even worse is higher and I just can't have that.

Because really, I know it wasn't Drew or Adam. And right now, I don't think it was Caine either, but I'm planning to hang on to my anger for a little longer. Just so the fear doesn't completely consume me, like it's threatening to do.

I storm out of his room, not waiting for him to get dressed to follow me. I don't know what I'm doing, or even where I'm going. Everything feels like it's consuming me, and I just need to get out. Someone was in my space. Touched my stuff. *Destroyed* my things. My safe place doesn't feel safe anymore.

As I quickly leave Caine's house, I swipe his keys from the entryway and don't think about what I'm doing or the fact that I've never driven a motorcycle before. I can figure it out, I'm smart, determined, and pissed the fuck off.

Once outside, I straddle the bike, finding the ignition easily, twisting the key and starting it up. I can't help the cackle that comes out of my throat. I remember how I've seen him get the bike to go and rev the engine just as Caine bursts outside.

"What're you doing, killer?" He sounds amused.

"Destroying your shit, too," I state firmly, knowing full well that if I manage to get this thing to move, I will end up with it crashed somewhere.

Caine steps up in front of the handlebars, and he puts his hands over mine where I'm white knuckling them.

"You can destroy anything of mine you want, I'll let you because I don't give a fuck about anything I own. I can replace any of it. But if you're planning on driving this into a wall or doing something that will end up destroying yourself, then I'm going to hop on with you because you're the one thing I can't fucking replace."

My mouth is agape as I stare at him. The seriousness of his tone has me pausing. I want to believe him. I want to believe he cares enough that he really would jump on the back of this motorcycle with me and let me run us into a wall. I want to believe he didn't destroy my house. I want to believe that maybe, just maybe, Caine is capable of being someone who has feelings.

Then the mixture of fear and anger takes over again, and I rev the bike even under his grip. It's a challenge, even though it's silent. I look directly into his light blue eyes, trying to see something there, something that tells me he did this. That says he's the one that broke into my house and that there's an explanation here.

There's not. Because all I see is how dead set, he is on letting me destroy anything I want.

I take the key out of the ignition and sit back slightly. Caine stands up to his full height. Without saying anything he stretches his hand out, and I set the keys in his palm. He doesn't pull his hand back, and that's when I realize that's not what he was gesturing for.

Putting my hand in his, he lifts me off the bike and brings me inside. "You're staying with me tonight, and tomorrow I'm going to find out who broke into your place, and I'll take care of it."

While I want to fight and argue with him, I can't. Because he wraps an arm around my shoulders and the way I easily lean into him scares me. Especially because the feeling of safety I get while he tucks me into his side feels odd to be getting from him.

I look up at him. "Sorry about your window."

He shrugs. "It's like you put your touch on the place. I like it."

I shake my head because only Caine would *like* property destruction.

Even as I get into his bed, I can't stop thinking about who destroyed my house. Uneasiness weighs on me and I struggle to fall asleep. That is until Caine takes advantage of having me in his bed and makes sure I have three explosive orgasms which at that point has me tired enough to finally fall asleep.

CHAPTER 52
CAINE

"We've got a problem," I announce as soon as I step foot in the gym. I don't care if other people are in here, the two that I need to talk to will know I'm only addressing them.

Adam stands up straight from where he's standing behind the front desk. "What's the problem?"

I glance around for Drew and finally see him unwrapping his hands as he approaches from where he was hitting the bag. "What's going on?"

I look around, and it's only Alexander and Cal here, fucking around in the cage, but I don't need them overhearing anything.

"Office," I state.

Adam closes the door once we're all inside and they look at me impatiently. I'm not one to draw out the suspense, so I cut to the chase, knowing they're going to flip out first and ask questions later.

"Someone broke into Max's place last night."

"What the fuck, who?!" Drew exclaims.

"Don't know. She thought it was me and showed up to my place. Broke a window and tried to steal my bike."

"How'd that go over with you?" Drew smirks.

I shrug. "I wouldn't have let her get far."

"Who the fuck would have broken in?" Adam finally asks, his tone is lethal.

I shake my head. "If I knew then I wouldn't be here telling you guys, I'd have already handled it."

This town is safe. During the tourist season in the summer, there are always a couple incidents, though that's to be expected. But right now, when it's the locals, we all look out for each other and crime isn't a problem. This was targeted, I just don't know why.

I'm not sure if she went to the cops. We sure as shit wouldn't, since they have it out for us anyway, thinking that we're violent criminals around here for some reason. Yet, in all the times that I broke into Max's house, I never caused any damage. Or did anything she didn't already want.

"Don't you always have eyes on her or something? Didn't you see anything?" Drew asks in an accusatory tone.

I clench my jaw when I think about what I saw when I watched the recording from the camera in her room. Hoodie up while he took a baton to everything he could. I assume it was a man by the height and build. He never once faced the camera, so I don't know who it was.

"No," I grit out reluctantly. "I didn't see anything."

I still don't want them to know about the camera, but now I'm wishing I had more around her house, which gives me the idea to do just that. Maybe they'll come back. I'm going to make sure to put a few more in throughout her house just in case.

"Where is she now?" Adam asks.

"The beach. She insisted on going alone, but I'm meeting her back at her house soon."

"We all should go," Drew insists.

"Why? Not like whoever broke in will be there."

Drew scowls at me, but I don't give a fuck. I just want to be able to hide some cameras without them seeing.

"We're going to get it figured out. We should make sure one of us is with her at all times until we do," Adam declares.

I nod. "Something we agree on. I'll be back in a bit."

I leave them there, probably to continue plotting something without me, which is fine. I'm going to do whatever I want to do anyway. Which includes going by my house to grab a couple more cameras that I have before going back to Max's.

Once I'm there, I look around at the damage. There's no doubt this wasn't random. This is sending a message to Max.

Someone did this to *her*. And it pisses me off that someone thinks they could do this to my girl.

I set up two cameras in the open living room, so I have a full view of the space. As I continue to look around, I hear someone approach. Max stands just inside the front door, and I can see the way she tries to hide her reaction to seeing her house like this again.

I close the distance between us. "We'll figure out who did this. Get whatever stuff you need; you're staying with me."

She rolls her eyes. "I don't have the energy to argue with you today, but that will change."

I follow her as she goes to her room, navigating the mess to collect some clothes to put in a bag. I notice how she doesn't grab a lot, and I want to tell her to pack up everything.

"I'll have to come back eventually," she tells me.

"Yeah, we'll see."

As we leave her house, her sass comes back when she says, "I'm not just staying with you. You're sharing me, which means I get to pick whose house I stay at."

I wrap my arm around her middle, yanking her back against me to stop her from walking away. "Doesn't matter whose house you stay at, I'll be there. I'll always be there."

CHAPTER 53
MAX

The past several days have been overwhelming with the guys refusing to leave me alone. While the sexual attention is something I'll never complain about, I miss the routine I'd made for myself. I miss the fact that I was finally feeling independent and then it was snatched away by someone who decided to break into my house.

Nothing's happened since, and I feel like it was a fluke. Just someone random, looking to rob me and maybe they got what they wanted. Even if none of us were able to find anything missing. I want to get back to how things were, and that has to start with being able to live in my own house again.

It's why I snuck out of bed this morning, making sure none of the guys woke up so they wouldn't stop me as I went back home. I hate seeing it like this, and I immediately start cleaning up. I'm going to have to replace so much stuff, it sucks that so much of the money I've managed to save is going to go into replacing everything, but I don't have a choice.

I'm sure the guys will want their spaces back, since it doesn't matter whose house I stay at, they all end up there with me anyway. Of course no one has complained—except Caine. He grumbles about wanting me to himself still. But he's getting over it for the most part, I think.

I manage to get the space cleaned up enough for now before I have to go to Uncaged for class. That's been another thing the guys have made sure of. They're all taking my training extremely seriously. All it took was Adam asking what would've happened if I was there when the person broke in, and then they were all on me about my training.

Not that I mind, the whole point of me starting at Uncaged was to learn to defend myself, and I've only gotten better. I just never want to use the skills I'm learning in any real-life situation if I don't have to.

⚜

I REALIZED at work that I'm out of clean clothes, and the annoyance at the fact that I can't just live in my own home takes over again. After I close the bar, I'm supposed to go to Drew's house, but I decide to stop at home first to get more clothes.

When I get inside, a chill runs down my spine. I know immediately that I should leave.

There's something wrong.

I'm just going to grab my clothes and get out.

I work quickly, grabbing the first things I find, not even bothering with a bag. I leave my room, and intend to get out of here right away, but a voice stops me in my tracks. A voice I have to be imagining. A voice I never intended to hear again.

No.

I'm hallucinating. It's just my fear playing tricks on me. There's no way. It's not possible.

But when he steps out into the light a bit more, I drop everything in my arms.

"Maxine," Carson sneers, looking me up and down, probably disgusted by the way I'm looking now. No longer a stick intended for him to break. I have weight on me, muscle from training and actually eating. But seeing him here, hearing him speak brings me back.

"Wha—" I can't even finish the question. I look toward the door, thinking about how fast I can leave. I'm faster, I have to be. I can fight him off, I've been training. I can do this; I can handle myself he won't–

"Don't even think about it." It's like he's reading my mind, and I swallow roughly. "Your fun is over. It's time to come home."

I raise my chin, preparing for a fight. "Then you're going to have to kill me, because the only way I'm going back is if I'm fucking dead."

He laughs. Carson laughs, and I know that this isn't going to be easy, but no matter what he thinks about me now, I'm not who I was when I left, and I'm not going down without a fight.

END OF BOOK ONE

Download Uncaged Obsessions

Read the first chapter HERE

ACKNOWLEDGMENTS

This book has tested me in more ways than one and truly would not have been finished without the love and support of the people around me.

Maeghen - This is your adopted baby and thank you for every single thing you did to help me with this book, including, but is not limited to: talking me off the ledge….multiple times. Alpha reading, pushing me to get my words in even when I don't want to. Thank you for everything and being my friend through it all! Love you!

Chelsey - Thank you for being the best PA I could ever ask for an my bestie! You also talked me off the ledge and stopped me from deleting this book many times. Thank you for encouraging every unhinged thought that went into this and the next one. I love you forever!

Ashley - You're my forever Booha and you listen to all my ideas and encourage them plus more. I'm sorry this wasn't the book you wanted me to write next, but I promise Jameson and Sutton will be next!

Sarah Beth - Girl…the fact that you've been with me since my very first book is insane. I'm so glad we found each other and I love you so much. Your love and support has been everything to me and I truly wouldn't be here if it wasn't for you!

Mikaela - Thank you for taking the chance on me with Chasing Books PR! Thank you for being there for me, everything you've done, the advice you've given and being there. You're the actual best!

Kay - Our sixth book together! Who would've thought?! Thank you so much for always being flexible with me and putting up with my chaos when it comes to editing. You're stuck with me for life and you know that.

Kim - Thank you for the gorgeous covers you've made for this duet! Seriously you kill it every single time and these ones are everything I could've wanted and more!

Thank you to all my beta readers, your comments and feedback kept me going! Anja, Emily, Lanae, Dani, Erin, Jaeann, Jessica, Katelyn, Leslie, Tiffany and Courtney.

And of course thank you to my street team, and ARC readers and every single person who has supported me you all have truly changed my life in a way I never expected. I am so beyond thankful for every single one of you. I also apologize for this cliffhanger…please don't hate me too much.

ALSO BY MADI DANIELLE

Denver Dragons Series:

The Hat Trick - A hockey why choose romance

The Power Play - A forced proximity hockey romance

Cross Checked - A friends to lovers novella

The Break Out - An enemies to lovers brother's teammate hockey romance

The Falling series

When They Fell - A friends to lovers romance

Who They Are - A cop romance

What They Feel - An enemies to lovers age gap romance

Signed Books available on my website:

www.madidaniellewrites.com

ABOUT THE AUTHOR

Madi is a romance author, wife and mother to one daughter and several animals. When she isn't reading or writing you may find her watching hockey or some cheesy movie. Madi has been writing since she was a teenager, but it took a backseat when she went to college and got her degree in Family and Human Services. After working as a social worker, she got back into writing as an escape and hasn't looked back since. Madi is originally from Arizona, but moved to Oregon to attend UO, which is where she still resides with her family.

www.ingramcontent.com/pod-product-compliance
Lightning Source LLC
LaVergne TN
LVHW010306070526
838199LV00065B/5459